DISЯUPTION

OTHER BOOKS AND AUDIOBOOKS
BY CLAIR M. POULSON

I'll Find You   *Checking Out*
Relentless   *In Plain Sight*
Lost and Found   *Falling*
Conflict of Interest   *Murder at TopHouse*
Runaway   *Portrait of Lies*
Cover Up   *Silent Sting*
Mirror Image   *Out Lawyered*
Blind Side   *Deadly Inheritance*
Evidence   *The Search*
Don't Cry Wolf   *Suspect*
Dead Wrong   *Short Investigations*
Deadline   *Watch Your Back*
Vengeance   *Fool's Deadly Gold*
Hunted   *Pitfall*
Switchback   *Kingfisher*
Accidental Private Eye   *Getting Even*
Framed

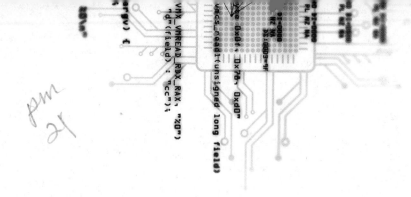

DISЯUPTION

a suspense novel

CLAIR M. POULSON

Covenant Communications, Inc.

Cover images: *Cute Little Boy Holding Book. Ginger Haired Kid on Chalkboard Background* © JNemchinova / iStock; *Portrait of Young Beautiful Girl* © dinachi / iStock; *London, United Kingdom* © Jack B / Unsplash; *Creative Dark Coding Texture with Text. Programming and Future Concept. 3D Rendering* © peshkov / iStock; *Unique Design Abstract Digital Pixel Noise Glitch Error Video Damage* © The7Dew / iStock;
Cover design by Toree Douglas and Kimberly Kay

Cover design copyright © 2021 by Covenant Communications, Inc.

Published by Covenant Communications, Inc.
American Fork, Utah

Printed in the United States of America
First Printing: August 2021

28 27 26 25 24 23 22 21   10 9 8 7 6 5 4 3 2 1

ISBN 978-1-52441-756-7

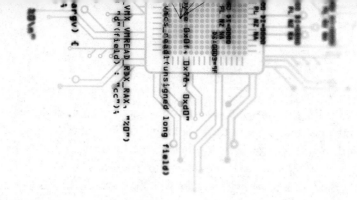

CHAPTER
ONE

"Do you still plan to take your brother to a movie tonight?" Pamela Dixon asked her daughter as Pamela and her husband, Roland, started to head out. They walked toward the mudroom, which was part of the large three-car garage. They both stopped and turned. "We won't be out as late as you if you do go, but we'll wait up for you."

"Just make sure it's a clean movie," Roland reminded them as he absently brushed at his short red hair with one hand.

"Dad, you know we will," Lilia said with a smile. At nineteen, she was pretty and about five feet, six inches tall, with a slender build and long brown hair.

Her parents smiled in return, their smiles filled with love.

Twelve-year-old Timmy looked from his dad to his sister. "We've never picked a bad movie." He had thick glasses and wore hearing aids tucked behind his ears, mostly hidden by his curly red hair. He blinked, his blue eyes appearing very large behind the thick lenses, which exaggerated the blink.

"As your parents, it's our duty to remind you," Roland said with a chuckle as he walked back toward his children and roughed Timmy's curly mop of red hair while adding, "and we always will. The dinner meeting with the senior partner of my law firm shouldn't be terribly long. We will not be late." He looked at his watch as he spoke. "It's nearly five, Pamela. We'd better get going."

The siblings exchanged glances, and then Pamela said, "You guys have a good time."

Timmy nodded with a big grin. "We'll tell you about it later," he said. "Like we always do."

Pamela and Roland took a moment to kiss each of their children on the cheek. Then the parents went out the door and into the garage. A moment later, Timmy heard the garage door open, followed by the soft hum of his parents' silver Lexus as it backed out, and then he listened as the door closed.

Through the living room window, he watched as the Lexus drove up the street. It was soon followed by another car with two men seated in it, both wearing ball caps. Timmy memorized the details of the car and noted the license plate as it passed by, something he often did. He watched until the car disappeared down the street.

"We need to leave by a quarter to six, Timmy," his sister said.

"I'm ready anytime you are, but we have a while," he responded.

"What were you watching out the window?" Lilia asked. "You seemed to be concentrating."

"It was a car, an older model Bronco, brown with some rust spots. It had California plates. There were two men in it. They both had ball caps on. The driver's cap looked blue, the passenger's red," he responded.

Lilia did not comment on his detailed description. She was used to it. Timmy had a brilliant, flawless memory and was often referred to as a child prodigy because of it. Lilia was very smart in her own way, but she had no jealousy for her little brother's intellect—most of the time, at least. Although they had disagreements at times, as siblings usually do, they were very close, and Lilia was often protective of Timmy.

"Why were you interested in the Bronco?"

"No one in this neighborhood has a car like that, Lilia," Timmy said. "I've never seen it before. It seemed out of place to me—that's all." They lived in a large, expensive home in one of the most exclusive neighborhoods in Salt Lake City, so people just driving through wasn't usual.

"Maybe the guys were lost, or maybe they work in someone's yard or something."

"Maybe," he agreed. "We have a few minutes, so I'll finish that calculus assignment Mom gave me this afternoon first. I don't have much left."

A twelve-year-old doing calculus didn't faze Lilia in the least. She'd gone to public schools, was on a scholarship at the University of Utah, and had always been quite popular. She'd had near-perfect grades in high school and still maintained them in college. Timmy's education, on the other hand, had started out a little differently. When Timmy was in first grade, his teacher thought Timmy was stupid because he seldom spoke in class and never raised his hand. The teacher had mentioned it to his mother in a phone call on the second week of school.

Pamela had explained that Timmy was actually quite bright, but since he was embarrassed about his above-average intelligence, he was usually very shy. She had assured the teacher that with his thick lenses and hearing aids, Timmy would have no difficulty functioning as well as anyone. The teacher had not sounded like she believed her. That was not, however, the only difference between Timmy's experiences at school and his sister's. He was also bullied relentlessly by other children.

Those two factors convinced his parents to start homeschooling Timmy. He didn't need much guidance. He could read at the speed of a rocket and still remember everything he'd read. And math was nothing to him, nor was any kind of science.

At age twelve, he could easily have qualified for admission to college, to any college, but as a twelve-year-old, his parents knew that would never work. Just because he had above-average intelligence, that didn't mean he had above-average social skills. He was still a young boy. So he continued to soak up knowledge at home.

Timmy also played with a couple boys from the neighborhood, rode his bike, played basketball in the backyard, lifted weights, worked on his karate moves for hours on end, swam laps in their pool, and read every book he could get his hands on—those that were approved by his parents, of course. He was very strong and stocky for his age. He was determined that no one would ever break his glasses, snatch his hearing aids, or beat him up again.

Just days before his parents pulled him out of school, Timmy had come home with broken glasses, a missing hearing aid, and bruises all over his little body. Before that week was over, both he and his sister were enrolled in karate classes. Neither of them had ever had occasion to use the skills they had acquired since no one bullied Lilia, and Timmy's social interactions were limited to church meetings and occasional meetings with other homeschooled children and his neighborhood friends. He was never picked on in those settings.

A half hour after their parents left, Lilia and Timmy were ready to go to their movie.

"Did you get the calculus finished?" Lilia asked.

Timmy frowned at her. "Of course I did."

They made sure all the lights were off, except the one over the front deck and the one in the mudroom. Lilia backed her robin-egg-blue Volkswagen beetle from the garage, down the drive, and onto the street. Ever observant, Timmy watched the garage door close, then looked to his right. He felt a slight stirring in his stomach when he saw that same Bronco with the California plates parked up the street a short distance. He was quite sure the same two men sat inside. He did not mention it to Lilia, not wanting to worry her. But it certainly looked out of place to him.

**

The movie was very entertaining, a comedy that had Timmy and Lilia still laughing as they left the theater. They stopped for pizza and then drove home.

"I thought Mom and Dad said they'd be home before us," Timmy said when the garage door slid up. It was very clear that the silver Lexus was not inside parked beside his mother's white Cadillac like it should have been.

"They must have been detained," Lilia said with no indication of concern.

But Timmy noticed something else amiss. "We left the front-deck light on," Timmy reminded her. "It's off now."

"It is? I didn't notice," Lilia said as she pulled her VW to a stop and killed the engine.

"The mudroom light is off too," he said.

Lilia made no comment but peered toward the mudroom. They both got out. Timmy opened the door leading into the kitchen and then stood there for a moment. The lights of the VW were still shining, but they automatically shut off moments after Lilia stepped up beside him and stopped too. "Timmy, what are you doing?" she asked. "Let's go in."

Timmy did not move, but he listened for several moments. Finally he said, "The deck light and mudroom light were both on when we left for the movie, and they aren't now. And that's not all. Our house is silent."

"That's because we beat Dad and Mom home," Lilia responded sensibly. "Are your hearing aids working?"

"They're fine. Listen, Lilia," Timmy said sharply, then stepped through the door and stopped just inside the kitchen.

Lilia followed and closed the door behind them. "It is very quiet in here," she agreed after a moment. "I don't even hear the refrigerator." She reached for the light switch and flipped it, but nothing happened. "The power must be out. That's why it's dark and quiet."

Timmy didn't respond immediately. He stood still, continuing to listen for any sounds. There was none. "The Stewarts' lights were on," he said, referring to their closest neighbor to the east. "So were the Johnstons'." They were the neighbors to the west.

"I didn't notice." Lilia put an arm around Timmy's shoulders. When she spoke, her voice cracked slightly. "But our power is out."

"We need to check the breaker box," Timmy said. "Turn the light on your cell phone on."

Lilia pulled the phone from her purse. "Siri, turn my flashlight on."

It came on instantly.

"Let's go outside and check the breaker," Timmy said.

"I don't know where it is."

"I do," Timmy assured her. "It's just beyond the back deck."

"I guess I've never paid attention," Lilia said with a chuckle, but she didn't fool Timmy. She was as nervous as he was. Something was seriously wrong in this big, silent house.

They hurried though the kitchen and into the wide, long hallway to the back door. Lilia unlocked and opened it. She stepped out ahead of Timmy. "Which way?" she asked.

"To the left."

They found the large breaker box. Timmy pulled a deck chair up to it so he could reach, and then he opened it. Lilia shined her cell phone light on the switches. For a moment, Timmy studied it. "The main breaker is off."

"Can you flip it on?" Lilia asked.

"Do you have a tissue in your purse?"

"Yes, but what for?" she asked in frustration. "Quit stalling. Just turn it on."

"I don't want to mess up any fingerprints that may be on it," he said.

"Fingerprints?" Lilia asked, her voice quiet and a tiny bit hoarse. "Why would that matter?"

"Lilia, someone turned the breaker off. I don't want to smudge the prints in case whoever it was didn't think to wear latex gloves."

"Trust you to think of something like that," she said as she dug through her purse.

She handed a tissue to Timmy, who then flipped the breaker on. It was still dark.

"It didn't work," Lilia said.

"It probably did. Let's turn on the lights by the door." Timmy led the way in the light of Lilia's cell phone.

A moment later, the deck was flooded with light. The two of them looked at each other for a moment. Timmy could see from the look on his sister's face that her fright matched his own. Finally, Lilia said in a slightly trembling voice, "Let's go inside."

They began to flip lights on all over the main floor of the house. They even stepped inside their father's home office and turned on that light. Lilia gasped, and Timmy felt the blood rush to his head. Their father's office had been torn apart. His law books were on the floor. The papers he usually kept so orderly on his desk had been swept off. The drawers of his filing cabinet were hanging open, the contents having been removed and scattered. The computer screen was smashed.

"We need to call the police," Timmy said.

"I'm calling Mom and Dad first," Lilia said. When both their numbers went to voice mail, she dialed 911 with trembling hands.

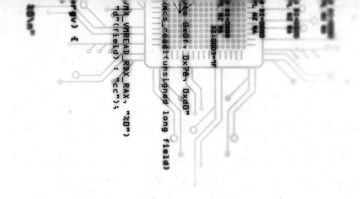

CHAPTER
TWO

"WHERE ARE YOUR PARENTS?" ONE of the officers who had just rung the doorbell asked when Timmy and Lilia both met them at the door. He was the older of the two officers, and he was looking suspiciously at the siblings.

"We don't know," Lilia said with a catch in her voice. "They're supposed to be here." Her eyes slid to the younger officer, whose frown seemed to indicate that he either felt like she should have known the answer to that question or that he didn't like the tone of his partner's voice any better than she did.

"I'm Sergeant Keith Hartling," the older officer said, his voice still a little bit gruff. "And this is my partner, Officer Erman. May we come in?"

"Of course, please do," Lilia responded. "We need your help." She led the officers into the large living room and asked them if they'd like to be seated.

The officers sat on a white sofa while Lilia and Timmy sat on a matching love seat. "I'm Lilia Dixon, and this is my brother, Timmy."

"It's nice to meet you," Sergeant Hartling said and turned to his young partner. "Write their names down, Officer." Then he turned back to the Dixons as Officer Erman hurried to do as he'd been instructed. "How old are you, Miss Dixon? Write this down too, Officer."

The young officer made no comment; he just began to jot down her name on a small notebook he'd pulled from a front shirt pocket of his uniform.

"I'm nineteen, sir."

"I'm a sergeant, actually. So you are out of high school but still living with your parents." It was not a question.

"I'm a pre-med student at the University of Utah," she said.

"I see. So you are old enough to take care of your handicapped brother without your parents being home." Again, it was not a question.

"I'm not handicapped," Timmy spoke up more boldly than he usually did. "I'm twelve years old, and I wear glasses and hearing aids, but I can do anything I set my mind to."

Lilia's eyes met the somber gray ones of the younger officer, but she noted a slight uptick at the corners of his lips. The sergeant, however, looked doubtfully at Timmy.

"My mistake. Please forgive me." The sergeant gave Timmy a lingering look before again addressing Lilia. "So why did you call the police? Are your parents supposed to come home when you tell them to? It seems to me that you're a bit bossy." He chuckled when he said that.

Timmy, who was fidgeting on his seat, his freckled face quite red, spoke up. "Lilia is not bossy. But we are both troubled about our parents. They told us they would be here when we got home from the movies, but they weren't."

"So they are late," Sergeant Hartling said as he stood up. "I suppose they'll be home soon. I'm sure they just got detained."

"We told the dispatcher this when we called. They would have called me if they were going to be late," Lilia said as she, too, rose to her feet.

"And why would they have done that?"

"Because that's the way they are. My dad's a lawyer. He and Mom had a dinner meeting with the senior partner of his law firm. It should have been over a long time ago."

"He's a lawyer, huh? Well, I know a lot of lawyers. They like to talk. I'm sure he and his colleague are chatting up a storm." The sergeant smiled. "Come on, Officer Erman. I think we're finished here. Miss Dixon, call us again if they aren't home by morning."

"But you don't understand," Lilia said. "Someone has been in our house. Dad's office was ransacked."

Timmy spoke up again, his hands on his hips. "When we got home, the house was silent," he said. "The house is never silent."

"Does your house usually talk to you?" Sergeant Hartling joked with a bit of a chuckle.

"And it was dark," Timmy added without bothering to respond to the sergeant's unnecessary question.

"So someone turned the lights off. I see it's light now. I guess you turned them on when you found it was dark." His voice was still a bit gruff.

Officer Erman bent toward Lilia and shook his head. "Sorry," he said very softly so only she could hear. "He's having an unusually bad day. His wife is very sick, and he's worried about her. He's anxious to get home and check on her."

"It's okay," Lilia responded just as quietly.

"We tried," Timmy continued, "but they actually didn't come on because someone had turned off the breaker. I didn't leave my fingerprints on it in case you need to check for the prints of whoever turned it off. After I flipped the breaker, the house wasn't quiet anymore. The refrigerator came on and started humming like it usually does."

The sergeant did not seem impressed, but Officer Erman clearly was. "Wait a minute, you guys. Are you saying that someone was in the house, did damage to your father's office, and shut the breaker off to kill the power to the house?"

"That's right," Timmy said. "You guys should look in Dad's office. It's a mess."

Sergeant Hartling took a deep breath, and then he said, "I guess we should, little guy."

"I also think you need to look for the car that was outside earlier—when Dad and Mom left and when we got home. The car looked suspicious to me."

"I suppose you're an expert," the sergeant said. He was gruffer than ever, and yet, his face wore a worried look. Lilia felt bad for him. She wondered what exactly was ailing his wife.

"I just know when I see something that seems out of place. Officer Erman, will you write down the description of the car if I give it to you?" Timmy asked.

"Of course." He still had the little notebook in his hand. "What kind of car was it?" he asked as the sergeant scowled.

"It was an older model Ford Bronco, brown with some rust spots. It had California plates. There were two men in it. They both had ball caps on. The driver's cap looked blue, the passenger's red."

"I don't suppose you got the license number?" Sergeant Hartling asked with raised eyebrows.

"Yes, Sergeant, I did," Timmy responded and rattled it off.

"Are you sure that's the correct number?" Officer Erman asked.

"You can be sure of that," Lilia said. "Timmy never forgets anything. He's especially good with simple things like license plates, phone numbers, names, and so on."

"Bright kid, are you?" Sergeant Hartling asked, not sounding quite so gruff. "How old are you, and what grade are you in?"

"I'm twelve, and I don't go to school. I'm homeschooled."

"But you must have an idea what grade you would be in," Officer Erman said.

"Actually, he's beyond high school. He's taking college courses now. He just finished an advanced calculus assignment before we went to the movies," Lilia said, unable to keep the pride from her voice.

Officer Erman shook his head in amazement. "Wow! Sergeant, I think we should look in Mr. Dixon's office."

The sergeant's brow was creased. Lilia could tell he was definitely worried about their situation now, and that made her worry even more. He followed Lilia and Officer Erman. She noticed that Timmy had crossed to the large living room window and parted the curtains.

"Look at the mess," Lilia said as she stepped into her father's large office. "They even broke Dad's computer screen. Everything is scattered around. Our dad always keeps his office neat and clean."

"I guess we'd better get some detectives in here," Sergeant Hartling said, more connected now. "Where's your little brother, Miss Dixon?"

"He stayed in the living room," she responded. At that moment, Timmy entered the room, a frown on his freckled face. "What did you see outside when you looked, Timmy?"

"It was that Bronco again," he said. "But only the guy with the blue hat was in it. And it had different license plates. They're Utah plates this time."

"Did you get the number?" Officer Erman asked.

"I did." Timmy recited it.

Despite his earlier negative reaction to the Dixons' complaint and his own personal worries, Sergeant Hartling was very interested now. "I'll step out and call for backup, and I'll run these two license numbers if you give them to me."

Timmy rattled them off again as Officer Erman wrote them on a separate page of his notebook. He tore out the page and handed it to his sergeant, who then left the room, punching numbers into his cell phone as he went.

"I'm sorry about the way Sergeant Hartling acted at first," Officer Erman said. "He's a good guy. Besides his wife being very ill, he's getting close to retirement. He was up for a promotion last week but just learned when we came on shift tonight that he was passed over again. He wanted to be a lieutenant before he retired. He's not usually as abrasive as he is tonight."

"At least he seems to believe us now," Lilia said. "Officer, we're both very worried about our parents. This is not like them at all."

"I believe you and so does Sergeant Hartling. And you can call me Stetson if you don't mind."

"And you can call us Lilia and Timmy."

Stetson smiled and looked right into Lilia's eyes. "Lilia. That's a pretty name. I like it."

She blushed. "Thank you."

"Now, let's talk about tonight in a little more detail," he suggested. "What kind of legal work does your father do?"

"It's some kind of boring corporate stuff," she said, wrinkling her nose. "But others in his firm do criminal defense work. He does some when they need him to." She bit her lip. "Before we go over more details, would you mind putting word out that our parents and their car are missing? I'm scared for them. This has never happened before."

"Sure, I can do that. Can you give me the make and model of their car, the license number, and a physical description of each of your parents?" Stetson asked.

Lilia turned to Timmy. "You tell him, Timmy. I don't remember the license number."

Timmy rattled off the descriptions and the license number of his father's car. After he had done that, Lilia went upstairs and came back a minute later with a picture of the couple. "You can take that, but we want it back after you find Mom and Dad."

"I won't need to take it with me; I'll just take a picture of it with my phone," Stetson said. "I can then distribute it as needed. Thank you."

They were still in the mess that was Roland Dixon's office when Sergeant Hartling came back in. "Okay, I apologize to you two. I didn't believe that you knew what you were talking about at first, and honestly, I've had a really bad day. I'm sorry. Timmy, both of the license plate numbers that you gave me are listed as stolen, and neither belongs on a Ford Bronco. I expect that it's stolen as well. A couple detectives will be here shortly, as will some technicians from our crime lab." He glanced at his young partner. "Stetson, we need to get a description of the car the Dixons were driving this evening and have it broadcast."

"I just did that," the officer said.

"Did young Timmy here give you their parents' descriptions too?" the sergeant asked.

"Yes, he was very detailed," Stetson responded.

"I'll need it written down for me."

"I already have it in my notebook."

"Good work. Okay, Timmy and Lilia, as soon as the detectives get here, they will want all kinds of information from you."

"We'll try to give them what they ask for," Lilia said. "We just want our parents to be okay."

The next couple of hours were stressful for both Timmy and Lilia as they answered the detectives' questions over and over again. The lead detective, Sergeant Mark Snow, assumed command of the investigation from Sergeant Hartling of the patrol division. Timmy was questioned closely, as some officers had a hard time believing that he was able to accurately recall so much detailed information. But not once did any of the officers trip him up in any way. His answers were always accurate, even though he was getting very tired. He was, after all, only twelve years old.

When asked about extended family, they told the officers that both their parents were from single-child homes and that all four grandparents had passed on. They had no close family to call.

***

Word traveled quickly throughout the neighborhood and the church ward, but when folks showed up at the house out of concern, the officers only allowed the Dixons' bishop and Relief Society president to enter. They comforted Lilia and Timmy and told them that they would make sure that, despite the fact that Lilia was nineteen, they were not left alone until their parents returned.

After a while, Lilia and Timmy sat together in the family room while the officers did their work in other parts of the house.

"You need to call Mr. Lundquist," Timmy said to Lilia. Harry Lundquist was the senior law partner. He'd scheduled the dinner meeting with their parents.

"I don't know the number. We'll need to go into Dad's office to get it, and I'm not sure the officers will let us do that," Lilia said.

"I know the number," Timmy said. "I should have had you call it earlier."

"I should have known you would," Lilia said. She would have smiled at her mistake, but there was no smile left in her, deathly worried as she was about her parents. She handed her phone to Timmy. "Here, you enter the number, and when he answers, I'll put it on speaker, and we'll both talk to him."

"Look. You missed a call from Mom while we were at the movies," he said when she handed him her phone.

"I noticed that earlier, but I was so upset I didn't think much of it," she replied. She took the phone back and looked at it. "Maybe she left a voice mail for me." She checked. There was no message, so she dialed her mother's phone, which she had already done several times, but got the same result: voice mail. She ended the attempt and handed the phone back to Timmy. "I wonder if she was going to tell us that they were going to be late, but if so, surely she would have answered my calls or tried to call us again."

"Let's call Mr. Lundquist," he said.

* * *

Harry Lundquist lived alone in a large house in the Salt Lake City avenues area, only a mile or so from Roland Dixon's house. His wife had passed away from breast cancer less than a year before, and his children were all grown and had homes of their own. His house felt empty every time he entered it, something he was having a hard time adjusting to. He had the TV on tonight, but it was muted. He found himself unable to concentrate on the program he was watching.

He was worried about Roland's family. Roland and his wife had both received calls while eating dinner with him at a downtown steakhouse. Roland had rejected the call, but when Pamela's phone rang, Harry had insisted she answer it.

She'd dug her phone out and accepted the call. Then her face drained of color, causing instant concern in Harry's mind.

"Who is this?" she'd asked. "Okay. We'll come right away." She'd ended the call and turned to her husband. "That was a neighbor. He said the kids need us. He didn't say why but said we should hurry home."

"Why don't you call Lilia and find out what the problem is," Roland had suggested. "They're probably at the movies now. I can't imagine why they would be at home. Maybe one of them got sick."

Pamela had made the call, but there had been no answer. "They must be at the movie still. Lilia would have silenced her phone in the theater. Maybe I should run home. Harry, would you bring Roland home when you two are finished?" she'd asked.

"Which neighbor called?" Roland had inquired.

"He said he was Gabriel Schiller. But the voice didn't sound right. He must have a bad cold. I'd better check," she'd said. Then to Mr. Lundquist, she'd added, "He's an elderly neighbor from across the street. He's a close friend of our family, the closest thing to a grandparent that the kids have."

Harry remembered the look of concern on both of their faces. The business he'd intended to speak with them about had to do with a major change in his law firm. He intended to give Roland a lot more authority and responsibility, something he knew a couple of the other partners would not agree with, one man especially, but Roland was an extremely bright and hardworking lawyer.

Harry needed him to have more responsibility, as it was getting more difficult for him to keep up with all he had to do following the loss of his wife.

"Why don't you both go. We can finish our business tomorrow night if you don't mind. Your family comes first. Call me if there's a serious problem."

They had not argued and left with their meals unfinished. Harry had finished his and then driven home. Neither Pamela nor Roland had called back, so he decided that it must not have been anything too serious. One of the kids must have developed a stomachache or something. Yet he was disturbed and couldn't shake the feeling that something more serious than that was wrong.

His cell phone rang. It was late, but he wondered if it might be one of the Dixons calling him at last. He did not recognize the number, but he answered with, "This is Harry Lundquist."

"Mr. Lundquist, this is Lilia Dixon. My brother, Timmy, is on the phone with me. The police are here at our home. Have any of them called you yet? Or have our parents called you?"

Lundquist felt an uncomfortable stirring in his stomach. "No, why would they be calling me?"

"They're trying to figure out where our parents are. They were having dinner with you early this evening, but they never came home."

Harry was shocked. It took him a moment to get his thoughts organized before he said, "Your neighbor called them away from our dinner. He said they needed to get home right away, that you needed them. Is that not true?"

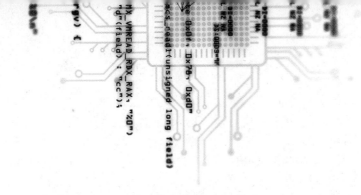

CHAPTER
THREE

FOR A MOMENT, THE LINE was silent. Harry must have upset Timmy and Lilia. He waited, and finally, it was Timmy who spoke. "Mr. Lundquist, which neighbor called them?"

"Do you have an elderly neighbor by the name of Schiller?" Harry asked.

"Yes, he's a widower," Lilia responded. "He lives right across the street from us. But we haven't seen him at all today. His first name is Gabriel. Gabe's a great guy and loves our family, but I doubt that he would know my parents' cell phone numbers. He still uses a landline and doesn't even own a cell phone or a computer."

"That's who your mother said called her." Harry hesitated. "Maybe I should be talking to a police officer."

"You need to," Lilia agreed. "But first, was Mom sure that's who she was talking to?"

Harry was an outstanding attorney, and he had learned over the years to guard his words. He didn't want to scare the kids worse than they probably already were. "Miss Dixon, will you please have a police officer get on the phone now?"

Timmy spoke up again. "Not until you answer our question. Was Mom sure it was Mr. Schiller?"

He could see that the kids were going to be stubborn. "She wondered if he had a cold."

"So she didn't recognize his voice?" the intelligent twelve-year-old asked. "Well, we know it wasn't him. Mom tried to call us. Lilia had her cell phone at the movie theater, but she had it muted. We didn't notice until a while ago, and so we tried to call her back, but it went to voice mail."

"I see," Harry said as his stomach churned. "So you really don't know where they are?"

"We don't," Lilia said. "And we're terribly worried."

"Can you get a police officer on the phone now? There are some officers there, right?" he asked.

"Yes, we called them," Timmy said. "Just a minute and I'll get one while you keep talking to Lilia."

"I take it your parents haven't ever done anything like this before," he said.

"Never, but here's the scary thing," she said. "When we got home, the house was dark and completely silent. Timmy figured out that the breaker had been turned off."

"Are you telling me that someone had been in your house while all of you were gone?"

"That's right. And let me tell you something else."

By the time an officer finally came on the phone, Lilia had told him all about her father's office, the old Bronco, the two men in the odd car, and the license plates. Harry pondered on how Timmy Dixon was indeed a smart boy, extraordinarily so. Then an officer spoke over Lilia's phone. "This is Detective Sergeant Mark Snow. I was told that you wanted to speak to me. I am in charge of the investigation."

"Thank you, Sergeant. My name is Harry Lundquist, and I am the senior law partner of Roland Dixon. Roland's children called me. Please, tell me what's going on there."

The two men proceeded to exchange information.

* * *

Timmy and Lilia were huddled across the room from the detective. He'd more or less shooed them away when Lilia handed him her phone. But there was no way she was going to let that phone out of her sight.

"I think we should go talk to Mr. Schiller," Timmy said.

"No, we should have the police talk to him," Lilia argued.

Timmy stubbornly shook his head. "They can too, but I want to first. Will you stay here so you can get your phone back from the officer while I go over there?"

"I don't think you should go right now," Lilia said sternly.

"You can't stop me."

"The police officers won't let you."

"They won't know," he said with a shake of his head. "I'll go out that west door and sneak across the lawn to the Johnstons' and then hurry over to Gabe's."

Lilia knew her little brother and decided it would do no good to argue further. "Don't let anyone see you. If he doesn't answer the door, come right back. Please don't be too long. I don't want to have to explain to the police where you are."

***

Without another word, Timmy slipped away. He took his time after he reached the shrubs that bordered the lawns between the two large houses. He carefully pushed his way through until he was on the far side and then looked around. He didn't see anyone near, so he headed for the street, staying close to the shrubbery, pretty much invisible in the dark shadows.

Once he reached the street, he waited for a minute. There was a police officer standing beside a patrol car, and he kept looking up and down the street. Timmy made a quick decision. He didn't want to be seen, so he worked back along the row of shrubbery and around the back of the house. He soon reached the next neighbor and scrambled over a fence that was between the two lots. He crossed through that big yard and again climbed a fence before making his way back to the street, staying close to bushes and shadows as much as he could.

Once he reached the street, he checked to make sure no one was looking, and then he ran across the street, up to an intersection, and around to the back of the houses on the street that was opposite his home. So now he was on the street north of the one he lived on and was out of sight of the police. He walked up the sidewalk until he could see the back of Gabriel's house. He had to cross through another yard to reach Gabe's back fence. He climbed over, and then he hurried to the back door of the house. Once there, he knocked loudly.

***

Sergeant Snow finished his conversation with Harry Lundquist, then looked around. When he spotted Lilia, he walked across the room to her and handed her back her phone. "Mr. Lundquist would like to speak with you again," he said. "Where's the redheaded kid?"

"Timmy was tired. He went upstairs to his room," she lied, uncomfortable about not being truthful but not finding a better option under the circumstances.

"Okay. But we will need to speak with him again in a little while," the sergeant said.

"Of course. I'll wake him if he's asleep when you need him," she said, hoping Timmy hurried.

She waited for a moment while Snow moved away, and then she put her phone to her ear. "It's Lilia again."

"Good. The police are putting out word for all officers to be looking for your parents, and for the old Bronco your brother spotted. Was he sure about the license plates?"

"Timmy does not make mistakes when it comes to remembering things. Yes, he's sure," she said.

"Lilia, how old are you?" Mr. Lundquist asked.

"Nineteen. Why?" she said.

"Well, there's something I need to tell you," Harry said. "I don't mean to frighten you, but I think you need to know that there have been some problems in my law firm. One of the attorneys resents your father, and I'm afraid that when he finds out what I was planning to tell your parents before they got called away, he will resent him even more."

"What were you going to tell Dad?" Lilia asked.

"Please don't mention this to him when he comes home," he said, hoping Lilia's parents would, in fact, come home. "I plan to promote him, if that's the right word. At any rate, he will soon be in a high position, beyond the other attorneys. He will be next to me in authority in the firm. That's all I'll say for now. But as I spoke with Detective Sergeant Snow, I mentioned that the one attorney who resents him may have sensed that some changes were coming. Although I don't know how, as I've been very secretive about this. And, ah, well, I'm not sure how he might react."

"Are you suggesting that he might do something to hurt Dad?" Lilia asked.

"I would hope not, but he could get nasty, I suppose," Harry said. "He is the main criminal defense attorney in the firm, and I've noticed a change in him over the past few months. I don't know what it's all about."

"Will you tell me his name?"

"Yes, under the circumstances, I think I should. I told Sergeant Snow, and I think that at some point he will be contacting him. His name is Saul Greenbaum."

"I've heard Dad mention him. He said he caught him in his office one day going through a file that was on his desk. When Dad asked him what he was doing, he swore at him and told him he was just checking something. Dad didn't mention it to you because he didn't want to create more tension in the firm. He only told me because he wanted me, and of course my mother, to know in case there were more problems and he had to go to you with it."

"Really? Your father never mentioned that to me. Anyway," Mr. Lundquist said, "I just wanted you to be aware of him, but it sounds like you already are. Please keep me informed of anything you learn about your parents. I'm sure they'll turn up pretty soon." He wished he could believe that, but he wasn't sure at all.

"I hope so," Lilia said with a catch in her voice.

* * *

Timmy was persistent. He knew that it was very late, but he felt an urgent need to speak with his elderly neighbor. When he didn't get an answer at the back door of Gabriel's house, he tried knocking on a couple of windows in the back, hoping that would wake Gabe up. Finally, a light came on in one of the rooms. Timmy hurried back to the door and knocked again. He could see another light come on, then he heard the lock slide back on the door. The door opened just a few inches, and to Timmy's surprise, the barrel of a pistol poked through.

"Who's there?" the old man asked, while he kept out of sight behind the door. "I'll call the police if I need to. Tell me who you are and then go away."

"It's Timmy Dixon," Timmy said boldly. "I need to talk to you."

"Timmy! What in tarnation do you want? Do you realize what time it is? I was asleep when someone knocked on the window. Was that you?" Gabriel asked.

"Yes, I'm sorry, but I have to talk to you. It's really important. Lilia and I are scared," he said.

"Then come on in," he said and swung the door wide enough for the stout little guy to slip through. Then he shut the door and locked it. "Sorry about the gun, Timmy. An old fellow like me can't be too careful these days, you know."

Gabriel laid the gun on a little table in a small room next to the back hallway and motioned for Timmy to sit down. "Tell me what has you so frightened. Does your father know you're over here?"

"No, we don't know where Dad and Mom are. They never came back from a meeting with Dad's senior law partner, and Mr. Lundquist doesn't know where they are either," Timmy said.

The old fellow leaned forward with arched eyebrows. "Why don't you tell me exactly what is going on."

So Timmy told him how the evening had started. "Here's the thing," he finally said. "Somebody called Mom's phone and told her that she and Dad needed to come home right away, that Lilia and I needed them. The man said he was you, Mr. Schiller."

A shadow crossed the old man's face. "I didn't call your mother. I don't even know the number of her cell phone. So I wonder who did. Surely your mother would have known it wasn't my voice."

"She didn't think it sounded like you, but she told Dad and Mr. Lundquist that you may have had a cold," Timmy explained.

"No cold. My voice sounds normal to you, doesn't it, Timmy?"

"Yes, sir, it does," Timmy responded. "When Mr. Lundquist told us that, we knew it couldn't be you. That's why I'm here. I'm trying to figure out who it might have been. It was someone who knew your name and that you are our neighbor."

Gabriel shook his head. Then he closed his eyes. Timmy watched as the old fellow seemed to be thinking, and he gave him time to do so. When Gabriel opened his eyes, he started to nod his head. "Timmy, I just remembered something. Yesterday morning, a man came to my door. I'd never seen him before. I told him I wasn't buying anything, but he responded that he wasn't selling. He just wanted to warn me of a scam that was going around the area. He said people were being told that they would make a bunch of money if they called a certain phone number. He told me the number but then said I should not call it under any circumstances.

"He told me that he could help me by giving me any new information that came to him and the team he was working with to stop the scammers. He asked my name, and I gave it to him. Then he asked for my phone number, but I couldn't help but wonder if he himself was a scammer, not someone he was supposedly warning me about. He left when I asked him to leave, and he was quite angry with me for not giving him my phone number. But, Timmy, my number is listed, so I suppose he can get it easily enough from the phone book."

"He probably just wanted your name," Timmy said. "And he used your name to frighten my parents into leaving their meeting with Mr. Lundquist. What did he look like?"

"I'm not very good at describing people, but he was probably around forty. He was taller than me and was wearing a red ball cap," Gabriel answered. "I think he had a brown shirt on, but I'm not sure. He certainly didn't look like a person who would be warning people about scams. He looked more like a crook."

Timmy felt his concern for his parents rising. He was convinced one of the guys from the old Bronco was involved. "Did you see what he was driving?"

"I don't see very well at a distance these days, but there was some sort of old car parked at the curb, a four-wheel-drive car. I'm pretty sure of that much."

"Thank you, Mr. Schiller. I need to get back to my sister."

"I hope your folks are okay," Gabriel said with a long face. "I'm so sorry if I helped in any wrongdoing."

"Oh no, Mr. Schiller, it's not your fault," Timmy said. "But thanks for telling me about that guy."

"I worry about you kids over there alone tonight. I feel like you're in danger. I have a lot of room. I think you should sleep over here tonight if your parents don't come home before the police leave. Will you do that?"

"I'll see what Lilia says," Timmy responded. "The bishop and Relief Society president have been there, and they did say that we should not be alone even though my sister is nineteen."

"I agree with the bishop. He's a wise man. Please stay with me. It would make me rest easier at least."

Timmy thanked him, and then he left out the back door and retraced his route to his house.

***

Lilia was waiting anxiously for Timmy's return. When he finally came, she could tell by the look in his magnified eyes through his thick glasses that he had learned something important. He relayed to her in hushed tones what Mr. Schiller had told him. "Our parents aren't just missing, but I think they may have been kidnapped," Timmy concluded, his voice betraying his age as sobs threatened.

He may be extremely bright and physically strong, but he's still just a kid, Lilia thought sadly. She put an arm around him and pulled him close. "We hope that's not true, Timmy. We need to pray."

They leaned their heads together, and Lilia offered a tender yet desperate prayer for the safe return of their parents. As soon as Timmy had whispered a tearful amen, he said, "I know that prayer will help us, but we need to do all we can to help them. If someone did kidnap them, we have to find out who did it and where they are. Heavenly Father will help us do that."

"And we have to find out why they were taken, if they were," Lilia told him.

"We have to find them and see if we can figure out why they were taken, if they were. We need to talk to Mr. Lundquist again, Lilia."

"I'm afraid that will have to wait until tomorrow morning, Timmy."

"No, we need to do it now. Let's call him again."

Lilia reluctantly pulled out her phone.

Lundquist answered on the first ring. "Have your parents returned?" he asked.

"No, but we wanted to tell you that Timmy talked to our neighbor Mr. Schiller. We thought you should know that he did not call my mother." She then told him about the man who had come to their neighbor's door.

"Thanks for telling me that. Don't hesitate to call me when you learn anything else," he said.

Lilia and Timmy still had their heads together and their backs to the room when they heard steps approaching.

"Are you guys okay?" Officer Erman asked gently. "This must be just horrible for you."

They both nodded. "It is," Lilia said.

"I'm sorry to intrude," he went on, "but I am worried about you."

"Thank you," they said in unison.

"I want to help if I can," Stetson said. He smiled at them. "I noticed that you were gone for a while, Timmy. And it wasn't up to your room, because I checked."

The siblings looked at each other. Finally, Lilia said, "Will you promise not to tell anyone?"

"I will only tell if the information is essential to the effort to locate your parents, and then only if it seems like there is no other way," he said.

Timmy was the one who made the decision to reveal his previous whereabouts. "I talked to our neighbor, Mr. Schiller. He lives across the street."

"Yes, I understand that he may have called your parents. Or that is what Sergeant Snow told me and the other officers a little while ago. We need to talk to him as well."

"You won't learn any more than I did," Timmy told him. "I went over there to talk to him because I wanted him to know what was happening."

"You've got to understand that Timmy likes to find things out by himself. It's just how he is."

"I see. What did he tell you, Timmy?" Stetson asked.

"Okay, I'll tell you." Timmy did just that, giving a complete report to the officer.

"We need to find those two men and their car. You were right to report seeing them. In my opinion, they are almost certainly involved in whatever has happened with your parents, and you are probably right about them calling your mother and pretending to be your neighbor."

Lilia looked at the handsome young officer's kind gray eyes, and she felt a shiver of attraction pass through her, but she quickly brushed it off. However, she instinctively felt like she could trust him more than the other officers.

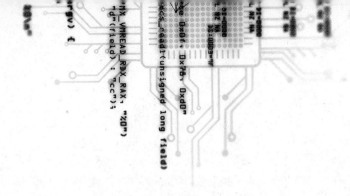

CHAPTER
FOUR

THERE WAS A TAP ON the window of the old Bronco. The driver, Louis, had been sleeping while parked in a desolate spot near the Great Salt Lake where he had been waiting for his partner to return in another car he had been ordered to steal. Their instructions were that this Bronco was to be left here when his partner picked him up. He opened his eyes. It was still dark, and it took him a moment to focus.

"Roll the window down. My cousin sent something for you," his partner, Benjy, shouted through the window.

"Good. So the boss is finally paying us for our work," Louis said greedily as he rolled the window down and peered at his partner's face in the dark.

"Yup, he sent this for you," Benjy said. He lifted his hand, but instead of a handful of cash, there was a gun.

Before Louis could even object, Benjy pulled the trigger, and Louis fell over into the passenger side of the car.

"Dead men don't talk," Benjy said with a laugh. "Sorry. It was good working with you." He put his gun back in his shoulder holster, straightened his red ball cap, and opened the passenger door of the Bronco. He retrieved Louis's wallet with gloved hands. Louis's ID, a forged one, was in the wallet when he checked. He also took everything else from his dead partner's pockets, including his pistol. He left the blue ball cap that was now stained with blood.

Benjy looked everything over carefully, and then he stepped back, shoved the door shut, and walked down to the water's edge, where he washed Louis's blood from his gloves. Then he walked back to his other stolen vehicle, one he would get rid of very soon.

* * *

The officers finally left. But Sergeant Snow told Lilia and Timmy that they could not stay in the house and offered to take them to a hotel. "We can stay at our neighbor's house," Lilia responded. "We'll be safe there."

So they went over to Gabe's house at about two o'clock. The two of them spent what was left of the night there. Gabriel made sure the doors and windows were all securely locked. They slept in rooms that were next to each other on the upper floor, directly over Gabriel's own bedroom. Officer Stetson, who went off duty at midnight, had promised to return in his own vehicle as soon as he could to keep watch outside during the night. It was a restless night, but from sheer exhaustion, Lilia and Timmy finally got some sleep.

When the siblings awoke in the morning, they smelled bacon. They dressed and hurried downstairs to find their wonderful old neighbor busily preparing a large breakfast. Officer Erman sat at Gabe's kitchen table, speaking to him. Stetson looked up as Lilia and Timmy walked in. "Hey, you two," he said. "Did you get any sleep?"

"Some," Lilia murmured. "You look tired, Officer Erman."

"Please, like I told you before, I would like it very much if you two would call me Stetson."

"Okay, Stetson," Lilia said, liking the feel of his name on her tongue. Despite her thinking that this was no time to let herself be attracted to someone, she was, and she simply could not help it. She smiled at him, and he smiled back.

"I am tired, but it's okay. I wanted to make sure you two were safe. Anyway, if I had been home at my lonely apartment, I wouldn't have been able to sleep worrying about you and your parents." He smiled again. "No one missed me since I live alone."

For some reason, those words about him living alone made Lilia's heart skip a beat and brought another tired smile to her face—he wasn't married. "Thanks for being here for us, Stetson. You didn't need to do that. Gabriel," she went on as she faced her neighbor, "you really didn't need to fix breakfast. We could have eaten at our house."

"I love you two kids and your parents. You are wonderful, thoughtful neighbors, and I want to do anything I can to help," he said. "You have a good friend in Stetson. He truly has your best interests at heart."

Lilia looked at Stetson, who nodded. Lilia read sadness and worry in his eyes. At least, she thought she did. His forehead was creased, and he slowly rubbed a hand over the stubble on his face.

"Stetson," Lilia said, "something is bothering you. Please tell us what it is."

"I'm sorry, but there is no word on your parents yet," he responded. "I've been speaking with Mr. Schiller about what you told me last night, Timmy."

"Call me Gabriel or just Gabe," the old man said.

Stetson nodded. "I promised Sergeant Snow that I'd get the information from Gabe." Timmy started to speak, but Stetson put up his hand. "No, Timmy. I did not tell Sergeant Snow or anyone else what you told me last night. That's why someone official needed to speak with Mr. Schiller since his name was used to get your parents out of the restaurant where they'd been meeting with Mr. Lundquist. That and the fact that you two decided to stay here. Sergeant Snow wanted to know why, so he asked me to interview Mr. Schiller for him this morning. I already relayed my report to Sergeant Snow."

Lilia had kept her eyes on Stetson's face. He seemed to be avoiding looking directly at her. He also looked uncomfortable, and that bothered her. Finally, she said, "Stetson, what aren't you telling us? Please, if there is something we need to know, just tell us."

He finally met her eyes. "The Bronco Timmy saw has been found near the Great Salt Lake in a desolate spot. We're lucky it was found so soon. The license plates on it matched the second set Timmy saw, and the California plates were on the floor in the back seat."

"That's good news, isn't it?" Lilia asked hopefully.

Stetson frowned. "I'm afraid not. It was a stolen vehicle taken from LA a week ago."

"So there's no way to tell who was driving it?" Lilia asked.

"Pretty much," he said as he looked away from her again.

"What about fingerprints, Stetson?" Timmy spoke up. "Won't that help you figure out who those guys are?"

"Well, yes and no," Stetson said evasively. The siblings looked at each other and then back at Stetson who sighed. "There's more I need to tell you. A dead man was found in the Bronco. He'd been shot. A blue ball cap lay on the front seat. It was bloody, as you can imagine. The man had no ID on him, and when the police ran his fingerprints, they got nothing. He was probably in the country illegally. The vehicle is still being processed, and maybe we can find prints to identify the other man—the one in the red cap. We can only hope."

Lilia glanced at her brother and could see that Timmy's mind was hard at work, his eyes shut tight, his lips pressed firmly together, and his fists clenched. She looked back at Stetson and Gabriel, who were both watching her little brother. No one said anything while his mind worked. Finally, he opened his eyes. "Someone must have hired him. He and his friend kidnapped Mom and Dad for someone else. I need to call Mr. Lundquist."

"Let's eat first," Lilia said. "Gabriel has it all ready."

"You guys start. Lilia, let me borrow your phone. I'll call him right now."

She reluctantly handed it to him, and Timmy began to make the call. No one ate. All three of the adults watched Timmy.

* * *

After a night of worry, tossing, turning, and moments of anger, Harry had finally showered and shaved. Shortly after, he entered his office. He said hello to his secretary, Rachel Kessler, and asked if there was anything urgent for him. Then he waited while she shuffled some slips of paper on her desk.

"Nope, there's nothing too urgent if you have something else going on. There is a note here that a Detective Sergeant Snow needs you to call him. He said it was important but didn't say it was urgent." Rachel had worked with Harry for over thirty years. She was in her sixties but was just as sharp as when he'd first hired her.

"I've been expecting that. I'll call him in a bit. Have you seen Saul this morning?" he asked. "I think he had a criminal matter he needed to be in court on."

"He called in an hour ago to say he wasn't feeling well and wouldn't be able to make it. Saul asked me to tell you he was sorry, and he wondered if you would assign someone to cover that small matter for him in court this afternoon." Rachel frowned. "He said the folder is on his desk. Jim and Randall are both here."

"I'll see who can handle it, Rachel," Harry said. "Jim might be best." Rachel was totally loyal to him. She knew things he didn't even tell any of his partners.

She got up and shut the door to her office, one that more or less protected her boss when he didn't want to be disturbed. She sat back down. "Harry, how did it go with Roland last night?"

Rachel was the only one in the firm who knew Harry had planned to move Roland up at the expense of the other attorneys. He knew she agreed with his plans. His cell phone began to vibrate as he asked, "Have you watched the news this morning?"

"No, why?" she asked.

He looked at the screen on his phone. "Come into my office. I need to take this, and then I'll explain what's going on." He accepted the call. "Good morning, Lilia."

"It's Timmy, but Lilia can hear you. So can Officer Erman and Gabriel Schiller, our neighbor."

"What's going on, Timmy?" Harry asked with a furrowed brow as both he and Rachel sat down. "I assume Officer Erman is with you on official police business, but why is Mr. Schiller with you? Isn't he the one who called your mother last night?"

Harry signaled for Rachel to be very quiet, and then he activated the speaker button on his phone so she could hear what Timmy had to say.

"You know he isn't," Timmy said rather sternly in his high-pitched voice. "We told you this last night. Someone pretended to be him. You said yourself that my mother wondered if he had a cold. But he doesn't."

"Do the police know who that someone is?" Harry asked as he watched the lines of concern etch his faithful secretary's face. "That's what I need to know."

"No, they don't. Now tell me more about Mr. Greenbaum, the lawyer you mentioned to us last night," he said. Rachel's jaw dropped, but she quickly put it back in place.

"What about him?" Harry asked. "I told you a little about him last night."

"We told you about Dad telling us about him looking at a file on his desk. When Dad told us about that the other night at dinner, he also told us that he felt like Mr. Greenbaum was causing problems for your firm. He said Mr. Greenbaum was acting very strange and that he always spoke rudely to Dad. Dad was afraid that he was up to something that could upset both you and my dad and possibly hurt the whole firm. Dad also said that he thought Mr. Greenbaum wanted him out of the firm."

"Your father told you all that?" Harry asked.

"Yes, he did. So did you talk to Dad about him last night before my parents got called away?" Timmy asked. "I know you told him that you were planning to give Dad more responsibility."

Harry met Rachel's eyes. She was nodding her head. Timmy was indeed a very intelligent and perceptive child. He thought for a moment about how to answer that question.

"Mr. Lundquist, are you still there?" Timmy asked.

"I am. Your father and mother left before I had the chance to explain what I needed," Harry said evasively.

"That is not what I am wondering about," Timmy said. "I think you know that." Timmy's voice was high pitched, that of a young fellow, but he spoke like a mature person.

"Yes, I do know that," Mr. Lundquist responded.

"Have the police called you yet?" Timmy asked next.

"A Detective Sergeant Snow left me a message to have me call him as soon as I can. I just got into my office and haven't had time to do that yet. But I will as soon as I finish talking to you," Harry promised.

"I need you to tell us more about Mr. Greenbaum," Timmy said. "Lilia and I both felt like you thought he could cause trouble and even put us in danger."

"Maybe we can get together in a little while," Harry said as he decided that he wanted Roland's kids informed as much as was reasonable. Timmy was far too smart to deceive, so it would be best to be up front with him and with Lilia, who was no dummy herself.

"Okay," Timmy said. "We would like that. Officer Erman just told us that the guy I saw with the blue cap was found dead in the old Bronco I saw drive past our house. Both sets of license plates were with the Bronco, so I know it was those guys. They don't know who the dead man is. I guess the other guy could be anywhere. But I think he knows where Dad and Mom are."

"I'm sure the police are looking into this whole thing," Harry assured Timmy, even as he felt in his gut that Saul had already caused trouble but that the police might have trouble figuring it all out.

"Call Sergeant Snow, and then will you call me and Lilia back so we can talk some more?" Timmy asked.

"Are you at home?" Harry asked.

"No, we are at Gabriel Schiller's house. We stayed with him last night, and Officer Erman stayed outside and watched for anyone who might be a danger to us," Timmy responded.

"I will come there as soon as I speak with the sergeant," Harry said decisively. "So don't go anywhere until I get there."

As soon as the call ended, Harry took a moment to explain to Rachel more about the trouble from the night before. Then he called the number he'd been given for Sergeant Snow. The sergeant answered and said, "Thanks for returning my call, Mr. Lundquist. Would it be possible to meet with you in person? I think we could communicate more effectively that way."

"I was just going to go over to the house of one of the Dixons' neighbors. The kids are there, and I need to speak with them."

"This would be Mr. Gabriel Schiller's house. Is that correct?"

"Yes, and Officer Erman is going to be there with them."

"Okay, I'll come there too, if that works for you."

"Please do," Harry said.

***

It was a clandestine meeting that Benjy was going to. After killing his partner, he'd spent a few hours in a hotel room waiting to hear from his cousin. He'd finally gotten the call and the meeting place was set up. It was out of the Salt Lake Valley, in a very remote area in Tooele County. He was driving the stolen car he'd used to meet his late partner at the lake, nervous that he'd not yet gotten rid of it. But that could wait until he finished the meeting he was eagerly anticipating. He pulled into a copse of trees. His cousin's car was already there. This would be the payout for his efforts. Too bad Louis couldn't have some of it, but his cousin only wanted to pay him.

Benjy got out of his car after pulling up next to his cousin's blue Escalade. "Did you take care of that little assignment for me?" his cousin, the man he knew as the boss, said.

"Yep, he was a little surprised," Benjy said, and he laughed.

"It's like I told you, I was afraid he would be a loose end that I could not afford to have running around."

"He's taken care of."

"Yes, thanks for that. You know though, I was a little surprised they found him so fast."

"Wait! What? How did that happen?" Benjy was genuinely surprised.

"You mean you didn't know?" the boss asked.

"No, I had to catch up on some sleep," Benjy said.

"I see." Benjy's cousin reached inside the fancy sport coat he was wearing. Benjy smiled. "So do I get Louis's share too?"

"Do you think that's fair?" the boss asked with no expression on his face.

"Sure do. I did everything you asked," Benjy replied. "And I know we didn't discuss it, but I expect you were going to give me a few thousand extra for taking care of the loose end."

Benjy was leaning back against the stolen car, smiling smugly.

"You'll get enough to last you for a long time. Here you go," his cousin said as he pulled his hand from inside his jacket.

Benjy barely had time to open his mouth in protest before two quick shots from a pistol closed his mouth forever. As his body slid to the ground, the boss said, "Can't have any loose ends, now can we? You were always a disgrace to the entire family."

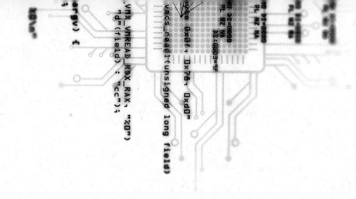

CHAPTER
FIVE

GABRIEL ANSWERED THE DOOR AND Harry Lundquist walked in, followed by Sergeant Snow. Within minutes, an intense discussion was underway. Timmy Dixon was involved, speaking like an adult in his twelve-year-old body and voice. No one commented about his thick lenses, his hearing aids, or his red hair and freckles. When he spoke, the adults in the room listened.

Everything known to date about the disappearance of the Dixons was discussed. The efforts the police were making were disappointing to Lilia. They apparently didn't seem to know quite what to do. They had been unsuccessful in identifying the man in the blue ball cap whose body had been found in the Bronco. The Dixons' silver Lexus had not been seen. Sergeant Snow was of the opinion that they must have driven it away from the restaurant themselves and been accosted somewhere else, the car then being stolen.

Lilia could tell by the tone of her little brother's questions that he was unhappy with what was being done to find their parents. Finally, he looked directly at Harry and asked, "What else can you tell us about the man who hates my dad?"

"Why do you ask about Saul?" Harry asked.

"You told us that you were going to make my dad's job more important, and that's why you were meeting with him and Mom. But you never did get into the details," Timmy said very seriously, his left eyebrow raised at an angle above the frames of his thick glasses. "I've told you some of what we heard Dad talk about concerning Mr. Greenbaum. Dad also said he was lazy. Is that true?"

"If your dad said it, then it must be true," Gabriel said. "Your dad is one of the most honest men I know."

"Thank you," Timmy said, and then, turning back to Harry, repeated, "Is it true?"

"Mr. Schiller is right," Harry responded.

"So that means that Mr. Greenbaum didn't work as hard as he should?" Timmy pressed.

"That's true, I'm afraid, but he is a very intelligent man and a skilled attorney. He does mostly criminal defense work, and he's had some impressive success."

Lilia could tell that Timmy was thinking deeply. For a moment he shut his eyes and squeezed his lips tight, and his fists curled tightly as well. Not a word was uttered for a minute or more, and all eyes in the room were on Timmy. Finally he opened his eyes and asked, "Did Mr. Greenbaum know what you were going to talk to Dad about?"

Harry took a deep breath, looked away from Timmy's intense little face, then looked back and said, "I don't think so. The only person, as far as I know, who knew the proposal I was going to make to your father was Rachel Kessler, my personal secretary. And she would not have told anyone. She is as honest as your father."

"But maybe Mr. Greenbaum did know," Timmy said, his words a statement more than a question.

"I don't know how he could have," Harry said.

"Did he dislike my father?" Timmy asked next.

"Goodness, Timmy, why all the questions about Mr. Greenbaum?" Harry asked. To Lilia, he seemed a little rattled, for he kept looking over Timmy's head and swallowing a lot.

"Well, did he?" Timmy insisted.

"I don't know. I guess that the two of them may not have been friends, but I couldn't say either of them openly disliked the other," Harry finally answered. His brow had beads of perspiration on it, and he rubbed at it with his hand. He stood up. "Timmy, you have raised some interesting questions. I don't think they have anything to do with what has happened to your parents, but I am going to try to get some feedback from some of the other people in my firm and see if they knew of any open hostility on the part of Saul toward your father. I hope you will all excuse me, but I need to get back to my office."

He left immediately after that. Sergeant Snow lingered a moment. After the door had closed behind Harry, he said, "Timmy, do you think that Mr. Greenbaum had something to do with your parents' disappearance?"

Timmy stood up and walked over to stand beside Lilia before he answered. "I don't know. But someone made them vanish. If not him then I think it may be another attorney in the firm. They didn't just leave on their own."

"Officer Erman and I have to get back to work on this matter," Sergeant Snow said. "Stetson, let's go. I'd like to meet with you at the station." He again addressed the Dixons. "Will you two let me know if you hear anything that might help me or if you think of something that hasn't already occurred to you?"

"Of course, if it will help," Lilia said. Timmy was mum and his eyes were closed. Lilia could tell with one look at him that his overpowered brain was busily at work. Gabriel Schiller saw Sergeant Snow and Stetson to the door.

As soon as they were gone, Timmy's eyes opened. "We need to go home. There is something I want to do."

"What's that?" Lilia asked as Gabriel looked on.

"I want to check some things in Dad's office in the house," he said.

"I'll come with you two," Gabriel offered.

"You don't need to do that," Lilia said. "You have already done too much for us. We'll be okay."

"You will come and stay again tonight, won't you? I'd never be able to sleep if you were in that big silent house of yours by yourselves," the old fellow said.

"Yes, we can do that," Lilia said. "Thank you."

Roland Dixon's home office was ordinarily tidy and well organized. As a busy lawyer, he brought a lot of work home. He had a file cabinet that contained quite a few files. But as Timmy knew, most of his notes and his work were kept on his computer, one he kept secure.

Timmy started by checking everything of his father's that had been shoved off of his desk. Then he looked in his desk. He could tell that things had been disturbed but hadn't been thrown around. While he was doing that, Lilia was checking each file that had been taken from the cabinet and then replacing them in the best order she could. Timmy pulled everything out of each drawer, taking them one at a time. In the bottom left-hand drawer he found some notes that his father had written to himself as reminders. Most of them had to do with cases he was working on and held little interest to Timmy at that point, he explained to Lilia, who had stopped what she was doing when he announced the discovery of the notes.

Lilia pulled up a chair and the two of them went over the notes together, one at a time. In each case, they had reference to something their father was reminding himself to do. They were generally not dated, but some did have dates written on them when he felt he had to take some kind of action on a particular day.

There had been nothing that caught Lilia's interest, nor had any of them so far caused Timmy to react. But Lilia let out a little gasp as Timmy held up the last note so she could see it. It had been at the bottom of the pile and was folded in quarters. However, on the outside was one word: urgent. It didn't appear to have been disturbed by whoever had messed up the office.

Timmy unfolded it, and at a glance, Lilia could see that it had been hurriedly written. The handwriting, though clearly their father's, was not as neat as usual. And it was written on a note pad that had the law firm's name at the top. "Dad only keeps pads like this at his office," Timmy noted as he pressed the note flat and then held it up. "I've seen them there. I've never seen one here."

"Are you suggesting that he wrote this at his office?" Lilia asked as she began to read the words written there.

"I think so. But he must have folded it and put it in his pocket and brought it home."

They both read the note, and then Timmy placed it on the desktop and closed his eyes. His fists were clenched and his lips tight together. Lilia was also busy thinking. The note was disturbing.

Lilia picked it up and read it again.

> *I need to be careful what I say to or about Saul. He has it in for me. I overheard him say to a client today when he didn't know I was close enough to hear him, "Don't worry about Roland Dixon. He won't be with the firm much longer." I need to speak with Harry about this. Maybe I'll call on him at home sometime soon.*

The note was dated April second. It made Lilia shiver with fright. Timmy had been right in pressing Mr. Lundquist about Saul. He hated their father. Timmy suddenly stood up. "Lilia, Dad wrote this note to himself the same day that he disappeared. He must not have known about the meeting with Mr. Lundquist then, so it must have been in the morning. And Mr. Lundquist must have told him during the day that he wanted to meet with Dad and Mom at a dinner that night."

"But it was at the bottom of the pile of notes," Lilia said.

"Okay, so when he got home, knowing that he would be seeing Mr. Lundquist that night, he had already made up his mind to mention Mr. Greenbaum at their meeting. So he stuck it at the bottom, which means to me that he considered it taken care of or at least that it would be when he and Mom met with Mr. Lundquist," Timmy reasoned.

"We should show this to Sergeant Snow and to Mr. Lundquist," Lilia said, feeling urgency roll the contents of her stomach around.

"Not yet," Timmy said. "Let's make three copies of this. We'll give one to the cops. You keep one and I'll keep the other, and we'll put this back right where we found it."

Lilia said, "I'll make the copies," and she stepped over to the printer/copy machine.

"I'll keep looking in these drawers. I'm surprised they haven't been messed up much. I still have two to go," Timmy said as he neatly replaced the notes back in the drawer he'd found them in. "We'll put that at the bottom like it was when you finish with the copies."

When Lilia handed him the note back, he was staring at a small metal box that he had just placed on the desktop. "What's that?" Lilia asked.

"I don't know, but there must be something in it that Dad wanted kept more secure than those notes." As Timmy spoke, he placed the Saul note back beneath the others and closed that drawer. "We need to find out what's in this metal box," he said as he straightened up and reached for it.

"It has a combination, Timmy. How can we get in it? It looks quite sturdy and would be hard to bust open," Lilia said.

"We need the combination," Timmy said reasonably.

"That could be anything," Lilia said with a scowl. "I don't see how we could ever guess it."

A smile creased her little brother's freckled face, and he ran a hand through his curly red hair. "Dad keeps all his passwords in his computer and on his phone in secure files," he said.

"If it's secure, how do we get into it? I mean, we don't even know the password to his computer," Lilia said, feeling very discouraged, for she couldn't help but think that there could be something very important inside of the small metal box.

"I know Dad's password," Timmy said.

"You do? When did he tell you? He never told me," she said.

Timmy grinned and looked up at her, his eyes large and sparkling behind his thick glasses. "I saw him type it in one day."

"Of course you remember it."

"Lilia, I always remember things. That's what I do," he said and moved over to his father's computer desk and then looked up at his sister with dismay. "I forgot about his screen. It's ruined."

"But you just said you remember things," she said a bit sarcastically.

"I do, but sometimes I get distracted. I'm distracted now. I can't be perfect," he said with a scowl at Lilia. "He has an old one in the basement. I'll get it. Be right back."

Timmy hurried away. Lilia was shaking her head. She could only hope the old screen still worked. Soon, Timmy was back. He unplugged the busted screen and hooked in the old, smaller one. "Now I'll get into his computer. This screen should still work. He only replaced it because he wanted a larger one."

Once he had it opened, he soon located the file that contained all their father's passwords. "I guess you know how to get into that too," she said.

Timmy nodded. "Of course. I notice things even when people don't think I'm looking."

"I don't think Dad and Mom realize how smart you really are . . . and how sneaky."

"I need to entertain myself," he said. "But I've never used what I know to get into this before, because I don't snoop just to snoop. But this is important." As he spoke, his hands were flying over the computer keyboard and a moment later, the file opened. "I hope the combination is in here."

He slowly scrolled down through the passwords. He didn't fool Lilia. She knew he could read at breakneck speed. What he was doing was memorizing them. He got clear to the bottom and said, "Here we are, sis. All it says is combinations and there are two. One is for this box, I think. The other one is for the safe in their bedroom behind that large picture of the Savior, but I already know that one."

"I'm not surprised," Lilia said sarcastically.

"I'm going to want to check more stuff on Dad's computer later, but right now, let's see what surprises this little box contains," Timmy said as he shut the computer down.

Lilia had tried to memorize the combination, but the last four numbers eluded her. They did not elude Timmy. He entered the twelve numbers and popped the box open. At that moment, Lilia's phone began to ring. She looked at it and said, "This is Gabriel. I better see what he wants."

She said hello and felt a chill come over her when Gabriel said, "Get out of the house right now! Go out the back and hide. Someone is trying to open your front door, and something makes me think he's not there on a social call."

"Shut that, and let's go," Lilia said urgently. Timmy had been watching her and had not yet looked into the small metal safe, for that was what it was.

"I better grab that note," Timmy said, and he hurriedly opened the bottom left drawer and grabbed it, shoved it in the safe, closed it, and followed his sister at a run through the house.

They had barely reached the door that led to the backyard when they heard the front door open. Lilia had not told Timmy what Gabriel had said, but he had obeyed without question. They slipped quietly out the back, locking the door behind them, and then ran for the back of the yard and into some thick shrubs near the fence.

Only when they were hidden deep in the shrubs did Timmy whisper, "Was Gabriel warning you that someone was getting in the house?"

"Yes, and he said to get out fast." She was breathing hard, as was Timmy. Their dash around the swimming pool and through the yard had been as fast as Timmy's legs would move. They were both keeping their voices very low. "I wonder who it could be."

"Did you get a look at him?" Timmy asked. "I was too busy trying to keep up with you to look back."

"I didn't," she said. "I don't think he got to where we could have seen him or where he could have seen us until we were outside. I'm sure we wouldn't have known him anyway."

"I wonder if he was wearing a red ball cap," Timmy whispered. "If I could just get a look at the guy's face, I would remember it, and I could draw it for the cops."

"But that's not possible. We've got to stay hidden. We can't take a chance on him seeing us. Whoever it is, he is dangerous, or he wouldn't have gone in our house like he did," Lilia reasoned in a whisper. "After he's gone, we can ask Gabriel what he looked like. At the least he can tell us if he was wearing a red ball cap and maybe even what he was driving. I can't believe, whoever it is, that he would open the door in the daylight and walk right in."

She looked through the gloomy light at her little brother. He had placed the small metal safe beside him on the ground. His eyes were shut tight. She had no idea what he was thinking, but it worried her. She spoke again, thinking that maybe she could get him out of his trance, as she always considered it when he was deep in thought. "Timmy, the guy had a key. He must have, because I know I locked the door after we came in. You know it too because you watched me."

Timmy did not move. His lips were pressed so tightly that they started to turn white. A couple of minutes passed. She didn't try to interrupt his thoughts again. She impatiently waited for him to speak when he was ready.

Finally, he looked across at her and whispered, "He got the key from Dad. He knows where Dad and Mom are."

Lilia's heart skipped a beat. "That's probably true," she responded softly.

"I've got to get a look at him," Timmy said.

"Timmy, no, you can't!" Lilia warned, her voice in a loud whisper now.

"I've got to. We need to know who he is. I can sneak around through the neighbors' yards like I did last night and go to Gabriel's. Then I can watch through his window. He might even have some binoculars I could use."

"Timmy," Lilia said in a warning voice, her eyes just slits as she spoke.

"I'm going," he said.

"But what about the little metal safe? We need to look in it," Lilia argued.

"I know, but right now seeing this guy's face is more important. I better hurry before he leaves and I miss seeing him," Timmy said as he started to stand into a stooping position.

"I'm coming with you," she said decisively. "I'll carry the metal box."

Lilia had put her phone on silent mode after they'd reached the shrubs. It vibrated in her pocket now. She hunched down beside the hedge she and Timmy had just crawled through into their neighbor's yard, pulled out her phone, and looked at it. It was Gabriel. She showed Timmy, then in a whisper she answered, "Hello."

"Did you guys get away okay?" Gabriel asked.

"Yes," she whispered.

"Stay hidden," he said urgently. "There is a second man just down the street near the property line between your place and your neighbor's house. He's standing beside a white car and is watching your house. I think they're together."

Lilia's heart spiked. She told Timmy what she had just heard. "Let's go then," he said, pointing to the next neighboring house.

But just then a gravelly voice said, "You stinking kids. I got you now."

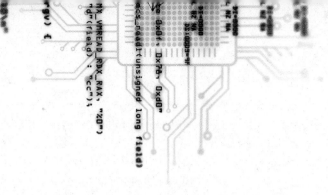

CHAPTER
SIX

THE MAN HELD A KNIFE, was dressed in blue jeans and a black t-shirt, was short, stout, had a shaved head, and sported a short beard. He was not wearing a mask, which was of great concern to Lilia, meaning he didn't care if they could recognize him at a later date. "You are coming with me now, or I will spread your blood all over your neighbor's lawn." His voice was very distinctive, with a gravelly sound to it like he needed to clear his throat but couldn't.

Timmy stood upright, flanked by his sister. There was clearly a lot this gangster didn't know about these two. But they soon educated him. "You first," Lilia said to Timmy.

As expected, the knife wielding man seemed to think that Timmy would try to run first, and she'd follow. He grinned wickedly at them. Timmy stepped forward and the guy stepped to the side. Then in a movement so fast the guy couldn't have reacted even if he'd known what was coming, Timmy kicked. His sneaker-clad foot caught the guy's wrist, the sound of breaking bones making the man open his mouth to scream even as the knife flew from his hand. But not a sound had come from him before Lilia's foot caught him violently on the side of the head, followed in a fraction of a second by little Timmy striking his throat with a well-aimed karate chop.

The guy fell with nothing but a strangling sound coming from his throat. Lilia sent another crushing kick to his head and all sound stopped. "I'll get his wallet and phone, you get the knife and the metal box," Timmy said. "I'll look for a gun too."

"I want a picture of him," Lilia said. "Then you won't have to try to draw it."

"I won't forget his face," Timmy reminded her, but she already had her phone in her hand. She rapidly snapped a couple of pictures, and then she grabbed the knife and box. Timmy got the wallet, found that the man didn't have a gun, and said, "That way." He pointed to the next neighbor's house to the west, which was some distance away as this neighborhood was an affluent one, the houses large and the properties quite sprawling.

All the time they'd been speaking in hushed tones, not knowing if the other man was still in the house or not. They ran through the backyard of their next-door neighbors, a middle-aged couple who had no children at home and who went to work every weekday morning. They didn't expect anyone to see them from that house.

Within minutes they'd reached the street, looked up and down it, and on Lilia's signal, they darted across. They slowed down after a minute and were soon knocking on Gabriel's back door.

He swung it open and said, "Oh, I am so relieved to see you two. That second man went out of sight along the hedge beside your house. I was afraid that he'd somehow figured out where you were."

"He did," Lilia admitted, "but we got away from him."

"Where is he now?" Gabriel asked.

"He was lying on the ground beside the fence when we left him. We need to call the police and see if they can find him before he wakes up," Lilia said.

"Wakes up? What are you talking about?" Gabriel's wrinkled old face was more wrinkled than ever as he lifted his eyebrows in surprise.

"We kind of knocked him out," Timmy said modestly as Lilia began to look at the contacts in her phone.

***

Officer Erman had just left Detective Snow's office. He was angry. Snow had thanked him for his help but then informed him that he had other duties to perform and to leave the investigation of the missing couple to him and his squad from this point on.

"I was just making sure they were safe," Stetson had argued. "I was off duty and won't be back on until tonight. And as you know, I was in my personal vehicle."

"I understand. Just don't do something that might mess up this case for me," Snow had said. "If for some unforeseen reason I need your help, I'll ask for it."

"I'm sorry, Sergeant. I didn't think I was interfering," he'd responded.

"Well, you sort of were. If I think they need protection, I'll arrange for it. Now go home and get some rest. I'm sure you need it," Snow had said.

"I got it," Stetson had said. "I am rather tired." He'd turned to the door to leave.

"Just a moment, Officer," Sergeant Snow had said. "There is one more thing. I saw the way that Dixon girl looked at you. And I saw you admiring her as well. She's off limits to you as long as this investigation is ongoing."

"I got it," Stetson had said again, rather embarrassed.

"Then beat it," Snow had told him with a surprising hint of a smile, and that's what he'd done. That smile made him feel a little less chastised. He knew Snow was an okay guy. He strode rapidly to the door and outside.

***

"I'm calling Officer Erman," Lilia said. Gabriel was moving his head slowly back and forth and Timmy was watching Lilia intently. "I've got it on speaker."

"Hello, this is Stetson Erman. Is that you, Lilia?" he asked.

"Yes, we need help. We just hurt a man who attacked us. Someone needs to get him before he gets away," Lilia said, the words tumbling rapidly from her mouth.

"Wait, where are you?" Stetson asked. "And are you both all right?"

"We are fine, and we are at Gabriel's house. There is another man in our house. We barely got out before he got us," she said.

"How did he get in?"

"He had a key, but hurry, and we will tell you about it all later."

"I'll get other officers on the way right now. I can't come myself, but I'll see that someone gets there soon," he said. "Don't leave Gabriel's house."

Timmy was already at the big window of the large living room that was directly across from his own front door. "Gabriel, do you have any binoculars?"

"Yes," he said, looking very confused.

"I want to see the guy who is in our house when he comes out so I can memorize his face," Timmy said.

That did nothing to relieve Gabriel's confusion, but it got the old man moving. He was gone for a couple of minutes. Lilia had joined her brother at the window and said, "I hope Gabriel hurries. Whatever that guy's doing in there might not take him long. That white car is still there, so I don't think the guy has left yet."

"He's probably doing what we did, searching Dad's office," Timmy said. "All they did before was mess it up."

Lilia said nothing more as they waited. She was thinking about Stetson. She would have thought he'd come running as soon as she told him what was happening, but he'd told her he'd send others. She was hurt. She'd thought he kind of liked her, and that he was concerned about her and Timmy's safety. She clearly had read him wrong. She tried to shove thoughts of him from her mind. It was immature of her to begin to fall for him like she had. She felt stupid but was determined not to let him get to her again, if she ever even saw him after this.

Gabriel shuffled back in the room, interrupting her thoughts, and handed a pair of binoculars to Timmy. It was none too soon, for about thirty seconds later, they saw the man that had tried to abduct them come stumbling into sight. As Timmy watched him through the binoculars, he described what he was seeing. "He's disoriented, I think. And he keeps grabbing his chest and his throat like he's having a hard time breathing."

"Yeah, I can tell that too. You must have hit him pretty hard in the throat," Lilia said.

"I was trying to. He wanted to make us go with him."

"Is that a knife you're holding?" Gabriel asked Lilia.

"Oh, yeah, sorry. I wasn't even thinking about it. Timmy kicked it out of the guy's hand. And you're probably wondering about this metal box. It's Dad's. We need to see what's in it when we get a minute," Lilia explained. "Oh, our front door is opening. The guy coming out has his cell phone to his ear."

Timmy said, "He's probably trying to call his friend. The guy's phone keeps vibrating in my pocket."

"I need to sit down," dear old Gabriel said. He shuffled to the nearest chair and more like collapsed than sat down.

"Sorry, Gabriel," Lilia said. "We'll explain in a bit."

"I can see that man's face really well," Timmy said. "I can see both of them. I can draw both faces unless the picture you took is good enough that I don't need to," he added, speaking to Lilia as he watched the men across the street through the binoculars.

"I wish the cops would get here. Those guys are going to get away," Lilia moaned. "They are both in the car now. It's leaving. Still no cops!"

Timmy watched the car until it was out of sight before pulling the binoculars from his eyes. "At least I got the make of the car and the license plate number. We can give that to Stetson when he gets here."

"Stetson's not coming," Lilia said, feeling a pain in her heart. "He told me he can't but that he'd make sure some other officers come."

Another five minutes passed before a cop car finally raced up the street and screeched to a stop in front of their house. Two officers piled out and, with drawn handguns, took up a position beside their car, using it as shelter from the direction of the Dixon house. Moments later, a second car joined them, and lastly, Sergeant Snow arrived.

"I'll call Sergeant Snow," Lilia said.

A moment later the sergeant's voice came on the call phone speaker. "Sergeant Snow," he said.

"Sergeant, this is Lilia Dixon. There were two men over there. One was in our house and one tried to kidnap my brother and me. But you're too late," she said, unable to mask the bitterness in her voice. "They're gone already."

"Okay, but we'll check the house anyway. You guys stay there. I'll come talk to you after we make sure everything is okay over there," the sergeant said.

"Let me go in the house with you guys," Lilia offered. "There's no danger now."

"We'll handle it. You need to stay put," Snow ordered and ended the call.

The siblings watched for a moment as the officers approached their house. Then Timmy said, "I am going to open the metal box again. I want to see what's in it before any of the officers come over here."

Gabriel, by then, had pretty much recovered from his shock, and he said, "Let's use the table in the dining room."

He led the way, and a minute later, Timmy had the little safe opened. Then he looked for a moment inside of it and finally began to pull items out one at a time. His father's note to himself about Saul was the first item he removed. Then he pulled an envelope out and discovered a couple of unexpired credit cards and the photocopies of three more.

"This won't help much," Lilia said as they looked over the cards and copies. "Mom and Dad can't use any of these cards, and the photocopies are probably of ones they had with them. Whoever kidnapped them probably took them."

"Yeah," Timmy mumbled.

"It might help the cops. They can try to find out if the cards have been used anywhere. Who knows, maybe one of the bad guys is using them," Lilia reasoned.

"Yeah, maybe," Timmy said. There were a few other papers in the little safe. Lilia assumed they were very important to her dad but meant nothing to her.

Timmy shuffled everything back into the box, and since there was still a little room, he also put the wallet and cell phone he'd taken from the would-be kidnapper in it. Then he shut the lid. It locked with a click. Lilia watched as he closed his eyes and balled his fists. He was back in thinking mode. She couldn't even guess what was going through that very fertile mind of his.

When he opened them after a couple of quiet minutes, he said, "I guess we need to tell the police about what we found in here."

When, a few minutes later, Sergeant Snow and a couple of officers came to Gabriel's house to talk to them, Timmy showed them the tiny locked safe. "Where did you get that?" the sergeant demanded. "I think you two have been over at your house. I told you to stay away, and I meant it."

"We needed some things, and still do," Lilia said as Timmy kept mum.

"I guess you don't know what's in it, not that it would be anything of use to us."

Timmy looked at Lilia with concern on his freckled face. She shook her head ever so slightly. She was sure he would get her message. When he spoke, she was proved right. He said, "What if there are credit cards or something like that in there?"

The officer scowled and shook his head. "That probably wouldn't help," he said.

"Can't you trace them if they are using their cards?" he asked.

"They wouldn't be. Whoever kidnapped them has got their cards, and I'm sure they would be too smart to use the cards themselves. Anyway, you're just guessing," Snow said.

"Could you tell what the guy did in our house today?" Timmy asked as he pulled the sergeant's focus away from the metal box and its contents.

"He made a mess of your father's office and of the master bedroom. I was surprised that there was a screen hooked to your father's computer," he said. "I wonder who hooked it up there." His eyes bored into Timmy's.

"I was hoping we could get into Dad's computer," Timmy said. "But it's password protected."

"And you with that supposed genius brain of yours couldn't figure it out," he said, finally smiling just a little.

"I didn't try," Timmy said truthfully, since of course he'd already known the password. "So what do you think the guy was after?"

"We suppose he was looking for something. Would you two have any idea what he may have been looking for?" Snow asked.

Lilia and Timmy looked at each other, and then she said, "No."

"That's no help, but I didn't really expect that you would," he said. "I don't want you two to go near that house again. You got lucky this time and didn't get hurt. You might not again."

Once more a silent communication passed between the two of them. Then Timmy said, "We saw the guys' faces and I got the make of their car and the license number."

"Now that could be of some assistance," Sergeant Snow said with a show of enthusiasm. "Why don't you describe them to me."

"I can draw you a picture of their faces, and we have a couple pictures of the guy who attacked us, but they aren't too good because it was after we'd beat him up," Timmy said.

The sergeant chuckled. "Yeah, I can just see you guys beating up a crook. No, just describe them to me."

Timmy did just that. But after, he repeated, "I will draw a picture of each of them and you can have them."

"Well, okay, but I don't know if that will be of much help," he said. "Now remember, you two, stay away from your house until we find your parents. They can stay here, can't they, Mr. Schiller."

"They surely may," he agreed.

Snow scowled at them for a moment, and his silent partners did pretty much the same. Then Snow said, "That knife on the table, is that what you guys took when you went in your house in case you had to defend yourselves? That was not smart. You guys need to be careful. You could get hurt."

"We took it away from the guy we beat up. It has his fingerprints on it. We were going to give it to you," Timmy said. "We took his wallet and his cell phone too."

Snow and the other officers chuckled softly. "You have a rather large imagination, young fellow. There is no way you took that knife from anyone, or a cell phone or wallet. We won't need that knife, but Mr. Schiller, you need to put it away and don't let these two take it again. We need to go now." And the three officers turned and left the room. A minute later, Timmy heard the front door close.

Timmy pounded his fists together. "He doesn't believe us, Lilia. Just because I'm a kid, he thinks I don't know anything. I'm glad we didn't show him what's in the box. The police will never believe us about anything, and they'll never find Mom and Dad. We are going to have to do it ourselves."

"Oh, now, Timmy," Gabriel said, "I don't think you should try to do that."

Timmy scowled at him. "Then who will find them?"

Gabriel didn't have an answer to that, but his wrinkled face looked more wrinkled than ever. There was a knock on the door, and he shuffled away to answer it. A moment later, he came back into the dining room followed by an officer they had not met before. "Hi guys. I'm Detective Diana Franklin," she said.

"Hi," they said in unison as they both looked her over. Lilia judged her to be around thirty. She was tall and slender with dark-brown, short hair, and brown eyes. She was very pretty. She smiled at them. That at least was a good sign.

"The burglar made a bit of a mess of your house, but Sergeant Snow doesn't want you to try to clean it up yet," she said. "We'll let you know when you can go back in there. I'm sorry. This must be so hard on you two."

"Yeah, he just told us we can't go in there," Timmy growled, his little face screwed up in anger. "It's our house, not his."

"It's out of concern for your safety. And believe me, Sergeant Snow and all the rest of us want you guys to be safe," she said. "We've got to find your parents, and we must do it quickly. Time is against us here."

"We know that," Timmy said, his face still angry and his eyes glaring through the magnification of his glasses. "Sergeant Snow doesn't want our help, and he needs it. So I guess you don't either."

Officer Franklin walked over to where Timmy was standing beside the dining room table. "If you have some suggestions, I'll listen to them. He's in charge of the case, but maybe I can sort of steer him in the right direction if you two have information that will help. He can be kind of gruff at times, but he's a good detective and he means well."

"We have some, but he laughed at me when I tried to help. So I think me and Lilia will just find Dad and Mom ourselves," Timmy said in a very determined voice.

Unlike the other detectives, Detective Franklin did not chuckle. Nor did she encourage Timmy and Lilia to attempt it on their own. Instead, she said, "Why don't you guys tell me what you know that you think will help us."

"Would you actually help us if we tell you?" Timmy asked. "Would Sergeant Snow let you?"

The detective smiled at him. "That's not what I said. You guys can help me. Got it?"

Timmy stared at her for a moment, glanced at Lilia, who nodded, and then he said, "Okay, got it."

"Lilia. That's your name, and yours is Timmy. Is that right?" Detective Franklin asked.

They both nodded. "I really would like to help you guys. I can't imagine what you're feeling. And I'm so sorry. I was told by Sergeant Snow to make sure you both stay safe. He's very concerned about you. So you will be seeing a lot of me. That being the case, I would like you to call me Diana and I'll call you Timmy and Lilia. Do you have any objections to that?" she asked as she looked into Lilia's eyes and then Timmy's. She seemed like a really good lady, and perhaps they could trust her. And yet Lilia couldn't help wishing it was Stetson here instead of her, but for some reason he couldn't come . . . or didn't want to, although he hadn't said that.

"Well?" Diana pressed.

"Yeah, I guess that would be okay," she said.

"Then maybe we'll be a team," Diana suggested with a smile.

Lilia tried to smile back. Diana obviously had no idea about her little brother. If the three of them were to be a team, it would be Timmy who was the real leader. She might eventually figure that out. Everyone underestimated him, but she had a feeling Diana might come to appreciate her little brother's exceptional intellect once she was exposed to it.

Diana turned to Gabriel and said, "I understand that you're going to let these guys stay with you for the time being."

"That's right," he said. "They can stay here as long as they need to. I have plenty of room."

Diana smiled again. "In that case, maybe you can be part of the team too," she said.

The old man smiled. "If you want me to be," he said.

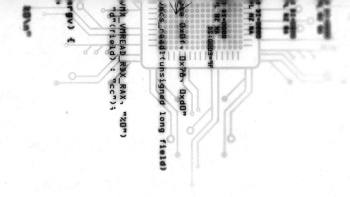

CHAPTER
SEVEN

THEY ALL GATHERED AROUND GABRIEL'S table.

"Okay, let's start with this knife here," Diana said. "Is that what you took with you when you went over to your house? Did you plan to defend yourselves with this?" She reached for the knife.

"Don't touch it!" the high-pitched voice of Timmy commanded. "There are fingerprints on it."

Diana drew her hand back and cocked an eyebrow at Timmy. "Would you like to explain?" she asked.

"You won't believe us, so you can think what you want," he said.

Diana eyed him warily. "I think there's something you guys are holding back. Would you care to tell me about it? If we are going to be a team, you need to trust me with what you know, or I can't help you."

Lilia looked at Timmy for a moment. Perhaps they should test this detective out, see if they really could trust her. Finally she nodded at Timmy and he said, "We took it from the guy who tried to kidnap us. I kicked it out of his hand and after Lilia knocked him out she picked it up and brought it with us. Sergeant Snow said he didn't want it because he didn't believe us. He thinks it's Gabriel's knife."

Lilia was watching Diana's face. The lady looked genuinely puzzled. Her eyes had first grown very wide, and then she'd begun to squint. She held that look as she said, "It does sound a little farfetched."

Gabriel spoke up. "That knife is not mine. You don't know these two very well, Diana. If you are going to try to help them, you need to know more about them. Timmy was bullied in school clear back in the first grade. Between that and the fact that he was way smarter than the teachers, his parents decided to homeschool him. Also, since he came home with bruises, broken glasses, and such, they decided that both he and Lilia should learn to defend themselves."

"Are you saying that these two are skilled in self-defense?" Diana asked, her eyes now growing wide again.

"They are amazingly good. I watched them a few times in matches. Neither of them could be beat by any of the other kids," Gabriel said, his face glowing with pride. "So you can rest assured, Detective, that they could easily have defeated the guy with the knife."

"I see there is something I haven't been told," she said. "Did you guys confront the man who broke into your house?"

Lilia spoke up then. "No, there was a second man. Gabriel warned us about him."

"Wait, let's go back to when you were in the house and tell me everything that occurred," she said.

"You probably won't believe us," Timmy said.

"Try me," she challenged.

Lilia looked at Timmy and then at Gabriel. They both nodded in agreement. "Timmy, you tell her," she said, trusting him to tell only what he felt the detective should know.

Timmy began and he told her most of what had occurred. He even told her about the small metal safe but did not tell her what was in it. Lilia was okay with that. He explained about Gabriel's panicked call for them to get out of the house. Finally, he told her how they had started to sneak back to Gabriel's house and about him warning them about the second man and how they came face-to-face with him.

"He pulled this knife on you?" she asked.

"Yes, and he threatened us with it. So I kicked his wrist and broke it, and he dropped the knife," Timmy said.

Diana looked doubtful. "See, I knew you wouldn't believe us," Timmy said.

"I didn't say that," she argued. "Tell me what happened next."

Diana listened as Timmy finished telling her about how Lilia kicked and knocked the guy out, and about taking the man's wallet and phone. "Then we came back here and watched as the two guys both left. Lilia had called Stetson, and he said he couldn't come but that he'd send some officers. I guess that meant you guys."

"Yes, it meant us, but it was an anonymous call that alerted Sergeant Snow. But you must be referring to Officer Stetson Erman," she said.

"He stayed outside the house last night to make sure the kids weren't disturbed," Gabriel told her.

"Sergeant Snow didn't tell us that. But he did say that Stetson was interfering, and he ordered him to stay off the case unless he was needed," she revealed.

Lilia, despite herself, felt a surge of joy go through her. Maybe he cared after all, she thought. "I wondered why he didn't come when I called him," she said.

"So you did call him," Diana said. "Then it must have been him who called the anonymous report in, but if so, he didn't say it was him so he wouldn't create more tension with Sergeant Snow. That makes sense. I know Stetson. He's a good officer and a great guy. Okay, so you guys beat this second bad guy up."

"That's right," Lilia said.

"I guess I believe you. I don't suppose you would care to demonstrate for me, would you?"

"Are you a black belt too?" Lilia asked with a tiny, mischievous grin.

"I'm afraid not," she said.

"Then we won't demonstrate on you, because you would get hurt," Timmy said.

"I'll take your word for it then. So tell me again exactly what happened in the encounter with the man whose name we do not know," she said.

"His name is Kris Shinn," Lilia responded.

"That's right. You took his wallet."

"Yes," Timmy responded. "I told Sergeant Snow that, but he didn't believe me. So I didn't show it to him."

"I believe you," Diana said. "Where is it now?"

Timmy patted the small metal safe and said, "In here with his cell phone and some things of my father's."

"I take it you can open it. Your father must have given you the combination sometime."

Timmy's little head shook, and he said, "I got it from his password list."

"And where did you find that?"

"In his computer," Timmy responded.

Lilia spoke up. "You don't know Timmy. Don't underestimate his brain power. I could never have done it, but he was able to break into Dad's secure file with the passwords in it."

"I am impressed," Diana said. The skepticism had again vanished from her face. "So would you let me take a look at what's in that little safe of your father's?"

Timmy got busy with the dials, and in a very short time, it popped open. He first pulled out the note that his father had written, and after explaining where he'd found it, he opened it and pushed it across the table to Diana, who read it, scowling as she did so. "This is serious. Does your father always write himself notes?" she asked when she pushed it back to Timmy.

"He does. Mom says he's done it since she first met him. She doesn't know why he does it. I guess it's a habit. I want to learn all I can about Mr. Greenbaum. I need Dad's computer to do it, but the detective said we can't go back in the house," Timmy said. Then he scrunched his eyes and said with determination, "He can't stop me."

"We'll get to that later," Diana said. "Let's see that wallet."

Timmy handed it to her. Diana examined it carefully. She was particularly interested in the driver's license. She tapped the picture on the license with a slender index finger and said, "Is this the same face you saw out the window and the one you saw when he confronted you?"

"Lilia, show Diana the pictures you took," Timmy suggested.

She did so. After studying them for a moment, Diana returned her phone and said, "This is the same guy as on the driver's license. But he looks a bit beaten up in the pictures." She grinned when she said it. "So we have the identity of one of the men. Is it by any chance the one who was not found murdered by the lake, the one with a red ball cap?"

"It's not him," Timmy said with conviction.

"Okay, so let's take a look at the phone. I suppose it's password protected."

"We haven't checked," Lilia said. She lifted it from the little safe and turned it on. "It is," she confirmed. "So I guess this is no good to us."

"There are ways to get into it," Diana said. "Maybe Timmy can do it."

Timmy took the phone, but after a moment he said, "I eventually could."

"How about if you let me take it? I'll work on getting it opened at a lab. I'll need a search warrant to do it, but I'm sure I can get one. So what else do you have in there?" Diana asked.

After looking at the credit cards and the photos of three more, she said, "It can't hurt to try to trace them, despite what Sergeant Snow says." She pulled out her cell phone and took pictures of all of them. "Okay, so I can work on trying to trace these and then see about getting into the phone. There are still more papers in there." She pointed at the little safe again. After Lilia explained that it was all stuff that had to do with their father's work, Diana decided not to look at any of them. "But we may want to later. Keep that thing secure."

"We'll put it in my wall safe," Gabriel suggested.

"That would be good," Diana agreed. "I think I'll go now. I'll get back with you guys. And please, don't take any more chances. I know you guys are good, but you can't kick a bullet." She started for the door but stopped and turned back. "About the wallet, if you guys want to keep it, I'm okay with that for now, but I should take a picture of his driver's license." After doing that, she left with another warning for Timmy, Lilia, and Gabriel to be careful. She also reminded them that she would come at a moment's notice if they sensed any kind of danger.

Gabriel said, "I'm a fan of the Second Amendment."

"Meaning you have a gun," Diana said with a grim smile.

"Guns," Gabriel corrected her.

"Keep them handy," the detective said. "Oh, and Timmy, there is something you can do for me. Draw a picture of the man who searched your house."

"I'll do it," Timmy promised.

After Diana was gone, Timmy said, "I know that we aren't supposed to go in the house, but we need more clothes, and I want to use Dad's computer."

"Also, Timmy, I think we should see what Dad and Mom have in their big safe," Lilia suggested.

Gabriel said, "Maybe I can go with you over there and bring a gun. It's legal for me to carry a concealed weapon, so I can't be arrested for that. But maybe we should wait until after dark."

"We can't wait," Timmy objected. "We have to find Mom and Dad, and every hour that we don't find them is worse for them—and for us." He removed his thick glasses and wiped his eyes with a finger, then put them back on. "I have a spare pair of glasses. When we go to the house, I should get them."

"Draw the picture first," Lilia suggested. "Then I will take a photo of it with my phone and send it to Diana."

Gabriel found him a sheet of paper and a pencil, and Timmy went to work. Fifteen or twenty minutes later, he showed his drawing to Lilia. "That's him," she said. "You did a really good job."

After she'd sent a photo of it to Diana, she said, "Let's go over to the house now."

* * *

Saul Greenbaum, who liked his men to call him Boss, was angry. "Can't anyone do anything right?" he asked. "You should have never let those kids get away once they saw you. I warned you that the Dixon kid is smart and that he has a perfect memory, or close to it."

"Sorry, Boss," Kris Shinn said. "Who knew they were so tough?"

Greenbaum glared. "I had to fire Benjy and Louis because they were so inefficient." He paused. Then he added, "They are both dead. Do I also have to fire you men? Look at yourself, Kris. You are sixty years old, but that is no excuse. You are in good physical condition. I can't believe you let a little twelve-year-old kid and a girl do that to you. You look pretty beat up. Having a broken wrist isn't going to help you."

"I can still do my job, Boss," he said.

"You better be able to. As for you, Rich, I think you missed something in that house. Sloppy work, that's all I can say. Do I dare trust you guys with another assignment?"

"You got it, Boss," Rich said. "We'll be more prepared this time. Whatever you need, we can do it."

"You better do what I say and not mess it up," Saul said, and then he explained what they were to do. "Can you do that?" he asked.

"Yep, we'll have them shaking in their shoes and running like scared rabbits," Rich said.

"They'll do what you want when we get through with them. You got my word on that," Kris added.

Saul smiled to himself. He had their attention now. "Give them these," he said as he handed over a couple of forged passports. "So you know what to do?"

"Yep, you got it, Boss."

"Okay, get out of here. I need to get over to the Matheson Courthouse."

The pair left and Saul smiled grimly. Since they knew how permanently Benjy and Louis had been fired, they wouldn't dare mess up this assignment.

* * *

The three of them were in the house. "I don't think anyone saw us come in here," Gabriel said. "I sure hope not."

"This is a mess," Lilia said. "Maybe I should try to clean it up a little."

"I don't think so, Lilia," Timmy said. "We don't want Sergeant Snow to figure out that we've been in here in case he comes back."

"Okay, so maybe later," she said. She hated leaving the house in a mess. "Can you open the safe in the bedroom?"

"Of course," Timmy responded. The three of them went in there together. "It's behind that picture of the Savior."

"I think I knew that," Lilia said with a sheepish grin. "Do I need to take the picture down?"

"Nope, watch this," Timmy said. He grabbed the lower right-hand corner and pulled. The picture swung out, revealing the safe. "Hinges. Now I'll open it."

The safe contained a number of things, including a lot of expensive jewelry. Lilia recalled seeing her mother wear some of it. She just hadn't ever known where she kept it. There was also a pistol and some bullets in there. She didn't know her dad owned a gun, but he clearly did. There were lots of papers, such as the deed to the house, the titles to the cars, birth and marriage certificates, passports, and so on. There was even a few hundred dollars in cash. Looking in it was a waste of time as far as finding any clues as to the whereabouts of their parents.

They next went to Roland Dixon's office, where Timmy fired up the computer. Lilia was getting nervous. "Maybe while you see what you can find out about Mr. Greenbaum, I'll watch out front. We don't want Sergeant Snow to find us in here. Not that I think he'll come back, but if he did, he'd be really upset with us, and we don't need that. We need to get along with him."

"Okay," Timmy said as he worked. "Hey, Lilia, just in case I don't have enough time in here, we could take your laptop and mine to Gabriel's house. Mine isn't as powerful as yours, but you have a really good one. We would need to download some programs from this computer to a thumb drive. Then we'd have what we need."

"I'll watch the front, Lilia, while you go get your computer," Gabriel said.

"Thanks, Gabriel," Lilia said. "Timmy, I'll grab yours too. Why don't you see if Dad has a thumb drive or two and download what you need."

"I'll do that first. He has several new ones in his desk."

Lilia came back in a couple of minutes with the two laptops and their charging cords. Timmy finished copying the last of the programs he wanted on the thumb drives and started to do an internet search on Saul Greenbaum when Gabriel came shuffling quickly into the room. "There's cops out front. I think it's the sergeant. They're heading for the door."

Timmy swiftly shut down the computer, Lilia turned off the lights, and the three of them hurried out the back door just as the front door opened. They hid in the shrubs again. "That was close," Lilia said.

"Yeah, just like when that other guy nearly saw us," Timmy added.

"Now what do we do?" Gabriel asked.

"We'll wait for them to leave, and then we'll go back in," Timmy said, his freckled face flushed with anger. "Those guys should not be able to just go in our house any time they want."

"Actually, they can," Gabriel said. "Especially if they have a search warrant, and I'm sure they do."

"I know about search warrants," Timmy said. "But what could they be after that they didn't find before?"

Lilia said, "I hope they don't go to your house looking for us, Gabriel, because they won't find us."

"They will know we aren't in your house, because they are in there now," Gabriel observed. "And unless they break into my house, they won't know we haven't gone somewhere in my car. It's in my garage, and there are no windows in it for them to look through."

The three sat in silence after that. The minutes ticked past. Lilia worried about Gabriel as he kept shifting his position. He was in obvious discomfort, but he did not mutter a word of complaint. Lilia was grateful for the old man. Without him, she didn't know what they would do.

Finally, after an hour, Lilia thought she heard a car start up in front of the house. "I'll go look and make sure they're gone," Timmy said, and before she could object, he darted out of the shrubbery. He returned shortly and said, "They're gone. Let's go see if we can tell what they were after."

They entered through the back door and instinctively headed for Roland's office. Lilia, the first one in there, gasped. "They took Dad's computer. They can't do that."

Timmy said, "I think if they had a search warrant they could."

"But why would they want it?" Lilia asked.

"Because they think it has something in it that might give them a clue as to why Dad and Mom were kidnapped," Timmy reasoned. "After all, besides looking into information on Mr. Greenbaum, I was going to do that."

"So that messes us up," Lilia groaned.

"Not really. I think I got everything downloaded that we need, and besides, I can get into Dad's computer from one of our laptops if I want to." He smirked. "Sergeant Snow isn't as smart as he thinks he is."

"They were in here a long time," Gabriel observed. "I wonder if they took anything else."

"Let's check," Lilia said. "Gabriel, you watch for them in case they come back. Timmy and I will look."

"There are a lot of his files missing that we put back earlier," Timmy observed. "I wonder if they are going to take his computer and the files from his office at work too."

"Probably," Lilia said. She was fuming. To her, their home had been invaded by too many people. She didn't like it, as it felt personal to her.

Ten minutes of checking throughout the house didn't turn up anything else that the officers had disturbed. They rejoined Gabriel at the front door, checked the street for traffic, and then hurried to the old fellow's house.

"You kids need to relax for a few minutes," Gabriel said when Timmy set up Lilia's computer on the dining room table and booted it up.

"There isn't time," Timmy said. "We've got to keep working. We've already lost over an hour."

"You need something to eat. Lilia, maybe you could help me fix something while Timmy works," Gabriel suggested.

"Let me know if you find something important," Lilia said as she left the dining room with Gabriel.

When they came back in with some sandwiches and milk a few minutes later, Timmy looked up from the computer and asked, "Gabriel, is your garage big enough to hold two cars?"

"It holds three, just like yours does, but I only have one anymore. Why do you ask?"

"We are going to need to go do some things tonight, and it would be nice if when we get back, we could park Lilia's car in your garage," Timmy said.

"Where do you have to go?" Gabriel asked, frowning.

"I want to talk to some people at the place where Dad and Mom were having their meeting with Mr. Lundquist."

"Oh, Timmy, that sounds dangerous."

"It'll be okay. I can't just sit and let time pass us by. I want to figure out what happened that night if I can."

Gabriel shook his head in dismay, but he finally said, "Where you two kids go, I go."

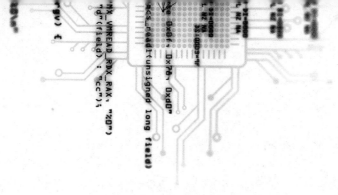

CHAPTER
EIGHT

TIMMY MUNCHED ON A SANDWICH as he worked at the computer. Gabriel, thinking that they might have a long night, went to his room to get some rest. Lilia sat in a chair next to Timmy, watching the computer screen closely.

"Look, Lilia. I just found something," Timmy said with a scowl on his face.

She looked closer. "Oh my goodness!" she exclaimed. "Mr. Greenbaum has a cousin who has been in prison."

"Yep," Timmy said smugly. "And look at this. He's only been out for a few months. He has a long history of doing really bad stuff."

"Is that picture of him?" she asked.

"It is," Timmy said, looking closer. "I wonder if Gabriel is asleep. He got a good look at the guys in the Bronco. Maybe he could tell us if this guy is one of them."

"I'll check," Lilia said, and a minute later, she came back with Gabriel.

Gabriel looked closely at the picture of Saul Greenbaum's cousin, whose name was Benjy Meyer. After a moment, Gabriel straightened up. He was smiling. "I'm pretty sure that was the guy in the red ball cap," he said.

"Good," Timmy said with a smug look on his face. "I'll bet the cops haven't figured that out yet, and they don't think I know what I'm doing. Now I need to see if I can find out who the one in the blue ball cap is, the one who was killed."

Gabriel went back to continue his nap and Lilia again joined Timmy at the computer and watched as he worked with the keyboard and mouse. For a half hour, the boy worked with total concentration. Lilia realized as she watched him how much she loved her little brother. Yes, he irritated her at times, but he was simply amazing, despite his hearing and sight impairments.

"Hey, Lilia, look at this guy's picture. He's on parole. And his parole officer is the same one that Benjy Meyer has." He looked up from the computer. "I think I'll call the parole officer."

"He won't tell you anything because you sound so young," she protested. "Maybe I should try."

"Or Diana could," Timmy suggested.

Just then, Gabriel came shuffling back into the room. "I can't sleep I'm so keyed up. My mind just keeps running and I can't shut it down. I guess I shouldn't complain. I usually can't get my brain to even start." He grinned. "You kids find anything else?"

"Yes, I have another picture for you to look at," Timmy said. He quickly brought up the parolee's picture, an ex con by the name of Louis Sutton.

After a moment's study, Gabriel said, "That's the guy with the blue ball cap. I'm sure of it. I may be old, but I have decent eyesight and a good memory for faces. Sorry, Timmy. I hope I didn't offend you."

"Of course not," Timmy said. "I think we should let Diana know about these two, and then we won't need to call that parole officer."

"I'll call her," Lilia said. A minute later, she said into the phone, "Diana, I'm glad I was able to reach you. We have figured out who the two guys in the Bronco are."

"You must be kidding me. Sergeant Snow and his men have spent hours trying to figure it out and they still don't know. Are you sure?" Diana asked.

"Oh, yes, we're sure."

"I'll be right there," she said. "You are still at Gabriel's, aren't you?"

She grinned and said, "Of course. Where else would we be?"

"Nowhere, I hope," she said. "I'll be bringing another officer with me. I hope it doesn't get us both in trouble." They made it in fifteen minutes.

Lilia felt a jolt when Stetson walked in with Diana. "I thought you couldn't have anything to do with our case," she said.

"I'm not supposed to, but Diana and I are friends. We belong to the same ward. Her husband is our Elder's Quorum president, and I am his second counselor. She is going out on a limb involving me, but I am on my own time. And I really want to help."

"I'm glad both of you are here," Lilia said. "You are both so nice. But I don't want either of you to get in trouble with Sergeant Snow."

"I came with Diana in her car, so even if he were to come to the area again, he'd have no reason to suspect that I'm here. So don't worry," Stetson said. "And just so you know, Diana filled me in on everything that happened with those two guys." He smiled. "I can't believe you guys were able to beat that one man up, the one whose name you believe is Kris Shinn."

A moment later, all of them entered the dining room, where Lilia's laptop was set up. Timmy was working on it at something else. When he saw Stetson, he said, "Hey, I didn't think you could help anymore."

"Diana asked me to, but whatever happens, Sergeant Snow mustn't know. It looks like you've been very busy, Timmy," he said.

"I have. I bookmarked what I need to show you, but first, Diana, do you know how the detectives got my father's computer?"

"Whose is that?" Stetson asked, pointing at the laptop on the dining room table.

"Is it Gabriel's?" Diana asked.

"No, it's mine," Lilia told them.

"Oh, I see," Stetson said. "But what makes you think the detectives have your father's? I certainly haven't heard about it if they do, but then I wouldn't, since I'm not part of the investigation. I suppose you'd know, Diana," he said.

"Yes, Sergeant Snow and another of our squad got a search warrant and picked it up a little while ago," Diana responded.

"We wondered if that's what happened. Let me show you what I've learned," Timmy said after getting a warning look from Lilia. She thought he was going to tell Stetson and Diana that they had been to their house.

Once again, she underestimated her little brother and his deceptive maturity. "We have a program on Lilia's computer that can team up with Dad's. That means that from right here, I can operate Dad's computer." Lilia noted that he didn't tell them how it got that ability, that he'd copied that program from their dad's computer onto a thumb drive and then loaded it onto hers.

"Okay, I'm familiar with that capability. But I still ask how you know," Stetson said, cocking an eyebrow.

"Look here," Timmy said with a smug face. "Someone at the police department is working on it right now. But I can't stay on here long and I won't do anything while I am. They would wonder what was going on, and I don't want them to know that I can do this or even know I can tell they have his computer."

"Okay, I see what you mean. You're right. Now, let's see your proof that you know who the men in the Bronco are, or were, in the case of the one in the blue ball cap," Stetson said.

Timmy broke the connection with his father's computer and went to one of the bookmarks in Lilia's. "This is the guy with the red cap," he said.

"I recognized him," Gabriel broke in.

"His name is Benjy Meyer," Timmy said. "He got out of prison recently." Timmy went to another bookmark. "And this is Louis Sutton. He has the same parole officer as Benjy."

"I identified him too," Gabriel said.

"And now, to the next bookmark," Timmy said. "Guess who Benjy's cousin is?"

Stetson and Diana both leaned down. "Oh my! Are you sure? That's Saul Greenbaum you're looking at there," Stetson said.

"I know it's Saul," Timmy said. "And I'm sure he's Benjy's cousin. I can show you guys how I figured it out if you want me to."

Stetson straightened up and said, "No, I'll take your word for it. How about you, Diana?"

"I believe you, Timmy," she said. "I guess you realize how serious this could be."

"I do," Timmy responded with sadness on his face.

"That's why he asked Mr. Lundquist about Saul," Lilia chipped in. "Dad was worried about him. You know that from the note we found."

Stetson rubbed his chin thoughtfully. He asked, "Are you two thinking that Saul Greenbaum could have something to do with whatever has happened to your parents?"

"I do," Timmy said again firmly.

"And I agree," Lilia said.

"I'm afraid it makes sense," Diana said. "I will need to give this information to Sergeant Snow. You understand that, don't you?"

"Of course. I want you to. If I told him, he wouldn't believe me. And he won't believe you if you tell him I was the one who figured it out. You will need to make him think you figured it out, Diana."

"I can do that," Diana said. "So what's next?"

"Lilia and I are going to go to the restaurant where Dad and Mom met with Mr. Lundquist and ask a few people if they remember seeing our parents leaving in their Lexus," Timmy said.

"Oh, I don't know if that's such a good idea," Stetson said with narrowed eyes.

"That could be dangerous," Diana agreed. "I'm supposed to keep you guys safe. I can't let you do that."

"We've got to," Timmy replied, his freckled face going red with frustration.

Stetson thought for a minute, looked at Diana, and then asked, "How about if I go with them?"

"If the sergeant finds out you've been there, it could get you in trouble and Diana too," Lilia warned. "I don't want you guys to get in trouble."

"Maybe a little bit, but I'm not too worried about it. I'll just stay there out of sight and back you up," Stetson suggested. "You'll need to stay together since you don't have a cell phone, Timmy. Lilia will need to be able to call me if the least thing goes wrong."

"I will need my car," Lilia said.

"It's still in the garage at your house, isn't it?" Stetson asked.

"Yes, but we can park it in Gabriel's garage once we get it."

"Or you can use my car," Gabriel offered.

"I like that idea better," Stetson said.

"I'd rather use my own car," Lilia said.

Stetson shook his head. "For now, we'll use Gabriel's. I don't want Sergeant Snow to think that you guys have been in your house. What do you think, Diana?"

"Even using Gabriel's car I think it's too risky," she responded.

"We are going to go," Timmy said stubbornly. "It's our parents who are gone, and I will do anything I can to get them back. I miss them, and I love them," he said as tears formed behind his thick lenses. He took off his glasses and rubbed his eyes.

Lilia said, "I agree with my brother. We are going." Her eyes met Stetson's and he winked at her! Her stomach went all aflutter. She was so glad he was willing to take the risk to help them. And she really liked the idea of him going with them.

Diana shook her head. "You are stubborn kids," she said. "But I think I understand how you feel. So how about we do this: Stetson can drive Gabriel's car and stay close in case you need him. And I will also be there in my car, so you will have double protection."

"You're willing to do that?" Lilia asked.

"Part of my assignment is to watch out for you kids. If somehow my sergeant found out what you were doing, I could tell him that you insisted and so all I could do is be there to make sure you stayed safe," Diana said.

"But what about Stetson?"

"No one needs to know that he's going too, or after the fact, that he'd been there. Is that agreeable to everyone?" Diana asked.

No one said it wasn't. "We can't go until later," Timmy said. "I think I'll keep looking for information about Mr. Greenbaum for a while."

"You do that," Stetson said, "and Diana can let Sergeant Snow know about the two guys you identified and about Benjy's relationship to Saul."

"That works for me," Lilia said. Timmy didn't respond as he was once again totally wrapped up in his search for information on Saul Greenbaum.

Lilia, Stetson, Diana, and Gabriel left Timmy to his work and went into another room. "That kid brother of yours is a genius," Stetson said.

"I know that," Lilia said. "And Timmy knows it too."

"He doesn't have a cell phone, does he?" Diana asked. "I haven't seen him with one or heard either of you mention one."

"I explained to Diana that I didn't think he had one when she was bringing me up to speed before we came here," Stetson said.

"He doesn't have one. But Mom and Dad have been talking about getting him one," she said.

"I think he needs one," Diana said. "Don't you agree, Stetson?"

"I do," he said.

"You are both probably right, but it's okay for right now," Lilia said. "He and I will stay together. He's smart, but he's still just a kid. With my parents gone, I've got to make sure he's okay."

They talked for a bit longer, but after a few minutes Timmy came running into the kitchen where they were seated around the kitchen table. He was bouncing with excitement. No one had to ask him what he'd learned. He burst right out with it. "Someone has been stealing a lot of money from clients of the law firm and from the law firm itself!"

"Wow!" Lilia exclaimed. "Is it Saul?"

"I can't tell who it is yet," Timmy admitted. "But I'll figure it out."

He sounds pretty confident, Lilia thought. Did their dad somehow find out about it? To her it looked more and more like Mr. Greenbaum would have reasons to have their father removed from the firm, or even removed altogether. Her stomach rolled at that dark thought.

"Stetson, Diana, do either of you know how to trace credit cards? You know, to see where they are being used?" Timmy asked. "I know someone in the police department knows how, because they've tried."

Stetson shook his head. "I'm afraid not. I've never had to do anything like that."

"I can do it," Diana said. "I wasn't the one checking earlier, but you make a good point."

"Will you check again?" Timmy asked. "If you can't, I will figure it out."

"You seem to know a lot about computers. And where did you learn to hack like you seem to be able to do?" Diana asked.

Timmy grinned. "I just figured it out. It's not that hard once you understand the computer world. So will you try to trace their cards?"

"I will," Diana said.

"Thank you. If Saul, or his cousin or someone else who helps him, has Mom's and Dad's cards, they might eventually use them. Maybe we could find them that way."

"What about the cards they didn't take with them?" Diana asked. "Do your parents have those numbers?"

"Probably," Timmy said. "I know what you're thinking, and I was thinking the same thing. We could see if Dad uses his. The bad guys couldn't because they wouldn't know the numbers."

"I'll check on that as well," Diana promised. "I doubt that your parents are where they could do that, but it's worth looking into."

A few minutes later Diana and Stetson left with a promise to meet them at six that evening.

"Timmy, I just thought of this right now, but did you get your spare glasses when we were at our house?" Lilia asked.

"I did," he said. He pulled the glasses case from his pocket. "I also got some spare hearing aid batteries."

"Would you like me to keep them someplace safe?" Gabriel asked. "They could get broken in your pocket."

"Can we put them in a drawer in your kitchen?" Timmy asked.

"That should work," their elderly neighbor said. He led Timmy to the kitchen, and Timmy deposited all but two batteries in the drawer Gabriel indicated. "I need to keep two with me just in case I need them. I never know when a battery is going to quit, and I really need my hearing aids to be working because I can't hear much without them."

After that, Timmy sat back down at Lilia's computer and began again on his unrelenting pursuit of useful information. He finally stopped and joined Lilia and Gabriel in the kitchen as they were getting ready to eat a meal that they had prepared. Lilia was worried about Timmy. She was afraid that he was overdoing it and that it was getting him down. He hadn't said a word about what he might have learned since Stetson and Diana left.

"You are getting too tired, Timmy," she said. "Maybe we shouldn't go tonight."

The little guy's blue eyes flared behind the thick lenses. "I'm okay," he said stiffly. "I am not going to quit until we find Dad and Mom." He paused, and then he added, "And get Mr. Greenbaum locked up in jail. I'm sure it's him who has caused all the trouble."

Lilia watched him for a moment as he fiddled with his food. If it wasn't exhaustion of either his mind or his body that had him looking discouraged and unable to eat like he usually did, then it was something else. She wondered if it was his failure to succeed in whatever it was he had been searching for the past couple of hours. Yes, that had to be it, she thought. She started to say something to encourage him, but then she decided not to.

Stetson and Diana were right on time. Diana went back out to her car as soon as Stetson, Lilia, and Timmy entered the garage. When the three left in the old fellow's car, a rather old but little used black Cadillac, Diana followed. Stetson was driving with Lilia seated beside him. Timmy rode in the back, and just like at dinner, he was silent, deep in thought. She wished she knew what was going through his amazing brain. But until he had something to tell her, he would remain silent. That she knew from years of experience. She again decided not to pry.

They found the restaurant, and Stetson let them out a half block away. "I'll be close," he promised. "So will Diana. You two be very careful. Please don't take any chances."

Lilia was feeling very uncomfortable, even a little frightened, but Timmy appeared to be just fine. As smart as he was, he may still not have the maturity to recognize how dangerous this could be. He led the way as they began their evening's work. They approached several people at businesses near the restaurant and showed them pictures of their parents and asked if they had seen them here a couple of evenings ago. They met with no success. Folks seemed concerned when they told them that their parents were missing, said they wished they could help, and were mostly sympathetic, but they were of no help at all.

An elderly, well-dressed couple was approaching the door to the restaurant from the parking area at the same time Timmy and Lilia reached the front doors. Timmy politely asked them, "By any chance, did you guys have dinner here the night before last?"

"Strange you should ask," the gentleman said. "But yes, we did."

"Maybe you can help us. I'm Timmy Dixon, and this is my sister, Lilia. We can't find our parents," he said.

"That's strange," the fellow said, concern creasing his brow. "Were they here the night before last?"

"We think so," he said, appearing to be unsure, exactly like Lilia was feeling at this point.

"We are Howard and Lindy Graham. Are you wondering if we saw them?" Mr. Graham asked perceptively.

"Yes, let us show you their pictures," Timmy said.

Lilia pulled them from her purse, as she had done a dozen times in the past few minutes. Mr. Graham took them and looked closely at both of them, handing each picture in turn to his wife. He was nodding and his wife did the same. "Isn't this the couple that we passed in the parking lot, Lindy?" Howard said to his wife. "I remarked to you about how red the fellow's hair was."

"I do believe they are the ones. Such a nice-looking couple," Lindy said. "The man with them didn't look nearly as nice. I'm sorry. I shouldn't have said that. I try not to judge people. The Lord tells us not to do that."

"But you do anyway," Howard reminded her with a smile. "Yes, we saw them. The fellow had red hair about the same color as yours, Timmy. I notice things like that."

"They were such a handsome couple," Mrs. Graham added.

Lilia's heart raced and Timmy's eyes went wide. "Did you see them get in their car? It's a silver Lexus."

"Oh yes, we surely did. I hope I didn't make you feel bad about what I said about the fellow they were with," Mrs. Graham said. "Your mother and father got in the front and their friend got in the back."

Timmy's little face went dark, and he said, "He's not their friend. Can you describe him to us, please?"

"If he was not their friend, then who was he?" Mr. Graham asked. "He didn't look like a very nice man, and your mother and father seemed a bit unhappy. They certainly were not smiling. Neither was the other fellow."

"We don't know who he was. Please, can you describe him?" Timmy asked.

"He wasn't dressed to be going into a nice establishment like this one," Mrs. Graham said with a shudder. "Why, if I remember correctly, he was even wearing a ball cap."

"A red one or a blue one?" Timmy asked before they could add any more description.

"What a strange question. Are you sure you don't know the fellow?" Mr. Graham asked.

"We don't," Timmy said, and then he looked at Mrs. Graham, waiting for an answer.

"It was actually red and was quite dirty, wasn't it, Howard?" Mrs. Graham asked her husband.

"Yes, it was," he responded with a frown. "Your parents were dressed so nice, but this guy had on a badly worn and dirty sport shirt of some kind and blue jeans."

"What color was the shirt?" she asked her husband. "Was it brown?"

"It may have been," he said.

Lilia, trying to keep her hands from trembling and not succeeding very well, reached in her purse again and brought out the two pictures she had of the man with the red ball cap, one that Timmy had drawn, the other one a copy they had made from the computer. She showed them to the Grahams.

Mrs. Graham handed Lilia back the pictures of her parents as Mr. Graham took the other two. His wife leaned close to him. They studied the two pictures for a moment, and then Mr. Graham said, "This could be the man. Is he a criminal of some kind?"

His wife spoke up. "They wouldn't know that, Howard. They said they didn't know that man."

"We don't know him," Lilia said, unable to mask the bitterness in her voice, "but we do know about him. He is a criminal. If our parents went with him, it was not willingly."

"When my father drove from the parking lot, did you see another car follow them?" Timmy asked.

Mrs. Graham's face went quite pale. "Yes. It was an old car, and come to think of it, the driver had on a blue ball cap. Oh, you poor kids. Did those men kidnap your parents?"

"They must have. Was it an old Ford Bronco that the second man was driving?" Timmy asked.

"It may have been," Mrs. Graham said. "Do you recall, Howard? I'm no good at car makes."

"Yes, as a matter of fact, it was," Mr. Graham said with certainty. "I usually don't remember things too well, but with the red hair and the difference between your parents and the other man, it left a huge impression on my mind."

"And on mine," his wife said.

"You have been a huge help," Lilia said as she took the pictures back and put them in her purse.

"We are so sorry," Mrs. Graham said, and her husband nodded in agreement. "You kids must be hungry. Please, come inside with us, and we'll buy you a meal."

"That's very kind," Lilia said, "but we ate already. We need to run now. There is a police officer who will be picking us up shortly."

"Could we have your phone number, Mr. Graham?" Timmy asked. "The police might want to speak with you."

"Do you have a pen and paper in your purse, Lindy? Maybe you could write all our phone numbers down for them and also our address," Mr. Graham said.

"That won't be necessary. If you will just recite them for us, Timmy will remember," Lilia said.

"Are you sure?" Mr. Graham asked skeptically.

"Oh yes, he never forgets anything. That drawing of the man in the red ball cap he drew from memory after having seen him only fleetingly," Lilia explained.

"That is quite amazing," Mrs. Graham said, and she proceeded to recite the numbers of their cell phones, their home phone, and their address.

As she was doing that, Lilia pulled out her phone and was calling Stetson. "We are in front of the restaurant," she said. "You can come get us now."

They thanked the Grahams, and in a matter of seconds, Stetson pulled up to the curb. "Let us know if we can be of any more help. We'll certainly be praying for you and for your parents," Mrs. Graham called back to them.

They jumped in the Cadillac and Stetson pulled back onto the street. Diana appeared right behind him in her unmarked patrol car.

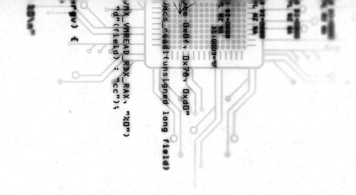

CHAPTER
NINE

"THAT WAS FAST, AND FROM the look on your faces, I'd say you guys learned something," Stetson said.

"We did," Lilia responded. "The man with the red ball cap made them drive him away in their own car and the guy with the blue ball cap followed them in the Bronco."

"Tell me all about it," Stetson said. "It sounds like you were guided by the Spirit of the Lord."

"We sure were," Lilia said. And then as Timmy sat quietly in the back, his eyes and lips tightly closed and his fists clenched, she recounted the entire experience to Stetson. She repeated it again when they reached Gabriel's house to Gabriel and Diana.

"Okay, so now Diana will need to give this information to Sergeant Snow. He'll be quite amazed that you identified both Benjy and Louis and that you now know they forced your parents to leave the restaurant with them," Stetson said. "She won't tell him I drove you there. She'll say that you went in Mr. Schiller's Cadillac with Diana near you at all times. We both need to leave now, but Diana will let you know how it goes with Sergeant Snow. She'll call me too."

Lilia's eyes met his and she got that tingle that was now becoming all too familiar, in a very nice way. They both smiled. "Thank you, Stetson," she said.

"You are welcome. The Lord is blessing you now. You are such a righteous young lady, and Timmy is a fine boy," he said. "I look forward to getting to know you better after this is all over for you."

"I won't be gone long," Diana said. "Keep a close eye out and don't leave the house until I get back."

"Thank you, Diana," Lilia said, and Diana and Stetson went out the door, with Gabriel locking it behind them.

Timmy missed all that. He didn't even see Stetson and Diana leave. He was back in Gabriel's dining room, absorbed with the computer. He didn't look up until Lilia came in and told him that Sergeant Snow and Diana had just arrived, that Diana had met briefly with him at the police station, and that they had then hurried over.

Timmy took a moment to shut down the computer. Lilia noticed that there were three or four thumb drives on the table and that he slipped them into his pocket before walking with her into the large living room where the sergeant, Diana, and Gabriel were waiting for them.

"You two need to sit down," Sergeant Snow said with a frown on his face. "I know you think you have some information for me, but I'm afraid I've got some for you. Mine is real and I'm afraid it's not good."

Lilia didn't like the sound of his voice, and she felt her stomach churn. But she and Timmy did as they were instructed. They sat together on a cream-colored sofa and waited for the sergeant to speak again. He also sat, as did Gabriel.

When he spoke, his voice was forceful and not the least bit tender. "Your folks left by their own choice. They were not kidnapped. I'm sorry, but they left you two to take care of yourselves."

"That's not true!" Lilia shouted angrily, coming to her feet. "Benjy and Louis kidnapped them at the restaurant and forced them to go somewhere."

"I know who you mean by Benjy and Louis, but I'm afraid you are quite wrong. I'm sorry to have to tell you this, but your father has stolen several million dollars from a very wealthy client of their firm and more from the firm itself. I just came from meeting with Harry Lundquist. He is understandably very disappointed in your father, but he agreed when I told him that I was going to get a warrant for his arrest. I am also getting one for your mother. She is an accessory to your father's theft," Sergeant Snow said.

"It's not true!" Lilia screamed while Timmy sat quietly on the sofa as she raged up and down the room, his eyes shut tight and his fists clenched.

Diana sat quietly, not uttering a word, but when Lilia caught her eyes, she shook her head ever so slightly.

"I'm afraid it is," Sergeant Snow said. "I'm sorry. There is very solid proof. Now, you say you had some information for us. I'll listen to it now, but I assure you it will probably not help your parents."

Before Lilia could scream another protest, Timmy opened his eyes, unclenched his fists, and said very softly, "We don't have any information for you. I'm sorry we bothered you. You may go now."

Lilia looked at him in surprise, but he simply nodded at her. She had no idea what was in his head, but she was not about to contradict him. She said nothing more.

"Do not go in your house until I tell you that you can," Snow said with too much firmness. "My detectives and I will be doing a further search there. I need to go now. But it will probably not be until tomorrow that we search again because we have so much else to do. But I say again, do not go in there, or the two of you will also be in a great deal of trouble."

Sergeant Snow got up to leave, and as he did, he said to Diana, "We will both go now. Like I told you at the station, these kids won't need you to stay close by anymore. They are in no danger." With that, Snow headed for the door.

"I won't be gone too long if I can help it," Diana said quietly. "I'm pretty sure the sergeant is wrong, but he won't listen right now."

"Come on, Detective," Snow called from the doorway. "We have work to do." She did as she was ordered, but it was clear that she was not in agreement with her sergeant.

As soon as the door had shut behind the officers and Gabriel had locked it, Lilia asked Timmy, "What were you thinking? We do have information for him. He's wrong. We know that."

"He doesn't believe anything we say, Lilia. We are doing better on our own," Timmy replied.

"Timmy, they have accused Dad of stealing a lot of money. I think it would be better to cooperate with them so they won't be so angry," she argued.

"Lilia, do you think Dad stole all that money and that Mom is supporting him in it?" Timmy asked.

"Of course not," she said.

"Well, Sergeant Snow and, even worse, Mr. Lundquist believes it. Anything we tell them will be ignored or we will be called liars," Timmy said as tears formed in the corners of his eyes. "It's not fair. You and I know that the real criminal is Mr. Greenbaum. Unless we prove what he did with the money he's made it look like Dad stole, and I'm sure he did that, then he and Mom will be caught and go to jail. I don't want them to go to jail."

Lilia was rendered mute. She simply rubbed tears from her own eyes.

"I need to get back to work, and the only thing I can do now is work with the computer. I know how to find things, Lilia. I have already done that, and I will do a lot more," he said.

"But Dad's files won't be enough, and neither will other records that you can access," she said softly.

Timmy simply said, "I can do what I need to, and I will. I just need time to figure it all out."

Lilia knew very well that the only way for her little brother to find information that would prove that Mr. Greenbaum was an evil criminal would be for him to be a hacker. She didn't want Timmy to get in trouble, but she knew him well enough to know that he would put himself at risk anyway and hack if that was the only way he could reach the truth. And she also knew that somehow he had figured out how to hack and wondered just how good at it he was.

Timmy went back into the dining room and once more booted up Lilia's computer. Gabriel had a sad look on his wrinkled face, and his head drooped. "I'm sorry, Lilia, but I'm afraid that your little brother is right. We need to let him look for information in whatever way he can. Your parents are some of the finest people I know, and they can't be allowed to be locked up over something they did not do."

Diana stopped by for a few minutes around ten. She said, "My sergeant and Mr. Lundquist are wrong. Timmy, I tried to tell him what you two learned at the restaurant. He told me it wasn't true. I asked him to at least check with Howard and Lindy Graham or let me do it. He said I was not to do that, that it simply wasn't true, and that the proof of your father's theft was rock solid. He accused me of being too sympathetic towards you."

"I'm glad someone is. Does Stetson know?" Lilia asked.

"I called him and told him. He's really angry. He said to tell you guys that he would do everything he could to help you, even if it costs him his job. Like me, he saw the two of you talking to the Grahams. We know what the truth is. However, we also understand Sergeant Snow's concerns. Mr. Lundquist showed him how the theft had occurred. It's hard to argue with that."

Diana and Lilia talked a while longer and then she said she needed to leave, but she told them to be very careful, for they were still in as much danger now as ever. Shortly after she left, Lilia got a call from Stetson.

He was fuming about the fact that both Sergeant Snow and Lundquist had been duped. "You guys need to be really careful and let me know of anything you learn."

She talked a while longer, and after Stetson had hung up, she told Timmy what both Diana and Stetson had said. "I wish they could do more," she said, "but I don't think they can. You need to keep working at the computer. You need to dig until you find something."

Timmy worked until after midnight that night, and he only quit when Lilia insisted that he had to get some sleep. She asked him if he'd found anything, and all he'd said was, "I'm still looking."

She had a feeling that he knew more than he was saying, but she decided to ignore it for now. They both went to bed. Whether Timmy slept or not, she didn't know, but she certainly didn't get much sleep. She'd tossed and turned all night, and whenever she did fall asleep, she would dream, and those dreams woke her up. She dreamed of visiting her parents in prison. She also dreamed that they had done wrong, and that she and Timmy would have to do the best they could without them. She even dreamed of Stetson, but the dream consisted only of him shaking his head and saying nothing to her. It was a really horrible night.

The next morning, she tried to help Gabriel fix some breakfast. But she couldn't get her mind to quit dwelling on her parents being accused of such a terrible crime. Timmy went right to the computer and started typing and moving the mouse around quite vigorously. When she asked him to come eat, he shut the computer down. She offered a blessing on the food at Gabriel's request and offered a prayer asking that the Lord would help Timmy find the information they needed to clear their parents of the accusations against them and to bless them both to be okay.

Timmy wolfed his food down and went straight back to the computer. Shortly before noon, he walked around for a minute, mumbling something under his breath. Lilia asked him what was bothering him. All he said was, "The police are not even looking at any other suspects in the theft."

"How do you know that? We haven't talked to any of the officers today," she said.

He looked at her and said, "I just know."

"You've hacked into the police computers, haven't you?" she asked in alarm.

"I just know," he repeated without either looking at her or answering her question. She let it go.

However, there was a knock on the door about ten minutes later. It was Sergeant Snow. Lilia called at Timmy that he was here and that he wanted to talk to them again. Timmy took a couple of minutes before he came into the living room. "Hello, Sergeant Snow," he said. "Have you found our parents?"

"I think you know that we haven't," he said darkly.

"I guess that's true," the little guy said without looking directly at the sergeant. "If you had, you would have called us, wouldn't you?"

"Yes, we would," Sergeant Snow said. Then he added, "Hey, Timmy, we are not your enemies. Your parents did something very serious, and you and your sister are victims of what they did. It's not my fault, and it's not Mr. Lundquist's fault. It is your father's fault. I know that is hard for you two to admit, and I understand that. I'm sorry, but it's true."

"It's not true!" Lilia said angrily.

The sergeant simply shook his head. "I'm sorry you are having such a hard time." He reached into an inside pocket of his sports jacket and pulled out a folded paper. He straightened it out. "This is a copy of the search warrant that I obtained to search your parents' house again. It also gives us the authority to search this house and seize your computers and search them. Why don't you bring them to me right now. I know you have them here because Timmy has been using them."

Lilia was alarmed, but Timmy simply said, "Sure, Sergeant, they are both in the dining room." He stood up. "We will need receipts for them," he said. "But I can tell you right now that there is nothing at all on either my computer or Lilia's that has anything to do with my father and what you have accused him of."

"We'll see about that," the sergeant said. "We have to be thorough. I'll also need the keys you guys have to your house."

"Why?" Lilia demanded. "You already took the only other set we have."

"Just turn them over to me, please," he insisted. Timmy looked on without a word. She finally got her purse and dug in it for the keys. She started to remove her car key, but he said, "Leave it on there. I am going to need to search your car as well."

"Why?" she asked. "Do you think I did something illegal too?"

"Does your father ever drive your car?" Snow asked.

"Once in a while, mostly to get it serviced for me," she said.

"Again, I have to be thorough," he responded.

"But I might need it," she said.

"Sorry, but without the keys to your house, you can't get it out anyway. If you need a ride, I'm sure Mr. Schiller will let you use his car."

She finally handed her key ring with all her keys over to him. Sergeant Snow gave her a receipt and headed for the door with the two laptops and the keys. "I remind you to stay away from your house across the street. You can't get in it now, anyway, but I don't even want you in the yard. My officers are already at work over there. I'll bring you another receipt for anything we seize."

With that, he left. Lilia was scared. Her face was pale, and her hands were shaking. "Timmy, they will be able to find out what you've been searching for."

He grinned at her. "No they won't. I'm not that stupid."

Timmy is not only "not that stupid," she thought, *he is a genius.* If he said they wouldn't be able to find anything, then she was sure they couldn't, but she could not imagine how that could be.

Timmy was moody for the rest of the day. He spent a lot of time with his eyes shut and his fists clenched. Lilia would love to have known what was on his mind. But when she asked him, he just looked at her and frowned. She worried about him, not sure what he might do.

He lightened up a little bit when Stetson showed up at the house for dinner, which Lilia had invited him to on one of several phone conversations they'd had. Gabriel had given the idea of Stetson coming for dinner his approval. Stetson had parked his car in Gabriel's garage so it wouldn't be seen if Snow came by. Although he told Lilia that he didn't think it mattered much anymore, as from what Diana had told him, Sergeant Snow was focused on nothing but finding and arresting her parents while also building his case against them.

After dinner was over and the kitchen cleaned up, the four of them sat down in the living room. "I'm sorry about the way things are going," Stetson said. "I've been poking around in an attempt to figure out what kind of evidence Mr. Lundquist gave Sergeant Snow against your father. But I've gotten nowhere. Diana tells me she has also failed to figure anything out, but Snow says that Lundquist is adamant that your father got away with millions of dollars."

"If I thought it would do any good I'd call Mr. Lundquist," Timmy said. "But he's apparently convinced that Dad is the thief. I need to find proof that it's Mr. Greenbaum who stole all that money. But Sergeant Snow took our computers. So I've had to waste this whole afternoon when I'm sure I could have found something by now."

"I guess you could buy a new computer," Stetson ventured.

Timmy shrugged but said nothing about that idea.

"So what do you think we should do?" Stetson asked.

Timmy shrugged his shoulders again and said, "I dunno."

"I have an idea," Stetson said suddenly, smiling.

"What?" Timmy asked.

"I could take you guys to a movie, and we could relax for a few hours," he said.

Timmy slumped in his chair. "You guys go. I'll just stay here. I don't think I want to see a movie."

"How about you, Lilia? Would you like to go with me?" Stetson asked.

"Are you asking me on a date?" she queried, unable to mask her pleasure at the idea.

"Sure, why not?" he said. "But I really would like Timmy to go with us. You guys both need a distraction from the stress you're under. Are you sure you wouldn't like to go with us, Timmy? There's nothing you can do here."

"That's okay. I think I'll do some reading," Timmy said.

"Okay, but we'll miss you," Lilia said.

Timmy actually cracked a smile then. "I don't think so. I would be a third wheel. I've seen the way you two look at each other. It reminds me of Mom and Dad."

Lilia could not suppress a blush, but Timmy turned his head and pretended he didn't notice. He stood up and said, "Thanks for dinner, Lilia and Gabriel. I think I'll go up to the room and read."

After he'd left, Stetson said, "He's pretty glum. Was he actually making progress before Snow took your computers away?"

"Probably, but he won't tell me what he'd learned," she said. "I've never seen him like this before. It scares me."

"Do you think that Sergeant Snow will be able to cause Timmy some trouble if he finds something on your computer that shouldn't be there, Lilia?"

"He didn't say so, but I think that Timmy must have known the sergeant was going to come for our computers, because I asked him about the same thing you just did and he was confident that there was nothing to be found," Lilia responded.

"That brother of yours amazes me. I wish we hadn't lost the computers, because I have a feeling he might have been able to turn this whole thing back on Greenbaum," Stetson said. "Should we go?"

Despite her worries, Lilia found that she was able to relax in Stetson's company. He was so good to her. She found herself developing feelings she'd never had for any guy before. It came as a surprise to her, for she had dated some pretty nice young men.

The two didn't get in any hurry to end their date. So it was quite late before Stetson finally stopped in Gabriel's sweeping driveway. He didn't bother to put his car in the garage this time. He walked Lilia up to the door. "Would you like to come in for a little while?" she asked hopefully.

"I would love to, but I think I should get home. I have to work in the morning. So I need some sleep. But thanks for helping me have a wonderful night," he said.

For a moment they looked at each other. Lilia hoped he would try to kiss her, because she would let him. She was not one who gave kisses out freely. But Stetson was special, she was thinking. She enjoyed being with him. But he did not attempt a kiss; however, he did put an arm around her shoulders and give her a hug. It felt really good to her.

They said their good nights with Stetson promising to check in with her when he had a minute during his shift the next day. "I want to make sure Timmy's doing okay," he said.

"He'll be fine," she said, not at all sure that that was the case.

She went in and listened at the door as Stetson drove away. Why couldn't things be different right now? she thought. If she'd met him when she was not under so much stress and worry, she had a feeling that things might progress quite nicely between them. But as it was, she wasn't even sure she'd have the chance to go out with him again.

She got a drink of water from Gabriel's kitchen. She was grateful to him, but she hoped that she and Timmy wouldn't have to be dependent on his generosity much longer. He was a wonderful old man, but it couldn't be easy for him where he had lived alone for all those years since he'd lost his wife.

She looked out the window at her house across the street. It was off limits. She couldn't get anything else she needed from her room. She couldn't even get her car. The house, one where her family had lived in love for all of her life, looked silent, dark, and lonely. She longed to go over there and walk around the outside of it, but she didn't dare. Sergeant Snow was pretty adamant about them staying away until he cleared it for them to return. She wouldn't be surprised if he had officers checking from time to time just in case her parents showed up. Tears suddenly filled her eyes, and she gave in to them and cried openly for several minutes.

She finally gained control of her emotions and turned and noticed a paper on the kitchen table that she hadn't noticed before. She picked it up. It was another receipt. Snow and his detectives had taken a number of files and papers from both the file drawers and the desk in her father's office. But that was apparently all they'd taken. She hoped that meant they had been unable to find anything that would further incriminate her parents. She didn't know what was in those files she had so carefully gathered up and restored to the cabinet following the two break-ins. She shoved it from her mind, folded the receipt, put it in her pocket, and shut out the kitchen lights.

She headed for the stairway. She decided to check on Timmy before going to the bedroom that Gabriel had so generously told her she could use for as long as she needed to. He'd told Timmy the same thing. She eased the door to his room open. The light from the hallway fell across his bed.

It was empty!

CHAPTER
TEN

PANIC SHOT THROUGH LILIA WITH a searing pain. Where could he be? She entered his room and searched. She looked in the almost bare closet and even under the bed. She went to the upstairs bathroom at the end of the long hall that led past her bedroom, suddenly hopeful that he was in there. It was also empty.

She checked the other rooms on that floor. He was not in any of them. She ran down the stairway and began to search down there. It was a large house with lots of rooms. She checked all of them but the one Gabriel was sleeping in. She even went out to the large garage. He was in none of those places. She went outside and spent the next ten minutes searching under every bush, behind every tree, in the small outbuildings, and all along the fence. He was nowhere to be found.

Lilia was scared now. She had told herself that he would be somewhere just sulking. But he was not. The only other place to look was in Gabriel's bedroom, but common sense told her that would be useless. Finally, out of sheer desperation, she looked across the street at her house. Maybe he was hiding over there somewhere. Despite the stern warning from Sergeant Snow, she crossed the street.

She looked around her, fearing unreasonably that an officer would be watching her. But no one tried to stop her. She ran around back after trying the front door and finding it locked, which is what she expected. Sergeant Snow had the keys now. She couldn't even get in her own house. Then she checked the shrubs in their front yard. She moved toward the back, testing each door of the five that were outside doors. All were locked.

She searched the yard out back as thoroughly as she had her neighbor's. She looked around all the trees, under the shrubs, and in the pool house. She even looked in the pool. There was a large shed that she searched. Finally, frantic, she began to check to see if any windows were open. But they were all secure. She couldn't tell with those on the second floor, but there was no way to get to them from the outside unless you had the skills of Spider-Man. Timmy could do a lot of amazing things, but Spider-Man he was not.

Timmy was simply gone. She trembled with fear for him. She fumbled in her pocket for her phone, sinking down on the grass and sobbing uncontrollably. She finally got herself under control enough to call Stetson. When he answered, his first words were, "Lilia, what's the matter?"

His voice was so tender that it brought the tears back and she couldn't say a word. She didn't need to. Stetson said, "I'm on my way."

She tried to talk again to tell him where she was, but she could not get past the sobs. So she simply put the phone back in her pocket. She couldn't sit here. Stetson would go to Gabriel's house. She had to get over there. She felt so weak with fear and sorrow that she could hardly stand up. Once she was on her feet, she started to stumble back across the large backyard to the house. She finally made it around it and to the front. She crossed the street and was surprised to see Gabriel standing at the door.

As soon as he spotted her, he shuffled in her direction. He threw his arms around her and asked, "What is the matter, dear girl?"

She blubbered, felt like a fool, but she couldn't stop the crying. In her mind, she had failed her little brother. Regardless of why her parents were gone, she had become responsible for him. He was a genius, talked like a very smart adult, was very athletic and strong for his age, but he was still just a young boy. He'd needed her, and she wasn't there for him.

"Stetson called me," he said. "You weren't in your room. So I looked around a little, called your name, but when I got no response, I came to the door and there you were stumbling to the street."

Once they were inside, he helped her to the living room, where she collapsed on the cream-colored sofa and buried her face in her hands. "Stetson will be here shortly," her elderly neighbor said. "So will Diana. Stetson called her too. I'll go check on Timmy."

"No!" she heard herself cry out. She began shaking her head. She tried to calm down. Gabriel stood watching her, concern etched deeply on his wrinkled face.

"Why?" the old fellow asked.

She was able to get one word out, "Gone," and fresh tears flowed. He headed for the stairway.

It was only a few minutes before Stetson came running into the house, followed by Diana. He spotted Lilia on the sofa and knelt in front of her. She reached her arms around his neck. He leaned close until their cheeks were touching. "What is it, Lilia?"

She looked up, met his concerned eyes, and said, "Timmy."

"What about Timmy?" he asked.

"He's not here," Gabriel said. "I just came from his room. He's not there. His jacket is gone. So are his shoes."

"That can't be," Stetson said.

"It . . . is . . ." Lilia managed to stammer.

Stetson pulled her toward him and held her tight. "Does he sleepwalk?" he asked her.

"He . . . never . . . has," she managed to say. Her voice was coming back. "I've . . . looked . . . all over."

Several minutes passed. The steady influence of Stetson helped Lilia gain control. She said, "I wondered if he could be in our house. So after I checked all around here, I went over there. I knew the doors were all locked and Sergeant Snow took our keys. I checked them anyway. I checked all the windows. The house is so silent, so dark," she said and found herself having to choke back another sob.

"Your little brother is pretty ingenious," Stetson reminded her.

Diana had been checking through the house and had just reentered the room. "I called Sergeant Snow. He's coming. We need to go in your house and make sure that he didn't somehow get inside," Diana said.

A moment later, Stetson's phone rang. He answered, and after a moment, he said, "Sergeant Snow, what Detective Franklin told you is true. I got a call a little while ago from Lilia Dixon. She was so distraught that she couldn't talk. It wasn't until Diana and I got here that she was able to tell us that she couldn't find her brother."

Lilia had moved close enough to hear what was said on the other side of the call. She didn't like what she heard. "That little brat can't be in that house. I have the keys. I took them because I knew I couldn't trust him or his sister. Detective Franklin knows that. I told her I'd come, and I will, but my guess is that he's being a spoiled brat hiding somewhere."

"Sergeant, he's nowhere on Mr. Schiller's property, nor anywhere around the Dixon's house. It's locked up tight," Stetson said. "Lilia even checked in their enclosed swimming pool. I think he could be in the house. He's a bright kid. Who knows what he can do."

"He's a spoiled brat, that's what he is. I'll come, but if he's in that house, I will place him in juvenile detention and keep him there until he turns eighteen! I'm not tolerating any further interference from him," Snow said. "I'm coming. I won't bother any of my crew. You and Diana can help me search, and we will search everywhere in that house that he might be hidden, although frankly, I don't believe he could get in short of breaking a window. My guess is that he's throwing a tantrum and has run away."

"Or maybe someone took him," Stetson ventured.

"Don't be stupid, Officer. He's run away. He'll come crawling back with his tail between his legs pretty soon," Snow said. "But I'll come like I told Diana I would, and we can check. Meet me over there in ten minutes. And I don't want that sister of his there. She is to stay at the old man's house."

"I'll see to it, Sergeant," Stetson said with a bite to his voice, and he ended the call.

Lilia tore herself free from Stetson and bounded to her feet. She had never been so angry in her life. "Timmy is not a brat!" she spat. "He's not spoiled. He would not just run away and put himself in danger. Not that he's afraid, for he is very brave, and he can defend himself very well, as he proved the other night. I'm going over there with you."

"I don't think that would be wise," Stetson said. "I can just see Snow arresting you. And believe me, a pretty girl like you does not want to end up in jail."

He called her pretty. That calmed her down. Maybe someday . . . She brought her mind back on track. "Okay, I'll wait here. I was just thinking that if I shouted for him, he would come out from any place he might be hiding, if he is hiding."

Diana had again started checking out Gabriel's house. She even looked in the trunk of his car. She had no better luck than Lilia had. When Stetson told her he was heading across the street, she joined him.

Lilia and Gabriel sat on wicker chairs on his front deck and waited for over an hour while Stetson, Diana, and Sergeant Snow searched inside the Dixons' house for Timmy. When they finally came back, Snow was seething. "He's not in there, Miss Dixon. So tell me where you think he might go. You must have family nearby, or he might have gone to a friend's house."

"We don't have any family," she said. "I told you that the night my parents disappeared. Timmy has friends, but none he would ever go to for help or whatever he might be seeking," she said.

"Are your parents from here in Utah?" Sergeant Snow asked.

"No, they were raised in Texas, but they left there shortly after they were married," Lilia said.

"I will need you to prepare a list of family and friends in Texas so I can send it down there to authorities and have them watch for your dad and mom and your little brother. And I will have an attempt to locate broadcast to the police both locally and all the way to Texas, and when we find him, I will lock that little brat up," the sergeant said.

"I can't make a list. I don't know anyone down there. I already told you we have no family anywhere, here or in Texas," Lilia tried to explain.

"There has to be someone. Think, Lilia. Surely they had friends they send Christmas cards to. Where in your house would I find a Christmas card list?" Snow said, clearly not believing her.

"You have to believe me. There is no one. I don't remember my mother ever sending Christmas cards after the last of our grandparents passed away," she said.

"Write down the towns where they lived. That will be a start. If your little brother is as smart as you say he is, which I seriously doubt, he would remember those towns and maybe try to find his way there," Snow insisted.

Diana and Stetson were listening to the whole thing, and all they could do was shake their heads. Finally, Lilia said, trying hard to control her temper, "I tried to tell you about Louis and Benjy, but you wouldn't listen. I have pictures of them in my purse. I'll get it and show them to you."

Despite his protests, she got the pictures Timmy had drawn and laid them in front of the angry officer. He glanced briefly at them. "They have nothing to do with this," he said.

"Sergeant, look closer," Stetson said firmly, "especially at the one in the blue ball cap."

"These are just drawings," he protested. "They mean nothing."

"Then look at these," she said and produced ones Timmy had taken off the internet. Stetson put a finger on one of the pictures. "This man was wearing a red baseball cap when both Gabriel and Timmy saw him in the Bronco on this very street."

"That has nothing to do with this case, Officer Stetson. Why can't you get that through your head?" Snow asked.

Stetson was not giving up, and Diana spoke up in support of him. "You need to listen to us," she said. "The guy in the blue ball cap is a parolee by the name of Louis Sutton."

"I know that. He was murdered on the shore of the Great Salt Lake, in a Bronco," the sergeant admitted. "We finally figured out who he is. But I'm telling you, that is all just a coincidence. He may have been on this street, but I honestly don't believe he had anything to do with the Dixons' disappearance."

Stetson pointed again to the picture of the second man, the one who had been wearing a red ball cap. "This man was in prison with Sutton and has the same parole officer. His name is Benjy Meyer. He is the cousin of Saul Greenbaum, a lawyer who had been causing trouble in the law firm."

"The senior partner, Harry Lundquist, realizes now that Greenbaum wasn't the problem, that Roland was," Snow argued. "And as for this Benjy, Saul's cousin, he's been a thorn in the side of Saul and his family for years. Saul explained to us that he finally fled from the state, and as far as he's concerned, it's good riddance."

Lilia stepped back into the fray, "Benjy and Louis kidnapped my parents from the restaurant. I have proof."

"That's nonsense," Snow said.

"Sergeant, I watched as Lilia and Timmy spoke to an elderly couple by the name of Graham who saw Benjy and Louis abduct them," Diana said. "I tried to tell you that, but you wouldn't listen. I have since spoken with them. They told me exactly what Lilia and Timmy claimed they said to them."

For a moment, Snow looked taken aback. Finally, he said, "I guess you and I better find them right now and talk to them. I'm sure you will find that they were either misunderstood or simply remembered wrong."

"It's the middle of the night," Diana said. "But I'll call them, and if I can wake them up, I'll tell them we're coming to see them tonight."

"Okay, I'll go along with you even though I think it's a wild goose chase," Sergeant Snow said. "Officer Erman, would you mind waiting here with Lilia and Gabriel until we get back? I'm sure we won't be long."

Lilia was so worried and upset over her missing brother that she couldn't even enjoy being with Stetson. But she did respond to what he had to say. He asked, "Timmy had a spare pair of glasses. Are they still here?"

"I'll look," Gabriel said, even though he was clearly exhausted. He was not used to being up so late at night, and that added to Lilia's worries. A minute later, he came back in. "The glasses and hearing aid batteries are there where he and I left them," he said.

"Then I don't think he ran away. He would have taken them with him," Lilia said with a catch in her voice. "That could only mean one thing. Someone took him just like they did my parents, and it was probably Benjy Meyer."

"I sure hope not," Stetson said.

As if they didn't have enough worries, Gabriel groaned and slumped to the floor without a word. Stetson jumped toward him and knelt beside him. He quickly checked for a pulse. "It's weak, but he has a pulse," Stetson said. "Gabriel, can you hear me?"

There was no response. Lilia didn't have to be told what to do next. She had her phone out and was calling 911. She explained to the 911 operator what had happened and gave her Gabriel's address. Then she knelt beside Stetson as tears began to flow, and she simply could not stop them. This was more than she could stand.

"Lilia, I'll stay right here with him," Stetson said. "You need to lie on the sofa."

"I can stay with you," she said between sobs.

Stetson straightened up, put his arms around her, and pulled her close. "I'm sorry," he whispered in her ear as he held her. "Gabriel will be okay. And we will find Timmy and your parents."

"I wish I knew that," she said, wiping her eyes.

"You've got to believe it," he said. Then he kissed her on the top of the head and said, "Now go lie down. I'll wait with him until the ambulance comes."

"Okay, Stetson," she said. "I'm so glad you're here. I don't know what I'd do if you weren't."

She stood up and he stood with her. "I'll be here as long as you need me," he said tenderly. "You are very important to me."

"Thank you," she said and let him help her to the sofa. As soon as she was lying down, he reached down and very gently touched her lips with his. Then he moved back to where Gabriel had fallen.

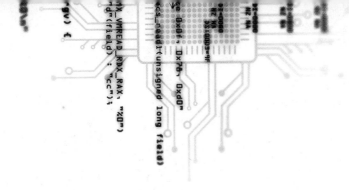

CHAPTER
ELEVEN

STETSON KEPT A HAND ON Gabriel's chest, making sure he continued to breathe. Although the breaths were shallow, they were steady. Gabriel remained unconscious. As he monitored the old man's condition, he thought about Lilia and her family. There was something about Lilia that had grown on him over the past days. He'd never known a young woman who affected him the way she did.

He prayed that her family would be spared and that he could one day get to know her better. Her sorrow had become his sorrow. Her fear had become his fear. Her love for her brother and her parents had become his concern as well. He also prayed for Gabriel. He was elderly, but totally unselfish. The stress of the past few days had been more than he could take. He could only hope that he would make it to the hospital and that he would be able to recover.

He finally heard a siren. He had the door open for the paramedics as soon as they came up the walk. He answered their basic questions and then turned Gabriel's care over to the professionals. At that point, he joined the beautiful girl on the sofa. He knelt beside her, took one of her hands in his and simply held it without speaking a word.

One of the paramedics called out to him and he laid her hand back on her stomach and hurried back to where the paramedics were getting Gabriel ready for transport to the hospital.

He was told that Gabriel was conscious and trying to speak. He leaned down and said, "Gabriel, it's Stetson. Can you hear me?"

"Yes," the old man said in a very weak voice. Stetson leaned closer. A hand touched his shoulder, and he was aware of Lilia beside him. "Tell the kids they can stay here as long as they need to," he said.

"I hear you, Gabriel," Lilia said as she also leaned close.

"If I die, take care of my place," he said.

"You are not going to die," Lilia replied.

"I hope not, but just in case."

"Okay, I will."

"Timmy and your mom and dad will be okay," he said.

"I hope so," she responded.

His head moved slightly, and then he drifted off again. Soon he was being carried out to the ambulance. The paramedics told Stetson that they would be taking him to the University Hospital.

***

A late-night meeting in a remote area of the state of Nevada was underway between Saul and his two henchmen, Kris and Rich. "Did you get the message relayed?" Saul asked, his eyes dark with suspicion.

It was Kris who answered. "We did exactly what you told us to do."

"How was the message received?"

"They didn't like it," Kris responded.

"Of course they didn't like it," Saul said sarcastically. "That is not what I want to know. Tell me what they are going to do as a result of your message to them from me."

"We didn't tell them it was from you, Boss," Kris said.

"Of course you didn't. You were told not to," Saul said impatiently. "What they are going to do is what I want to know."

"They cried a lot and got very angry with us," Kris said.

"You men aren't listening to me. Are Mr. and Mrs. Dixon prepared to do as you told them to?" Saul asked.

The two men looked at one another for a moment, and then Rich said, "I'm pretty sure they are. They don't want their children hurt."

"That's getting close to what I want to hear. But you are still not quite there. Are they going to leave the country using the passports I told you to give them and not attempt to contact their children, the authorities, or anyone from our law firm?"

"That's right," Rich said.

"Okay, very good. I don't want them found dead, for that would only make the authorities doubt what I've told them, and anyway, I don't want any heat on myself," Saul told them. He rubbed his forehead with a white handkerchief and then continued. "Did you make sure they got on a plane for Europe?"

"Of course we did. That's what we were told to do," Kris responded.

"Do they understand that their lives and that of their two spoiled children are at stake if they don't continue to do as I asked you to tell them?"

"They do," Kris said.

"Do they also understand that they are both wanted here for stealing from my law firm and one of our clients?"

"Mr. Dixon said he didn't steal anything," Rich said.

"I am not interested in what he says about that. He did it, and the only way for the two of them to stay out of jail is to disappear somewhere in another country," Saul told them coldly.

"Mr. Dixon asked us how they were supposed to live without an income and no way to get money from their accounts," Kris reported.

Saul laughed. "They are free to use their credit and debit cards if they dare. You told them that, didn't you?"

"Mr. Dixon said he couldn't do that, because those transactions could be traced and they would be arrested," Rich responded.

"I guess that's a risk they have to take. Did Mrs. Dixon say anything?"

"All she did was bawl," Kris said with an evil grin. "That's what you wanted, wasn't it?"

"Pretty close. Okay men, here is the cash I promised you." He handed them each twenty-five crisp one hundred dollar bills. They greedily stuffed them in their pockets. "I think that's all for now. You may go. If I need you again, I'll call you. Go now." They both turned away and started for their stolen car.

Saul coldly shot both men and left their bodies where they fell after stealing their IDs and taking back the money he had just given them. As he looked for a moment at their bodies, he repeated his favorite phrase. "Dead men tell no tales." He laughed. "If anyone ever finds your bodies, they will never know who you are or what you were doing out in this forsaken place. Better you die than the Dixons since the cops couldn't care less about your deaths, but they would work very hard at discovering who killed the Dixons, which is why I prefer they simply flee and look guilty."

* * *

That same night, a young couple, after eating a romantic dinner at a restaurant in Tooele, went for a drive in their Jeep out in the surrounding area. They soon became lost. After wandering for over an hour in an attempt to find their way back to town, they came upon a grisly scene. There was a dead body next to an old vehicle. It smelled bad and was quite bloated. It looked like it had been there for a while. They were so distraught that they lost the nice meal, did not even get a description of the vehicle, and tried to find their way back to town. They had no cell service for the next couple of hours. Finally, around three in the morning, they were able to call 911. They could not tell the officer that called them shortly after that the location of the body.

That meant they had to go to the sheriff's office and then ride with a couple of deputies back toward where they had been. It took a couple of hours, but they finally arrived at the scene.

The body was just as awful as they had remembered. The only piece of clothing that was easily recognizable was a badly soiled red ball cap that was on the ground a couple of feet in front of the body. The body was starting to decompose, according to the deputy. And rodents had chewed on the face and hands.

***

Gabriel was resting comfortably in the hospital when Stetson and Lilia went to see him at about nine o'clock in the morning. The doctor told them that he would be fine, that he was just stressed and both mentally and physically exhausted.

He was awake and smiled briefly when the two of them stepped into his hospital room. "I'm so sorry, Gabriel," Lilia said. "This is my fault. I should never have stayed with you. I will find someplace else until . . ." She began to sob and was unable to finish her comment.

Stetson tenderly put an arm around her shoulders and said, "You understand what she means, Gabriel."

The old man nodded the best he could on his pillow, but then he said, "Lilia, please, don't stay anywhere else. I need you more than you know. I love your family, and my life is worth nothing if you won't let me help in any way I can."

"But we have stressed you out. And it's not going to be easy until, well, you know," she replied.

"My dear girl," Gabriel said with a shaky voice but eyes that pierced hers, "you must have faith. Your parents and your brother will be found. Don't give up on any of them. In the meantime, please stay at my house."

Lilia, with tear-filled eyes, nodded and said, "Okay. Thank you."

Stetson took her back to Gabriel's house and held her hand as he walked with her inside. His phone rang. He glanced at the screen and then answered it. "This is Officer Erman. Lilia and I just came from the hospital where we visited Gabriel. He's going to be okay."

"I'm glad to hear that, Stetson," his caller, Detective Franklin, said. "I'm just calling with a bit of news." She then told him about the body that had been found during the night and concluded with, "There was a red hat near it."

"That could be the other man that Timmy identified," he said.

"Yes, Benjy Meyer. Timmy's picture was enough to allow us to make an identification. He was shot, just like his partner, Louis. But we don't believe it was with the same gun," Diana said. "The body had been there a while. So we know it could not have been him that kidnapped Timmy Dixon."

"Someone did," Stetson said.

"I wish that Sergeant Snow would seriously consider that instead of so stubbornly believing that Timmy ran away," Diana said. "By the way, how is Lilia holding up?"

"She's a strong girl. But this is not easy on her," Stetson said.

"She needs to be strong," Diana agreed. "I also called you to tell you that Sergeant Snow wants me to look in the Dixon house again and see if by any chance Timmy has been back there. Would you mind helping me?"

"I'd be glad to," Stetson responded. "When?"

"In about fifteen minutes, if that works for you."

"Come here to Gabriel's house. I'll wait for you. And I think we should take Lilia with us. She's alone here and I know she would feel better just going in her house," Stetson said.

"That works for me as long as we don't tell Snow. See you in a few minutes," she said, and the call ended.

After Diana got there, they talked in front of Gabriel's house for several minutes. Diana said, "Sergeant Snow was surprised when the body of Benjy was found. Knowing that he is Saul Greenbaum's cousin has got him and the rest of our squad rethinking their conclusions."

"Diana, I don't for one minute believe that Lilia's father stole that money. But until we can prove that someone else did, it doesn't look good for him. In my mind, that someone else is none other than Saul Greenbaum."

"Sergeant Snow didn't come with me because he was going back to the firm to speak with Lundquist. I'm hoping that Lundquist realized that Saul could be the bad guy, like I understand he used to think," Diana said. "Anyway, at least it's got Sergeant Snow thinking. Should we go ahead and go over to Lilia's house?"

Lilia and Stetson did not hold hands as they crossed the street, but she walked very close to him as the two of them followed Diana. She had the key, and she opened the door. Since all they were doing was trying to see if Timmy was by any chance hiding in the house, the search didn't take long, although they looked in any hiding place that a twelve-year-old genius might try hiding from someone intruding into his house. But he was not to be found in there. Finally, Diana said, "I guess that's it then. I will report to Sergeant Snow that he is not here."

Lilia had participated in the search, but she saw something the two officers did not. They spent very little time in the basement, but Lilia had felt a quickening of her pulse as she stayed behind the others, lingering for a moment down there. Things had been disturbed. She realized that it could have been done by previous searchers, so she said nothing to Diana or Stetson, but in her mind an idea began to form.

She followed them out of the back of the house, watched as they searched the pool house and the tool shed. She knew that Timmy, if he was even around, would not hide in those places. So while the officers searched, she lifted her eyes and began to scan the trees in the back of the yard. She didn't expect anything, and so she was surprised when she caught a bit of brown high up in one large tree. It was barely visible through the thick green leaves, but it was not quite the right color for the bark of the tree.

Her heart began to pound. She looked away as Stetson and Diana approached her. And once again, she said nothing about what she thought she had seen and what she was thinking. Soon, the three of them walked around the large home and across the street to Gabriel's house.

* * *

Several minutes passed. Timmy, high in the tree, sat still and silent on his perch. Finally, feeling that the intrusion was over, he descended from the tree, ran to the house, and opened the same basement window he had earlier used to flee the house when he could see that the officers and Lilia were going to go inside. He made sure it was locked behind him. There was no way he could have let them find him there. He proceeded to go up the stairs from the basement to the main floor and peered through the drapes in the living room. The officers were just getting in their cars to leave. He let out a sigh of relief. Then he returned to the basement and looked carefully around to see if anyone could have figured out that someone was staying there.

His eyes strayed to the window he'd used as the way into and out of the house. If anyone would have noticed, it would have been Lilia. It was her eyes that had stopped and stared for a long, tense minute as he had tried not to flinch. He had to take action. He hoped it would work. He had much to do.

***

Lilia was alone in Gabriel's large house. It was silent except for the humming of the refrigerator and the gently blowing air conditioning. She shivered involuntarily. She missed having Stetson's steadying presence with her. She'd been alone for several hours after Stetson had left last night. But she felt more alone than ever now. And she knew why. Her mind was on her family and what she had observed over at her house.

She didn't know what to do. It was too quiet, and the silence grated on her frayed nerves. She tried praying and found some comfort in that. Then she pondered what she had seen. The impulse she kept getting and had to put down was to go back over to her house. But she didn't think that was such a good idea until she was able to solidify what was running through her mind.

She was extremely tired, and she finally stretched out on the sofa in the living room. She wished Gabriel was here. She felt like she could talk to him about what she'd observed. She'd wanted to mention it to Stetson, but she didn't want him doing anything about it until she was sure of it.

She eventually drifted off. When she awoke, a couple of hours had passed. She felt somewhat rested. Her mind again went to what she had observed. She decided that she needed to talk to someone about it, and that someone had to be Gabriel. She retrieved his keys from a hook in the kitchen and went out to the garage. She headed for the University Hospital in his Cadillac.

When she arrived there, she sat in Gabriel's car for a couple of minutes, trying to convince herself that she really should talk to Gabriel. She'd come here for that purpose, so she decided she would do it. She pulled the keys from the ignition and reached for the door handle. As she did so, her phone began to ring.

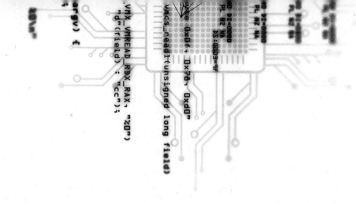

CHAPTER
TWELVE

LILIA DID NOT RECOGNIZE THE number that appeared on her screen. She debated not answering the call, feeling that it could be one of the many super irritating spam calls that she got quite regularly. But she decided to answer it, and if it was spam, she would quickly end the call.

"Hello," she said.

"Lilia," a voice she recognized and loved said quietly. She was stunned, and for a moment, she didn't know what to say. The voice went on. "Are you there, Lilia? Please, I need to talk to you."

"Timmy?" she asked as she leaned back against the seat of the black Cadillac.

"Yeah, it's me. I'm okay, but I have to talk to you. I'm hiding so that Sergeant Snow can't stop me from hunting for Mom and Dad," he said. "I'm sorry if I scared you. I was just so confused and upset. Will you forgive me?"

"Yeah, you did scare me. I thought you'd been kidnapped," she said as both relief and anger surged through her. "And of course I forgive you, but don't ever do that to me again."

"I'm sorry, but I didn't dare tell anyone. I was afraid you would try to stop me. But when I saw you looking up into the tree where I was hiding, I realized you probably thought it was me. And it was," Timmy said.

"What were you doing up there?" Lilia asked as her heart rate slowed and her breathing evened out.

"I saw you guys over at Gabriel's. When you all looked at our house, I realized you might be coming over, so I went out a basement window and climbed the tree. That was where I was hiding the first time officers searched after I came over here," he said.

"How did you get a phone?" she asked, puzzled.

"I remembered that Dad and Mom had one of Grandma Dixon's from after she died. I guess they forgot to cancel it. I was hoping that was what happened. I was pretty sure they hadn't thrown it away, so I looked for it. I found it in the basement in a box with other electronic stuff. The charging cord was there, so I plugged it in. This phone is not password protected, so I had no trouble getting into it once I got it charged," Timmy said. "Are you mad at me?"

"Yes, I am. You could have told me what you were going to do and why," Lilia said. "But mostly I'm glad you're okay. But I don't see how you can find Dad and Mom."

"You would have tried to stop me," Timmy told her again.

"You know it," she retorted, but her anger was fading as relief pushed it away.

She heard her twelve-year-old brother chuckle. "I'm using this phone. But that's not all. Dad's old laptop computer was in the same box."

"Let me guess. You've got it working too."

"Yep," Timmy said.

"So why didn't the cops take it like they did all the other stuff they took?" Lilia asked.

"I think it was because most of the stuff in the box looked like junk. They didn't realize that the phone and computer were in it. They were under a lot of other stuff, and I think they dug down a ways and then quit," he said. "I'm glad they did. I knew these were in there, so I just hoped they hadn't taken them," Timmy said.

"I guess you got lucky," she said. "So have you done any good yet?" She was hopeful but would be surprised if he'd found anything useful to them.

"Mom and Dad are in England," he said with a touch of pride in his young voice.

"What? How did you figure that out?" she asked, shocked.

"You remember those credit card numbers in the metal box we found, don't you?"

"Of course I do," she said.

"Well, I figured out how to trace them."

"How did you do that?"

"It was easy. I hacked into the police computer again, and, well, without going into all the details, I was able to see how they did it. But of course they didn't have these numbers, or at least they didn't use them. Sergeant Snow didn't figure they were of any value," he said.

"So they are in England?" Lilia asked. "Are you sure?"

"Yep, they are. I have a couple of addresses where they used them," he said.

"Can you get ahold of them?" she asked.

"Maybe, but I'm trying to decide what to do."

"Let's decide together," she suggested.

"I don't want Gabriel to know that you know where I am. If you left to come over and join me, he might figure it out," Timmy said.

"Not for a day or so, he won't," she said and explained why.

"Oh no! I hope he's going to be okay. I tell you what. Maybe you can come tonight. Come after midnight. There's one of the basement windows that I can open for you," he said. "It's the—"

"I think I know which one it is. I'll tap on it to let you know it's me."

"How do you know?" Timmy asked, sounding slightly alarmed.

"It was unlocked."

"Did the officers notice it?"

"Nope, and I didn't tell them," she said. "I'll text you when I get ready to come over."

A few hours later, Lilia and Timmy were huddled in the basement where lights wouldn't show to the outside. That was where Timmy had been hiding out—except for the relatively short periods when he was in the tree.

"Dad must be forgetful," Lilia said. "He must not have known that he hadn't canceled Grandma's phone and just kept paying since it was on the same bill with all of ours. I guess that's what happens when you have a stressful job like Dad's."

"I guess. Anyway, I have a phone now and it works okay."

"So what have you been doing over here? Surely you haven't been on the computer all that time," Lilia said.

Timmy reached into a box near the blankets he'd been using to sleep and pulled out his triple combination. "I've been studying the scriptures," he said.

"Wow. That's great. You already know more about the gospel than I do, and I study every day for a few minutes."

Timmy shrugged. Then he added, "I've also been working out. At least Snow didn't take my workout equipment. I also went for a couple of late-night swims in the dark. I need to stay in shape."

Lilia studied her brother for a moment, and then she said, "You are certainly in good shape. I need to work out more." Then she shifted the subject. "Let's think about what we need to do next."

"Lilia, I think I might know where Mom and Dad are staying. You remember when they took us to Europe a couple years ago. They stayed in a hotel in London that they really like. I'll bet that's where they are. They used the credit card at the restaurant there. I know it's the same one."

"Didn't they use it to check into the hotel with?" Lilia asked.

"No, but I found where they took some cash from an ATM. So they probably used that," he said.

"Timmy, why don't they get a hold of us? If they aren't being held captive, they could have done that," Lilia suggested. "It doesn't make sense to me, and it scares me. I don't want Sergeant Snow to be right."

Timmy answered with, "Our dad and mom are honest. There has to be another reason. What if they don't dare try to contact us?"

Lilia took a deep breath. "You mean like what if Mr. Greenbaum threatened to do something to us if they did?"

"Exactly. They would go to jail if they were found by the police, even though they have been framed by Mr. Greenbaum. I've been working on that, and I'm getting closer to proving that he was the thief," Timmy explained. "I still have more work to do on that."

"So what should we do?" Lilia asked her little brother. "Should we maybe go to England?"

"That's what I've been thinking," Timmy said. "I think we should go soon."

"Then we need airline tickets."

"We can use the same card Dad and Mom have been using to get them. Let's do that."

"I'll start calling right now, but I need you to give me the number," Lilia said.

"Don't use your phone. We can do it on the computer," Timmy said.

Within a half hour, they had tickets secured for a flight to London. They had to be on the plane at ten p.m. It was after midnight as they were huddled in their own home. It was very early Sunday morning. "I wish I dared go to church today, but I don't want anyone to tell the cops that I'm really not lost. But I think you should go, Lilia. You could take Gabriel's car."

"I think I'll do that," she said. "Now that we have a plan, I'll go back to Gabriel's and sleep. I'll call you when it's time to leave. I'll come over here, and we'll take my car. Sergeant Snow isn't as smart as he thinks he is. He doesn't know I have another key to it hidden in the garage." She chuckled. "Gabriel will need his car when he gets out of the hospital."

"What do we tell him?" Timmy asked.

"We can't tell him anything," Lilia responded. She thought for a moment and then said, "Okay, so we'll leave him a note on his pillow and just tell him that both of us are okay, but we felt we needed to hide out somewhere else for a while," Lilia suggested.

"I guess that'll be okay," he agreed. "But we also need to tell him to destroy the note."

"Yeah, that sounds good. Let's pack our suitcases right now and put them in the trunk of my car. We'll need our passports, Timmy. They are in the safe with Mom and Dad's. I wonder how they got to England without them."

"I'm sure they must have some forged ones. But don't ask me how they got them. Anyway, I'll get ours from the safe when it's time to go," he said.

Less than an hour later, the small suitcases were locked in the trunk of Lilia's car, and out of an abundance of caution, they locked the spare key to her car in the safe as well. Then Lilia hugged her brother. "Don't you dare go anywhere again without telling me," she said. He promised, and she went back to Gabriel's house.

***

Saul Greenbaum was seething with anger. He was pretty sure that someone had hacked into his computer. He couldn't tell if the hacker had learned anything, but it worried him. Timmy Dixon was very bright. He was missing, he'd heard, but he had a feeling he wasn't really missing. He and his sister were up to something, and he simply could not allow that. He had to do something about those kids. He'd have left them alone if that nosey kid hadn't messed around. And the more he thought about it, the more he figured it was him doing the hacking.

He waited outside Gabriel Schiller's house in one of several cars he used when he needed to be unrecognized. It was an old Buick that had been his mother's car. He also had his late father's car as well and a couple that his men had stolen that he kept stashed in a private storage facility. He knew he wouldn't likely find Timmy, but finding Lilia would not be a problem. At a little before ten on that Sunday morning, one of the doors to Gabriel's garage opened and out came his black Cadillac with Lilia Dixon at the wheel.

He followed her when she headed down the street. If she stopped somewhere that he could snatch her without being seen, he would do that. If not, he would get her when she got back to Schiller's house.

***

Lilia's phone began to ring. She retrieved it from her purse and answered. "Lilia, a car is following you," Timmy's frantic voice told her. "It's been parked in front of Gabriel's house for a while. I don't know how long because I just looked out a few minutes ago. I got the license number. It's an old blue Buick. A man is driving. I didn't get a good look at him. Please be careful."

"I see it back there now," she said. "I won't stop until I get to the church. I'll come straight back afterward. Don't worry, I've got this, Timmy."

"Well, I am worried," he responded. "Let me know what he does."

"I will," she said.

The rest of the way to the church, she kept an eye on her rearview mirror. The Buick followed her all the way. She parked as near the chapel as she could and waited until some other people started toward the front door and then joined them. Even though she had told her little brother not to worry, she could hardly bear the tension she was experiencing. She was terrified. It didn't help that everyone wanted to talk to her, to console her and to offer help.

She made it through sacrament meeting and then decided to go home. She texted Timmy and told him to watch for her. She didn't see the Buick and began to relax. But a couple of blocks from home, she spotted it. When she turned into Gabriel's garage, the Buick passed on by. That did not in any manner reduce her anxiety.

She entered the main house from the garage and was surprised to see Timmy waiting for her. "You shouldn't have come over. You could have been seen," she scolded.

"I know you could handle that guy by yourself if he tries to come in the house, but with two of us he hasn't a chance," Timmy said.

"And then he'll know you aren't lost," Lilia reminded him. "I may be able to beat him and even tie him up, but let me do it alone if I can. You stay close but out of sight. If I need help, then you can help me."

Timmy shook his head. "We don't know who it is. He might have a gun."

"You stay right inside that doorway, and if he pulls a gun or knife on me, I'll back over there and then you can do your thing," she suggested more calmly than she felt.

The two of them watched from through a slit in the closed blinds. The minutes ticked by much too slowly. Two. Three. Four. Five. Finally, Timmy said, "I'll check the back of the house."

A minute later, he came running. "He's coming to the back door!"

"I should have figured that," Lilia said. "Let's get back there. We can make this work without you being seen yet—I hope."

Lilia waited near the door and Timmy hid just inside the nearest room. They waited another minute, and then another. The tension was almost more than Lilia could stand. What if there was a second person?

Finally, when she thought she would burst with anxiety, she heard the doorknob being fiddled with. It was locked, but she was certain that would make no difference to whoever was there. There was a faint scraping sound in the lock, and then the knob turned, and the door slowly began to open.

A head peeked in. Mr. Saul Greenbaum. The tension fled and anger took over. Fueled with adrenaline, Lilia was ready for him. He looked back and forth and then silently stepped inside. He had a gun in his hand. But not for long. Lilia kicked the gun free, and then she followed up with a swift barrage of kicks and hits that sent Greenbaum to the floor. He didn't move once he'd landed.

Lilia leaned over him. He was unconscious and injured. Timmy joined her. Together they checked him out. He was breathing and his heart was beating. She felt relief at that. However, they found that she had broken his arm just above the wrist, had bloodied his mouth, and both eyes were changing color.

"Boy, Lilia, you really let him have it," Timmy said.

"I shouldn't have, but I lost my temper and I just kept hitting and kicking. We've got to call someone," she said.

"First, we tie him up," Timmy suggested.

"For sure," she said. "I'll stay here, and you find something."

Saul still had not stirred when Timmy returned. "Will this work?" he asked as he showed Lilia a roll of gray duct tape.

"Perfect," she said. Saul regained consciousness as they were busy taping him with many layers. Timmy stepped away so he would not be seen. Lilia soon had his feet and hands bound so that all he could do was twist around, which he did. "Do I need to knock you out again?" Lilia asked coldly.

No verbal response. But his continual struggles were a response all the same. She coldly kicked him on the side of the head, not too hard, but hard enough to stop him from moving. She rolled him on his side and taped his arms behind his back with a dozen wraps of tape around his stomach. She did the same with his legs. Then she blindfolded him with a cloth so he couldn't see, and Timmy rejoined her. He came fully conscious again and began to curse.

His mouth got duct tape as well.

Lilia put her finger to her lips, making sure that Timmy didn't say anything. Then she spoke to Saul. "You stole money from the law firm. You will admit that now," she said. "I'll remove the tape from your mouth if you agree to that. Just nod your head the best you can so I'll know you are going to do that."

Rather than nod, he shook his head. She fought to control her anger. "Now tell me where my little brother is. I know you kidnapped him." She smiled at her brother as she spoke. He grinned.

She pulled the tape from his mouth. He cursed. She let him but said, "Where is Timmy?"

"I don't know," he said.

"I don't believe you," she shot back.

"I'll kill you for this," he said.

Lilia had her phone recording. She had turned it on after putting a strip of tape over his eyes. That way he wouldn't know what she was doing with her phone. She was glad she was recording when he made that threat. She wasn't through. "Did you kill my mom and dad?"

"They are as good as dead," he said. "So are you and Timmy."

"Where is Timmy?"

His language was horrible.

"Where are my mother and father, Mr. and Mrs. Dixon?"

He interrupted his cursing long enough to say, "I'll never tell. I was going to let them live, but now they are going to die because you did this to me."

Lilia was so angry that she kicked him again after shutting off her phone. He screamed, and she reapplied the tape to his mouth. She signaled to Timmy to follow her. "I should call Diana, but we need to give ourselves some time. We need to be gone from here before the police show up."

"Let's get his cell phone before we go," he said. "I need it."

Lilia did not argue but ran back and retrieved the phone from inside Saul's suit coat and rejoined Timmy. They checked the street out front, left the door unlocked, and fled across the street and around their house.

Once inside they retrieved the car keys and passports from the safe as well as some of the cash their parents had kept in there. Then Timmy said, "We can't take your phone. They will trace it. Let's disable it and lock it in the safe."

"Okay, but, Timmy, where is the metal box with Dad's papers and stuff in it?"

He grinned. "It's in a plastic bag up in the tree. It can't be seen from the ground." Then his freckled face grew very serious. "Lilia, what if the cops or Saul's friends come in and break into the safe?"

"They would get my phone and . . ." She hesitated, watched Timmy's face, and then she said, "I get it. Should we put them up in the tree as well?"

"Yes," he said.

"Okay. But let me send this recording to Diana first."

After Lilia sent the recording to Diana and Timmy put the items in a garbage bag, Timmy ran outside. Lilia followed, watching nervously all around.

He scaled the tree like a monkey. He disappeared from sight in the high, thick branches. She waited, and then after a couple of minutes, he descended from the tree. "There, they won't get wet, the wind won't blow them down, and they are safer than if they'd been in the safe."

"Okay, let's head inside while I make a call on the landline." She called Diana. "Detective, this is Lilia Dixon. Mr. Greenbaum broke into Mr. Schiller's house and attempted to kidnap me at gunpoint. He failed. He is bound and gagged near the back door."

"I'm on my way," the detective said.

"Did you get the recording I sent you?" Lilia asked.

"Just a moment," the detective said. A couple of minutes later, she said, "Yes, I got it."

"Thank you. Will you watch it?"

Lilia waited while Diana watched the recording.

"I'm shocked," Diana said finally. "Did he know you were recording him?"

"Of course not; I blindfolded him. I'm still alive, but I can't say if my parents and Timmy are or not. Do you have enough to arrest Mr. Greenbaum on?"

"More than enough, and now I'm on my way."

"Thank you. I'm about to fall apart. Please hurry." With that, Lilia ended the call. She really was so stressed she was half sick to her stomach.

The siblings got in Lilia's blue VW, and two minutes later they were several blocks from their home.

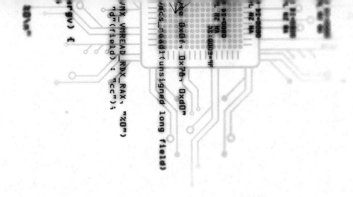

CHAPTER
THIRTEEN

STETSON ANSWERED HIS PHONE AS soon as he saw it was Detective Diana Franklin calling. "Hey, Diana, what's up?"

"I need your help," she said.

"Is it urgent, Diana?"

"Very much so. I'm on my way to Gabriel Schiller's house. Lilia called. She's really upset and claims Saul Greenbaum tried to kidnap her at gunpoint but failed."

"I'll come right now," he said, and he ran for his car. He was off duty but had a patrol car at his apartment. When he started the car he could hear Diana calling for additional backup. When the airwaves were clear he signed on and said, "I'm heading to that location."

He arrived at about the same time as Diana and another backup patrol car. He jumped from his car and met the other officers. Diana took charge as she said, "I hope there is no danger in there, but just in case, we'll treat it as a live incident. Stetson, take the back door." She went on to assign the other officers to cover two more doors and she took the main entrance.

Stetson ran around back and onto the rear deck. There he slowed down and approached the door. With his service weapon drawn, he stood at the side of the door and reached for the doorknob. To his surprise it was unlocked. He shoved it open and peered in. He grabbed his portable radio and said, "One person bound on the floor just inside the back door. Am I clear to enter?"

Diana's voice came on and she spoke. "Yes, I'm in the front door now."

The other officers reported meeting locked doors. So she instructed them to come to the back and enter carefully with Stetson. He waited until they showed up and he could see Diana coming his way with her gun also drawn. He went in and checked the bound man on the floor. "He's alive," he reported, and then he shouted, "Lilia, it's Stetson. We are here. You can come out now."

There was no response. Diana then instructed Stetson and one of the other officers to join her in a search of the home while the second one stayed with the bound man. "Stetson," she said. "I don't like this. There could be another person here holding Lilia."

That was his thought, so urgently, speedily, but also cautiously they began to search. It took ten minutes to clear the entire house and the garage. They met back by where the bound man lay. He was conscious and trying to squirm, but he was having very little success.

"Lilia is gone," Stetson said, fighting to keep his emotions at a professional level, even though he was frightened for the girl he had come to like more than just a little.

"A second suspect must have got the drop on her and taken her," Diana said. "We need to make sure who we have here and see if we can get him to talk."

It only took a moment to determine that it was in fact none other than Saul Greenbaum. Stetson unbound the man's legs from behind his back, and then he and two other officers lifted him to his feet. At that moment, in came Sergeant Snow and another detective. Saul, though awake and trying to resist, was clearly injured.

Diana quickly told the sergeant what was happening. Then she pointed at the pistol that lay several feet away. "That must be his gun. It will have prints on it as he has no gloves on. I don't see his cell phone. If he had one, that is."

Diana continued, "Lilia Dixon is not here. Both the front and rear doors were unlocked. He must have had someone else backing him up, so I can only assume that Lilia is now in the hands of more criminals."

"I guess you're right," Snow said. "This house is now a crime scene. I take it that Mr. Schiller is still in the hospital."

"He is," Stetson responded, "but can be released later today. I was told that when I called a little while ago."

"Okay, so let's process the scene and then clear the house for Schiller so that it will be okay to allow him to return."

At that point, they carried Saul Greenbaum from the house and shoved him into the back seat of a patrol car, still bound by his arms, feet, and mouth. "Have medical personnel at the jail check him over and administer any aid he needs. I think he has a broken arm or wrist," Sergeant Snow said.

He then gave orders for two men to search for the car Saul had come in if there was one, although he said, "I'm afraid the second person probably took Miss Dixon in that car. I can't believe I was so wrong all this time. I feel like a fool."

None of the others commented, and they were assigned to search the house for anything that looked like it could be related to the kidnapping of Lilia Dixon. Snow turned to Diana. "Detective, you come with me. We'll see if we can interrogate Greenbaum at the jail after he is patched up. Officer Stetson, I would appreciate it if you would stay here and assist the detectives as needed."

Despite the conciliatory tone of the sergeant's voice, Stetson felt like he was being shoved into the background. But that was no surprise as Snow had resisted having him involved in the case. He wasn't asked to do anything, so he slipped into Gabriel's kitchen and dialed Lilia's phone. It went to voice mail. No surprise. He felt sick at heart and to his stomach as well. He could not believe this was happening.

He sat down at the table feeling useless and began to pray, pleading with the Lord for Lilia and her family. He had barely finished when his phone rang. He looked at the screen and was shocked to see Saul Greenbaum's name on the screen. He wasn't sure if it would be wise to answer it or not. He stared at it as it rang.

***

Lilia waited as the phone continued to ring. Finally, when she was about to give up on Stetson answering, she heard his voice. It was a simple, "Hello."

"Stetson, this is Lilia. Can I trust you to tell no one that you've heard from me? It's very important."

"Lilia, where are you? Are you safe or is someone holding you?" he asked.

"Please, Stetson, I need you to promise that you will keep what I have to tell you totally secret. I'm fine but . . . well, there's something I need to tell you. Please."

"Okay, Lilia, I promise," he said.

"I have not been kidnapped. But my life is in danger. Do you know about Saul Greenbaum?" she asked.

"I know you beat him up pretty badly," he said.

"I was defending myself. But I'm glad I hurt him. He is a really bad man. I'm sure he has a lot of others who are working for him. My life and those of my family are in danger. I know he will get out of jail on bail, and when he does, he said he would kill us," Lilia revealed.

"Can you prove he said that?" Stetson asked.

"Yes. Diana has a recording I made of Saul after I had him subdued and his arms and feet taped with duct tape," she said.

"So she will share that with me?" he asked.

"I think so. It's pretty awful."

"Where are you?" Stetson asked her. She had Saul's phone on speaker so Timmy could hear what was being said. He shook his head at Stetson's question.

"I can't tell you that," she said. "But I am safe."

"How did you get Saul's phone?" he asked.

"I took it from him," she responded. "What did you think?"

"I guess that's what I thought," he said. "How did you get into it? Surely it was password protected."

"Timmy figured it out," she said.

For a moment, Stetson was silent. Finally he asked, "Is . . . is Timmy with you?"

"He is, but you can't tell anyone," she said. "He and I have some work to do. I wish we could count on the police and Mr. Lundquist to believe us about Saul and quit blaming my parents for his crime. I will make sure that until that happens, no one will know where we are."

"I think Sergeant Snow is coming around to that. Lilia, I'm afraid for you guys. Please, tell me where you are and I'll meet you," he said. The urgency in his voice increased her fears of Saul and those in league with him.

"I'm sorry, but I can't tell you that. Timmy and I are okay. We are going to find our parents if we can," she said.

"Lilia, you know that's impossible, don't you? I mean, Timmy is extra smart and all, but even he can't do something the police can't do. We are trying everything we can to find them," Stetson said. "You two will only put yourselves in more danger."

"Stetson, if I hadn't known Saul was looking for me, he would probably have killed me. But Timmy saw him and warned me. I was able to use the training my father made me take to stop him. However, I can't depend on that if any of his people find us," she said.

"Lilia, please, listen to me. I will help you. Don't shut me out. Tell me where I can meet you, and I'll protect both of you while the search for your parents continues," he said. He was begging, and it made her feel bad. He went on, "I promise. No one needs to know that I know you and Timmy are safe."

"Safe for now," she corrected him. "We have got to find our parents. They are not safe."

"Lilia, listen to me. I hate to have to say this, but you need to realize that your parents are probably already dead. I don't want you to die too," he said, his voice sounding desperate now.

"I can't use this phone much longer. Sergeant Snow will probably start trying to trace it to find me, since I guess he thinks I've been kidnapped."

"He may already be doing that. The detectives need that phone, Lilia. It may have evidence that will prove your point about Saul," he argued.

"That's why we have it," she said. "Now, we have to go. And remember, you promised."

"I know," he said, and she ended the call and handed the phone to Timmy. "Can you make this so it can't be traced?" she asked.

"Of course," he said. "I'll still be able to retrieve whatever information he has on it later. I'll do it right now."

"I think it was a mistake calling Stetson on this phone. Not that I don't trust him, but it was a mistake. I'm going to see if I can find a pay phone somewhere. I know there aren't many of those anymore, but I need to talk to him again. I know we can't use Grandma's phone, because that needs to be kept secret."

She drove in silence while Timmy did his thing to the phone. Finally he said, "Okay, that's fixed. Where do you think we can find a pay phone?"

"We'll check some convenience stores first," she said.

"Okay, but we can't spend too much time, Lilia. They might figure out that your car is not in our garage, and then they'll be looking for it. We need to get to the airport as soon as we can. Anyway, our flight is in three hours."

"You are a genius, little brother. We don't need to look for a pay phone. They have them in the airport. Let's head there now," she said.

Timmy laughed. "I'm not all that smart. I honestly didn't think of that. Anyway, I can't wait until we are on our way to England. I can't wait to find Mom and Dad. I miss them so much."

The laughter died away, and Timmy had to wipe away a tear. It was infectious. Lilia's eyes filled as well. "This is so hard, Timmy. I don't know what we'd ever do without our faith."

"We forgot to pray before we left," he responded. "I'll say a prayer while you drive." And that is what he did. He asked the Lord to watch over the two of them, their parents, Gabriel, and their police officer friend, Stetson.

When he'd finished, he said, "I wish Stetson could go with us. It would be safer, don't you think?"

Lilia was surprised at his suggestion, but the idea appealed to her. But she gave a practical answer. "He wouldn't want to go and probably couldn't even get time off from his work."

"As soon as we get to the airport, let's call him again. I think we should ask him. He likes you a lot, Lilia, and I know he would want to protect you," he said as she blushed. It made him grin. "I know I'm just a kid, but I get it with you two. I'm not blind and I'm not dumb."

"That's for sure," she agreed. "Sometimes you are too smart for your own good."

***

Stetson's phone rang. It was an unlisted number. As before, he hesitated to answer, but he had a feeling that he should. "Hi, Stetson," Lilia said as soon as he'd said hello.

"Where are you?" he asked.

"I can't tell you unless you agree to what I am going to ask you to do," she said.

He did not hesitate. "Tell me what you want me to do, and I'll do it if I can," he said.

"Come with Timmy and me," she said.

He was stunned. But he knew that there was nothing he'd rather do right now. "Okay, if I can get some time off. Where are you going, and for how long?"

"We are going to another country, and we are scared. We don't know for how long," she said.

He could hear the trembling in her voice, and he didn't have to think twice. He was learning to care deeply for that girl, and he would do anything to keep her and her brother safe. "Give me ten minutes and then call me back," he said. "I need to arrange for some vacation time. I have a lot coming. How about if I ask for two weeks? Will that do?"

"I hope so," she said. "We don't have a lot of time. I'm going to get you a ticket right now and then call you back. You'll need a passport. You do have one, don't you?"

"I do. I'll get busy and see if I can work it out." The call ended and he called his sergeant's cell phone. When Sergeant Hartling answered, he said, "Sergeant,

I have had an emergency come up. I have some vacation coming. Can I have two weeks starting now? I hate to throw this at you, but I really need to leave the state for a few days to help some loved ones out." That was not a lie. He loved the Dixons as if they were family. One of them . . .

"I guess I can work it out if it's important to you," the sergeant said.

"Thank you so much. I'll talk to you later," he said and hung up before Sergeant Hartling could change his mind. He quickly packed a bag, grabbed his passport, and answered his phone as it began to ring. "I can go," he said as soon as he was sure it was Lilia. "Did you get me a ticket?"

"I did," Lilia said. "But there is one thing. You can't bring your cell phone. We don't want anyone to know where we're going, and they could track you."

"I've got to have a phone," he said.

"Shut yours off, leave it at your apartment, and buy another phone on your way here. Come to the airport, terminal two. We'll meet you there. Stetson, thanks, but please hurry. We don't have a lot of time." She hesitated for a moment and then added, "You're the best."

With that, she ended the call.

Stetson, despite the enormity of the danger facing Lilia and her family, could not suppress a smile. With it lingering on his face, he shut off his phone, put it in a bedroom dresser drawer, and left the house.

He hurried, taking time to get a phone with a new number. As promised, Lilia and Timmy were waiting for him at terminal two. Lilia rushed up to him and hugged him tightly. Timmy bashfully also hugged him. He tousled the kid's red hair.

"Let's get your luggage checked," Lilia said. "Oh, is that all you brought? You can carry that on. We packed light too. So we don't have to check anything either."

"Thanks for getting me a ticket," he said. "I'm surprised you could get me on the same flight."

"We got lucky, Stetson. It was the next to the last seat. Thank you for coming. Let's hurry."

"Stetson," Timmy said as they hurried along, carrying their carry-on luggage, "What's your new phone number?"

Stetson opened the phone he had just bought and then recited the number, not in the least surprised that Timmy did not write it down. Later, while waiting at the gate to board their flight to London, Stetson noticed Timmy busy working a phone he held. He hadn't known that the kid had a phone, and he threw a questioning glance at Lilia. She explained about the phone. Then they both watched Timmy.

"What's he doing?" Stetson asked.

"He's contacting a hotel in London," she said.

"Making reservations for us?" he asked with raised eyebrows.

Lilia shook her head. "No, he's leaving a message for them to give to our parents."

Stetson's eyebrows shot even higher. "You're kidding, right? You guys can't possibly know where they are."

"We think we do," she said. "Don't ever underestimate my little brother."

Stetson was stunned. A couple minutes later, Timmy walked back to them and sat down next to Lilia. "I hope they get it," he said to her.

Timmy opened his bag and pulled out a small laptop, which he booted up and began working on. "I thought Snow's detectives took your computers," he whispered to Lilia.

She smiled. "Sergeant Snow thought so too." She offered no explanation.

He had a ton of questions to ask, but he didn't have time before they were told to board the plane. As was to be expected, his seat was not anywhere near theirs, so to his frustration, the questions had to wait.

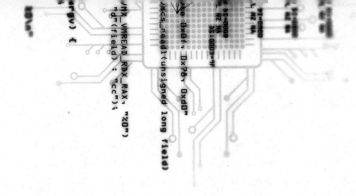

CHAPTER
FOURTEEN

DETECTIVE DIANA FRANKLIN WAS SUMMONED to Sergeant Snow's office. He waved her to a seat. As soon as she was seated, he said, "I just wanted to bring you up to date on a few things. The bullet that killed Benjy, Greenbaum's cousin, was fired from the gun he used in his attempt to kidnap Lilia Dixon."

She was astonished. Snow gave the information a moment to sink in before he added, "It seems that Mr. Greenbaum is a very dangerous man. It is now believed that he framed Roland Dixon for the theft of the money from the law firm. But we don't yet have proof of that. I spoke with Mr. Lundquist this morning."

"Does he now believe that the Dixons were kidnapped, as Lilia and Timmy claimed?" Diana asked.

"He does. And he is afraid that they are dead, which is reasonable in light of this new information," the sergeant said. "Mr. Greenbaum, for as bright as he is supposed to be, has made some serious mistakes. One of them was trying to kidnap the Dixon girl. As you already know, we found the car he drove when he made that attempt. It's filled with his fingerprints and some we can't identify."

"Are you charging him with murder?" Diana asked.

"Yes," he said.

"So he shouldn't be getting out of jail anytime soon, if at all," she said with a smile of satisfaction.

Sergeant Snow did not smile. "He's already out. He posted a hundred thousand dollar bail before we figured out the murder and could get him charged with it."

"Oh no!" Diana exclaimed. "He threatened Lilia and her little brother as well as her parents. We have that recorded."

"And since we think he had a confederate who kidnapped Lilia, it only seems logical that they are holding Timmy as well," Snow said. "I'm afraid that we probably have more murders by now. It makes me sick. I'm afraid I made a terrible mistake. I read this whole thing wrong. Most likely the entire Dixon family is wiped out, and that horrible man is free."

Diana dropped her head into her hands. "I really messed up. I tried to keep track of those kids, but I sure did a bad job of it."

"You did the best you could. You are only one person," Sergeant Snow consoled her. "And I'm the one who took you off the assignment when we believed that the Dixons had absconded with the money. I wish we would have had enough manpower to put around-the-clock surveillance on them. In retrospect, we should have done it even though we are shorthanded and didn't think it was necessary. It's too late to worry about that now."

"What do we do next?" Diana asked.

"You have a new assignment. Try to locate Mr. Saul Greenbaum. We took his passport, so he can't leave the country, but that doesn't stop him from leaving the state, Detective. His phone is gone and seems to be out of service. The best lead I can give you is his car, his personal vehicle, a dark-blue Cadillac Escalade," Sergeant Snow said. He slid a piece of paper across his desk to her. "This has his vehicle license and VIN numbers on it, and a couple of credit cards we know he uses."

"Okay," she said, feeling overwhelmed. "I'll do my best."

"I know you will, Detective. But you will need some help. I have the rest of our crew tied up along with some other detectives in the department. I have permission to use someone from patrol. Contact Sergeant Hartling and tell him that he is to let you use Officer Erman. He has an interest in the case, and I believe he is an okay officer. He will be assigned to you full-time until further notice. Keep me posted."

The interview was over. Diana left the office, went to her own cubical, and dialed Sergeant Hartling's number. He picked up after a couple of rings. She identified herself and said, "I have orders to use Officer Erman as my partner for a while. I am assigned to locate and arrest Saul Greenbaum."

"I'm sorry, Detective, but I'm afraid that isn't possible," Hartling said. "He had a personal emergency arise, and I allowed him two weeks of his personal leave time to deal with it."

Diana was deflated. She liked and trusted Stetson. And he was familiar with the case. Someone else would need to be brought up to speed. "What was his emergency?" she asked.

"He didn't say, exactly," Sergeant Hartling responded. "He only told me it had to do with some of his loved ones."

"Would you object if I tried to call him and see if he would possibly be able to make himself available to help me?" she asked.

"Feel free. Do you have his cell phone number?"

"I do."

"Okay. Maybe where he has developed some ties to the Dixon family he would help you. Tell him it has been authorized."

"Thank you, Sergeant," Diana said. "I'll see if I can persuade him."

She next called Stetson's cell phone. It went directly to voice mail. She left a message for him to call her. Then she talked to Sergeant Snow again and told him about her inability to contact Stetson but told him that she would keep trying.

"I hope you reach him. In the meantime, I'm afraid you'll have to work by yourself. If I can free up one of the other officers, I'll give you some help, but right now I don't see that happening. I suppose we could ask for someone else from patrol, but Stetson is the right fit with his previous involvement in the matter, even though I wasn't happy with him inserting himself at first," Sergeant Snow said honestly. "But I have formed a different opinion of him since then. I'd take him as a permanent addition to my squad if I could swing it."

"Okay, I'll get to work. But I'll keep trying Officer Erman," she said.

Diana used the computer for a while, attempting to get a trace on Saul Greenbaum's Cadillac. She found that it was parked at his home. She decided to go there, even though she knew it would be too simple if she found him there, as he had another car. He surely wasn't so dumb that he'd be at home anyway. He had to know murder charges would be coming his way as well as attempted kidnapping ones.

Saul lived in an upscale neighborhood in a very nice house. She rang the doorbell. It was answered by an attractive young lady in her early twenties with bright green eyes, short brown hair, and a slim figure. "Hi, I'm Detective Diana Franklin. I need to speak with Mr. Greenbaum," Diana said, flashing her badge.

"I'm his daughter, Sydney," the young lady said. "Dad's not at home. He and my mother are not on speaking terms since she divorced him a couple of years ago. She sent me to ask him some questions for her, but he's not here. I don't know where he is."

"Are his cars here?" Diana asked, even though she was already pretty sure the Cadillac was. At least it was just a few minutes before.

"He has two cars," Sydney said. "A Cadillac and a Porsche. They are both in the garage. I have no idea where he would have gone without them. I tried calling his cell phone, but it goes to voice mail. I called his office. They sounded kind of . . . well, secretive. But they claim he hasn't been in for a couple of days."

"Sydney, have you spoken with your dad in the past few days?" Diana asked.

"No. I don't like my father. He was never a good dad and he treated my mother like dirt. But at least I can still talk to him if I have to even though Mom can't," Sydney said.

"I see. Well, I really need to speak with him," Diana said. "If I give you my number, would you have him call when you see him?"

"Is Dad in some kind of trouble?"

"Have you not heard the news lately?"

"No. I don't care much about the news, to be honest with you. Neither does Mom."

"Do you live with your mother?" Diana asked.

"Right now I do. I've been working in Provo, but I quit my job and came back here to try to help Mom. Dad really ruined her life. I mean, she's an emotional wreck. Do you know my dad?"

"We've met," Diana said, hoping not to have to expound on how appallingly her father had acted when he was dragged from Gabriel Schiller's house.

A car pulled into the wide circular driveway and parked beside Diana's unmarked police vehicle. "Here's Dad now," Sydney said. But she gasped when he got out of the passenger side of the car. "Dad, what happened to you?" she asked, wide-eyed. "You look awful."

Diana was on high alert as soon as Saul began to advance to the sidewalk, his right wrist and arm in a cast, his face a mass of bruises, with both eyes partially shut and very swollen. "Sydney, you are not welcome here anymore. I hear you've moved in with your mother again. I can't forgive you for that."

What a greeting, Diana thought. What a bad time not to have backup. She needed to arrest him and take him in.

He got within three or four yards of the women on his front deck before he suddenly shouted, "What are you doing here, Detective? Get off of my property."

Diana was aware of another man, a big fellow that looked dangerous both from his size and the look of his face, approaching. He'd apparently been the driver of the car. The smart thing to do now was to retreat, she thought, call for backup, and then arrest Saul. She said to Sydney, "It's nice to meet you. I need to go."

Sydney looked at her with fear in her green eyes. "No, it's okay. Why don't you stay and talk to Dad." Her lips then formed the word, *please*. Now Sydney was in a tough spot. This girl no longer wanted to see her dad any more than Diana did, but she was the cop, and she had a duty to protect as well as to arrest.

She stepped back beside Sydney, and the two of them faced Saul and the very large and slowly advancing menace, who was now on the sidewalk and looking the size of Goliath. Her heart in her throat, she said, "Mr. Greenbaum, I need to speak with you."

Saul uttered some words that were consistent with the horrible language on the recording that Lilia had made and that he had used when dragged from Gabriel's house. Then he reverted to clear English. "I am a free man, Detective. Get off my property."

"I'm afraid I'm going to have to arrest you," she said.

"What now?" he demanded. "I am an attorney and a mighty good one. I know my rights, and you have no right to arrest me again."

"Dad, what have you done?" Sydney asked in a very shaky voice. Diana did not glance at her. She was keeping her eyes on Saul and his chauffeur or bodyguard, or whatever he was.

"Nothing that concerns you. Go in the house while I deal with this cop," he ordered.

Sydney, to her credit, did not move. In fact, she sidled closer to Diana.

"Sir, you are under arrest for the murder of Benjy Meyer," Diana said as she pulled out her handcuffs, hoping they'd fit over the cast on his arm, but she was almost certain they wouldn't.

"He's Dad's cousin," Sydney said, her voice not much more than a whisper.

"Sydney, Benjy is fine. This cop is bluffing. Go in the house while I straighten this out with Detective Franklin," Saul said.

Sydney, to Diana's dismay, said, "Okay, Dad." She slipped away from Diana and went into the house, shutting the door behind her.

"I am not going anywhere with you, Detective," Saul said. "I don't know what you're talking about. I haven't seen Benjy in years. He's sort of, you know, the black sheep of the family. But I'm sure he's just fine."

"Tell you what, why don't we go down to the station and talk about it," Diana said, swallowing her fear and speaking with authority.

"That is not going to happen," he said coldly.

Diana tried to distract him by saying, "Where is Timmy Dixon?"

What little of his eyes that was visible through the bruises narrowed. "I don't know anything about him. Now, I am going to give you one more chance to leave my property."

Diana wanted to do just that, and if it weren't for the frightened young lady in the house, she would have done so. "I can't do that," she said as she stepped close to him. "You are coming with me."

The massive man on the sidewalk said nothing, but his mere bulk and dangerous face were enough to tell Diana that she would never get past him with Saul, and possibly not even without him. When, a heartbeat later, a gun appeared in the giant's hand, she knew it. The giant said nothing, but Saul turned his head and looked back.

"Tiny, this woman is leaving. Let her, unless she tries to put those handcuffs on me. Not that she can with my broken arm. But don't shoot her. Just hit her hard with your fists."

At that exact moment, Diana heard the door open behind her. To her surprise, Sydney said, "Dad, tell your goon to put his gun down. More cops are coming."

From the look on Saul's battered face, it was clear that Sydney had a weapon. Saul said, "Sydney, that is a mistake. You couldn't shoot anyone if you had to."

Sydney stepped out and again stood next to Diana. "You are wrong. I will shoot both of you if I have to. Detective Franklin wouldn't be placing you under arrest for killing Benjy unless you actually did it."

"Shoot them," Saul suddenly shouted. Sydney's gun was very loud in Diana's ear when it went off. Tiny the giant dropped his weapon and grabbed his stomach, screaming with pain. Just then sirens sounded a couple of blocks away. Saul backed up, stepped off the deck, and said, "Get in the car, Tiny." He bent and with his unbroken left hand picked up the giant's gun. "I'll kill you both," he said as the sirens sounded closer.

Diana didn't remember dropping her handcuffs and pulling her concealed weapon. But it was in her hand. She took aim, but before she could fire, a little boy peddled up the sidewalk, just beyond the driveway. A ricochet could hit the kid. She didn't dare shoot. Apparently Sydney didn't either. The big man, blood soaking his hands from holding his stomach, lurched back to the car, and using one bloody hand, climbed in the passenger side.

"Little boy, get away from here," Diana shouted, but the boy seemed mesmerized and didn't move. Saul backed toward him. "Mr. Greenbaum, are you okay?" the boy asked innocently.

"I'm fine, but these people want to shoot me. Come here, Jackie."

"Get away, Jackie!" Sydney shouted. "My father will hurt you."

But the boy seemed to know Saul better than he knew his daughter, and he dropped his bike and stepped to the curved driveway. "That's a good boy, Jackie. Open the door for me, please."

Patrol cars were now screaming up the block. Jackie opened the door. Saul slammed the kid over the head with the gun, then dragged him into the car with him and somehow managed to get it into gear. "Tiny, grab this kid," he shouted as he began to drive wildly around the curved lane and onto the street.

Diana thought for a fleeting second about shooting at the car's tires, but a miss could injure or kill Jackie. So she could only watch as the car drove away. Officers piled out of the two patrol cars, guns drawn, and told Sydney and Diana to drop their weapons.

"I'm the one that called for you to come!" Sydney said urgently. "It's the guys in that car that you want. They just kidnapped a little boy."

"I'm Detective Franklin," Diana said.

That seemed to do it, and the officers holstered their weapons. Diana wanted to pursue the fleeing Chevy. She was terribly afraid for little Jackie. "I'm going after that car. One pair of you stay here, the other ones follow me, but don't use your guns. There's a little boy in that car. Sydney, tell them what just happened," Diana said and ran to her car and squealed out of the driveway and onto the street.

One of the patrol cars followed her. She got on her radio and gave the dispatcher her location. "I am in pursuit of a gray Chevy Sedan, an older model with Utah plates. A little boy is a hostage in the car along with a man who is wanted for murder." She gave the address, and then she told them that another unit was behind her.

She had the gray car in sight now, but it was driving very erratically and dangerously fast for the neighborhood. Fear for little Jackie surged through her. Somehow, they had to save the boy.

Saul tried to turn a corner way too fast and ran into a fire hydrant. Water shot up. Saul jumped out and stopped a yellow sports car by waving his gun around. Diana slowed down and approached the intersection with her gun in one hand. The driver of the sports car got out with his hands over his head.

Saul got in and took off again. A rubbernecking driver plowed into the old Chevy.

She could hear Jackie screaming. The driver of the rubbernecking car was shoved against the back of his seat by airbags. He made no movements. The passenger was trying to get out, blood streaming down her face. The yellow sports car disappeared. Diana knew what she had to do. There were injured people who needed to be attended to, the foremost in her mind being Jackie.

The officers in the patrol car had also stopped. They all got busy. Diana radioed her position, gave a brief description of the yellow car, and requested ambulances. Unless someone spotted the sports car and soon, Saul was going to get away. But there was nothing she could do about that. She ran to the wrecked cars, getting soaked from the huge spout of gushing water, and looked in. Jackie was pinned between the big man and the dashboard. Tiny wasn't moving. Jackie continued to scream.

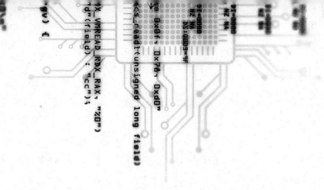

CHAPTER
FIFTEEN

DIANA, ATTEMPTING TO IGNORE THE water that was hammering down on her, slid into the driver side of the car and shouted, "Jackie, I'm a police officer. I have help coming. Can you move at all?" The other car had slammed into the side Saul had been in. Had he not gotten out in time, the chase for him would have been over.

Jackie's screams stopped, and he looked with glazed eyes at Diana. "Help me," he moaned.

She reached for his hand and tried to pull. But Tiny had him lodged tightly between his huge bleeding stomach and the crumpled dashboard. "I'll be right back," she told Jackie. "I'm not leaving you. I will get you out of here."

With the help of a couple of strong patrol officers, they managed to get the passenger door open. Diana was glad it was an older car, for it did not have automatic seats and they were able to slide the seat back. She was then able to gently lift Jackie away from the body of Tiny, who was clearly deceased, and get the boy into an ambulance.

She was surprised as she was helping with the driver of the rubbernecking vehicle to hear a familiar voice say, "Detective Franklin, is there anything I can do to help?"

She looked up into the tearstained face of Sydney Greenbaum. "No, we've got it, Sydney, but thanks for saving my life."

"I knew Dad was a monster," Sydney said, "but a killer?"

"I'm sorry," Diana said.

"Is that giant guy dead? I see that no one is bothering with him," she said, her voice shaky.

"He is."

"I killed him," Sydney said, and fresh tears descended in torrents down her pretty face.

"No, your father is responsible for his death. You had no choice, and anyway, for all we know, it was the crash that killed him," Diana said. "You are a hero today, and don't you ever forget it."

"I bet you thought I'd caved in to Dad when I went in the house," Sydney said between sobs.

"I wasn't thinking a lot about anything other than how I was going to get out of that situation with my life. You solved that for me. Thank you."

"You are soaked, and so are those other officers," Sydney observed as she slowly regained control of her emotions. "Was Jackie okay? I saw him being loaded in an ambulance."

"I'm sure he's hurt bad, but he'll live," Diana said. "My question is, are you okay?"

"I will be," she said. "I guess Dad got away."

"For now," Diana told her. "I think these other officers have things under control here now. I need to go change into some dry clothes and get back to my office. Thank you again, Sydney. I owe my life to you."

Diana finally arrived back at her desk, dry but emotionally torn. Sergeant Snow joined her there. "Are you all right, Detective?" he asked.

She nodded. "I'm fine. I'm just sorry I messed up so badly."

"I'll need a full report from you, but I already know that you acted with heroism, and I want to thank you for that."

"But you don't even know what happened," Diana said.

"Actually I do. I spoke with Saul Greenbaum's daughter a few minutes ago. She came in looking for your boss." He chuckled. "She's certainly nothing like her father. She told me what took place in some detail."

"But Saul got away, and I had him right there," Diana said.

"If it hadn't been for the man he called Tiny, you would have brought him in. You are probably wondering if there is any update on him," Sergeant Snow said.

"I am," she responded. "I am going after him again. That is, unless someone caught him."

Snow shook his head. "He abandoned the stolen sports car he left the accident scene in, carjacked another car, and fled. The driver of that car was unconscious. She was found lying in the street. No one could tell anything about that last car he stole. So for now, he is simply out there somewhere."

"At least I can find people who may have seen him with that cast on his arm and his battered face," Diana said.

"Yes, that will help. But I need to find someone else to give you a hand. I'm sorry I sent you into such a dangerous situation by yourself. Have you heard from Officer Erman yet?"

"No, but maybe I'll go to his apartment and see if he's there," she said.

"Let's ping his cell phone. Maybe that will help. His sergeant didn't know where he was going or what the emergency was," Snow said. "You can fill me in later on the attempted arrest today even though I did get a pretty full story from Saul's daughter. Let's go to my office, and we'll see if we can locate Erman's phone."

Ten minutes later, Diana was headed for Stetson's apartment. His phone was there, so he probably was too. She smiled through fatigue and frustration as she thought about how he would probably react when he found out all that had happened that day that he had missed out on.

She parked as close as she could to Stetson's apartment. She'd never been there before, so she searched for the number, found it, and rang his doorbell. When she got no response, she knocked on the door. While waiting, a lady came by and told Diana that he wasn't home, that she'd seen him leave with a bag that looked like he was going on a trip. Diana thanked her and went back to her car wondering why he would go on a trip, no matter the emergency, without his cell phone. She didn't know Stetson well, but she knew he was a bright and conscientious man. Worry bugs started skipping through her brain.

She called Sergeant Snow, reported what she'd learned, and decided to make a trip to the Dixons' neighborhood. She wasn't sure what she thought she might learn, but she felt compelled, so she went. She parked in front of Gabriel Schiller's house. She walked to his front door and rang the bell. After waiting a minute or so, she rang it again. He was old and barely out of the hospital, so she didn't expect him to come trotting to the door. She was patient.

Finally, the door opened, and Gabriel said, "May I help you?"

"We've met before," Diana said. "I'm Detective Diana Franklin."

Recognition sparked in his eyes and he invited her in. "I hope you're here with good news about my neighbors. I am sick with worry. I love that family," he said. "I fear for their lives. One of your colleagues told me about that awful man and how that brave girl knocked him down a few levels. I just worry that someone took her, both her and Timmy."

Diana directed the old man to his living room, telling him, "I just have a few questions for you, and I'll let you enjoy the rest of your afternoon," she said as she interrupted his flow of information. She was afraid he'd have gone on talking forever, and she had certain questions she needed answered.

Once he was seated, she sat near him. "You have been wonderful to those kids," she said. "I just wanted to pick your brain. Did Lilia ever say anything that might lead you to believe that she knew more than she was saying about her parents?" She knew it was a shot in the dark, but maybe he'd heard something that would help her. There was no doubt in her mind that Saul would leave no stone unturned in searching for the children unless he already had them and both they and their parents were dead. But the fact that he'd made the threats he had to Lilia gave her hope that he hadn't, so far, killed any of them.

The old fellow rubbed his eyes. "Not really," he responded. "But I've been thinking a lot. Those kids are bright. Timmy, of course, is a genius. He needed a computer to do his work, his research, or whatever it was he was doing. When you police officers took their computers, he was crippled in a way."

"I can imagine that," Diana responded.

"He needed one, and I have tried to believe that he wasn't kidnapped but just went in search of somewhere that he could use a computer without anyone knowing," he said.

"Did his sister wonder that too?" Diana asked. "Or did she maybe know what he was up to?"

"She may have wondered, but I don't think she knew. She could not have faked the worry and strain she was under."

"Gabriel, is there any chance that Timmy would have gone back to his house, despite Sergeant Snow's orders to the contrary?" Diana asked.

He said, "You officers took the keys."

"Yes, but he's smart," Diana said.

"You searched the house," Gabriel said, "and didn't find him in there. But . . ." He did not complete his sentence and closed his eyes, appearing to be in deep thought. What he said when he opened them surprised her. "He can climb trees like a monkey." That made no sense to her. She made no comment. Either Gabriel was losing his train of thought or he had an idea in his head. She let him think some more.

"Let me suggest a theory," he finally said. "Timmy is a genius, but he's also a young boy. I remember once, a couple years ago, when he got angry about something his parents had done. He disappeared. They searched frantically. They asked me to help. I looked up at those huge trees in their yard and wondered, since I'd seen him climb them a few times, if he was up there hiding." He stopped and smiled.

"That was where he was. It was almost impossible to see him in the thick branches and heavy leaves, but when I suggested the idea to his parents, his father called to him and told him to come down, as if he actually knew he was up there, which he didn't. It worked, and pretty soon, he appeared, slithered down, and started crying. He apologized and everything was fine."

Diana's mind leaped ahead. She had an idea that Gabriel might be onto something. She didn't say anything except, "Keep thinking and talking. I'll keep listening."

Gabriel again closed his eyes. When he spoke again, he said, "Timmy was—no, he *is* an observant child. If he happened to have found a way into his house, he would be smart enough to make sure no one caught him in there. He probably had a plan in place to keep from being caught. If so, he would slip away before anyone could get in, even though you officers had the keys. And it would be logical to believe he might have climbed one of those trees and watched until he felt it was safe to come down again."

Diana grinned at Gabriel. "You aren't a retired detective, are you? That's some pretty good reasoning."

"No, I was a businessman. A pretty successful one, if I do say so myself. I would never have been able to afford this house on what you officers make. Anyway," he said, "I think that with what I've just suggested, maybe you should go over there and take a look."

"I will do that," she said. "Would you like to come along? If you are strong enough, that is."

"I'm fine now, and I was hoping you would ask," he said.

They tried the front door and all the rest of the doors that led to the outside. Diana wasn't surprised that they were all locked. They circled the house and began to check the first floor windows. Gabriel crawled awkwardly into some shrubs to a window that was mostly concealed by the plants while she stood and gazed past the pool house to the large trees.

Suddenly, the old man called out to Diana, "He's been in the house. I found a window that he managed to get open. I can see that someone has crawled around back here."

"That's great. Can you get in, or should I try?" she asked as she ran to where he was concealed.

"I don't think I can manage that," he said. "Give me a second here and I'll come out."

She waited, and a minute later, Gabriel crawled out. "Will you help me up?" he asked.

She grabbed one hand and helped him to his feet. "That's not something I have done for a long time," he said. "You go ahead if you want to. I left the window partly open. You can go in, can't you?" he asked.

She patted his shoulder and said, "I can legally, I can physically, and I will. You wait at the back door and I'll let you in."

"I'm not a police officer. I don't want to break the law," he said.

"You won't be, since I will be using your assistance. Give me a couple of minutes." With that she crawled into the bushes, crawled through the window, shutting it behind her but not locking it. She hurried up the stairs to the main floor and let Gabriel in. He was clearly exhausted, so she had him rest in a recliner while she looked around.

Timmy, if he had been in there, and she was quite certain that he had been, had been very careful not to leave signs of it. If he had been in his room, she couldn't tell it. The one clue she found was in the basement bathroom, which had a shower. She checked it closely and discovered that the soap in the soap dish was still slightly damp. That was all the confirmation she needed.

There was a pile of blankets on the floor in the farthest room in the basement. They were neatly folded. She suspected that he'd used them and then folded them carefully each time he was finished sleeping. She spent the better part of the next hour searching the basement, as that, in her mind, was where he would most likely have spent the majority of his time.

There were cardboard boxes there. She looked through them. The largest one had miscellaneous items, and she stirred through them for a moment, then stopped and went to another, much smaller box. She found nothing of interest in it. She started to walk past the large box and stopped, looking at it for a moment. She had not looked all the way to the bottom of it. Would her colleagues perhaps have done the same thing she did?

She once again started digging down through that box. At the very bottom, she found what looked like an ear buds cord. She had one similar to it. She set it aside and looked further. There were a couple of CDs. She rubbed her chin. She put them back, and then she finished looking through the box. She found a set of old hearing aids but nothing else of interest.

Diana, a trained investigator, put her mind to work. She was quite certain that the only one in the family who wore hearing aids was Timmy. Could these be old ones of his? She examined them more carefully, envisioned Timmy's head, and remembered that the ones he wore fit inside his ears. She lifted one and put it behind one of her ears. The tube fit easily into the part she inserted in her ear. These were too large to have ever fit Timmy. She put them in her pocket along with the small phone cable.

What else, she wondered, might he have found in here? She had a feeling that he'd found something. Could there have been an old computer? If so, he would almost certainly have been able to use it. She shook her head. Even if that were the case, she was no closer to figuring things out than she was before.

She thought about the trees. They needed to be searched, even though she had no idea what she would find. Unless . . . the metal box, the contents of which she hadn't seen, came to her mind. She was pretty sure it was not in Gabriel's house. It wasn't in this one, unless it was in the Dixons' large safe. She couldn't get into that, but the department would be able to find someone who may be able to. Timmy would have known that. She thought about the trees again.

She heard shuffling steps and turned to see Gabriel approaching her. "Find anything that's of any use?" he asked.

"Not much, but did you ever meet any of Roland's or his wife's parents?" she asked.

"They're all dead now, but Roland's mother hasn't been gone for more than a year or two. She visited quite often from her home in Texas, long visits. She died on one of those visits. She was a nice lady. Why do you ask?"

"Do you know if she was hard of hearing, you know, like Timmy is?"

Gabriel nodded. "She wore hearing aids. Big things—behind her ears."

"Like this?" Diana asked as she retrieved the aids from her pocket where she had put them earlier for the very purpose of showing them to Gabriel.

"Yes, exactly like that," he said. "I'll wager those are hers."

"Did she have a cell phone?" Diana asked.

"She did. And she usually had it plugged in one ear with some kind of device when she used it. I recall her taking one hearing aid out, putting it in her purse, and then using the phone," Gabriel responded.

"Could this have been what she used?" she asked as she produced the cord she'd found in the box.

"Yes, I'm sure that's it," he said. "But is that of any use?"

"I wonder," she said, "what happened to the phone."

Gabriel shook his head. "I think I see where you're going with this. Are you wondering if our young genius found it?"

"If he did and we had the number, we could try calling him," Diana said thoughtfully. "It's a long shot, but I wonder if I should get a search warrant and check all of Roland Dixon's phone records."

"I think you should try," Gabriel agreed.

"Now, let's go back outside and see if we can spot anything up any of those trees," Diana suggested.

She made sure the window they had entered through was closed but not locked, like they had found it. Then they locked the house and walked past the pool and pool house to the tall trees that lined the back of the Dixons' large yard.

"The tallest and thickest of the trees is that one," Gabriel said. "I don't know what kind it is, but it's the one I've seen Timmy go up. He climbs it like a monkey. You know, Detective, he's not only smart, but he's also extremely athletic and very strong for his age."

The two of them looked high into the branches, but they were very thick, and it was hard to tell if there was anything up that high. "I wonder if there is a tall ladder somewhere," Diana said. "I think if I could get up as high as the lower branches that I might be able to go a little higher and maybe spot something."

"I have a ladder that extends to twenty feet," Gabriel said. "I haven't used it for many years, but I still have it. It's in my shed out back of my house."

"Twenty feet," Diana mused. "I think that would do it. Let's go get it."

The ladder was quite heavy, but Diana was able to carry it. She waited beside Gabriel's house while a car passed. She didn't want to be seen if she could help it. Gabriel stood at the street and watched for cars and anyone coming out of any neighboring houses, which was unlikely this time of day. Most of the houses on the street were large, with expansive yards. A car went by, and as soon as it was at the end of the block, Gabriel signaled to Diana, who hurried as fast as she could while carrying the bulky ladder. She reached the back of the Dixon house just as another car entered the street. When Gabriel caught up, he told her, "I'm quite sure no one saw you."

She put the ladder down for a moment and rested her burning muscles. Then she packed it to the tree she wanted to try first, although she supposed Timmy may have hidden something up in any of the trees. This one, however, seemed the most likely due to its height and density of the limbs and leaves way up there. Gabriel helped her extend the ladder to its full twenty feet and maneuver it into place against the tree trunk. They had to place it between some of the lower branches. It felt quite sturdy.

Diana said, "Wish me luck," and began to climb. Luckily, she was not afraid of heights or she may not have been able to do this.

Gabriel kept his hands on the ladder while she climbed. When she reached the top of the ladder, she was into some thicker branches. This is where it got tricky. She took a deep breath, offered a short prayer, and stepped from the ladder onto a branch. She was soon ten feet beyond the ladder, and at that point she saw what she was hoping to find. There was a black, heavy-duty garbage bag just a short ways above her, nestled against the trunk in some really stout, leafy branches.

Once she reached it, she wondered how in the world that kid had made it up here with it. There was no way she could go back down and take it with her. She called down to Gabriel, who she could barely see. "I've found a large garbage bag. I'm going to sit up here and go through it. It's more than I can carry down."

She sat in a relatively safe place, where Timmy had most likely sat. By parting the branches a little, she could see the yard, the pool house, the pool, and the back of the house. She nodded to herself. Then she untied the bag and reached in. The first thing she pulled out was the little metal safe. Of course it was locked. She rummaged around some more. He had a jacket in the bag and a small pair of binoculars. Then she found a cell phone in a small freezer bag. She looked it over carefully. It had been disabled, but the battery was also in the bag.

There were a couple of thick novels, a book of very advanced crossword puzzles, and a pencil. They must have been here to help him pass the time. She half expected to find a small computer or tablet, but there was nothing like that in there. She put everything but the metal box and the freezer bag with the phone in it back in the large bag. She put the phone in a pocket, but the little safe was too big for that. She retied the garbage bag to the tree.

The metal box was a problem. But she was determined to get it down. She finally placed it on a limb below and, being careful not to dislodge it, climbed down past it, and then placed it on another limb below her. She succeeded in reaching the ladder in that fashion. Then, once she was on the ladder, she placed it at the top and started down. She stopped while it was still within reach. There was now no place where she could place it without it dropping now.

Diana said to Gabriel, "I've got the metal box here. I'm going to try to climb down and still hold it. I hope I don't fall."

"Why don't you drop it. Better taking a chance on damaging it than on you falling," Gabriel said.

"That sounds good," she replied and reached down as far as she dared and let the box go.

"Whoops," she said when it hit. The little box had hit on one corner and popped open. "I guess it wasn't as sturdy as we thought. At least we got it open," she said with a grin and descended to the ground.

She took a moment to catch her breath, and then she said, "Let's get this ladder down, and then I'll gather up the stuff that spilled from the little safe."

They did that and then Gabriel suggested, "Let's leave the ladder here, and we can come get it after dark."

Diana was fine with that. But they did place it a short distance back into the trees where it was concealed. Then she turned her attention to the little safe. "I can't believe it popped open," she said as she picked it up. "It looks like it hit just wrong, or right, I guess would be more like it. It bent it and popped the lock out when it hit on that corner."

"It won't lock again," Gabriel noted.

"Which is fine. Let me gather this stuff up and go back to your house to look at what we've found."

"Okay," he agreed.

Diana was thoughtful for a moment, and then she said, "Hey, I need to go back in the Dixons' house. There's one place I never looked, and I need to. It's the garage."

"I'll wait here," Gabriel said.

Diana returned to the window, opened it, climbed through, and hurried up the stairs and to the garage. She found what she had suspected she'd find. It was an empty spot where Lilia's car was parked before.

Once she was back outside, she said to Gabriel, "Lilia's car is gone. She must have had a second key. She and Timmy have gone somewhere in it, but I can't imagine where. It worries me. At least it gives me hope that Saul doesn't have them stashed somewhere. Let's hurry to your house and check out the things we found."

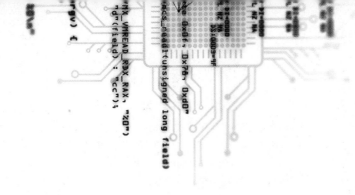

CHAPTER
SIXTEEN

"That's the hotel where we stayed when we visited England with our parents," Lilia told Stetson as they rounded the block. They had the taxi drop them off at the entrance. They got out, Lilia paid the driver, and they turned to the hotel.

"I hope they got my message," Timmy said. Lilia glanced at him. His mouth was puckered, and she could see from his eyes that he was worried. He'd told Lilia on the plane that he wasn't sure what they'd do if he had guessed wrong.

They went inside and straight to the registration desk. Stetson spoke politely to the man at the counter. "You have a couple staying here by the name of Dixon. These two are their children, and we are supposed to meet them here. We sent a message to have given to them. Is there any way you can check and see if they got the message?"

"Let me see what I can find out," the hotel attendant said. He disappeared through a door. Five minutes had passed before he came back out again. "They got your message, but they have checked out."

"Thank you," Stetson said as he looked at the faces of Lilia and Timmy. They were both rubbing their eyes, trying to keep the tears at bay.

They all stepped away and walked over to some soft chairs that were in front of a huge fireplace and sat down. "I scared them," Timmy said. "They must have thought it was fake, that Mr. Greenbaum sent it. I was afraid that might happen."

"At least we know that they were here," Lilia said. "I guess that's something."

"But where would they go from here?" Timmy asked. "I've got to think about this for a minute." He entered his thoughtful mode. Stetson reached for Lilia's hand and squeezed it gently. They watched the young redhead. Finally, he opened his eyes. "I'm not thinking very well, but I think I know what to do now. I need to see where they used their credit card next."

"If they dare use it," Stetson said. "If they think the message was fake, then they must wonder how Greenbaum found them."

"I'll try anyway," Timmy said. "It's the only thing I can think of." He pulled his bag onto his lap and retrieved his father's old laptop. "I need Wi-Fi."

"You guys stay here, and I'll go to the desk and see if they will give the password to me so we can connect," Stetson said.

As soon as he stepped away, Lilia felt a wave of fear that Stetson's nearness had kept at bay. She turned and watched him, not wanting to lose sight of him. He walked confidently across the lobby and spoke to the fellow at the desk again. The man nodded, wrote on a piece of paper, and handed it to Stetson.

"That was easy," he said as he handed the paper to Timmy.

***

"The kids and someone I don't know just entered the hotel, Boss."

"Are you sure it's them, Fredrick?" Saul asked into his latest phone.

"Yes. There is a redheaded kid with thick glasses and a very pretty girl with long brown hair. They are approaching the registration desk. I've never seen the guy before. Quite tall, very well built."

"I don't know who that would be. Doesn't matter anyway. Do you still have the Dixons in sight?"

"Sure do, Boss. They are in the gift shop."

"Okay, Fredrick, this is better than I could have ever hoped for. That kid may be smart, but he has stepped into a trap which you will spring. I want all of them together. Stay on the phone with me for now."

"You got it, Boss."

"You better not mess this up," Saul warned. "If you do, you will regret it."

"No worries, Boss. I got this."

***

"We don't know who that man with them is," Pamela whispered. "It scares me."

"Let's just watch for a minute. Maybe he's okay, but I can't imagine it. If Saul has had our kids kidnapped to get to us again, so help me . . ."

"Roland, the kids look scared. I wonder if there is someone else here," Pamela said. "I can't believe one man can cause so much heartache as Saul has."

Roland and Pamela Dixon were standing behind a magazine rack in the hotel's gift shop. They moved back and forth and continued to whisper. "Sweetheart, we've got to have faith. We'll get together with them again. We've been telling each other that all this time. I can't believe they found us here. It had to have been Timmy's doing. The message might really have been from him."

"Or maybe Saul was the one who sent it."

"But how in the world did Saul find us? We've been so careful."

"We didn't think he'd look anymore. After all, he gave us passports to leave the country. I thought that would be enough to satisfy him," Pamela said, her voice filled with fear.

They continued to watch. The kids and the man with them stood up. The man put his arms around their daughter's shoulders and pulled her close. She looked up at him and then touched his cheek with one hand.

"Pamela, it looks to me like she likes that guy," Roland said.

"Or is she being forced to act like that?" Pamela responded. "You know Lilia. She can be a good actress when she wants to—or when she has to."

"I hope she's not acting. We'll keep watching, but so help me, I can't let those kids leave here."

"That would be dangerous, Roland."

"I've been a coward, Pamela. I'm through running. It's time to take our lives and our family back despite Saul's threats."

"If they leave, we could follow them," Pamela suggested.

"Maybe. We'll see. That guy is a strong-looking man. I wouldn't stand a chance if I had to fight him."

Roland watched for a moment, and then he said, "I wish I'd taken the time to learn karate like the kids did. They are both so good. I could have been, but life got in the way. I was way too busy. I regret it."

"Maybe the kids can take that guy down," Pamela suggested hopefully.

"Unless he has a gun. And unless there is someone else watching them and they know it," Roland suggested. "I don't think they'd risk that."

"I just want to take them in my arms and hold them," Pamela said, fighting back a sob.

They watched as their children and the stranger walked around in front of the huge fireplace. Lilia and the stranger were holding hands now. *The guy looks nice, but at one time, so did Saul*, Roland thought.

Suddenly, his wife gasped. "Roland, look!"

He looked in the direction she was pointing. A large man with a beard and long hair appeared from somewhere. "He doesn't fit in here," Pamela said with a sob. "He looks dangerous."

He walked right over to their kids and stood looking around. The young man with Lilia let go of her hand and stepped between the kids and the other guy. For several minutes, nothing happened. Lilia whispered something in the ear of the good-looking guy they were with. He nodded and stepped next to the big man.

* * *

Lilia listened as Stetson spoke to the rough-looking fellow. "Hello, sir. Are you from around here?"

When the guy responded, it was with an unmistakable English accent. "Yes. I live a few miles away. I do some maintenance work for this hotel. I'm waiting for my buddy to meet me here, and then we will be going down to the basement. You are American, I see."

"We are. We're looking for some friends that were supposed to meet us here. I don't suppose you've seen them," Stetson said.

"My name's Lenny, and you are?"

"Stetson, and this is Lilia and Timmy."

"Nice to meet you folks."

"Same here."

"Describe them for me," Lenny said.

"The man is about five feet, eight inches and 160 pounds. He has red hair like the kid here," Stetson said pointing at Timmy.

Before he could describe Pamela, Lenny said, "He's with a pretty lady, not very tall, with short brown hair?"

"Yes, you've seen them?" Stetson asked.

"I have, matter of fact. Hard to miss that red hair—or the pretty lady. Saw them right here in the lobby. They were looking at a note the guy was holding and kind of shaking their heads. They didn't look very happy. Worried, I'd say," Lenny responded. "Hope they show up. This kid's got to be the fellow's son. Hey, there's my helper. Gotta go. Maybe I'll see you around."

The man shook hands with Stetson, nodded and smiled at Lilia and Timmy, and hurried away. He met up with a much smaller man with shorter hair. They headed for the elevators.

Stetson stepped back to Lilia and Timmy and said, "Well, that worked out okay. Nice guy."

"I know we shouldn't ever judge a book by its cover, but that guy looked scary," Lilia said as the phone in her purse began to buzz. As she dug their grandmother's phone from her purse, she said, "No one knows this number. I don't know if I dare answer it."

"I guess you better, or do you want me to?" Stetson asked as the phone continued to vibrate.

Without hesitation, Lilia handed it to him. "Hello," he said.

***

"Stetson, is that you?" Diana asked in surprise. She was at her desk and had barely received the information she'd been seeking on the Dixons' phone account. She had just dialed the number of the one phone that she was unfamiliar with.

"Diana! What the heck." Stetson sounded like he was stunned. Not that she wasn't.

"I've been looking for you," she said. "I was told that you and I were to team up and find Saul. I tried to go it alone and nearly got myself killed. The guy's out of control, to say the least."

"Diana, how did you get this phone number?" he asked.

"It took some work, but it was listed as one of the phones on Roland's AT&T account. I had reason to believe Timmy had it," she said. "Where are you, and how did you get that phone?" Diana was shaking her head, and she could visualize Stetson doing the same somewhere in the country . . . or the world. "On second thought, let me fill you in on what's going on, and then you can explain what you're doing. I hope we can team up and stop Greenbaum."

***

Pamela and Roland looked at each other, shaking their heads. "That man must not be as dangerous as he looks," Roland said. "Maybe that fellow is actually with the kids. Maybe we should go see them now."

"I don't know," Pamela said. "I'm still nervous. Just because that guy seems okay doesn't mean there are not others around."

"Pam, all we've done for days is look at everyone we see with suspicion. Saul would never have let us leave the country if he didn't think he had frightened us enough to do what he said or face something terrible happening to Lilia and Timmy," Roland reminded her again.

"Roland, Lilia must have her phone. If they weren't forcing the kids to come here and meet us, then why would they let her keep it?" she asked.

"But she handed it to the fellow and he's the one talking on it," Roland said, puzzled.

"It was in her purse," Pamela reminded him.

"You're suggesting that if she has it, they might have followed her here," Roland said. "Or maybe the kids really did figure out where we are? Although I can't imagine how. But there was that note."

"Do you forget that we have a son with a computer for a brain?" she asked with a worried frown.

Just then, the attendant in the gift shop approached them and told them that unless they were going to buy something, that maybe they should leave. "I don't want you discouraging other customers from coming in here. You've been standing here a long time," she said sternly.

"I'm sorry. We are watching those kids and that man over by the fireplace," Roland said.

"Are those your children?" the lady asked, her sternness fading away. "That boy has the same color hair as you do."

"I'm sorry if we are creeping you out, but this is a difficult situation. Two of them are our children, and they may be here to meet us, but we don't know the stranger with them. They could be in terrible danger, and so could we," Roland said.

The lady blinked her eyes and said, "Maybe I should call security."

"Would you do that for us? We want to gather our children together with us, but the threats and dangers are enormous," Roland said. "We are not even sure how the kids got to England let alone to this hotel. Even though the fellow with them seems friendly, we can't be sure."

"Oh, you poor folks," the lady said. "I'll call security right now."

She stepped away and made a call, and then she stepped back to them. "It's fine for you to wait right here until an officer joins us. I hope he can help you."

"Thank you," Roland said. "We are uncertain what to do."

It wasn't more than a minute before a slender young man in a security uniform rushed into the gift shop. "You called for help, Flora. What seems to be the problem?"

"These folks have a dilemma, Art," she said. "Maybe you can help them."

Art turned to Roland and said, "What seems to be the problem, sir?"

Roland explained in some detail as Flora listened. Her eyes grew wide, and his eyebrows arched. "So you don't dare approach the kids in case the man with them is not really a friend?"

"No, my kids are very skilled at defending themselves. What we worry about is that the guy has backup here who will come and attack all of us. We want to go to our children in the worst way," Roland explained. "But we are afraid to; afraid we might get them hurt."

"Okay, how about if we do this? We'll wait while I get a couple of my fellow security officers here, and then I'll go over and ask your children to come to the gift shop," Art suggested. "That way, if someone is watching from somewhere here in the lobby or even through the outside doors, we'll have plenty of help to protect you and your family."

"That would be great. But hurry, please. We don't want the kids and the fellow with them to leave."

The officer spoke into his radio. The response was that two others would be there within a minute at the most. Good to their word, two more uniformed men approached at a jog and then entered the gift shop. Art explained the situation, and then he said, "So I'll go over there and see if I can get them all to come in here. Then if the man is a threat, we will detain him and call the police."

Roland and Pamela looked at each other, nodding their heads but unable to keep the worry lines from their faces. "Okay, go ahead," Roland said.

***

"Hey, look, there's an officer of some kind heading toward us," Lilia said.

Into the phone, Stetson said, "I will call you back in a moment. There is an officer, possibly hotel security, headed our way. Maybe we can enlist his help." He ended the call and then suggested very firmly, "You two stay behind me and let me do the talking."

He stepped a couple of steps forward, but he didn't have to summon the man to aid him, as the fellow walked straight toward them. His eyes were moving back and forth as if watching for someone, just like they'd been doing.

"Hello, sir, my name is Art. I'm with hotel security," the officer said. "Do you folks need assistance?"

"We are glad to see you," Stetson said. "I'm a police officer, and these two are in danger. We are looking for their parents."

"Do you have some ID?" Art asked.

"Of course," Stetson replied and pulled out his police ID and shield.

Art studied it carefully. Then he handed it back. "I will need the three of you to accompany me to the gift shop. I have some backup in there. I believe we can help you."

Stetson said, "Okay, Lilia and Timmy, we'll take our bags with us. You stay right with me. Be prepared to fight if this is a trick of some sort."

"It's no trick, Officer," Art assured them. "But I certainly understand why you are being cautious."

That caution flew into the wind the moment Lilia spotted her parents standing behind a neck-high magazine rack. "Mom!" she shouted and flew into the gift shop as her mother flew out.

It was an amazing reunion. Tears flowed, cheeks were kissed. Hugs were long and tender. Stetson stood back with Art and kept an eye open all around. Finally, Lilia ran from the gift shop and grabbed his hand. "You've got to meet my parents."

***

"They are all together now, Boss. They are in the gift shop."

"Perfect. Kill them, Lefty, and don't mess up. Call me when it's finished."

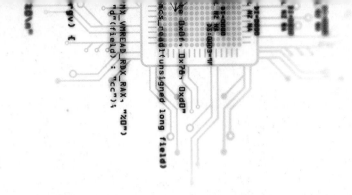

CHAPTER
SEVENTEEN

A NICELY DRESSED MAN WALKED past them and into the gift shop carrying a briefcase.

"I don't have a good feeling," Stetson said to Art as a tremor passed over him. "Something is wrong here."

"Stetson, it's okay now. This is my mother, and this is my dad," Lilia said, and then her eyes followed Stetson's. The man sat his briefcase down and picked up a magazine. But a second later he put it down and started for the exit.

"I don't like this. We need to get out of here right now!"

"No, it's okay," Lilia insisted.

Timmy, on the other hand, sided with Stetson. "Let's go."

"We are watching out for you," Art said. "I don't see any danger."

"That man's briefcase!" he shouted. "Run, everyone!"

The power of his voice started a mad dash from the gift shop. Timmy still held his bag, as did Stetson. Lilia's was forgotten in the panic. The attendant followed them, as did the security officers.

Stetson's eyes were on the man who'd left his briefcase. He was running hard toward the exit. "Hurry!" Stetson shouted.

A second later, there was a loud explosion, so powerful that they were all knocked to the floor. Burning debris rained down on them. Stetson jumped to his feet while the debris was still falling. Quickly, he accounted for the Dixons. They were all on the floor, but he could see that they were all moving. Lilia started to get up. "Stay down," he ordered.

Behind them, two security guards lay still, and farther back was the gift shop attendant, bloody and motionless. Stetson checked for pulses. They were all alive. He didn't see Art at first. Then as the debris settled, he saw him. He'd been the last to leave the gift shop, like he couldn't believe Stetson. People ran toward them, screaming and shouting.

Stetson took a quick look around. The nicely dressed man in the business suit was nowhere to be seen, having apparently reached the exit and gone outside. Stetson ran the last few feet to Art. A jagged stick of wood, probably from a display case, was embedded in his back. There was nothing that could be done for him. Saul had cost another innocent life.

***

Diana was getting very worried. Stetson hadn't yet called back. She finally redialed the number of Grandma Dixon's phone. It rang several times before Stetson finally came on. "Sorry, Diana. There was a bomb, but the Dixons are all alive. One security officer is dead, and there are other people injured. I've got to help them. I'll call you back."

Just that fast he was gone again. Diana was shaking. How in the world did Saul's evil influence reach so far? It couldn't be a random bombing. She looked at her watch. It was ten after seven in the evening. She consulted Siri, and the automated voice told her it was ten in the morning in London.

She dialed Sergeant Snow's cell number. She'd seen him leave the station a few minutes earlier. When he answered, he asked, "Are you making any headway, Detective?"

"All of the Dixons and Stetson Erman are in London. They just survived a bombing, but there were some casualties," she reported. "Stetson is pretty sure that Saul was somehow behind it."

"What in the world are you talking about?" Sergeant Snow demanded. "What is Stetson doing in London? Who told him to go there?"

"He's on leave, remember, and I think he just saved some lives."

"I'm coming back in. Assemble the squad for me. And see if you can find Sergeant Hartling. It's his man that's in England, so I want him involved. I'll call the lieutenant," Snow said, his voice a rapid staccato.

Diana did as she was asked, and within a half hour the entire squad was there, along with officers from another squad of detectives. The lieutenant was in charge, but all he did was call the meeting to order and then turn it over to Sergeant Snow. He gave a quick overview and then asked Diana to report on what she'd done and how she had been able to locate Stetson and the Dixon kids.

She kept listening for her phone, hoping for a call from Stetson as she reported her activities of the day. She didn't give the details of how she'd learned that Timmy had a phone, but she explained just enough to let the other officers know she had been convinced that he had somehow obtained one.

She was still speaking when her phone rang. She looked at it and said, "This is Officer Erman calling from London. I'll put it on speaker so we can all listen." She then answered, speaking down at her phone, which now lay on the table in front for her. "Officer Erman, thanks for calling back. My phone is on speaker. Let me explain who is here." She did that, and then she asked, "So what's happening where you are?"

Before Stetson had a chance to say anything, Sergeant Snow demanded, "What are you doing in England? Who told you that you could go there?"

Stetson, when he replied, talked quite calmly. "First, let me report that other than a few minor bruises and small cuts from flying debris, the Dixons and I are all okay. We are surrounded by dozens of London's finest and are safe at the moment." There was a slight pause, and then he said, "Sergeant Hartling, you approved my leave time."

"Yes, I did, but all you told me was that you had an emergency with some loved ones," Hartling responded.

"That's right. I just didn't tell you who they were. Now you know," Stetson said. "Sergeant Snow, you have seriously underestimated the genius of young Timmy Dixon. He found his parents, but if I hadn't been here with them, that family would now be dead." At those solemn words, no one in the entire room said a thing for a full minute, and then Stetson said, "I'll keep you informed of anything important." With that, he abruptly ended the call.

It was Sergeant Hartling who broke the silence that followed. "That was good work on Stetson's part. I will be putting him in for a commendation." No one responded. So he added, "I am going to cancel Officer Erman's leave and have him continue to work in London or wherever he has to in order to continue to keep that family safe. While I'm at it, I am also going to recommend that Detective Franklin receive a commendation."

Lieutenant Bob Gibson had been silent, but he spoke now. "I agree with Sergeant Hartling on the commendation and on having Officer Erman continue to protect the Dixons. Sergeant Snow, I am going to order Detective Franklin to get a ticket to London and fly there as soon as she can. Two officers are far better than one, and they can watch each other's backs as well as the Dixons'."

Snow stuttered for a moment, and then he said, "I have her assigned to find Greenbaum, and I don't want to change that assignment."

"She found him, and it nearly got her killed," Lieutenant Gibson shot back. "She is going to London. In the interest of safety and plain good sense, you are to issue her a new phone and a new number, and I don't want anyone but you, me, and Officer Erman to have that number."

Snow frowned for a moment, and then he said, "Okay, I'll get a couple of others tracking Greenbaum. But it won't be easy. My squad is awfully busy."

"Sergeant Hartling, I hate to do this to you, but I think Homicide needs Erman worse than you do. I'm going to recommend that he be promoted to detective and assigned to Sergeant Snow's crew. You won't oppose me on that, will you?" the lieutenant asked.

"I'll miss having him, but I certainly understand. He's young, but he's one of my best officers. I believe he will be a great asset to you," Sergeant Hartling said.

"I'll get the official approval in the morning, and with your support, it won't be a problem. As of right now, he and Detective Franklin are partners, and we will consider him a detective," Lieutenant Gibson said firmly.

* * *

"I got them, Boss," Fredrick Bole, one of his men in London, said.

"Are you sure?" Saul asked. He was getting increasingly unsure about the capabilities of the men he'd surrounded himself with in his criminal enterprises. Of course, he should not have been surprised, as most of them were men he'd defended in court and then drafted into his secret criminal organization, sometimes having to resort to blackmail to get them to work for him.

"The bomb went off just like I planned," Fredrick said. "I got away in plenty of time."

"Fredrick, have you seen the bodies?"

"Well, no, but I'm sure—"

Saul angrily cut him off. "You go back and make sure. If by any chance even one of them survived, you take care of the problem. Do I make myself clear?"

"I'll check, but I'm pretty sure they're all dead."

"Pretty sure isn't good enough! Call me back when you can confirm it, and be quick about it."

"You got it, Boss," Fredrick said.

* * *

Stetson was busy getting Roland's and Pamela's luggage, what little they had, from storage at the hotel. Lilia's bag had been destroyed in the blast. Stetson had never set his down before he gave the order to run. Timmy had saved his bag, even though it had slowed him down the second or two it took him to pick it up, which could have proved fatal, but the Lord had protected him.

"Thank you, Officer Erman, for saving our lives," Roland said as soon as they had the bags secured. "Now what do we do? We are in your hands."

"First, we get out of this hotel and go as far away as possible," Stetson said urgently. "The guy who tried to kill us will almost certainly try again if he finds out he didn't succeed. We can't take any chances. Let's get a cab and get out of here."

"But the London police expect us to show up at their station and give full statements," Roland protested.

"We'll worry about that later. Right now, we need to get a move on. Your lives are what I care about."

Lilia clung to his hand, Timmy to his mother's, and they all hurried from the hotel. They were all able to get in a cab and soon were on their way. They were all very somber. Timmy rode with his eyes shut, his fists clenched, and his mouth clamped tight. Lilia wondered what he was thinking about. One thing she knew for sure was that something was developing in that shrewd mind of his.

"How did Saul ever find us?" Roland asked after a couple of minutes. "He told us to leave the country and never come back, or he would have the children murdered. His men sent us on our way. Why did he bother to look for us again?"

Timmy's eyes opened. "Dad, did they give you guys the bags you have?"

"Yes, of course, that and passports in our own names," Roland responded.

"Then there's a tracking device somewhere in your stuff," Timmy said.

Stetson slapped his leg. "That's got to be it."

Pamela spoke up. "They didn't ever plan to let us live, did they?"

"Probably not," Stetson agreed grimly. He leaned toward the cab driver and said, "Cabbie, pull to the curb and stop here. But don't leave us. We need to check something. Will you help us get some of our luggage out? We need to look through it."

The only bags that needed checking were the two that belonged to Roland and Pamela. There was no concern about Timmy's or Stetson's, and Lilia's had been destroyed in the bomb blast. Stetson took them to the sidewalk and began to look through Roland's first. There was not a lot in there. Saul's henchmen hadn't given them much to travel with. But it was not the clothes that interested him—it was the bags.

He slowly and carefully felt the seams, then every square inch of material, and finally, he stared for a moment at the handle. A close inspection revealed that it had a tiny slit on the bottom side that had been glued back together. He didn't have a knife, but the cabbie did. It was a small but very sharp pocketknife.

He opened the handle with the knife and found a small metal object wedged inside. He popped it out and looked at it. Timmy leaned close. "That's a tracking device," he said. "I saw one just like it on the internet. I know it's small, but if you cracked it open, there would be a bunch of tiny wires and other stuff."

"What kind of stuff?" his father asked.

"It's hard to explain. I'll show you sometime on the computer."

An identical device was found in the handle of Pamela's bag. Stetson held the two of them in his hand and said, "Timmy, how about if we see what's inside of these right now?"

"You would ruin them," Lilia said.

Timmy scowled at her. "I think that's what we want, isn't it? They are the reason that guy found Mom and Dad."

Stetson thought his reasoning was right on, and he said so as he helped repack the bags. Then he put one of the little tracking devices on the sidewalk and stomped on it. Nothing much happened. The cabbie offered him a hammer. That did the trick. Timmy curiously studied the contents while Stetson destroyed the other one. Then he took the one back from Timmy and gave it another hard whack.

"Okay, guys, that should do it. Let's find us another place to stay." The cabbie pulled up to a nice hotel several miles from the one they'd been in. He pulled away, and the Dixons reached for their bags. "Just a minute," Stetson said. "Let's catch another cab."

"What for?" Timmy asked.

"That cabbie seemed like a nice guy, but he knows where he picked us up, and if by some chance the guy in the suit and he happened to get together . . . Well, I just think we need to be doubly cautious now."

No one disagreed with Stetson, so they caught another cab and found a hotel several miles farther away. As they were getting out that time, Stetson's new phone rang. The number to it was only known by Diana, and yet he did not recognize the number calling. He knew it wasn't hers. "Hello," he said cautiously.

"Stetson, it's me, Diana. Sergeant Snow issued me a new phone."

"What's wrong with your other one?" he asked.

"Lieutenant Gibson was afraid I would be tracked by Saul or his people, of which there must be a lot. Of people, I mean."

"Why would you be tracked, or is Saul targeting you now?"

"He probably is, but I'll be on a flight to London in a while, Detective."

"My title is officer, yours is detective. Anyway, why are you coming to London?" Stetson asked. "I think I may have made our superiors unhappy, so I'm guessing you are coming to escort me home."

"Sergeant Snow was a little upset, but he got over it," Diana said. "He's been complaining about not having enough help on his squad. When he was told by Lieutenant Gibson that he was assigning you as my partner and as part of his squad, he calmed down. And no, your title is changing. As soon as the upper echelon approves it in the morning, you will be a detective. Lieutenant Gibson said he's referring to you as that now."

"That's a surprise," Stetson said as he caught Lilia's eyes. He could tell that she wondered what was going on. So he said to her, "I'm a detective now, and Diana is coming to meet us." Then back to the phone he said, "So when exactly are you coming?"

"I have a flight in about five hours," Diana responded. "I'll be landing at Heathrow." She told him the approximate time.

"Okay, when you get there, I'll tell you where you need to go, and it won't be to where we are now, but we'll meet you and bring you here, and then we'll decide what course of action we need to take. Until then, my goal is to keep everyone safe," Stetson said.

A few minutes later, they were all in their hotel rooms, one for Stetson and one right next to it with a connecting door for the Dixons.

* * *

Saul was simmering. His broken arm ached, and there was still pain in his face from the battering the Dixon girl had given him. But his anger was over more than that. He had just heard from his man in London, Fredrick Boles. The news wasn't what he had expected. Apparently, the bodies had all been removed by the time Boles got back, and he didn't dare ask anyone who was killed.

"My guess is that you messed up, Fredrick. If there were a bunch of dead people, they wouldn't have been removed this quickly," he had said.

"I'm telling you, Boss, there is no way anyone got out of that gift shop alive. They had no idea that I'd set a bomb down in there. It blew the place to pieces. They are dead. Guaranteed," Fredrick had said.

"You do what it takes to find out for sure. I want to know that I'm rid of them," Saul had growled at him.

He was sitting now in a cheap motel room that was so awful that it grated on his nerves. Luxury was what he needed and deserved. As soon as he could get another passport, and it wouldn't be too long, he was going to London. His man Fredrick better hope the Dixons were no longer a problem.

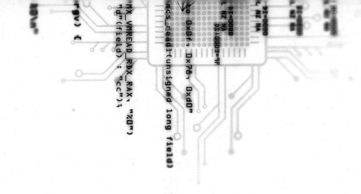

CHAPTER
EIGHTEEN

DIANA ARRIVED WITHOUT INCIDENT AT the address that Detective Erman had given her. With him in the taxi was the Dixon family. Stetson told her, "We are sticking together. I'm not taking any chances leaving them by themselves."

"What are your plans now?" she asked.

"We were waiting for you before we decided what to do," he admitted. "We know for sure that Saul has someone here in England. What we don't know is if he has more people here looking for us. For a Utah attorney, he sure seems to have a lot of criminals working for him. He's a regular crime boss."

"If, as you suspect, he is the one who stole the money from the law firm, then he has almost unlimited funds," she said as she climbed into the taxi with the Dixons. She said hello to Timmy and Lilia, and then Lilia introduced her to their parents.

There was no discussion regarding future plans as they traveled to their hotel. But once there, when Diana mentioned that she'd get a room before they sat down to plan, Stetson said, "No need for that, Diana. I'll see what you think, but I believe we need to move on. Where we go next is the question."

"I can see the wisdom in that," she said.

Minutes later, they were all gathered in Stetson's room. They began to discuss their options, all but Timmy, who was hard at work on his computer again. Diana asked, nodding at where Timmy was sitting cross-legged on Stetson's bed, "What's he working on?"

"He's trying to find what Saul has done with the money he stole," Stetson said.

"Can he do that?" she asked.

Stetson chuckled. "He found his parents here in London. I wouldn't put anything past him."

"This may be one thing that's beyond his ability," Lilia said doubtfully.

Timmy looked up and with anger in his eyes said, "Lilia, sometimes you make me mad. Have faith in me."

"Sorry," she said. "But it does seem like a rather impossible task."

"Maybe to you, but not to me," he snapped.

Stetson attempted to stop what he saw as a developing argument between the two of them by saying, "It can't hurt for him to try. So Lilia, where do you think that we should go?"

She looked at him, frowned, and then said, "Why do you ask me? Ask Timmy. He's the smart one."

"Hey, Lilia, calm down," Pamela interjected. "We need to focus on what we do next."

"Okay, sorry," Lilia said, and she attempted a smile. "It's just all so discouraging. All I want to do is to go home and be together as a family. I want my life back. I want our lives back."

"We all do," her father said. "And what you just said sort of makes sense to me."

At that point, Diana spoke up. "What do you mean, Roland?"

"What Lilia said is that we should return home. That's what I'm thinking as well," Roland said.

"I wasn't being serious," Lilia said. "I'm just so sad that we have to go through all this because of one man's greed. Yes, I'd like to be home, but I don't want us to be in more danger."

"We can't run forever, dear," her mother said.

"It seems to me that Greenbaum knows you guys are here in London. If he is intent on catching you again, I suspect that he'll concentrate on finding you here," Diana said.

Stetson, who Diana noticed seemed to be in deep thought, cleared his throat. Everyone looked at him. "I've been thinking about the bomb. The guy that left that briefcase ran out of the hotel when the bomb went off. He may think that he killed us all. If he does, Saul might be calling his people back to Utah."

"But what if he figured out that we weren't killed?" Roland asked.

"Then he'll be looking for us here in London," Pamela said. "I think we need to at least leave England."

Timmy, who none of them had paid any attention to for the past two or three minutes, said, "Hey, guess what. I just got into the computer system at the hotel where the guy tried to bomb us."

"That's great," Stetson said. "What have you learned?"

"They have a list of who died and who was injured, and we are not on it," he said. "The police have the list, but they are not releasing it and have told the hotel not to."

"I guess that's a good thing," Stetson said. "Timmy, what else have you learned?"

"They think they know what car the bomber got away in," he said. "It was a white Subaru, fairly new. It's a rental car."

"Do you know which rental agency it came from?" Stetson asked.

"Yes, and it was rented three days ago to some guy by the name of Fredrick Boles," Timmy revealed.

"Do they have any pictures on the hotel computer system of the guy who left the bomb?" Stetson asked.

"It's the guy we saw in the suit," Timmy responded. "They don't have a picture of his face because he was being careful to keep it turned away while he was in the lobby. They also had a camera outside that caught him getting into the Subaru and driving away, but again he did not look toward the camera."

"Anything else?" Stetson asked.

"That's all so far, but if you want me to, I'll keep checking," Timmy said.

"Timmy," Lilia began, her earlier sharpness toward him tamped down, "You were able to find all that out. Do you think Saul or anyone who works for him could do the same thing?"

"He seems to have some resourceful bad guys helping him," Timmy said. "So yes, Lilia, I do think that he could have someone who could figure out the same thing I have."

Diana had been quietly listening to the conversation. She said with her brow wrinkled, "I think that we need to assume that Saul knows you guys survived. If so, the guy in the suit driving the Subaru will be looking for you."

"I agree," Stetson said. "Even if Saul doesn't already know, he probably soon will. Good work, Timmy. So where do we go now? Any ideas?"

"I think we should go home," Timmy said. Then he grinned one of his triumphant little grins. "I also looked at your police system, Stetson."

"Oh, have you now?" Diana said with a grin. "So what do you think our bosses are doing?"

"As near as I can tell, they think Saul will come here to England," Timmy said.

"He lost his passport," Diana reminded him. Then before anyone could respond, she said with a sheepish grin, "But I suppose he could get a forged one."

"Let's get out of London," Roland said decisively. "He can't track us anymore, so we can go wherever we want now and not have to worry about him or some of his guys being right behind us."

"There is one thing I keep putting off," Stetson said. "We do need to talk to the police here. Now would be a good time to do that. I have the number of one of the officers who responded to the hotel. I'll call him right now."

***

Fredrick Boles finally found the courage to return to the hotel where he had set the bomb off. He chose to go in slacks and a sweater instead of the suit he'd worn before. He combed his hair differently and put on a pair of dark glasses. Despite the doubts that Saul had, he was still confident that he had killed all of the Dixons. But Saul wanted to know for sure before he caught a plane to London.

Fredrick's computer skills were okay but not great. He had tried and failed to hack into the hotel's computer system. He'd thought about calling the police but didn't think they would tell him. He'd checked the news and there was nothing about that bombing except that there had been one and that there had been casualties. Numbers and names were not released.

Frustrated, he got into his rental car and headed to the hotel. His life would be in jeopardy if all the Dixons were not dead before Saul came to England. He parked a couple of blocks from the hotel and began walking. He was nervous and perspiring, but he tried to hide it as he entered the lobby.

The entire area around the gift shop was still taped off, and a couple of police officers were busy sifting through the debris. He didn't go any closer, but instead he went to the front desk. "May I help you?" an attractive younger lady asked.

"I have some friends staying here that I'm supposed to meet. Their names are Roland and Pamela Dixon," he said.

Her eyes narrowed. "Surely you know what happened to them?" she asked.

"No, I'm sorry, but I don't," Fredrick said. "I just arrived from Paris this morning. Are they okay? I've been worried because they aren't answering their phones."

The lady tapped at her keyboard and then said, "They checked out."

Fredrick waved a hand toward the other side of the lobby where he'd planted the bomb. "Are you sure they were okay when they left?" he asked.

"Yes, I am. Someone set off a bomb. They left, and that's all I can tell you."

Fredrick's stomach clenched. He'd failed. That was not good. He had to find the Dixons soon because if he didn't finish the job, Saul would be furious, and that was dangerous for him. He started for the door, grumbling over his bad luck. It just didn't make sense that the bomb didn't kill the Dixons. He'd made it strong enough to do a lot of damage, and he was no novice at making bombs. That was the reason Saul had sent him to England on this assignment.

He stopped short of the large exit doors and looked back toward where the gift shop had once stood. Indecision kept him standing there, but finally he decided to have a look at the damage his bomb had caused. He walked toward the area and stood outside the police tape, looking at the damage. He was a former military demolitions expert. He knew what he was doing. There was a lot of damage, about the amount he'd figured his bomb would cause. He couldn't see any way that anyone who was in that gift shop could have survived when his bomb went off.

An officer came through the debris and told him he would need to leave. "Sorry," he said. "I'm a demolitions expert, and I just wondered what happened here."

"You can see what happened. Some idiot decided to set a bomb off while there were people inside the gift shop," the officer said.

"How many people did it kill?" Fredrick asked, trying to look innocent.

The officer shook his head. "Sorry, but I can't tell you that. You'll need to leave now."

"I was just curious. Hope you catch the guy that did it," Fredrick lied.

"We will. You can be assured of that," the officer told him. "You need to leave."

Fredrick slowly walked away from the carnage he had caused, feeling quite proud of himself. He had barely reached the large exit when a pair of policemen entered the hotel. Before he had time to react, the two of them grabbed him and slapped handcuffs on his wrists. "Hey, what's going on here?" he demanded as panic set in.

"You need to come with us," one of the officers told him.

"What for? I haven't done anything."

"Let's go. We'll talk about it at the station," the second officer said.

"You've got the wrong man. I was just in here to look at the damage. I'd heard about it and was curious. Is that against the law?" Fredrick asked.

"If you're the one who set the bomb, it is."

Fredrick began to struggle, but the two men dragged and carried him out of the hotel as he loudly protested his innocence.

* * *

Stetson led the way into the station, where he told an officer at a desk that they were there about the bombing. He was told that it would be just a moment. The officer disappeared and came back a minute later with a large man in plain clothes. He was well over six feet and looked to be in his forties.

"Hello, folks, we've been hoping you'd soon be here. I'm Detective Inspector Dennis Kinser with homicide," he said. "And you are?"

"Detective Stetson Erman, Salt Lake City, Utah, homicide investigator, and this is my partner, Detective Diana Franklin," Stetson said, feeling a little strange about his new title.

"These folks must be the Dixons," Detective Inspector Kinser said with a smile.

"Yes, Roland and Pamela and their children, Lilia and Timmy," Stetson said.

"Glad you folks are here. Come on back."

Once they were all seated in a small conference room, the inspector said, "You are rather lucky to be alive. I'm not sure how you managed it. As you probably know, a security officer and the gift shop manager were not so fortunate. The security officer died immediately, and the gift shop manager died at the hospital several hours later. Another security officer is in critical condition and may not pull through."

Lilia spoke up and said, "Detective Erman told us to run, so we did."

"Why did you tell them to run?" the inspector asked with his brows drawn together.

"I saw the guy put his briefcase down, and he left rather abruptly. It didn't feel right to me. With all the trouble the Dixons have been put through, I wasn't about to take any chances," Stetson said.

For the next few minutes, the inspector asked questions while the detectives and the Dixons answered them the best they could. Finally, Roland asked, "Inspector Kinser, are there video recordings of the bombing or was the bomber by any chance caught on camera?"

Stetson and Diana had cautioned the Dixons not to mention anything about Timmy's hacking, and Roland had been careful in his question to the inspector. The inspector said, "Funny you should ask. We have footage of the bomber and of you folks as well. The bomber kept his face turned away from our cameras, so we didn't get a good shot of his face. We did get a good look at the car he drove away in."

"What kind of car was it?" Timmy asked with a straight face.

"It was a white Subaru." The detective inspector smiled. "It was rented by a man whose name is Fredrick Boles with a Denver, Colorado, address. Does that name mean anything to any of you?"

Both officers shook their heads, but Roland Dixon was deep in thought. "Roland, you look like you might know something," Stetson said.

"I think I do," Roland responded. "Two or three years ago, if I'm remembering the guy right, he was charged in a bombing in Denver. Most of us in the firm are licensed to practice law in Colorado."

He fell silent as he again began to think. He was rubbing his chin and blinking his eyes rapidly. No one attempted to interrupt his thought processes. Finally he said, "Yes, I'm pretty sure that's the name."

"Is he in prison?" Detective Inspector Kinser asked.

"No, he was acquitted."

"Dad, he was represented by Saul Greenbaum, wasn't he?" Timmy asked, his freckled face very serious.

"As a matter of fact, he was," Roland said. "Saul got him off. What made you think of that?"

"Well, Dad, I've been doing a lot of research on Mr. Greenbaum. I read about that case while we were in the hotel room."

"And why were you doing that, young man?" the inspector asked rather sternly.

"Because he is the one who has caused Dad so much trouble. He's a very bad man," Timmy said with a scowl.

"I can vouch for that," Diana said. "He intended to kill me and almost managed it."

"I will need to hear more about that," Kinser said. "But first, Timmy, are you good with computers?"

"I do okay," Timmy said modestly.

"You remembered the name from reading about it a few hours ago?"

"Timmy remembers everything," Lilia said proudly, her earlier disagreement with him forgotten.

"Smart kid, I take it," the inspector said.

"You could say that," Stetson responded blandly. "So Greenbaum got this Fredrick guy acquitted, and now Fredrick's in London driving a rental car."

"And he owes Saul big time," Diana said quietly.

"Timmy, did you see the man's face when he brought the briefcase into the gift shop?" the inspector asked.

"Yes, and I can draw it for you if you'd like me to."

"Are you sure?" the inspector asked doubtfully.

"He can do it," Lilia said.

"Let's wait and see if we need it," the inspector said.

"I can do it fast," Timmy said.

"Well, okay. As I think about it, that could be very helpful. Let me find you a pencil and paper."

After the detective inspector left, the others talked about what they had learned. "I saw the guy's face, and so did Timmy. Did any of you other three see his face?" Stetson asked.

"We were too busy being grateful to see each other again," Pamela said. "All I could see were the faces of my children."

"I suppose your people are looking for Fredrick and the Subaru," Stetson said when the inspector came back in a couple minutes later.

"Of course," he said as he handed Timmy the paper and pencil. Timmy went right to work. "I'll tell you more after I see what this young fellow comes up with here."

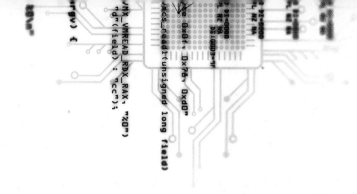

CHAPTER
NINETEEN

TIMMY DREW RAPIDLY, AND BEFORE he was even finished, Stetson said, "That's the guy. Good job, Timmy." The inspector watched as the face came alive on the paper. Stetson was watching his face. A small smile formed there, and he nodded as the sketch was completed.

Timmy grinned as he handed the finished sketch to the inspector. "That's him," he said proudly.

"Indeed it is, young man," the inspector said. He looked at Stetson and then at Diana. "I've been holding back some information. Now that I have this sketch, I can compare it to the video shots we have, and I can even do better than that. Mr. Fredrick Boles thought that by wearing dark glasses and dressing in slacks and a sweater that he would not be recognized when he returned to the hotel and began asking questions."

"When did he go back there?" Diana asked.

"A little over an hour ago. Just before you folks came in. He asked a lady at the registration desk if his friends, the Dixons, were there. She told you had checked out. That seemed to upset him. As soon as he left the desk, she called me on my cell phone. She had recognized him, or thought she had."

"Sometimes crooks do the dumbest things," Stetson said, shaking his head.

"Yes, and that's not all. He walked across the lobby to where the gift shop used to be and spoke with one of my officers there. He was asking what had happened. One of my officers on duty there also recognized him from the videos and called me. The guy then tried to leave the hotel, but two uniformed officers arrested him just before he got outside," the inspector said.

"So he's in custody? Will we be able to speak with him?" Diana asked.

"I hope so," the inspector responded. "We also found the Subaru. It was a couple of blocks from the hotel. It's being impounded as we speak. And we have his cell phone now. That will be of great help to us, and possibly to you officers as well."

"Oh, yes," Diana said. "It could contain a lot of helpful information, I'm sure."

"Now, Detective Franklin, tell me what exactly happened with you and this Saul Greenbaum character and how he might have done you harm," Inspector Kinser said.

* * *

Saul was waiting with his brand-new forged passport to board a plane to London. He'd purchased a laptop, which was a little difficult to use with one arm in a cast, and was doing a search on it now despite that handicap. He was very adept in the use of computers, more so than anyone in the law firm, and that included the senior partner, Harry Lundquist. He hated the man and had been thinking over the past few hours of ways to hurt him. He just wished he could depend on the crooks he used to do his dirty work, but unfortunately, most of them were not terribly intelligent.

He was busy reading news reports from London, and in none of them did it mention who had been killed or injured in the bombing of the hotel where he'd tracked the Dixons. He cursed the police. He was quite certain that they were withholding information. For the hundredth time, he tried calling his demolition expert, Fredrick Boles.

Fredrick had been successful in bombing a business in Denver in which a number of people were seriously injured, but Saul had, by hook and crook, managed to get him acquitted. The guy had done a very good job in that bombing, and he owed Saul a good, clean bombing this time, but he was becoming increasingly doubtful that it had been that good. If it wasn't, Fredrick would be eliminated. Saul had no use for anyone who didn't perform to his standards.

He spent a few minutes as he waited checking his bank balances in a half dozen offshore accounts. What he found alarmed him. One of the accounts showed evidence to his expert eye of having been tampered with. He looked up the balance and was shocked to find that it was at zero. That couldn't be! Angry and worried, he checked the others. Everything was fine with them. Surely there had been a mistake made on that one account. He would have to follow up on that later, as he was out of time now. First-class passengers were being told to board.

He picked up his carry-on luggage and the computer bag. He hadn't checked any bags. He wanted to proceed directly to the bombed hotel as soon as he arrived in London. He had to find out for himself if Fredrick had succeeded or failed. For some reason, one that frustrated him, his tracking devices on the Dixons' bags were no longer working. That made no sense to him. Roland was way too stupid to ever figure it out. Then a troublesome thought occurred to him. Perhaps their bags had been destroyed in the blast. He'd have to find that out when he got to London.

As he settled in his seat, his thoughts returned to Harry. He was almost certain that Harry had meant to promote Roland over him. The only thing that persuaded Harry to doubt Roland was the theft of the money, which Saul had so expertly tied to Roland. There was no way that Harry or anyone else would be able to figure out what he'd done. That he was quite sure of.

What he wasn't so sure of was Harry's mindset. He'd succeeded in turning him against Roland quite easily, but could he be turned back? He didn't think it would be wise to let that happen. As he sat there on the plane, waiting for it to pull away from the gate, an idea came to him, and he made a phone call. Talking very low, he gave an order to his man on the other end. "Let me know when you have him. I'll give you further instructions at that time."

With that item checked off, he thought about that lady detective. She may have spoiled his chances of ever running the firm, but then he guessed he could live with that. He would simply not return to the United States to live. If he made visits there, they would be short and secretive. He had enough money for him to live in luxury for a very long time. But that woman had to be dealt with. No one did to him what she did and lived to tell about it. He made another call, quietly gave another order, and then closed his phone and rested his head back on the headrest. No one messed with Saul Greenbaum who wouldn't regret it. No one.

***

Timmy had plugged his computer into a socket in the conference room where they were still waiting. After learning that they were going to be there for a while, he and Stetson had gone out to the car they'd ended up renting and brought the computer inside. Timmy was restless without it. There was so much he wanted to do, he'd told Stetson. So now he was busy typing, working the mouse, and trying to keep up with his own supercharged mind.

Lilia was watching him. She adored him, but she also had to admit that he did at times get on her nerves. She also felt a twinge of jealousy. Why had he gotten that genius brain and not her? She didn't get that thought often, but it did happen. It was happening now. She wondered what he was looking for at the moment, so she moved around the large table and sat beside him.

"What are you looking for, Timmy?" she asked.

He looked up at her and smiled, making her feel guilty. "I'm messing with Mr. Greenbaum's life," he said, but to her disappointment, he did not expound. So she looked over his shoulder and watched the laptop screen.

Timmy went from one thing to another so rapidly that she couldn't tell for sure what was happening. Then he slowed down and studied what was in front of them. It was some numbers, very large numbers. His finger stopped and the mouse was stilled. She leaned closer. The numbers came into focus. They were dollars—lots of dollars.

"What do you have there, Timmy?" his father asked as he tousled his red hair.

Lilia stood up and straightened her back. "It's something to do with money."

Timmy looked up and grinned. "I'm messing with Mr. Greenbaum. He shouldn't be so mean to you, Dad." He gave no further explanation.

However, there was soon a crowd looking over his shoulder, his mother and both detectives having joined them. He once again began to type and move the mouse around. Suddenly, the large sum of money disappeared. He clicked for a moment more and then sat back with a sigh. "I wonder where Mr. Greenbaum is now," he said.

"What did you just do?" Stetson asked.

"I'll tell you later. I need to check something else right now," Timmy said with a gleam in those magnified eyes of his.

Lilia knew from long experience that to question Timmy any further right now would do no good at all. He'd tell what he'd done when he was good and ready, and not a moment before.

Just then, Detective Inspector Kinser entered the conference room. "If you folks would like to come with me now, I want you to look at the man we arrested. He'll be behind a one-way glass."

Of course, no one but Timmy and Stetson could identify him as the man who had left the briefcase in the gift shop. But they all recognized him from the sketch that Timmy had drawn. "Is that the man you saw?" the inspector asked.

"It is," Stetson said.

"Yes, that's him," Timmy agreed with a smug smile.

"Your sketch was certainly an accurate likeness of him," the inspector said. "How do you remember his face so well?"

"I don't know," he said modestly.

"Don't let him kid you. He has a photographic memory," Stetson said. "He also did some drawings at the beginning of our case that were a big help."

After a few moments, they were taken back to the conference room. "We are going to interview Fredrick, and if you detectives would like to be in on that, you are welcome to," the inspector said.

"We'd like that very much," Diana said for both of them.

"Also, we are getting the paperwork approved to search his phone. I suspect there may be some things that will be revealed that might help you in your case in Utah. We will share that with you."

As Stetson and Diana followed Detective Inspector Kinser back to the interview room, Diana leaned over to Stetson and said quietly, "I'll be surprised if we get anything from him, but I guess we can hope. His phone is our best bet."

Fredrick had nothing to say regarding the bombing, but he did listen carefully as Diana asked, "Do you know a man named Saul Greenbaum?"

"He's the attorney that helped me in a case in Denver where I was wrongly accused," the prisoner said. "He proved my innocence."

"Have you been in communication with him recently?" she asked.

"No, and I can't call him to come help me here because he can't practice law in England. I wish he could," Fredrick said. "He's a brilliant attorney."

Stetson was content to let his experienced partner take the lead, and she next asked, "When was the last time you spoke with him?"

Fredrick squirmed uncomfortably on his hard seat and pulled against the handcuffs. Finally he said, "I haven't heard from him since my trial. I had no need to speak with him after that."

"Mr. Boles, you appear to me to be a smart man. Why would you lie to us when you know that your phone is in the possession of Detective Inspector Kinser? You do know that he will be able to see all your phone calls and texts and be able to receive detailed information about those communications from your cell phone carrier, don't you?"

Fredrick said nothing, but he was sweating profusely. Diana glanced at the inspector, then back at the prisoner and asked, "What was the offense that Saul Greenbaum successfully defended you on in Denver?"

Fredrick was a fairly smart guy, but like most criminals, he was not smart enough. He made a huge mistake when he answered her question. He said, "You already know that, I'm sure, but I was accused of setting off a bomb that injured some people. Of course, it wasn't me." At that point, his brain caught up with his mouth, and he said, "I am not a bomber and I am not a killer. I don't know anything about any bombing here in London."

Another quick glance at the inspector brought a nod from him, and Diana continued. "You were arrested today at that very hotel where you had asked about some people by the name of Dixon. Do you know the Dixons?"

"No," he said.

"You were looking at the extensive damage that the bomb caused in that hotel. Isn't that the case?"

"I was simply curious," he said. Once again his mouth outran his brain. "I am a demolition expert, and out of curiosity I wanted to see what kind of damage had been done. I can't believe anyone would be stupid enough to set off a bomb in a hotel with people around. I hope you guys catch whoever did that. I take my training and experience very seriously, and it angers me when someone who has been trained as I have would stoop to such terrible behavior."

At that point, the inspector jumped back into the questioning since Fredrick had so stupidly admitted to being a demolition expert. He asked, "Mr. Boles, witnesses have informed us that they saw you set the briefcase down and leave the gift shop just moments before the explosion. Furthermore, we possess video footage we obtained from the hotel management that clearly shows you carrying the briefcase into the gift shop and leaving without it. It also shows you hurrying out of the hotel and getting into a white Subaru, which is now in our possession. Are you sure you wouldn't like to come clean with me now and tell me what happened, why you detonated that bomb?"

"I didn't do it," Fredrick said, but the pale color of his face and the fear in his eyes told a much different story.

Diana kept the pressure on him. She asked, "What did you do that Mr. Greenbaum knows about that would send you to prison for life if he ever revealed it?"

Fredrick visibly shrunk within himself. But he didn't answer the question. She then said, "He's blackmailing you, isn't he? And possibly he threatened you if you didn't kill the Dixons."

The prisoner's face went even whiter, and he began to tremble. Diana kept up the pressure. "Two men who worked for Mr. Greenbaum by the names of Benjy and Louis were shot and killed. Did you know that?"

Fredrick tried to speak, but all he could do was stutter. The inspector leaned close to his face and said, "You better get a hold of yourself and speak to us about what you know. For example, you did know Benjy and Louis, didn't you?"

Fredrick nodded, and Diana asked another question. "Did Greenbaum threaten to kill you if you didn't get rid of the Dixons?"

He finally recovered his lost voice, and he said, "I am a dead man. Inspector, he is coming to England to find me. Please, you have to protect me from him."

"You'll be quite safe in our jail," the inspector assured him.

After that, Fredrick broke down and confessed to the bombing and to being told to do so by Saul. He was shaking and perspiring, and there was no color left in his face. With a weak voice and without looking at any of the officers, he asked, "Did the Dixons die?"

"They did not. In fact, one of them drew this sketch for me a short while ago." The inspector dug through a file he was holding and pulled out the drawing that Timmy had made. "Do you recognize this man?" he asked.

In a low and hoarse voice, Fredrick said, "That's me."

Stetson cleared his voice and the prisoner looked at him. He said, "You have been very helpful. It's Saul we are after. You say he's coming to London. That tells me that you talked to him on the phone. Of course, that will all show up when your phone is searched. What I would like to know is this: did Saul mention any other people whom he wanted removed? You know what I mean. Did he order you or did he tell you of anyone else he was ordering you to kill or even hurt, someone besides the Dixons?"

"No," Fredrick said. His voice was stronger when he gave that answer, and it appeared that he was most likely telling the truth.

After the interview was over, Stetson and Diana rejoined the Dixons in the conference room. They told them what had occurred in the interview. Stetson stressed the fact that Fredrick Boles had been told to find and make sure that the Dixons were dead and that if he failed, he would pay a very steep price. "He told us that he knew that Greenbaum would have him eliminated for failing," Diana revealed.

"Now what do we do?" Lilia asked as she held tightly to Stetson's arm.

"We keep away from Saul, that's what we do," he said.

"Are we going home?" she asked.

"Not yet. The inspector asked that we stay nearby. I think Scotland is nearby enough. Should we go there?" he asked.

"I think we should," Diana agreed. "But first I want to see what Mr. Boles's phone reveals. For example, maybe we can learn what Saul's new phone number is and try to locate him with it."

At that moment, the inspector joined them. "We're working on getting the information from Mr. Boles's phone. But we already have a list of numbers he's been in touch with. Use this as you see fit. Also, if you folks would feel safer leaving London, that would be fine, but please stay in Europe for a few days if you can," he said. "If I come up with anything else once we get information back from his phone provider, I'll see that you get it. I have your numbers. I want to thank you for your excellent work today, Detectives. Thanks to you, we have Mr. Boles's confession."

"We just got lucky," Diana said modestly.

"I can't agree with that. You were smart in your questions. Thank you again. And I'll be in touch. You folks may leave now, with my thanks to all of you."

After he'd gone, Stetson said, "We have a rental car. We can drive north toward Scotland. Are we all agreed on that?"

They were, but Timmy, who had continued to work at his computer, said, "I hope Gabriel's okay."

"I've worried about him too," Lilia agreed. "Do you think it would hurt to call him?"

"Not from our cell phones. We can't be too careful. But I wonder if the inspector would let us make a call on his phone?"

They located him in his office, and he handed his cell phone to Lilia. "Go ahead. It's the least we can do for you."

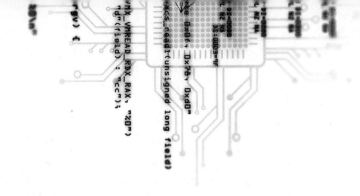

CHAPTER
TWENTY

GABRIEL SCHILLER WAS NOT FEELING well. Worry about the Dixons was wearing him down. He wasn't sleeping well, and he found it hard to eat. He was afraid of a heart attack. He wished he had some way to contact them.

He was staring at his TV set when his phone rang. He looked at the number on it. It was clearly an overseas number. He answered and felt a huge relief come over him when he heard the sweet voice of Lilia Dixon. "Gabriel, I'm sorry we haven't called sooner, but we haven't been able to."

"Are you and Timmy safe?" he asked.

"Yes, and thanks to Timmy, we were able to find our parents. We are together now in England."

"Oh, my dear girl, you have removed a dark cloud from my mind. I love you folks and I have been so worried," he said as he absently ran a hand through his thinning hair.

"Well, we are okay now, but we were wondering about you. How are you feeling?" Lilia asked him.

"Better now that I've talked to you. When will you be coming home?"

"We don't know that yet," she said. "Hopefully it won't be very long. Is our house okay?"

"I haven't seen anyone around it. I've walked over several times and looked things over. I don't believe there has been anyone there. I'll continue to watch. It's so good to hear from you," he said.

"Well, we need to go now. You won't be able to reach us on this phone, because I'm using one that I borrowed from a policeman here in London. But when we can we'll check back with you. We love you, Gabriel."

"And I love you, all of you," he replied. "Oh, there's someone at my door. I guess I should answer it."

Lilia felt a lurch in her stomach. "It's about two o'clock in the afternoon here. What time is it there?" she asked.

"It's about nine. I should go to bed now. But first I better see who is at the door."

Then he heard the commanding voice of Stetson as he said, "Lilia, let me take the phone." Then to Gabriel he said, "I've been listening to you and Lilia talk. Gabriel, don't answer your door."

"Why not?" he asked innocently.

"Do you ever have people come to your door this late at night?" Stetson asked.

"It is a bit unusual."

"We will call and get an officer to come to your house. You lock yourself in your bedroom and wait for us to call you back. Be sure and have a gun handy."

There was now a loud knocking on the back door. "They are at the back door now."

Stetson said, "Keep your phone on and go to your bedroom. Are your guns in there?"

"One of them is."

"Good, hurry now." Gabriel quickly did as he'd been instructed. As he locked the door, he heard a loud crash, the sound of a window being smashed. "They are breaking in," he said as he collapsed on the recliner in his bedroom.

"Diana is on another phone. She's getting help headed your way. Keep this phone open," Stetson instructed him.

A couple of minutes passed. Then Gabriel whispered into the phone, "They're at my bedroom door."

* * *

Stetson could hear the pounding, but all he could do was stand there and pray. A moment later, he heard a crash, and then Gabriel screamed. He heard a thump like the phone may have fallen to the floor. It still worked, and Stetson helplessly listened as Gabriel shouted that he had dropped his gun and was being carried from the room. A moment later the phone went silent.

Diana, who had been calling from another room, rushed in. "There are officers on the way," she said.

Stetson, with a catch in his voice, said, "It's too late. Someone has taken him. He dropped his gun. He must have been shaking so hard he couldn't use it."

Lilia began to cry. Stetson handed the phone back to the inspector. "What was that all about?" the inspector asked.

Stetson explained, and then he said, "Saul is out of his mind. I can't even imagine what he has planned for that innocent old gentleman."

They traipsed back to the conference room. "Saul just had someone kidnap Gabriel," Lilia said as she rushed to hug her parents, tears streaming down her face.

Timmy looked up from his computer. "Saul must be in the airplane, because his new phone goes to voice mail." He tapped his phone, which was beside him on the table. "I've tried calling him twice. I'll keep trying."

Diana's phone rang a few minutes later as they were in the rental car, heading north. She glanced at the screen and said, "It's Sergeant Snow."

Then she answered. Stetson listened the best he could while concentrating on his driving, making sure he kept to the left side of the road, which wasn't easy. In fact, it was quite confusing. He did hear her say, "Oh, no!" at one point. And again a moment later, she said, "What's he going to do?" And finally, she said, "Let me know how it goes."

After the call ended, Diana, who was in the back seat, leaned forward and said, "Mr. Lundquist got a call from a voice he did not recognize. He was told to let the caller know within twelve hours where Pamela and Roland are. He told them he didn't know and had no way to find out. Then the guy said he had better find out and let him know or the old man, meaning Gabriel, I'm sure, would die."

"We'll have to tell Harry," Roland said. "I can't let anything happen to him. He is totally innocent. It will have to be me instead of him."

"Dad, you can't do that," Lilia wailed from the front seat.

Stetson calmly but firmly said, "All of you listen to me. We are going back to the police station. We'll tell Inspector Kinser what's happening. And then we'll let Sergeant Snow and Mr. Lundquist know where we'll be. But it won't be we, it will be me. I don't want any of you in danger. I need to set Saul up."

"Stetson, you can't do that. It will be too dangerous," Lilia said as she clutched at his arm.

"He won't be alone. I'll be with him," Diana announced.

"No, Diana, you will need to stay with the Dixons. But I'm sure the inspector will give us some men."

"And a weapon," Diana said. "You and I aren't even armed."

"We'll ask him. I'm sure he'll help out however we need. After all, it's to his benefit to make sure there are no more deadly crimes happening in London," Stetson said.

The inspector was more than helpful, and he volunteered himself to be with Stetson at the hotel room they agreed on. Diana and the Dixons would be nearby with a couple of London officers with them for added security.

It was late in the evening by the time it was all arranged. Then Diana called Sergeant Snow. "We're all set," she said. She explained the plan they had made.

Snow responded with, "Lundquist's caller warned him that any attempt to involve the police would be fatal to the old man."

"We've got to fool Saul or whoever he sends. It's the only chance we have of saving both the Dixons and Gabriel," Diana said. "Call Lundquist and tell him the location and that Roland and Pamela will be there by themselves. It's the only thing we can do."

A half hour later, Sergeant Snow called Diana back and said, "I gave Lundquist the information. He didn't like it. He told me that he guessed it was all he could do, but he didn't want to endanger Roland and his wife again. He expressed regret that he'd ever believed Saul but that he'd had some pretty firm evidence that Roland had stolen the money. Now he knows that's not true."

"Okay, but he needs to do exactly what the kidnapper tells him to. That means he has to give him the information about the location. He also has to express to the guy that he couldn't risk the old man's life, that it was better to give them the Dixons," Diana stressed.

"I don't think it's going to work," Roland said. "It has to be me. There is no other way."

Stetson raised a hand and pointed a finger at Roland. "That will never happen. We'll take our chances."

"Hey, guys," Timmy called out. "Mr. Greenbaum is at the airport."

"My men are in place there," the inspector informed them. "They will follow him but not arrest him at this point. My orders to them are to keep him under constant surveillance and to keep me advised of his location at all times."

"They don't know which flight he's on. Heathrow is a huge airport," Stetson said.

"Your boy genius here just narrowed it down for us. We know he just arrived. Is that true, Timmy?"

"Yes. And he's still on the plane," Timmy said. He told them the flight number.

"All right then, we'll find and follow him," the inspector said with total confidence. "In the meantime, you wait here. We won't go to the hotel for a couple more hours yet."

* * *

Saul was still sitting in his first-class seat. He was on the phone with one of his men in Utah. "Did you get the old man?" he asked and waited while he was told yes. Then he said, "Does Harry know what he's to do?"

Once again he was told yes. Then he said, "As soon as Lundquist calls you with the information of the Dixons' location, take care of G. Do I make myself clear, Jeremy?"

"Of course," Jeremy said.

Satisfied that Gabriel would be taken care of, Saul dialed the phone number of Fredrick Boles. The call went to voice mail. That disturbed him. Fredrick had been told to keep his phone free for his call. He didn't think he'd intentionally let the call go to voice mail. That got Saul thinking. It seemed unlikely, but he supposed he could be in the custody of the police. If he was, it could also mean that he would possibly be in trouble when he got off the plane, and he could not risk that.

There was only one thing Saul could do. He sat right there on his seat while the rest of the passengers left the plane. A flight attendant stopped beside him. He was lying back, groaning as if in pain. He was told that he needed to leave the plane right then. "I'm sick. I think it's a heart attack. I need an ambulance. Please, hurry!" he said, inserting as much pain into his voice as he could manage.

The flight attendant reacted with concern and haste. A few minutes later, Saul was strapped to a gurney and carried from the plane and rushed to an ambulance down on the tarmac. At his request, his carry-on bag and his computer were also delivered to the ambulance. When they reached the hospital with him, he sat up. "I think I'm okay now. I'll just walk in there by myself and have the doctors check me out."

It had been quite clear from what the ambulance personnel were saying and how they were acting that they had already figured out that he was faking an illness. One of them said, "Sir, why did you fake a heart attack? This has been a lot of trouble for us."

"I'm sorry, but I was desperate. I had a phone call from one of my associates here in London that there were a couple of men who were going to grab me and take me by force. I have enemies, as you can see from my battered face and broken arm. It was the only thing I could think of to keep from getting someone hurt. I'm sorry, but you probably just saved my life. I'll cover all your expenses."

There was some argument, but finally the ambulance attendant said, "Okay, you get out then. But first I need your name and address and where we can send the bill."

Saul gave them what they asked for—sort of. The name was the one on his passport, which was not Saul Greenbaum, and the address was totally bogus. He grabbed his luggage and computer and walked away from the hospital, chuckling to himself.

His next move was to flag a taxi and have it take him to a hotel where he could get a room and prepare for what he needed to do later.

***

Timmy closed his computer and put it in its bag. "You need to let Mr. Lundquist know that the law firm's money is safe now."

"What are you talking about, Timmy?" his father asked. "Have you done something illegal?"

Timmy, with a very serious face, said, "I don't think I'll say what I did. But the money Mr. Greenbaum said you stole, that he really did steal, is now safe. But Mr. Lundquist needs to know it. Someone should call him."

"This is crazy, Timmy," Lilia said with a fierce scowl.

"Are you saying I'm crazy, Lilia?" he asked with a flare of temper.

"I didn't mean it like that, and you know it," she said angrily. "You are the opposite of crazy, and we all know that. But just because you're a genius doesn't mean you use good sense all the time."

"I can't help it that I'm not as old as you," he retorted. "I just do the best I can. I did what I needed to do, what no one else could do. So don't worry about it."

Their mother intervened by saying, "All right, kids, that's enough. Timmy, what did you do?"

His temper cooled as quickly as it had flared. He grinned. "I'm not saying. You don't want me to go to jail, do you?"

"Timmy, you must not break the law. I know we have a lot going on right now, but that is not an excuse for you. The last thing we want is for you to get in trouble," she said.

"I'm sorry, Mom, but I didn't say I did something illegal," he responded.

"All right, Timmy, we'll leave it at that," Stetson said in good humor. "What we don't know won't hurt you. But your mother is right. You've got to be wise in your actions and honest."

Timmy nodded but said nothing.

"About Mr. Lundquist," Diana said. "I think you're right, but we can't call him directly as we don't want to take the chance of anyone figuring out one of our phone numbers."

"I would like to call Mr. Greenbaum too, but I know I can't," Timmy said.

"Do you want to rub it in his face?" Lilia asked, but without animosity.

"Yeah, I do. He and that money have caused our family a lot of trouble," Timmy said.

"Well, with a little luck, he'll be in custody soon," Stetson said. "The inspector said he'd call and let us know as soon as he's been arrested."

"I'll call Sergeant Snow right now. It's late there, but I think it's important enough to disturb him," Diana said.

She made the call, and Snow answered instantly. She put the phone on speaker and then said, "We are expecting a call soon to let us know that Saul Greenbaum has been arrested at the airport. We know the flight he was on landed not long ago. I'll let you know when we know more. Also, I have reason to believe that the money Saul stole is now secure and out of his reach. Would you call Mr. Lundquist and let him know? That's all I can tell you for now."

"How do you know that, Detective?" the sergeant asked.

"Like I said, that's all I can tell you at the moment. I don't suppose you know anything else about the kidnapping of Mr. Schiller," Diana said.

"Not a thing," he said. "We gave Lundquist the information you gave us, and we've heard nothing more. I'll try to call him now and get back to you."

They all waited after that for a call from Detective Inspector Kinser. They were all restless. Even Timmy, who was not on his computer, was pacing around the room. Suddenly, he dropped to the floor and began doing pushups. Lilia counted softly as he did one hundred, then two hundred, and finally stopped at two hundred fifty.

He got up, grinning. "Your turn, Lilia," he said.

She looked at him rather sternly for a moment, but then she said, "I don't work out as much as you do, but I'll see how many I can do."

She dropped to the floor and began. Grinning, Stetson kept track. She stopped at one hundred. He said, "That's pretty impressive, Lilia."

She walked over to him, looked him in the eyes, and with a big grin she said, "If you can do more than me, I'll kiss you."

"I can't turn down a challenge like that," he said, and he began. He stopped at one hundred fifty. He stood up and said, "I think that's enough for now. Pay up, girl." She did, right there in front of her parents, her brother, and two police officers.

Diana's phone rang. She answered it and went pale.

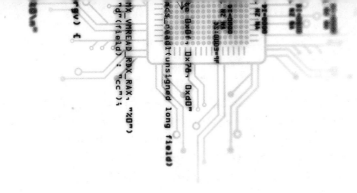

CHAPTER
TWENTY-ONE

"Did you just say that you can't locate Harry?" Diana said after putting her phone on speaker. "Isn't he at home?"

"His cars are there, but he isn't," Sergeant Snow said. "His phone goes to voice mail. We don't like the look of this. We've tried tracking his phone, but it's apparently in his house."

"You better go in," Stetson said.

"We need justification," Sergeant Snow reminded him.

"If all that has happened isn't justification enough, then I don't know what it would take," Stetson replied with a bite in his voice. "Maybe he's asleep, or sick, or injured."

"We could call his son, I suppose," Sergeant Snow said.

"Then do it, but please don't waste any time."

"What about his wife?" Diana asked.

"He lost her to cancer a while back," Roland said. "It's been terribly hard on him. He hasn't been the same man as before."

Stetson looked at him, and what he saw was alarming. "You'd better lie down, Roland. I think this has all been too much for you."

"I'll be fine," he said.

"Roland, lie down," Pamela said firmly. "Please, honey."

So he plopped down on one of the two beds in the hotel room they were using as temporary quarters. Then Diana said to Sergeant Snow, "Sorry about that. Mr. Dixon is a bit pale, and I don't blame him. Will you let us know as soon as you go into Harry's house?"

"I will, and you need to let me know as soon as Saul is in custody. Also, you need to be ready as planned in case someone is coming to get the Dixons. It may not necessarily be Saul himself," Sergeant Snow said. "So you need to be ready in case anyone comes."

After that call was over, Lilia touched her mother on the shoulder. "Mom, you lie down by Dad. You have both had more stress than I can even imagine."

Pamela voiced no resistance to that suggestion. Timmy, in the meantime, had once again been on his computer. He looked up from the small desk where he was sitting and said with a frown on his freckled face, "Mr. Greenbaum is not at the airport anymore."

"Can you tell where he is?" Stetson asked. "Hopefully he is in custody by now and on the way to the police station."

Timmy shook his head. "I don't think so." He pointed at the screen of his laptop. "According to this, he is several miles from the airport, and from the map I looked at earlier, it's nowhere near the police station."

Diana said with urgency in her voice, "I'll call the inspector."

She had the phone on speaker, and they all heard her say, "Did your officers miss Mr. Greenbaum when he got off his plane? According to our resident expert here, Timmy, he is a long ways from the police station."

"I'm sorry. We've been really busy. I was going to call you in a few minutes. It seems that he somehow convinced the flight attendant on his plane that he was having a heart attack. They took him down to the tarmac and sent him to a hospital in an ambulance. We've got officers checking every nearby hospital. He isn't at any of them. We finally located the ambulance that took him, and they say he told them he was in danger and couldn't get off the plane safely any other way than to fake a heart attack. He walked away from the ambulance. They have no idea where he went."

"Timmy, tell the inspector where Saul is right now."

Timmy did that, and then he said, "He's not stationary. He must be in a car."

Diana asked, "Can you get some officers to that area? Meantime, we will get in place in case he or someone else comes to the rendezvous point we passed on to Mr. Lundquist."

"Okay. I'll send my officers there right now. One of my men also just managed to begin tracking the suspect. Keep me informed," the inspector said and ended the call.

Stetson was just heading out the door when he heard Diana's cell phone ring. "Hang on," she said. "It's Snow." She took the call and then said, "It's Detective Franklin. I hope you have good news. We sure could use some. Saul got away from the airport without getting arrested."

"That is indeed bad. I also have bad news. We are in Harry Lundquist's house right now. He is alive but barely. He's been badly beaten. They just left with him in the ambulance," Sergeant Snow reported.

Roland moaned and sat up. "That's more of Saul's doing."

"That's for sure," Stetson said.

"We are getting a search warrant for his house and computer, but we can't find his phone. It will be a little while, but if we find anything that points us to who did this, I'll let you know."

"They will kill Gabriel," Lilia said tearfully.

Stetson pulled her close and held her for a couple of minutes, and then he said, "I better go meet the London officers. I'll take a taxi and leave the rental car for you guys so you can go somewhere else if you think you need to. Timmy, keep me posted on Saul's location."

* * *

Saul was on his phone. He'd given up trying to reach Fredrick, but he had another man in London who had fled the states after Saul got him acquitted on a murder charge. He called that man now and reminded him, "You are in my debt, Ollie Sparrow, and don't try to deny it. I am in London, as I know you are. I need your help and I need it now."

"I paid you a lot of money for defending me," Sparrow said. "So don't say I owe you. I'm trying to go straight now. I don't need trouble."

"You are trying to go straight," Saul said with a sneer. "Well goody for you. But if you will recall, I took some real chances getting you off on that murder charge. You and I both know you did it. No other lawyer would have gotten you off. I did more than what the pay you gave me covered."

"I paid what you asked, and it was a lot. So don't try to tell me I owe you. I gotta go now."

"Ollie!" Saul said angrily. "You listen to me and you listen well. Remember the name Farner? What was it you called him? Was it Slim or something like that?"

"What about him?" Ollie asked, but Saul smiled as he noted the caution that had crept into Ollie's voice.

"You admitted to me that you killed him. You do remember that, don't you?" Saul asked. "I wonder if the Salt Lake police would like to know who killed Slim."

"Hey, you can't tell anyone about him. I told you that in confidence," Sparrow protested.

"His death had nothing to do with the case I was defending you on. Anyway, at this point there are things more important than attorney-client privilege. I'll call anonymously, tell them where to look for evidence, and tell them that it was that unsolved case that inspired you to move to England," Saul said. Then, very snidely, he added, "And don't expect me to believe that you have gone straight in England. I'm sure that I could drop your name and a few things about you to the police here and you would find them on your tail in a heartbeat."

"So now you are blackmailing me?" Sparrow asked.

"Ollie, Ollie, how very silly of you to use that term. You owe me and I have an assignment for you. We need to meet and we need to do it in the next hour. I'll give you an address and wait for you there," Saul said.

Ollie Sparrow did not respond. So after a minute or so, Saul said, "Okay, forget it. But don't think that I won't do exactly what I told you I would." Saul could all but see the big man's shoulder's slump. He could imagine Ollie running his hand through his long, thin brown hair. He waited, and finally Ollie said, "Where do I meet you and what do you need done?"

"I'll tell you that when we meet," Saul said. "It is nothing you can't easily handle with your experience and expertise."

"Where do we meet and when?" Ollie asked, defeat in his voice.

Saul gave him the address of a local restaurant and said, "I'll be inside having a cup of coffee. You come in and come to my table."

"Okay, so did you say in an hour?"

"I did, but it's fifty-five minutes now, and Ollie, when you come, make sure you are armed."

"Boss, you know I can't have a gun in England," Ollie whined.

"Dear Mr. Sparrow," Saul said in a low voice. "I know that such a little law like that wouldn't bother a man like you. Bring a gun, a handgun. In fact, bring one for me. I wasn't able to bring one on the plane. We may not need them, but we need to be prepared. And one more thing: bring a couple of your friends. I will pay them well for helping. Ollie, I mean it. Bring them and make sure they're armed. Do I make myself clear?"

"Yes, sir," Ollie said. "I'll bring a couple of guys that I know, but it may take me a little longer."

"No longer. This can't wait. Get them, bring them, bring guns, and don't be late."

"I don't like this at all. I haven't been arrested since I came to England, and I don't want to be now."

"Quit whining. Just come with some help. If you don't, I will make you regret it. And you know that I can do that with just one phone call," Saul reminded him.

"I'll come, but when I get this little job done for you, I won't owe you anything, and you will forget all I ever told you when you were my attorney. So you will wait for me there?"

"I will be here when you get here," Saul said and terminated the call.

There was no way he was staying in any one spot very long until the Dixons were terminated. As soon as that was done, he would ditch his new phone, buy another one, and leave England. He honestly didn't think there was any way anyone could know about this phone and be tracking him with it, but he was not planning to take any chances. He was going to protect himself until he could get out of this country and take advantage of the millions of dollars he had stashed away.

* * *

Stetson met seven officers in plain clothes who had been sent by Detective Inspector Dennis Kinser inside of the lobby of the hotel where he had reserved a room. He told them that they needed to be prepared for violence. "That seems to be the only thing these people of Saul's understand," he said.

One of the officers, a young constable by the name of Arnold Roper, asked, "Inspector Kinser told us it could get ugly. Do you know how many people are coming?"

"I don't have any idea. You see, gentlemen, we were told to have a couple by the name of Dixon here or an innocent man in the United States who has been abducted will be killed," Stetson revealed. "If they come, it could be one or it could be a dozen. We really don't know. Although I would be surprised if it's more than three or four who actually show up. But we have to be prepared for anything once they arrive. When they discover that we are not the Dixons, anything could happen. So we must be prepared to shoot if we have to."

He asked the sergeant in charge of the London officers, Sergeant Watkins, a burly man with a hard face and deep voice, to assign four of his men to be outside where they could watch the entrances—front, rear, and sides. Then Stetson said, "If any of you see this man, let me know immediately."

He showed them a picture of Saul. "It would be best to take him and the men with him before they reach the room, but just in case, there will be three of us up there. I will expect you to follow them up and back us if you can't stop them first. Now, I may know before any of you when Saul gets here, as I have someone tracking his phone. So does your inspector. They are both in close contact with me. If I get word that he's here, I'll let you all know and maybe we can stop him and whoever's with him before they actually get into the hotel. Any questions?"

There were none, so the sergeant gave the order to his men, then Stetson and the others, including Sergeant Watkins, moved to the elevator and rode up to the room Stetson had checked into earlier using Roland Dixon's name.

They looked the room over carefully. Then Stetson said, "Okay, one of you will be out of sight behind the door here." He pointed to the spot. "The other one will be in the bathroom with the door open but out of sight of the entrance to the room. Each of you is to have your firearms in your hands as this will probably become very dangerous very fast. Is that okay, Sergeant Watkins?" he asked.

"It seems okay to me. I'll be the one in the loo," he said. Of course, Stetson knew that he meant the bathroom. After all, he was in England.

They took up their positions and began what could be a long wait.

* * *

Saul was sipping a cup of steaming coffee. He kept looking at his watch. Ollie was late. He began to steam as much as the coffee was. Ollie would pay dearly if he didn't show up with some recruits very soon. The idea of being stationary here for very long made him nervous. He kept reminding himself that no one could possibly know where he was. But he was nervous, nonetheless. He'd checked into a hotel room minutes before coming here and had left his few belongings, including his computer, there.

Just as he was pulling his phone out to call Ollie, the big man poked his head in the door and looked around. As soon as the two men's eyes met from across the room, Ollie walked across the floor to his table. The two did not shake hands or speak any niceties, as there were no longer any niceties between them.

"Where are your men?" Saul demanded, barely able to keep his anger in check over the delay.

"Outside in a car belonging to one of them," Ollie answered, his own temper clearly at the surface. His face was red and his eyes were glaring.

"My gun?" Saul asked.

"In the car," Ollie answered.

"Okay, let's go." Saul left his steaming coffee at the table, but he did not leave his own steam, nor did he leave any money for the pub.

The car in question was a Land Rover, old and dented but sufficient for the job at hand. Before he got in through the front passenger door, which was hanging open, he held out his hand and said, "The gun."

Ollie reached inside and one of the occupants in the back seat handed one to him. He in turn handed it to Saul, who hid it in front of him as he climbed in beside the driver. The first thing he did was check the gun. It was loaded and looked okay. Then he turned to Ollie, who had gotten in the back seat. "Only three guys?" he asked with a snarl. "I only got one good hand, you know."

"I see that, but it's all I had time for. It's not like you gave me a lot of notice," Ollie said.

"Okay, it will have to do. Let's go." He told the driver the address of the hotel they were going to, and the Land Rover pulled onto the street.

It took fifteen minutes to reach the Dixons' hotel.

* * *

Lilia was leaning anxiously over her little brother's shoulder, watching the computer that was faithfully tracking Saul's movements. Both of their parents were lying down, totally exhausted and worn down by the high level of stress they'd been subjected to.

At this point, all the stress that Lilia was feeling was for the man she was falling in love with. Stetson was the one going into a dangerous situation. All she could do for him was pray, and she was doing that.

"Lilia," Timmy said, "Saul is almost at the hotel where Stetson is meeting him. You better let him know."

She did not need to be told twice. She called Stetson, and as soon as she heard his voice, she said, "Saul is almost there."

"What direction is he coming from?" he asked.

She looked at the computer and wasn't sure, so she asked Timmy the same question. "He's coming from the east, moving west," he said. "He's really close now."

Lilia relayed the information to Stetson, who said, "Thanks. Update me as soon as he stops."

"I will, and Stetson, please, please be careful," she pleaded.

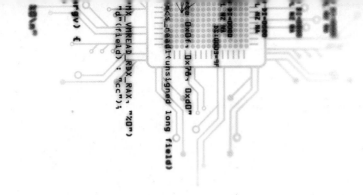

CHAPTER
TWENTY-TWO

STETSON GAVE THE UPDATE TO Sergeant Watkins, who in turn radioed the information to his men. Then he said to Stetson, "If he's close, maybe we should go outside with my officers and confront him there."

Stetson's phone rang before he could answer. "Stetson, he just stopped. As near as Timmy can tell, he's right at the hotel."

"Okay, thanks," he said.

"He's out of the car and walking," she said.

"We'll get him," he said and ended the call.

Leaving an officer in the hotel room just in case, he and Sergeant Watkins ran for the elevators as Watkins alerted his officers. Stetson had never had such a long elevator ride in his life. At least that's what it felt like to him. It finally stopped and the door opened. Standing at the next elevator was Saul Greenbaum and three tough-looking men.

Watkins's officers were trailing a short distance back. Stetson could tell by the looks of concern on the faces of the men that they had not been able to do a thing. His eyes shot to the doors across the lobby. An old Land Rover was parked right outside the doors. Saul and his henchmen, he concluded in a fraction of a second, had come in that vehicle.

Saul glanced around, and then the door to the elevator in front of him opened. Saul rushed in with his men right behind. A woman screamed as Saul threw her from the elevator. Sergeant Watkins and his men rushed to the elevator. A shot rang out as the door started to shut. An officer went down. Sergeant Watkins fired into the elevator, and a man went down in there. The lady was on her feet, running and screaming.

Stetson punched the button of the elevator he had just left. The door opened, and he jumped in, followed by Sergeant Watkins and three of his men. The others were bent over the downed officer.

Watkins radioed the man in the room up above and warned him. He said, "Leave the room and position yourself next to the elevators. We need to know which floor the elevator closest to the west stops on."

Stetson could not hear the response, but he had a sinking feeling that Sergeant Watkins had guessed correctly that Saul would stop at a different floor. Several heart-thumping seconds passed before the sergeant's radio came to life. It was the voice of Constable Roper who said, "It stopped on the sixth floor."

Stetson punched that number on the pad in his elevator, and a moment later it rumbled to a stop, just as Constable Roper's voice over the radio said, "It's going back down."

Stetson hit the ground-floor button on his elevator. There was no way to know which floor Saul might get out on, but he suspected it would not be the bottom floor. He punched the button and his elevator stopped at the fourth floor. "I'm heading for the stairs," he shouted.

"I'll go on down," Watkins said, but then on his radio he told the young constable to take his man and head for the stairs. The door had closed before he had a chance to hear Constable Roper's response. Having earlier made sure he knew where the stairs were, Stetson ran that way, nearly running into an older couple who appeared to be headed for the elevators. He had his handgun out and shouted as he passed the couple, "Police. Go to your room and stay there."

He hesitated at the top of the stairs and listened. He could hear steps coming down. He looked up and saw the young constable running down, and then he started down himself. A man came into view. It was not Saul. It was a big man who had a gun in his hand. Stetson did not hesitate, nor did the constable. Two bullets tore into the big man, who went backwards and began to tumble. A second man appeared above them on the stairs. He got a shot off. Stetson felt a sting in his left thigh, but it didn't stop him from firing. The second man went down.

Stetson stopped when he reached the big man. There was no pulse, so he signaled the others to continue down the stairway. The second man was still alive and raised a gun from his crumpled position on the stairs. The constable fired and the man lay still.

Stetson, feeling a burning pain in his left leg, leaped over the second dead man and continued down. When he reached the bottom of the stairs, he carefully pushed the door open. Seeing no one, he stepped out, followed by the other officer.

The stairs were some distance from the elevators. He told Constable Roper to watch the stairs. "Someone could have gotten off at one of the floors and could still be coming down," he said. Then he and the other constable ran for the elevators on the main floor of the hotel. They heard gunfire as they rounded the corner. In front of the elevators, another constable was down. So was another of Saul's henchmen.

"Where's Saul?" Stetson shouted as he approached.

"He got to the door and out of the hotel," Watkins said. "One of my guys pursued him. This man's hurt bad. You go. I'll get help on the way for him."

"That's all there is," he said to Constable Roper as they ran for the large glass front doors. "Call your man at the stairs and tell him to come on down to the main lobby."

The constable did that, and by the time the two of them had crossed the lobby and reached the exit, the second officer could be heard running behind them. Stetson knew he was hurt, but he gritted his teeth and ran through the door and watched as the old Land Rover hit the street and merged recklessly into traffic.

His phone rang. "Saul is headed west," Lilia's voice said. "He's going fast."

Stetson debated getting a cab but knew it would be fruitless even as he said to Lilia, "He got away from us, but his gangster friends didn't. Tell Timmy to keep track of him if he can."

"He's stopped now. He's only a block or two from the hotel," Lilia said.

"Constables, one of you come with me, and the other one, go join your sergeant," he ordered.

As he limped up the street, trying to ignore the pain, he glanced over as Constable Roper jogged alongside him. Stetson still had a gun in one hand and his phone in the other. "He's right ahead of you," Lilia said. "Be careful."

There was no Land Rover in sight. But lying on the sidewalk with a man bending over it was a cell phone. "Don't touch that!" Stetson shouted, and the man jumped back as if stung by a hornet.

He knew whose it was, and that meant that Timmy could no longer track Saul. He'd gotten away and would still be a threat. Very likely, old Gabriel Schiller was condemned to die. He said, "Lilia, Saul threw out his phone. I've got it now. I'll get back to you."

Timmy came on and said, "I need it. If we can get into it, we will know who he's been talking to in Utah, and maybe I can trace that, and they can catch the guy who has Gabriel."

"It's open right now," Stetson said, and he quickly looked under recent calls. The most recent were London calls. But one other number, a United States number, showed up several times. He recited it to Timmy.

"I'll get to work on it now," the boy said.

Then Lilia's name came on the phone, but Stetson had a hard time hearing her. The pain in his leg was intense and getting worse by the second, and the adrenaline rush that had kept him moving was over. Constable Roper grabbed his arm and said, "Sit down, Detective. You're losing a lot of blood."

He heard Lilia scream, "Stetson, are you shot?"

Constable Roper took both phones from Stetson's hands as he sank to the sidewalk.

"He is shot," Roper said into Stetson's phone. "So are several others."

A different voice spoke. "This is Detective Franklin. Who am I speaking to?"

The last thing Stetson remembered before passing out was Roper identifying himself.

***

Diana said, "You all need to come with me. We've got to get to Stetson. We need to hurry."

By the time they arrived at the hotel, there were cop cars and ambulances all around the main entrance. They could not get close. "Stay with me," Diana said, feeling frantic. She didn't like the idea of taking the Dixons to the scene of what must have been multiple shootings, but she couldn't see any other option.

She identified herself to officers who were positioned at the door. She asked about the American detective. She was told that he'd been taken to a hospital. She asked, "Where is Constable Roper? That's who told me that Detective Erman was shot. Erman's my partner."

As soon as she was told that he was inside the hotel, she had the Dixons follow her. What they found there was a lot of activity. There were people on the floor being treated by paramedics. One was covered with a blanket. She felt an almost overwhelming sadness come over her.

An officer approached her and said, "Ma'am, we have a situation here. Please go back to your rooms, all of you."

"I'm Detective Franklin. My partner is Detective Erman," she said.

The man's eyes became very alert. "I'm Sergeant Watkins. Erman has been taken to the hospital. Who are these people?"

"The Dixons," Diana said as she heard Lilia softly sobbing right behind her.

"Is Stetson going to die?" Lilia blurted.

"No, he will be okay, young lady. We need to find you folks a place to wait. We have a lot to do here. Actually," he said after a moment of hesitation, "there is a room on the seventh floor that none of the violence occurred in or near. It's registered to the Dixons. Come over to the registration desk and I'll get you a key card and you can go on up. It's on the seventh floor, room number 721. One of the elevators has a body in it, so that one is closed, as are the stairs. Take the farthest elevator to your left as you approach them. I'll send Constable Roper up with you, and he can tell you what happened here."

Before they ever reached the room, Diana had Sergeant Snow on the phone. "Do you have Saul in custody?" he asked before she had a chance to explain anything to him.

"He got away. There was a lot of shooting. Stetson was wounded. I'll know more later, but let me give you one thing to work on. Saul threw the phone away that Timmy Dixon was using to track him with. We have the phone number of the man who took Gabriel." She recited it to her sergeant, and then she said, "The Dixons and I are at the hotel where the operation went down. There is a constable following us to a room. He will fill me in as soon as we get there."

"I will want to be included on that," Snow said. "So call me back. Meantime, I'll get someone working on this phone number."

"Okay, thanks, but one more question. Do you have an update on Harry?"

"I don't, but I will get back with you on that," the sergeant said.

It was only a couple of minutes before Diana had her sergeant back on the line. "We're ready—are you?" she asked.

"I'm ready, let's hear this," Sergeant Snow said.

For the next ten minutes, they listened to the constable explain what had happened. Everyone was listening, with one exception. Timmy was hard at work on his computer again. Lilia was listening, but her mind was mostly on Stetson. She was as concerned about him as she would have been if he was a member of her family. She realized that he had become just that important to her in the past few days. She silently prayed for his recovery.

Once the whole story had been told and Constable Roper had answered all their questions the best he could, Diana said, "Now we need to find out how Stetson is doing. I can see that you are worried sick, Lilia. But we have to believe that he is going to be okay."

Timmy, silent and concentrating on his own work, spoke up then. "I know where that guy is who Saul's been talking to."

That got Diana's immediate attention. "Where is he?"

Timmy gave her an address. Diana called Sergeant Snow back and passed the address on to him. "I'll get officers there right now," he promised. "I'll get back with you, Diana."

***

Gabriel Schiller was feeling very ill. He wasn't sure he would survive the situation he was in even if the cops found him soon. One of the men who had taken him from his home was a violent, dangerous man. The other one, much younger than the first, was the one he saw regularly. He didn't seem much like a hardened criminal, but Gabriel had to believe that he was. The young man referred to himself as Jeremy. He was the one who brought him food and seemed somewhat sympathetic to his situation. He was the only one Gabriel had seen after the two of them had brought him to this unknown place.

The young man walked in now. He had his phone in his hand and was talking to someone. He had a frown on his face. He was saying, "I thought you said after you had the Dixons taken care of."

Gabriel could not tell what was said on the other end of the call, but he could tell that it was a man's voice and that he was enraged. Jeremy responded to whatever had been said with, "Sorry, Boss. Yes, he's still right here." Another pause, then, "Wait, you mean you didn't get the Dixons after what you made me do for you?"

He was standing just inside the heavy door that he'd kept locked since bringing Gabriel in here. He appeared to be around thirty. Gabriel judged him to be around five feet, ten inches, a handsome, slender fellow with dark blond hair that fell just over his ears and to his collar. He was frowning and kept shifting from foot to foot like he was worried about something. Finally he spoke. "Okay, I will take care of him for you," he said. "Sorry I misunderstood." With that, the call ended.

Gabriel was frightened beyond words. All he could do was sit there in the chair he was bound to and tremble and pray. He was certain that he was about to die. Jeremy said, "I have to make a phone call."

He punched in a number. After a moment, he said, "Sydney. This is Jeremy Dinzley. I need your help."

Gabriel listened while whoever the Sydney Jeremy had called responded. Then he said, "It's your father. He threatened me if I didn't do something for him. I can't do what he wants, but I've already done too much."

Jeremy listened again. "I know. But your dad got me out of some trouble, and he says I owe him."

More listening, then again he spoke. "Your dad will kill me if I don't do what he says. But I can't. Please, Sydney. I know I broke up with you, but I wish I hadn't. Your father threatened me if I continued to see you. I still love you, Sydney. Please, I desperately need your help."

After another spell of listening, Jeremy said, "Thank you. I'll pick you up at your mother's house and explain what's going on. I just hope you can tell me what to do."

The young man was in tears when he finished that call. He stepped closer to Gabriel, and after wiping away his tears and blowing his nose, he said, "Saul wants you dead. I'm supposed to kill you and get rid of your body. But I'm not a killer. I'm sorry I got you into this mess. Saul is a terrible man."

Gabriel found a reason to have some hope for his life, the beginning of an answer to his desperate prayers. This young man wasn't as bad as he'd feared. He was finally able to speak. He asked, "Who is Sydney?"

Jeremy rubbed his eyes. "She is a girl I was going to marry until Saul stopped it. She is Saul's daughter. She's not at all like her father. She's a little younger than me and lives with her mother. She and her mother are both afraid of Saul."

"Has she ever been in trouble?" Gabriel asked, his voice very weak and getting weaker.

"No, never. She didn't realize what an evil person her father was until after we had dated for a few months. I'd been in a little trouble before I met Sydney, and Saul told me that if I didn't stay away from Sydney, he would see to it that I went to jail," Jeremy said. He looked absolutely wretched, and he sank to the floor in front of Gabriel.

"Surely that wasn't the only reason he made you kidnap me, is it?" Gabriel asked perceptively.

Jeremy's chest heaved and great sobs erupted. It was a couple of minutes before he was finally able to speak again. "Saul told me that Sydney would disappear if I didn't do as he told me to. He repeated that to me again just now. Believe me, sir, he would do it. He's that evil. He loves only his horrible self."

"So it's either my life or the life of the girl you love," Gabriel said with a catch in his voice.

Jeremy nodded. "Yes, but I can't kill you, and I can't let Sydney's father kill her. I'm supposed to pick her up at her mother's house. I'll bring her back here. She's smart. Maybe she can figure something out." Great wracking sobs again made his whole body tremble. Finally, he gained control of his emotions and got to his feet. "I'll be back." With that he left, shutting the door behind him.

For the first time since he'd been put in this little room, Gabriel did not hear the door lock. If he could just get out of these ropes . . .

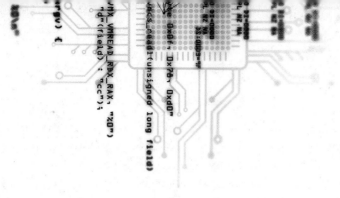

CHAPTER
TWENTY-THREE

TIMMY WAS NOW TRACKING THE phone that Saul had called several times. None of them knew if that was in fact the phone number of the person who was holding Gabriel, but it was all they had to go on, so that is what he was doing. Lilia tried to keep her mind off what was going on downstairs in the hotel lobby. It was the second time in such a short while that lives had been lost in hotel lobbies here in London. It made her sick to think about it and made her even sicker to think about Stetson.

She'd tried his phone several times, even though she didn't know if he even had it anymore. If he did, he simply may be too badly injured to answer it, despite Constable Roper telling her it was just his upper leg, that he would be okay. It was the loss of blood that had been the biggest concern, he'd told her.

She tried again. Same result. She wished she'd thought to ask Roper if he knew whether Stetson's phone had been taken with him to the hospital. But she had not thought of that until he'd gone back to help with the crime scenes below. They had all been told to stay in the room with Diana until further notice.

Timmy called out, "He's leaving that place I traced him to. I'm still trying to get an address."

"He or she," Diana said. "We don't know if it's a man or a woman."

"I guess that's right," Timmy admitted. "I'm going to see where he or she is going now, and maybe when he or she stops again, I can figure it out." He again concentrated on his computer.

Diana called Sergeant Snow again. Maybe he was having better luck than Timmy at pinpointing the location where the phone had been temporarily stationary.

***

Sergeant Snow answered his phone as soon as he saw it was Detective Franklin calling. "What have you heard concerning Stetson?" he asked.

"Nothing," she said. "Lilia is worried sick. She's been trying his phone every little while, but he either can't answer or it isn't with him."

"I think she can quit worrying. From what that constable said, I don't think it's too serious. They may have to give him some blood and do some stitching, but that's probably all," Snow said.

His words echoed Diana's thoughts, so she let it go and asked, "Anything on that phone number we gave you?"

"Yes, and it has taken us clear down to Juab County. We think we're close now. I'll let you know," he said.

"Juab County?" she asked with a furrowed brow. "That's not what Timmy is seeing. He wasn't able to pinpoint an exact address, but Gabriel's still in the Salt Lake area, he thinks."

"Maybe the kid isn't so smart after all," Snow said a little too derisively. "I'll let you know as soon as we find the location."

"Are you sure you have the right phone number?" Diana asked.

The sergeant recited it back and Diana groaned. "That's one digit off," she said.

"It's what you gave me," the sergeant said.

Diana didn't argue with him, she simply said, "I must have given it to you wrong." Even though she was quite certain she hadn't. She gave it to him again.

"Okay, we'll head back north while we see if we can find this one and get to tracking it."

"Any word on Mr. Lundquist yet?" Diana asked.

"No, but I'll follow up as soon as we find Schiller—if we do." With that, Sergeant Snow ended the call.

Timmy said excitedly, "I have an address now. He's stopped there."

As soon as he told her the address, she said, "I'll call Snow back and let him know. They need to get someone there right away."

* * *

Sydney headed hesitantly for the door when the bell rang. She'd been in deep thought ever since Jeremy had called. She'd loved him at one time, but his sudden desertion of her with no explanation had soured that love. She'd been thinking about what he'd said while she was waiting for him. She had been infused with anger both at Jeremy and at her father. In her opinion, Jeremy should have been honest with her. She was hurt that he hadn't been.

On the other hand, as she reached for the doorknob, she felt a surge of the old affection when she realized that Jeremy may have saved her life. The deep anger was at her father. He had apparently threatened to do something to her if Jeremy didn't break up with her.

She swung the door wide, and what she saw was a miserable man, who she could see had been crying. She impulsively opened her arms to him, and he fell into them. They held each other tight for a long moment as she realized that she didn't detest this man. In fact, she felt a spark of that old love for him hit her right in the heart.

She pulled away from him but grabbed his hand and pulled him in and shut the door. Then they embraced again. He sobbed, and that got her to sobbing as well. Finally, he said, "Where's your mother?"

"She's out of town with the company she works for now. I just got home from work when you called me. Jeremy, I can't believe all this is happening."

"It's true. I'm so sorry," he said. "I don't deserve to even be around you, but I didn't know who else to call."

"Tell me exactly what's going on, what my father has caused now," she said as she checked her purse. "My pistol is in there," she said. "I just wanted to make sure. You have a gun too, don't you?"

"I do. Can we talk on the way to where the old man is? He must be scared to death, and he's a decent guy. Your father used him to try to get to the Dixons again," he said.

Once they were in Jeremy's car, he told her everything, holding nothing back. She listened, her heart aching for Jeremy while filling with intense anger at her father. After he had finished, she said, "Jeremy, we have to protect that old man. What did you say his name is?"

"Gabriel Schiller. If you can believe this, Sydney, after kidnapping him and holding him in that dirty room, he asked me to call him Gabriel."

"Do you?" she asked as she wrinkled her brows.

"Of course. Like I told you, he's a nice man. So I think you should call him Gabriel too."

"Okay, I'll do that. But we have got to protect him from my father," she said with her eyes narrowed. "We cannot let him cause that man's death. He's done far too much damage already. Did I tell you that I saw him try to shoot a cop, a nice detective lady?"

"No," he said. "You better tell me about it. We are almost there."

She quickly recited what had happened at her father's house and why she had gone there at her mother's request. She concluded with, "Jeremy, my father killed a man in cold blood. He is responsible for the death of Tiny, and he would have killed Detective Franklin if he could have."

When she had finished, Jeremy said, "Sydney, your father is dangerous, and if he finds out that you helped me today, he'll come after you. We've got to protect you too."

"And you," she responded. "I know he will want to destroy you. I wonder where he is. He had a cast on one arm that covered his wrist. It was broken. But I'm sure he wouldn't let that stop him from doing whatever he wanted to do."

"I don't know where he is at the moment, but the last I knew he was in London," he said honestly. "But he could be on his way back here for all I know." He pulled around to the back of the old, abandoned house where he'd been holding Gabriel. But before he opened his door, he looked at the girl he'd once loved, the girl he still loved, and said, "I'm sorry for what I've done and how I've hurt you. I know you can never forgive me, but thanks for helping me now."

She gazed at him for a minute with tenderness that shocked him. "Jeremy, I most certainly can forgive you. This may surprise you, but I don't think I ever stopped loving you. We can talk about that later. Right now, let's take care of protecting Gabriel."

Jeremy was shocked, he was elated, and he hated himself for the things he'd done. He'd never thought he could ever forgive himself, but he thought, as he smiled at Sydney, if she could forgive him, then maybe he could eventually forgive himself.

Once inside the house, Jeremy opened the door to the bedroom where he'd been holding Gabriel prisoner. The old man was slumped over in his chair, drooling from his mouth but not moving. In alarm, Jeremy ran to him. He was shaking with fear when he felt the carotid artery. To his great relief, the old man's heart was still beating, but it was not a strong beat.

"He needs to go to the hospital," Sydney said as she helped Jeremy untie him.

"I haven't heard from the guy who helped me kidnap him. He could be keeping track of what I'm doing, for all I know," Jeremy said as he and Sydney lifted Gabriel and began to carry him from the room.

"We'll have to watch for him. Who is he?" Sydney asked.

"All I know him by is Snitch. He's a large guy with a scar on his left cheek and the tattoo of a snake on his left arm. He wears his hair in a ponytail," Jeremy said.

"What else can you tell me about him?" Sydney asked, breathing hard but helping Jeremy to keep moving the old man to the back door. He wasn't very heavy, but he was dead weight, unable to help himself since he was not conscious.

"His hair is black, and his eyes are dark brown or black. He's left-handed and very strong. He must be over fifty years old," Jeremy said.

"How does he dress?" she asked.

"He was wearing blue jeans and a dirty blue button-down shirt when we picked Gabriel up. And let's see, he had a bandana on his head. It was blue, I think."

"What does he drive?" she asked.

"He has an old faded-blue Chevy Impala. That's the car we used the night we got Gabriel."

"Okay, so now we can both watch for him," Sydney said.

They struggled to get Gabriel through the door and into the back seat of Jeremy's gray Jeep Wrangler. Sydney sat in the back with Gabriel and cradled his head. Jeremy started the car when suddenly Sydney said, "Jeremy, I think you should leave your phone. We could be followed by the GPS capability in it."

"Oh my, I hadn't even thought about that."

"We can use mine, so we'll be fine. Frankly, I'm not letting you out of my sight again. I lost you once and I'm not going to lose you again. So throw yours into those bushes beside the house there where it won't easily be seen. Then drive fast. Let's get Gabriel to the nearest hospital."

As she spoke, he tossed the phone into the bushes. "That would be IHC in Murray," he said as he rolled his window up and stepped on the gas pedal. "It's only about ten or fifteen minutes from here."

Jeremy's heart began to race when he spotted a pair of police cars that were speeding toward him with sirens blaring and lights flashing. They didn't even slow down as they passed him. "It's good you threw your phone out," Sydney said. "I'll bet they're headed to that house we just left in Millcreek."

"I owe you again, Sydney," he said as his heart slowly returned a little closer to its normal pace.

He drove for three or four minutes, keeping a close watch in his rearview mirror. His heart began racing when he saw an older, faded-blue sedan about a half block behind him. He couldn't tell the make, nor could he see the driver. "I may be wrong," he said as calmly as he could to Sydney, "but Snitch may be behind us."

"Okay, well, we'll do what we have to if he tries to stop us from taking Gabriel into the emergency room. Do you know how to get there?" Sydney asked.

"Not exactly, but I'm sure the signs will direct us."

"I know how, so I'll guide you. In the meantime, I'm going to call the hospital and have them meet us outside with a stretcher."

It was with a great deal of relief that Jeremy saw the stretcher and two people in hospital garb awaiting them when he pulled in. Sydney explained to the folks there that they had found the old man unconscious in front of a house in the Millcreek area and had brought him in, afraid to wait for an ambulance because he looked so bad and his heartbeat was so weak. She explained, upon questioning after he'd been wheeled inside, that she didn't know where he lived, but that he had ID on him, which was true. She also explained that neither of them was related to him or knew him personally.

Jeremy was pacing, clearly worried, so Sydney hurried her answers as they moved him inside. Sydney followed them while Jeremy parked his car. Soon he was able to join Sydney inside the hospital. The emergency room doctor and nurses were busy working on Gabriel, so they moved into the waiting area. Jeremy said, "That blue car passed right by as we turned into the emergency room area. I got a better look at it and the driver. There is no question that it was Snitch, which makes me worried about Gabriel's safety in here. But I didn't see him again when I parked."

"Let's give it a few minutes and see if some cops show up. I'm sure the emergency room staff will call them. Once we see them coming, we can leave and try to get away from Snitch in case he's watching for us." With that decided, they sat back and waited, both nervous but united in their desire to see that Gabriel was kept safe.

***

Sergeant Snow and several officers surrounded the house that the signal had led them to. He announced their presence with a bullhorn and told whoever was inside to come out. When there was no response, he tried the front door. It was locked. "Let's try the back door as well," he said. Leaving a couple of officers watching the front, they circled around to the back. That door was not only unlocked but was hanging open.

He entered cautiously and soon learned that the house was deserted, but in one bedroom there were some ropes that were lying on the floor next to a soft chair. There was a wastebasket near the chair. It held some empty fast food containers. "He was here," he announced. "But according to the GPS reading, the person who Greenbaum had been calling is still here. It doesn't make any sense."

Sergeant Snow's phone rang. It was the dispatcher telling him that a man by the name of Gabriel Schiller had been delivered to the hospital by a young couple in a private vehicle. "Are they still there?" he asked.

He was told that the nurse who called said they were waiting in the waiting room. Apparently they claimed to have seen him lying on the ground in front of a house in Millcreek and had brought him to the hospital themselves as they didn't dare wait for an ambulance.

"Let's go, folks. Gabriel Schiller is at the IHC hospital. A young couple brought him in," he said.

Leaving two officers to secure the house, he headed for the hospital.

* * *

A nurse came into the waiting area and addressed Sydney and Jeremy. "Mr. Schiller is being stabilized. You folks saved his life and are to be commended," she said. "I'm Nurse Maria Campbell. I'll need to get your names and contact information. And since the police are on the way, it would be best if you waited here so you could talk to them."

Sydney and Jeremy were prepared for this, and Jeremy told them they were Mr. and Mrs. Randy and Sybil Jones. He gave a false address and two equally false phone numbers. The nurse thanked them and left, reminding them that the police would be there shortly.

"Very well," Jeremy said. "We'll be here. We sure hope the old fellow makes it."

They did not wait, however. Instead, they hurried out to the parking area and got in Jeremy's Jeep. "Where should we go?" he asked as soon as they were both seated in the car.

"To my house, but we can't let Snitch follow us. Once we get there, we'll hide your Jeep, and if we need to go anywhere else, we'll use my car."

They did see Snitch's car again, but he was not in it. It was parked on the street about a block from the hospital's emergency entrance. "We need to alert the police that he may be in the hospital. But we can't use my phone. We'll need to find a pay phone, and that isn't easy anymore," Sydney said.

Ten minutes later, they had made calls from a pay phone to both the 911 operator and the hospital. That done, they drove to the house where Sydney lived with her mother.

CHAPTER
TWENTY-FOUR

SNITCH, WHOSE REAL NAME WAS Sandy Horentz, was seldom called Sandy. Snitch was a name he was proud of. He'd earned it by snitching on other criminals to both the police and more frequently to men who directed the various criminal enterprises in and around the Salt Lake Valley. He only had one rule that he lived by when turning on others, and that was that it had to in some way benefit him, even if it was just a small thing.

It was with that in mind that he called Saul Greenbaum's number. It was his intention to tell Saul that Jeremy had taken the old man to the hospital and that he was with none other than Saul's own daughter. He knew that Saul would award him generously for that information, for he had done so for similar information in the past.

He'd sat back and simply kept an eye on Jeremy, letting Jeremy make the calls when necessary to Saul since the kidnapping. The number he was calling was the one Jeremy had informed him was a new phone of Saul's, as it had gotten dangerous for the boss to keep his old one. Broken arm and all, Saul had arrived in London. So Snitch believed that was where he was, or at least had been recently. He also knew that Saul needed to be informed about the treachery of both his daughter and Jeremy, the man he'd ordered to never ever make contact with Sydney again.

He had watched as Jeremy and Sydney left the parking area and headed south on State Street. He had thought about following them again but decided against it. In his judgment, the most serious problem was right here at the hospital.

He tried Saul's number three times but got only voice mail. He was anxious to snitch on his treacherous young partner. He finally left a message for Saul. "Boss, this is Snitch. I have some very important information for you," he said. "You have a traitor in your organization. Call me as soon as you can for directions on how I am to proceed."

That finished, he continued to go about what he felt Saul would have wanted him to do had Saul been able to talk to him. Gabriel Schiller had to be silenced. Then, if he was still unable to talk to the boss, he would go after Jeremy and silence him as well. He knew right where to find Jeremy. It was quite simple, really. He would be at Saul's ex-wife's house where his daughter Sydney lived. He wouldn't touch Sydney unless he was ordered to do so by Saul. But Jeremy would be eliminated regardless, for he had no doubt that would be what Saul wanted.

Snitch entered the hospital and told them at the reception desk that he needed to see his beloved uncle who had just been delivered to the emergency room in critical shape. They would not tell him anything about Schiller, and that made him angry. But he did not let his anger show. He'd sneak around in the hospital until he could locate him, he decided. Then he would take care of the old man once and for all.

* * *

Sergeant Hartling responded to the hospital, along with numerous other officers from several agencies. The description of the dangerous man that an anonymous caller made to both the police and the hospital was very detailed. It was actually Sergeant Hartling who spotted the man the caller had referred to as Snitch skulking around in the hospital.

He got on his radio to alert other officers of the suspect's location. Two more officers were nearby and joined Hartling. He pointed out the man and they all started in his direction. Snitch spotted them and veered away from them. While the sergeant kept Snitch's location current for other officers, he continued to follow him. He and the other two conferred briefly and decided it would be best if they could follow him until he was outside of the hospital before attempting to arrest him. Snitch reached the front doors and hurried toward the parking lot. Hartling and the officers began to run. Two officers approached Snitch before he reached the parking lot.

Then Snitch did the unthinkable. He grabbed a young lady who was dressed in shorts and a tank top around the neck, pulled a gun, put it to her face, and then shouted, "You pigs back off, or I will mess up this pretty girl's head really bad."

Sergeant Hartling felt sick. If the suspect got away, he would most likely come back after old Mr. Schiller again, or send someone else. On the other hand, he might kill the girl. It was a no-win situation for the police. He closed in on Snitch while the other officers did the same, hoping beyond hope that he could talk the guy into letting her go. "Let her go, Snitch," he said.

"No way, you stupid pig. I mean it. I'll kill her and a lot of you if you don't back off. Now!"

Hartling was close enough to see the terror in the girl's eyes. She couldn't be but sixteen or seventeen years old, old enough to drive but way too young to die. He knew the drill. The girl's life at this point was the most important consideration. This had just turned from a protection mission for Mr. Schiller to saving the life of a teenage girl. He tried again. "You are only going to make this worse on yourself," he called out. "Let her go, Snitch."

"So you can shoot me? I ain't stupid. She's going with me. Now all of you get back!" he shouted.

"Stand back, men," Sergeant Hartling said, fearing that the girl was going to die if they didn't.

The officers moved back and left Snitch and his hostage a clear trail into the parking lot. Hartling knew where Snitch's car was. All the officers had been given that information. It was about midway from the doors to the far end of the parking lot, and right in the middle. It was an older faded-blue Impala.

He also knew something that Snitch did not know, and under the present circumstance, what had seemed like a good idea just minutes ago now seemed like a very bad one. The air had been let out of Snitch's tires. That car wasn't going anywhere. What Snitch would do when he figured that out was anyone's guess.

Snitch repeatedly warned the officers to give him lots of room. It appeared that he was becoming increasingly unstable, and that couldn't be helpful to the girl. There was now enough distance between the officers and Snitch that they could not hear what he was saying to the girl. But Sergeant Hartling figured it out when Snitch and his young hostage veered to the north. They must be going to her car, not his. So the flat tires wouldn't matter now.

Hartling and the other officers, which was a growing number as more came from inside the hospital and joined them, continued to follow Snitch but did so cautiously. Hartling didn't know who the other officers were, as several agencies were represented. He was probably outranked by now, but he had to keep control. This was not the time to make a change of command.

He soon figured out that it was a yellow Volkswagen Jetta that the girl had driven to the hospital. Even though he was a ways back, he could see her digging her keys out of her purse while Snitch continued to hold the deadly weapon to her head. He snatched the keys from her hand and forced her into the passenger side of the car and then shoved her until she moved across into the driver's seat.

He started to climb in after her, but suddenly he held his gun up and fired in the general direction of the officers.

No one was hit, but a car not thirty feet from Sergeant Hartling was. As luck or Snitch's intentions would have it, the bullet penetrated the gas tank and there was a huge explosion. The sergeant and several other officers were knocked to the ground. Another round was fired, and a second car exploded. The two explosions caused a third car to explode as the heat raged from the burning fuel. Officers were either running back toward the hospital or simply dropping to the ground either injured or attempting to protect themselves.

Fiery hot debris and metal and glass fragments rained down on the officers and on a couple of innocent civilians who were in the worst place they could have been.

In the confusion of the blasts and the screams of agony from injured people, the yellow Jetta got away. Hartling was stunned from the blast. His ears were ringing, and his face and hands were in pain, probably burned. He was pretty sure something was sticking in his back. It hurt like mad.

Other officers and civilians were moaning in pain. Hartling tried to get to his feet, but he stumbled and fell back down, bashing his head on the pavement. More officers approached at a run and began to assess the injuries of those who had been knocked down. Sergeant Hartling was told to lie still on his stomach, that he did in fact have a jagged bit of metal protruding from his back.

Sirens sounded, and a couple of police cars roared past and left. He supposed in his now slow-functioning brain that they were in pursuit of the Jetta. But at this point, Hartling feared, despite the pain he was in, that Snitch and his young hostage would be hard to catch. If the guy was as hardened as he appeared, he would simply carjack another vehicle and then another until he was able to hide somewhere with his young hostage.

Teams of medical personnel from the hospital arrived on the run. IHC was going to be very busy for a while. One nurse attended to Hartling. As she did, he was thinking about the gun the hostage taker had fired. It had to have been a very large caliber pistol, and in retrospect, it seemed to Hartling that Snitch had in fact hit exactly what he'd been aiming at. It was not an accident that the cars' gas tanks had exploded.

***

Jeremy and Sydney had arrived safely at her mother's house. His Jeep was now parked in the spot in the garage that Mrs. Greenbaum's car would ordinarily have occupied. The two of them had hurried inside. "Let's turn on the TV and see if there is anything on there about Mr. Schiller," Sydney said and proceeded to grab a remote. She sat on a sofa and patted the cushion beside her. "Come on, Jeremy, sit by me."

To Jeremy's surprise, KSL, the local station Sydney had turned to, was fully involved in reporting on a major event at the IHC hospital. They were stunned as they watched the TV coverage of burning cars, several injured police officers, and even some unlucky civilians. The gunman, identified only as Snitch, and his teenage hostage had escaped in a yellow VW Jetta, which had been found abandoned a mile or so from the hospital. Another car had been taken, the driver having been thrown to the ground by Snitch, and then with the girl in that car, he had driven away.

They sat glued to the TV, mesmerized by the mayhem. The girl, they learned after a few minutes, had been identified as sixteen-year-old Athenya Edler. A picture of her had been obtained and was flashed on the screen. She was a short, pretty, blonde girl with blue eyes. At the time she was taken, she had been wearing a pair of blue shorts and a red tank top. Her hair was long and in a ponytail.

"I can't believe this is happening, and all because of my father's greed. I hate him," Sydney said with undisguised venom.

"Hey, I wonder if Snitch knows where you live," Jeremy said as the news continued.

"Oh my gosh!" Sydney reacted. "I'll bet he does."

"We better get out of here, don't you think?" Jeremy asked.

"Yes, I think we should," Sydney responded. "I can't believe that Snitch did exactly what my father did the day he killed that big guy, Tiny, and almost killed Detective Hartling."

At that exact moment, there was the sound of a shot being fired, and the front door was slammed open. Drunk with rage, Snitch came in, pushing a terrified girl in front of him. "Help me," she cried weakly.

"They can't help you," Snitch growled. "That guy right there is gonna die. And as soon as her daddy calls me, she's gonna die too. That's why we came here."

Sydney, to Jeremy's surprise, said bravely, "Let her go, Snitch. You have us now. You don't need her. Anyway, you got away. Isn't that what you wanted?"

"I'll decide when to let her go, if I do at all. She's a female, and females have big mouths. I let her go and she's gonna tell the cops where I am."

"You aren't going to stay here, and you know it. Let her go, and we'll go with you."

"I ain't stupid."

"You are if you don't let Athenya go," Sydney said.

"Oh, so that's your name, little girl. You are Athenya. Well, I don't know, maybe I don't need you anymore," he said.

"That's right. Let her go, and you can take us wherever you want to. We'll go willingly if she's released," Sydney said.

"Well, okay. I only need one hostage."

"You will have two," Sydney said.

"No, just one. I gotta kill Jeremy. He betrayed the boss. And the boss don't like traitors. You should know that, girl. After all, he's your daddy," Snitch said with an ugly smirk. "Okay, go, little girl, run now before I change my mind."

Athenya ran out the door. Snitch was now holding his large caliber pistol on the two seated on the couch. "I guess I just as well shoot you right now, Jeremy. And then me and your girl here will go for a ride."

"In what?" Jeremy said as he heard a car start up out front. "You left the keys in that car and that girl just stole it."

Snitch was only distracted for a moment, but that was a moment too long. His life ended before he even realized what had happened to him. Sydney had removed her pistol from her purse and didn't even hesitate to send Snitch to the afterlife. She had finally got the man back that she had loved so much, and no way was she going to lose him to a lowlife gangster.

For a few moments, both of them stared at the dead man, whose blood was staining the tan carpet. It was Sydney who spoke first. "I had no choice, Jeremy. I lost you once; I don't intend to lose you again."

"We've got to call the cops, Sydney. Then I will be going to prison," he said.

"Not if I can help it," she retorted fiercely. "My dad forced you. You either had to kidnap Gabriel or my dad would have killed you or had you killed, and he would have killed me too, like he told you he would. I'll explain that to the cops and you'll be okay."

Jeremy slowly shook his head. "I'm afraid it's not that simple, Sydney."

"We'll get you the best lawyer we can find, and even though you may sit in jail for a while, you'll get off with a very light sentence," she said confidently. "They will have to look at what you've done today, saving Gabriel's life while risking your own. It will count for a lot, I promise you."

"I hope you're right, but I don't think I want to be here when they come," he said.

She reached back in her purse and pulled out her keys. "Here, take my car. Call me later when you find a place to hole up for a while. I'll get a lawyer, and you can turn yourself in when he has a deal made with the prosecutor."

"You will need your car, and they will find mine here and then you'll be in trouble. I gotta take my chances and drive my own Jeep," he said.

"Okay, I guess."

"Anyway, I don't have a phone, remember?" he asked.

"Take mine," she offered.

He shook his head. "I can't do that. I'll figure out what to do, but I need to leave now. That girl, Athenya, she'll tell the cops about me being here. They'll be coming anytime now. I'll call you when I can find a way to."

"I guess you're right," she said.

"Sydney, all this news is out there. Your dad will hear. And when he does, he'll order another of his seemingly endless stream of bad guys to kill you. Why don't we both go."

"Is that what you want?" she asked.

"I think so," he said. "I want to be with you."

"We can't just leave this guy here like this for the cops to find."

"Sure we can. Here's what you can do. Leave a note saying that you shot Snitch in self-defense and then left because you knew your dad was going to have someone else come here and kill you."

"Okay, if you think we should do that," Sydney said.

"I do. Let's take both cars and then we'll leave mine in a large parking lot somewhere and go away together in yours," he said.

She faced him. He stepped toward her. She looked up at him. He looked down at her. They slowly came together, and the kiss that followed was filled with hope and love. Then they stepped apart, she grabbed a pad of paper, wrote the note, placed it on the sofa, and the two of them, in separate cars, left her mother's home.

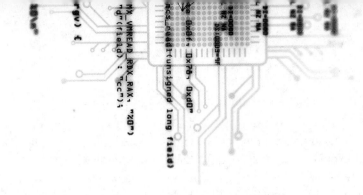

CHAPTER
TWENTY-FIVE

SAUL WAS IN A PARTICULARLY foul mood. It was not just because so many of his well-laid plans had gone awry or that his injured arm hurt like crazy and even itched under the cast. No, it was because he had just spent the past half hour trying to access his bank accounts. They all appeared to be closed. That made no sense. He needed his money. He would have to call one of the banks and give them a going over that they wouldn't forget.

Even the account he had thought was empty was now actually closed. He had no access to any of his accounts. Heads would roll when he got to the bottom of this, and he would get there. He was Saul Greenbaum. No one got away with messing with him.

He once again tried Jeremy's phone and got nothing. That young man had better not have messed things up. He had a job to do, and it had better be done. He again tried Snitch's number, and it also went to voice mail. Snitch was one of his most dependable men. It made no sense that he wasn't answering his phone. He'd worked for Saul long enough to know that he would not always be calling from a familiar number. Snitch should be answering.

A secretive trip back to Utah was not something he wanted to do, but if he had to, people would pay with their lives for causing him the inconvenience. That included anyone who crossed him, even his daughter, who was turning out to be more like her mother all the time.

He was tired of having to buy new phones, and yet when he was unable to contact Fredrick, he felt like he had to buy another one again, for the cops would try to keep track of him. He allowed himself a small smile. This time, he had purchased a cheap phone, and it had no GPS feature. It couldn't be tracked.

He tried Ollie Sparrow's number again, and when it didn't go through, he was pretty sure that Ollie had either been killed or captured in the abortive

attempt at the hotel where the Dixons were supposed to have met him. Anger
and hatred burned through him. Roland Dixon had to die. If not for him and
his attempts to gain favor in Harry's eyes, things would still be fine. He regretted
letting the Dixons go before. He would never be so stupid again.

Saul paced back and forth in his motel room, a dingy affair that was beneath
his dignity, but circumstances had been such that he felt another change of
location was necessary. Soon, if things didn't improve, he'd be on his way back
to Utah. Once there, he would be like a tornado. He'd move swiftly, deal out
deadly justice, and be gone before anyone could even guess he was back.

He looked at his phone again. The list of people who could be persuaded
to assist him was dwindling. He tried two more but didn't get an answer. It
was galling. He guessed he would have to finish off the loose ends himself and
then leave the country permanently.

Then he remembered the money situation and his gut churned. The thought
that all that money may have slipped away from him was maddening beyond
anything he'd ever experienced. But then, perhaps it was okay. It could be that
the cops had been snooping around his accounts and they had been closed as a
precaution by the bankers. Yeah, that was probably it. None of the banks would
have been able to reach him with his change of phone numbers. That thought
made him feel better. He would try to put it right the next day. He could certainly
put fear in the various bankers he worked with if he needed to do that.

**

Sydney and Jeremy had been talking their situation over. Jeremy would be in
trouble no matter what they did, but they both felt that punishment could be
contained to a short stint in prison.

"I think you'll be okay no matter what, Sydney," Jeremy said. "You are the
one who shot Tiny, but it was the way your dad drove that actually killed him.
You also had to shoot Snitch. The cops owe you big-time for getting rid of those
two. We don't have to let the cops know we were running from them. It would
be reasonable to say that you were running from more people who might be
planning to aid your father."

"That's true. And one cop, Detective Franklin, would have been dead if
not for me. I need to try to talk to her. Maybe that's the place to start," Sydney
said.

"It sounds good to me. Now, I need a phone," he said.

"I wonder if the cops found yours there at the house we got the old man
out of," she said thoughtfully.

"Are you thinking we should go back and try to find it?" Jeremy asked. "I don't know if that would be such a good idea."

"Wait a minute. Think about it, Jeremy. They will already have assumed that you got rid of it. They won't be trying to track you with it again. So you could go ahead and use it," she reasoned.

"Unless they've found it already. Okay, I like your thinking, Sydney. Should we go look for it now or after dark?"

"After dark, for sure. We'll take my car," she said. "Meantime, I'm hungry. We have to find something to eat."

"It will be risky," Jeremy cautioned.

"I don't think it will be too risky," she replied. "Right now the police have about all they can handle with the explosions at the hospital and with Snitch's body—if Athenya called them."

"In that case, let's venture out," he agreed. "But we need to be quick about it."

***

Athenya was in a patrol car with Sergeant Snow. She had driven around the city in turmoil for a while, frightened, sad, and lonely. Her mother was in the hospital. Her dad was who knows where. They hadn't heard from him in a very long time. She had no one else in the area to turn to. She realized that she was lucky to even be alive. She was unsure of how the cops would treat her. But she'd finally decided that she had to call them. Until she was sure her mother was okay, she wouldn't dare try to see her mother. Her mother was very ill, and Athenya was afraid she would be terribly worried if she knew what had happened to her. It would almost certainly make her mother's condition worse.

Athenya had finally made the call. Her call had been routed to Sergeant Snow, and he had met her about a mile from the hospital. He called in another officer to deal with the stolen car she'd been driving, the last one her kidnapper had taken before he'd let her go. She had said to Sergeant Snow, "I don't know what happened in that house after I was able to leave. But I think that awful man may have killed those two people. He'd even shot the lock out of the door when he found it locked. He was very angry and acting all crazy."

"Can you direct me to that house?" he'd asked.

"I think so," she'd said.

That was what she was doing now. She'd been pretty sure she could find it but had become disoriented a couple of times. Then she remembered seeing some stores nearby that included a Target. They found that, and when they did she said, "Okay, I know where to go now." A couple of minutes later, she said, "I'm pretty sure this is the street." Suddenly, she pointed and said, "It's that house right there. You can see from here that the door is shattered where the guy shot the lock out."

Sergeant Snow pulled up and parked. "Yes, I see the door," he said. "You stay here in my car while I check things out," he said.

He was gone for a couple of minutes, but when he came back out, he was on his portable radio. He stopped beside the car, and she opened the door just as he said, "That's right. There's a dead man in the house. He's been shot. Better get some officers here right away. We need to check out the rest of the house."

Athenya stepped out. "He killed the guy he called Jeremy, didn't he?"

"No, this guy looks more like the man who blew up the cars and then kidnapped you."

"Does he have the tattoo of a snake on one of his arms?" she asked. "And is he big with black hair in a ponytail?"

"Yes, you have nothing more to fear from him, Athenya. As soon as more officers get here, I'll have someone take you to where your car was taken after it was located. There is no reason you can't have it now. Then you can drive to the hospital and see your mother," he said. "I'm sorry that you have gone through so much."

"Every time I think of that guy grabbing me, I start to feel sick," she said, trembling.

"I suppose you will for a long time. You may need some counseling to help you through this. You can talk to your mother about that," Snow said. "Of course, we will be contacting you later in case we need any further information from you."

* * *

Jeremy and Sydney rolled slowly past the old house in the Millcreek area. There was no sign of police there even though there was police tape around it. They turned and went back. "Okay, I can slip under the tape and look. I think it went into those bushes right there." He pointed and she stopped the car. He slipped out.

He crawled into the shrubbery and began to search. He didn't see it right away even with the small flashlight that Sydney had given him from her jockey box. He stood up and signaled her as they had arranged earlier. Then he waited, and in a moment, he heard his phone ringing. He went back into the bushes a few feet from where he'd been and picked up his phone.

Grinning, he again stooped under the police tape and jumped into Sydney's car, and she drove off. "I'm glad the cops didn't have it, or they might have had your number now," he said with a chuckle. "But I've got it now. What's next?"

"I'm going to call Detective Franklin, and we'll see what happens after that."

* * *

Diana's phone rang, breaking the boredom that was prevailing in the hotel room and the angst she'd been feeling since she'd received a short phone call from Sergeant Snow. "Hello," she said.

"Detective Franklin, this is Sydney Greenbaum. I hope you can help me."

"Why, hello, Sydney! I haven't ever properly thanked you for saving my life the other day. What you did was both brave and selfless. Thank you. Now, what can I help you with?"

"I guess you know all about what's happened today. I suppose you were there," Sydney said.

"I know a little, but I wasn't there. My sergeant called me. It sounds pretty bad. Are you okay?" Diana asked.

"Not really," Sydney responded with a catch in her voice. "Why weren't you there? I thought every cop in the valley was involved."

Diana was very cautious. This girl had bravely defended her from her father and his henchman Tiny, but she was Saul's daughter. She had to keep that in mind. So in answer to Sydney's question she said, "I'm out of the area on an assignment."

Sydney was no dummy. "It has to do with my father, doesn't it?" she said.

"Well, yes, to a degree," Diana hedged. "But let's talk about you. Are you somehow involved in today's tragic events?"

"I'm afraid so," Sydney said. "I mean, I wasn't there, but I sort of got sucked into things afterward. Did you know about the girl who got kidnapped?"

"Yes, but I don't know the details," Diana said.

"Well, my boyfriend and I were at my house, my mother's house, as you know, and the guy brought the girl inside after he shot out our lock. He threatened to kill me and my boyfriend. I talked him into letting the girl go, and he did, but she took the stolen car he'd brought her here in," Sydney explained. "That distracted him, and I shot him."

"Oh my goodness! Was he another of your father's gang of outlaws?" Diana asked.

"Yes. He's called Snitch. He was one of the men who kidnapped the old man on my father's orders."

"I see. Did he die?"

"I am a good shot, even in a hurry," was Sydney's bland response.

Diana understood exactly what that meant. Snitch was dead. Her father would be livid. She asked, "Who is your boyfriend and why was his life threatened?"

"This is where it gets tricky," Sydney said. "Please, the help I need is for him. We are both in danger. I have no idea how many other people my father has out there, but I'm sure he has some of them after us."

"Why is it tricky? I mean, I understand that you must both be worried, but I get the feeling that there's more to the story than you're telling me," Diana said. She had signaled to Stetson, whose leg was much better now, to step close to her. He had done that and was now listening with his head close to Diana's.

"Please, if I tell you, don't tell anyone else unless you agree to help him," Sydney said, her voice strained with emotion.

"I'll do what I can. That's all I can promise. Is he with you now?"

"Yes, but no one knows where we are. We are so scared."

"First, from what you tell me, you shot this guy, did you say he's called Snitch?"

"Yes, I don't know his real name."

"But you shot him in self-defense. Is that right?"

"Yes."

"Tell me what happened and how your boyfriend is involved, and I'll do what I can to help," Diana promised.

"Okay, here goes. I'm trusting you," Sydney said with a bit of a catch in her voice. It took her a moment before she proceeded. When she did, she unfolded the entire story.

Diana listened without interruption, as did Stetson, although of course, Sydney did not know that he was listening. When she'd finished, Diana said, "Okay, so your friend did help in the kidnapping, but he was blackmailed by your father to force him to do so. In the end, he saved the life of Mr. Schiller at the risk of his own, with your help, of course."

"Yes," Sydney responded.

"So that was why this guy Snitch was after your friend. Do I have that right?" Diana asked.

"Yes, you do."

"Okay, I think I understand. But I need to caution you that your friend, whose name I still don't know, will probably be arrested and charged. What I can do is attempt to get him a much-reduced sentence or even probation. I will do what I can in that regard, but I don't know how much influence I have. I do think, though, that if Mr. Schiller lives, he will also go to bat for your friend."

"He's got to live," Sydney said, her voice breaking with emotion.

"Yes, he does. Now let's talk about what we do next, Sydney. First, we need to contact Sergeant Snow. He's my immediate supervisor. You may have to turn yourselves in to him. You need to talk about that and let me know what you decide. Are you willing to tell me where you are?" Diana asked.

"I can't. Not yet," Saul's daughter responded.

"I understand, and that will make it easier for me when I call Sergeant Snow. He'll ask me where you are, and I can truthfully tell him that I don't know," Diana said. "Call me back shortly."

"I don't need to call you back. We know this has to happen. We've had several hours to think about it and discuss our options and know this is the best," Sydney said. "But I can't lose him forever. I love him. I lost him once, thanks to my horrible father, and I won't lose him again. I can't."

"I understand. So let me call the sergeant. As I recall, you know him."

"Yes, and he was nice to me when he took me in to the station to give my statement after I shot Tiny."

"All right. I'll get back with you. But you hang in there, girl. We'll somehow get you through this. And be very careful, because you are probably right in assuming that your father has more men who will come after you," Diana said. Moments later, the call ended.

* * *

Sergeant Snow had never had so much going on at one time in his entire career. He had finally gotten back to his office after making sure that Athenya was safely back to the hospital with her mother when he was handed a note.

He read it and groaned. It stated that Mr. Lundquist requested his presence at the hospital, this time it was the University Hospital, and that it was extremely important. Everything was extremely important, it seemed. With a sigh, he went back out to his car and drove in that direction. He was thinking about Lundquist. This request, on its face, was both good news and possibly bad news. The good news was that Lundquist had regained consciousness at last. The potential bad news, to his way of thinking, was that the fellow didn't expect to live and had to tell him something that was very urgent.

As he was driving, his cell phone rang. *What now?* he wondered with a groan.

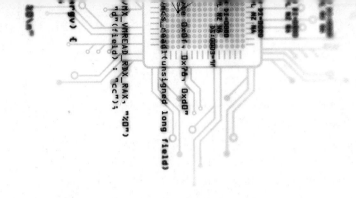

CHAPTER
TWENTY-SIX

THE CALL WAS FROM ONE of his detectives in London, Diana Franklin. "Are you busy?" she asked.

"I've never been busier, and I have a feeling you are going to add to that," he said.

"Yes, I'm afraid I am," Diana said. "Can we talk right now?"

"I'm driving to the University Hospital on an urgent request from Harry. I am still a little way from there," he said. "So what have you got?"

She wasted no words in laying out the situation with Sydney Greenbaum and her boyfriend. He let her tell him the entire story, and then he said, "I'm just pulling into the parking garage at the hospital right now. Where are Saul's daughter and her friend?"

"That she wouldn't say," Diana told him.

"I guess I expected that. Let me see what Harry wants and then I'll call you back. But one thing is for sure, and that is what you told Miss Greenbaum. She must meet me tonight at the station, and for the sake of her friend, I think he should come in too. And I will not forget that despite everything else he may have done, he did save the life of Mr. Schiller. You can call her and tell her that. Then wait for me to call you back."

"Is Harry doing better?" Diana asked as Snow got out of his car and started toward the elevators, his phone pressed to his ear.

"He must be if he requested to see me. But on the other hand, he may feel like he's going to die and wants to dump something of crucial importance into my overflowing lap. Talk to you later, Detective."

He sighed and shook his head at the same time as he approached the elevators. This Dixon matter was getting more complicated by the minute. What he wouldn't give to get his hands around Saul Greenbaum's neck. He had caused more death and mayhem than was realistically believable, and yet it was true. All the things he knew of that Saul had caused were real problems. He couldn't help but think that there were a lot more he didn't yet know about.

Sergeant Snow soon learned that Harry Lundquist was in the ICU. Snow was, after a short delay, allowed admittance. It was a place he was very familiar with, having gone there to interview shooting victims and others who were in bad condition during his years on the police force. He entered Harry's room and observed that he was hooked up to a cluster of machines. He had lines and tubes coming from his body for purposes that he could only guess at.

Stepping close to the bed, Sergeant Snow said softy, "Mr. Lundquist."

The attorney opened his eyes and focused them, after a little effort, on Snow. Then he said, "Thanks for coming, Sergeant. There is something I need you to do for me, if you will."

"I'll do whatever I can," Snow said as he observed the grayness of the man's face and the ugly bruises on it. One leg was in traction, and there was a temporary cast on one arm. He had been beaten very badly. Who knew what kind of injuries had been inflicted inside his body.

"I don't know if I will live. Even if I do, it will be a while before I can resume the leadership of my law firm," he said. Then he coughed and closed his eyes. A spasm of pain crossed his face, and then he again opened his eyes. "There is a document in a safety deposit box in the bank. It is notarized. I need for you to get it and make sure that Mr. Dixon, if he can be found, gets a copy of it. I want the original kept in the bank."

"Which bank?" Snow asked.

Harry told him and then said, "My key to that box is in the possession of my legal secretary. It is in a safe in her home. You will need to go there and get it from her and then get the document and make a copy." Harry then recited her address and phone number. "Will you take care of this for me? Roland and my entire staff need to know that Roland is now the boss. I don't think I have any other bad fruit in my basket, but after what Saul has done, I can't be sure. That will be for Roland to sort out—if you find him alive, that is. I surely pray that you do."

"I'll take care of it, and to ease your mind, Roland Dixon and his wife are safe and well at the moment, no thanks to your rogue attorney. Saul Greenbaum is on the run with warrants out for his arrest. He will be locked up for the rest of his life when he's found. He has caused a lot of death and destruction," Sergeant Snow said. "But we will hunt him down and bring him to justice."

"I regret that he ever convinced me that Roland was stealing from us. Of course, I know now that Saul did it. His actions could cost us a lot of clients, ones we need to stay in operation as a law firm. Roland is my best partner, and the document gives him the full authority to run the firm in my absence," Harry said. "He will figure out how to convince our clients to stick with us. I wronged him and hope he will be able to forgive me."

"I'll take care of it, and there is something else I need to tell you. I don't know how he did it, but Roland's genius son, Timmy, says that all of the stolen money has been recovered. I just don't know where that amazing boy has secured it, but I've learned these past few days that the kid can do just about anything he sets his mind to."

"You have no idea the relief that gives me. If anything will keep me alive, it's knowing that the Dixons as well as the money are safe. Saul's capture will help too. Thank Roland and Timmy for me when you can. Right now I better rest." And with that, Harry's eyes closed, and it appeared that he was already asleep before Snow turned away.

Sergeant Snow left the room, his mind in a whirl. He had way too much to do, but doing this errand for Harry had just become the most important. He drove toward Rachel Kessler's home. As he drove, he called Detective Franklin back.

***

Diana had spoken with Sydney again, and she and her boyfriend had been very calm. Sydney had said, "We have talked it over some more. I think that my friend would be safer in jail than not right now. He doesn't agree. He thinks there could be someone in the jail who might act on my father's behalf and that he could possibly be killed. I've argued with him, but his mind is firm, and I have to follow his wishes. But I will meet Sergeant Snow."

Diana had also said, "You know, Sydney, your father's reach seems to be pretty extensive. I would tend to agree with your friend. So I'm glad I don't know his name or where he is. But tell him to be very careful."

Sydney had responded to that with, "Believe me, he will. Thank you."

It was not long after that when Diana's phone rang, and she anxiously answered it. She listened as Sergeant Snow told her what he had learned from Mr. Lundquist. Then he said, "I'll send a copy of the power of attorney or transfer of power or whatever it is as soon as I can. But I want you to tell Mr. Dixon about it."

"Okay, I'll do that," she said.

Snow told her that the firm would be totally under his direction. "Wow. That will blow him away," Diana said.

"It's a huge responsibility for him, but Lundquist believes that he is up to it," Snow said. Then he changed the topic of discussion to Sydney Greenbaum. "Have you spoken with Sydney yet?"

"I have. She will meet you whatever time works for you at your office. I know it's getting late there, but she's anxious to tell you what she knows."

"I hope that includes the identity of her boyfriend. In fact, I hope she brings him with her."

"She would take him, but he won't agree," Diana said. "He's afraid that Mr. Greenbaum's reach is so broad that he could have him killed in the jail. He won't even begin to agree to turn himself in, and she won't say where he's at."

"Maybe she'll change her mind when I get a chance to talk to her. Okay, now back to Lundquist. I think there's a big chance that he may not survive. So it's very important that you and Detective Erman keep Mr. Dixon safe. The future of the law firm and their many clients is in his hands."

"We'll do our best," she said, and the call ended.

Stetson had not listened to the call, as he'd been away from the room, checking the hotel lobby and the area out front for any suspicious people and speaking to the two constables who had been assigned to provide security for the Americans. He hadn't been long out of the hospital and was in a lot of pain and was using a cane, but he hadn't suffered any permanent damage. He should have been in bed sleeping, but restlessness kept him going. He came back in just as Diana's call ended. "What was that about?" he asked.

"That was Sergeant Snow. Sydney Greenbaum is going to meet with our sergeant, but her boyfriend is not going to turn himself in. But that wasn't all." She turned to Roland Dixon and said, "Harry Lundquist is critically injured. He gave our sergeant some instructions regarding a document you need to know about. He will send me a copy of it for you as soon as he has a chance."

Before she could finish, Roland asked, "What is it about? Has he fired me?"

"Not by a long shot," she said. "He has given you total control of the firm in his absence. In the event he doesn't live, it gives you permanent control from then on."

Roland's face went white. For a moment, he couldn't say anything. But finally he asked, "Why me?"

"Because he has a great deal of confidence in you," she said. "He asked Sergeant Snow to let you know how sorry he is for letting Greenbaum turn him against you. As to why you, he apparently doesn't know for sure who else in the firm he can trust a hundred percent. He thinks Saul was the only bad one, but he can't be sure. Anyway, you are now in charge."

"I wonder if Harry can legally give me that much authority," Roland said.

"He must think he can," she replied.

"Yeah, I suppose so." Roland was thoughtful for a moment, and then he said, "He does own the majority of the firm and is by far the senior man there. Someone may fight it, but as long as he's alive, there isn't much anyone can do."

"Folks," Stetson said. "We need to make a decision. Once Inspector Kinser gives us permission to leave London, where should we go?"

"Home," Timmy said.

"Well, now, I don't know . . ." Stetson began, but he cut himself off when he saw the look of hope on Lilia's face.

"I think we should go back too," Roland said, and that brought a smile to his daughter's face. "As soon as I have a chance to read that paper Sergeant Snow told Diana about, I may realize that I have no choice if the firm is to be put back on solid ground, and we have a lot of clients who need that to happen."

"Let's just do it, Roland," Pamela said. "The Lord has spared our lives, and I don't believe he would have done that if he was going to let us be killed now."

"We don't have to wait, do we?" Timmy asked.

"I do want to see that power of attorney or whatever it is first," Roland said. "We can surely wait a few more minutes. Anyway, it's rather late to be leaving now. Stetson, you need to rest. You may think you're okay, but you lost a lot of blood, and I know you're in pain."

Stetson managed a grin. "They pumped more blood into me, and I have this cane. I'm good to go. I just don't think I should drive."

Lilia said, "I'll say you shouldn't. I want to go home, but why don't we all get some rest first."

"I can sleep while we travel," Stetson objected.

Diana took charge and said, "Let's look at the document when I get it and then we'll decide for sure, if you feel like you can travel, Stetson."

"I can travel," he said, even though his face showed that his recent foray down to the lobby and around had been very hard on him.

No one spoke for several minutes. Timmy was not on his computer. He was sitting with it on his lap on the floor with a very long face. Lilia led Stetson to a bed and made him lie down. She then knelt on the floor beside him with her head against his shoulder. Roland was pacing while his wife simply stood and watched him with love in her eyes.

Diana was watching all of them, thinking about how much she'd come to care for each one of them. She was worried. With Stetson injured, the bulk of the responsibility for protecting them had fallen on her shoulders. She was determined not to fail them.

Finally, she heard a text come in. She opened it. Roland walked over to her, and she said, "Yes, it's the document. I'll open it."

She did, and he said, "Forward it to Timmy's computer, where it will be easier to read." So she did that, and at Roland's request, Timmy opened his laptop and found the document. Roland sat next to Timmy on the floor, and Timmy pushed the computer onto his father's lap. He read quietly for two or three minutes.

When he finally looked up, he said, "I guess this is it. I'm in charge of the law firm. I've got to get back to Salt Lake. But I don't know that all of you need to come."

Diana responded firmly, "Roland, whatever we do, we all do it together. That's all there is to it."

Stetson's eyes were closed, but he said, "Then let's see about getting back to Utah."

At that point, no one disagreed. The only question now was when they should leave. Diana said, "I'll call the inspector and let him know."

She did that, and after explaining why they wanted to return, he said, "Let us make the arrangements for you, and then we'll take you to the airport and stay with you until you are on the plane. I want to make sure you have no other difficulties while you're in my area." He paused just briefly before asking, "Is Detective Erman up to this?"

"He says he is," Diana said.

"All right. You're safe there in your hotel rooms for now. Why don't you all get some rest. I'll let you know as soon as your travel arrangements are made," Inspector Kinser said. "By the way, we have made no progress on locating Mr. Greenbaum. But we are looking hard."

***

Sydney was nervous when she had to leave Jeremy. She'd missed him so much for so long that now, by a miracle she had not expected to ever experience, he'd come back into her life. She greatly feared losing him again. They were sitting on the edge of the bed in the dingy hotel room they'd rented, their arms around each other.

"I hope you can trust Sergeant Snow," Jeremy said. "I know I'm going to have to face up to what I've done, but I'm not sure they won't put me in prison for a long time. The more I think about it, the more I want to just run."

"Not without me, you won't," she said. "I think we can trust the authorities. I sure hope so. We've actually helped them a lot. But if you decide you simply won't turn yourself in for fear of what my father could cause to happen to you in jail, then we'll go away together."

Sydney's heart ached over the sadness she saw in Jeremy's eyes. She honestly hadn't realized how much she loved him and had missed him until he showed up in her life again.

"Let me know when you leave the police station," Jeremy said. "I just hope they don't arrest you."

"They can't arrest me," she insisted. "I haven't broken the law."

"You killed a man," he said.

"You don't need to remind me of that," she said as she tightened her arms around him. "I keep seeing his leering face, and that of Tiny. It will be a long time before I get over what I did, what I had to do."

"Sweetheart, you may never get over it," he said. "But what you did made the world a safer place. You better go now. You don't want to irritate Snow. I worry enough about what they might do to you as it is."

Sydney pulled away and stood up. "Now I'm worried," she said. "But I am going to go. I gave my word."

Jeremy stood as well. Sydney hugged him again, kissed him, and then with solid resolution, she left the motel room, making sure it was locked behind her. She was about halfway to the police station when she had a disturbing thought. Surely Jeremy wouldn't, out of sheer desperation, leave the motel room. She slowed the car as indecision entered her mind, but then decided she couldn't go back. So she drove on.

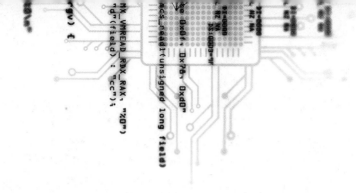

CHAPTER
TWENTY-SEVEN

SAUL GREENBAUM WAS TRYING TO get a flight back to Utah while doing all he could to avoid the London police. He could not get a straight answer on where his money had gone, and he only had about fifty thousand dollars in his personal accounts in a couple of different banks in Utah. So far, as near as he could tell, that money was untouched. He needed that, and he had some debts to settle that were not financial. He still had two or three more guys he thought he could bully into helping. Even then, he needed to be in Utah to accomplish what he needed done. So despite his misgivings, that was where he was going.

He had made some attempts to disguise himself. He thought he'd done pretty well. He'd bought a fedora, a hat like he'd never worn before, had dark glasses, shaved his head, and shaved off his neatly trimmed beard. He wore a loose jacket with extra-long arms to hide the cast on his left arm. He hoped to soon have a flight arranged. He wanted his money back, the money he had risked so much for, and someone was going to make that happen or pay with his or her life.

***

Sydney was more fearful now as she was walking from her car to the police station than she had been when she faced down both Tiny and Snitch. Both of those times, it had all happened so fast that she didn't really have a lot of time to get scared—she just felt the adrenaline kick in and did what had to be done.

She knew she'd made the right choice in both of those cases, but doubts assailed her mind the closer she got to her meeting with Sergeant Snow. Jeremy may be right, and she could get arrested. She stopped just outside the door and considered her options. She could go pick up Jeremy and run, or she could go on inside.

She really had no doubt about what she should do. So she gathered the courage she needed and proceeded into the station. A couple of minutes later, she was with Sergeant Snow. He gave her what she could tell was a very tired smile, and he asked her to sit down. "Miss Greenbaum, I appreciate you coming in. I wish your friend would too. He's in trouble, but he did a brave and selfless thing in saving Mr. Schiller's life. I just spoke to the old gentleman on the phone. He's stable there in the hospital in Murray and was able to take my call. There is no question that you and your boyfriend saved his life. He knows it, and he made sure I knew it."

"I'm just scared for my friend, Sergeant, and he's scared. I'm glad that Mr. Schiller is doing better. It really frightened me when we were taking him to the hospital. I wasn't sure we'd be able to get him there on time," she said.

"He's grateful, I can tell you that. So are my colleagues and I. Now, let's go over the events that occurred at your home earlier today. As in our previous interview, when you had to shoot the guy called Tiny, I will need to record this," Snow said. He fiddled with his recorder for a moment, and as he did, he said, "May I call you Sydney?"

"Yes," she said, her voice cracking.

He smiled that same exhausted smile and said, "You can relax, Sydney. I don't bite. Honest I don't."

She forced a weak smile and said, "I can't help it. I could have died today."

"I understand that," the sergeant said. "And I suppose that you are worried that I might arrest you. Well, don't worry. I don't plan to do any such thing, as I'm quite sure you will be able to justify your actions like you did before."

She nodded and he started the recording. After giving the introductory information that he needed, he began to question her. He was gentle and did not try to rush her. She was soon much more relaxed and was able to give him a decent rendition of the events that had been thrust upon her. For over a half hour he continued to ask questions and in turn listen to her answers.

Finally, after ending the recording, he said, "Sydney, you are a brave woman. Not many could have handled the situation like you did. You are to be commended."

"Thank you," she said. "But I know I'll have nightmares for a long time to come. I already have been having a hard time sleeping because of Tiny."

"That's quite normal. I would recommend that you get some counseling as soon as you can," he said.

"I guess I can do that, if it will help."

"Oh yes, it will help. Believe me, I know what I'm talking about. Don't allow yourself to suffer when there is help available," he said.

"Thank you," she replied. "I will when I can. Right now, I'm just afraid that my dad will show up, and I know what he'll do to me if he finds me."

"You are safe from him for the time being, Sydney. He is not even in the country right now, although we don't know how he managed that. We took his passport. He should have never been able to get on a plane."

"That would never stop him," she said. "I'm sure he got one forged with a false name."

"He must have done, but if he's smart, he won't come back here. He's facing several murder charges now. Some are for men who had helped him kidnap the Dixons."

"He killed them?" she asked as she felt her fear level rise substantially.

"He did, and we have some solid evidence. He wasn't nearly as smart as he must have thought he was."

Sydney felt a chill come over her body. "So even though I'm his daughter, he really would kill me if he could, wouldn't he?"

Sergeant Snow slowly nodded. "Yes, Sydney, I believe he would. I would suggest that you find a place to stay for a few days. I don't think you will want to go back to your house right now."

"I don't, that's for sure," she agreed. "I guess my mother shouldn't either. She doesn't even know what's happened. She will be so angry with my dad. She bought that house without any help from him. She's worked so hard to be self-sufficient."

"Actually, she does know what happened," the sergeant said. "In cases like this we are very thorough. I'm sorry if that upsets you, but I had one of my officers call her. We told her to not hurry back but to let us know when she was coming."

"I can't believe she hasn't called me," Sydney said.

"We asked her not to until later tonight. So you should be hearing from her pretty soon. Sydney, there is one more thing. I suppose you have the weapon you used today with you. I know it's not the one you used in the incident with Tiny because we still have it. I'm afraid I will need this one too."

Reluctantly, she pulled it out of her purse and handed it to him. He wrote her a receipt and then said, "Thank you, you may go now, Sydney, and be careful, please."

She left the police station feeling extremely vulnerable. She couldn't believe she hadn't thought about them seizing her gun, but she should have. Now she was in a tough situation. She still owned another gun, and she guessed she'd have to get it. The only problem was that it was at her father's house.

She'd left it there when she and her mother had first moved out. She'd been only sixteen at the time, but it was hers. However, her father had forbidden her to take it. She was pretty sure she could find it, for he kept his guns all together in a gun case in his home office. If it wasn't there, he might have one she could take. She certainly had no feelings of guilt about taking one of his if that's what she needed to do.

She thought about stopping and talking to Jeremy first but decided to just get it done. She was very vulnerable without a weapon. For all she knew, one of her father's henchmen could be looking for her right now or might even be following her. She shivered at that thought and kept a close watch in her mirrors. She couldn't see anything to alarm her, so with renewed determination, she drove straight to her father's house.

She drove past it once, just checking it out. Then she turned back, pulled into the curved driveway, and stopped. She opened the front door with the key she still had. She wasted no time but went straight to her father's home office. The large cherrywood gun case was exactly as she had remembered, and it contained a variety of rifles and shotguns and three pistols. She took the one that was hers and started walking away, but suddenly she turned back on a whim and took the other pistols.

She found bullets for each of the guns, put hers in her purse and the others in a paper sack she found in his kitchen, and headed out to her car. She put the two pistols of her father's in the trunk, and before she shut the lid, she stood there for a minute thinking about her father. If he came back, he would want to arm himself; she was quite sure. She decided to make that hard for him. She left the trunk open, hurried back inside, and came back out a minute later carrying all of his rifles and shotguns. She dumped them in the trunk and shut it. She looked around. She hoped no one had seen her. She hadn't seen anyone, so she felt like she'd be okay.

She drove toward the little motel, which was several miles away, thinking about Jeremy. She hoped he would be okay with what she'd done in taking the guns. She parked in the parking lot behind the motel and out of sight of the street. She glanced around the parking lot and felt a knot form in her stomach when she didn't see Jeremy's Jeep parked there. She ran around to the front of the motel and to the room and unlocked the door. He was not there.

She broke into a sweat. She'd been sure he'd wait there for her. She stepped in, shut the door, and glanced around the room. There was a sheet of paper on the bed. She picked it up and read it, then slowly sank to the floor and held her knees. The note had been written by Jeremy. He told her he was sorry for leaving but was afraid not to. He promised that he would contact her sometime soon and told her not to worry about him. The last thing that he'd written was that there was someone he needed to see and that he was going to do that now.

She was still sitting there when she heard voices outside her door. She jumped up and ran to the door and looked through the peep hole. Two officers stood there with their pistols in their hands. One raised his hand and knocked. She ran back across the room, grateful that they'd obtained a ground-floor unit. She slipped the old window open and climbed out. She ran to her car, glad she'd parked back there, jumped in, and drove toward the street.

Before pulling away from the motel, she looked back just long enough to see that the door to her room was hanging open. She gunned her car and sped away. The police must have followed her. For all she knew, they had seen her take her father's guns. Anger at Sergeant Snow rushed through her.

As she drove, she thought about how nice he'd been to her. She couldn't believe that all during that interrogation, he'd been planning on letting her lead them to Jeremy so he could be arrested.

She pulled her phone from her purse as she drove. She called Jeremy's number. As she feared, it went to voice mail after several rings. She left a message on his voice mail, telling him that he'd done right in getting away, that the cops had come after him. Then she begged him to call her so they could get together and decide what to do next.

***

Sergeant Snow was feeling guilty about leaving Sydney with the impression that he was not going to try to arrest Jeremy, even though he had not actually told her that he wouldn't. It was only after she'd been gone for several minutes that he made the decision to send a couple of officers after him. In his mind, he felt that by arresting her friend he might actually be saving the young man's life. It was too late by then for them to follow her from the police station, so he'd sent them to her father's house, thinking that she might go there looking for a gun, for he could see that she was not happy about him seizing her weapon, and yet she had not been devastated, which gave him the idea that she might go after one of her father's guns.

The officers reported that they had located her car as she drove away from Saul Greenbaum's house, had followed her to a little motel quite a number of miles away, and had waited until after she'd gone inside. Then they'd gone in.

"She was gone?" he asked when they told her the room was empty when they entered but that a window was open. "You didn't cover the back of the motel?" he scolded.

They were sheepish, but one of them handed him a paper that he told her they'd found on the bed. He read it and pounded one fist in the other. It was a note from the man who must be her boyfriend. His name was Jeremy, and the note was to Sydney, explaining that he didn't dare stay there. He excused the officers, and in a way, he felt okay about Jeremy being on the run. He didn't blame him. He might have done the same if their roles had been reversed. Exhausted both mentally and physically, he left for home. He needed to get some rest.

* * *

Sydney couldn't believe she'd failed to get the note Jeremy had written from where she'd dropped it on the bed. She tried to remember his words. As she recalled the last phrase, she felt a shiver of excitement run through her. She had an idea where she might find him.

* * *

Jeremy was nervous. He knew he couldn't stay here too long, and yet he hoped that Sydney, as smart as he knew her to be, would take the clue he'd given her in the note and act on it at once.

He and Gabriel had visited for several minutes. "I am so relieved that you are going to be okay," Jeremy told the old fellow.

"You saved my life. I told Sergeant Snow that I owe you my life," Gabriel said.

"No, I only saved you from what I caused in the first place," Jeremy said.

The old fellow smiled. "I can see the kind of man you are. I have a feeling that Mr. Greenbaum forced you to do what you did. I forgive you," Gabriel said. "Will you tell me what he did to make you help that other man kidnap me?"

"It's only an excuse," Jeremy said. "I shouldn't have done it."

"Please tell me," Gabriel said with some urgency in his voice.

So Jeremy did so. He was totally honest in the things he'd done in the past that Greenbaum helped him get through. Gabriel listened without interruption. At one point, Jeremy thought he'd gone to sleep. But when he paused, Gabriel's eyes opened. "Keep going," he said.

When Jeremy finished telling him about the threat on Sydney's life, one by her own father, if Jeremy didn't help with the kidnapping, Gabriel groaned. It alarmed him. He leaned over and asked, "Do I need to get a nurse in here?"

Gabriel said, "No, no, young man. I didn't mean to groan like that, but I couldn't help it when you told me how what you did was to save the life of the girl you love. How could any man do such a thing or even threaten to do it to his own flesh and blood?"

The door opened to his room, and a sweet voice said, "May I come in?"

Jeremy's heart leaped with relief. "I wasn't sure you would know what I meant in that note. I'm so glad you did."

Gabriel said, "Please come in, young lady. Thank you for what you did for me."

Sydney took hold of Jeremy's hand and smiled down at the old man. "You're welcome, Mr. Schiller," she said.

"Please, call me Gabriel. That's what my friends call me, and you are both my friends," he said.

They visited for a couple more minutes, and then Jeremy said, "We need to go now, Gabriel. Thank you for letting me confess to you. I feel so much better now."

Sydney leaned down and kissed the forehead of Gabriel. As she stood back up, he asked, "What are you two young people going to do now?"

Jeremy said, "I don't know for sure. I want to turn myself in, but I'm afraid to."

"Follow your heart, young man," Gabriel said. "It will lead you in the right direction."

They left then, and in the hallway, Jeremy said, "I'm so glad you understood my note. I just had to come see Gabriel."

"I understand, but if I figured out what you meant, I think Sergeant Snow might figure it out too."

"How? Don't you have the note?" he asked in alarm.

"No, I was in such a hurry that I left it on the bed when I went out of the window," she said.

"What? Why did you do that?" he asked in alarm.

"I was scared," she confessed. "I'm sorry. But the police are after you. Let's get out of here, and then we can decide where to go once we are away from the hospital. I'll tell you all about my time with the sergeant, but first we need to go somewhere, and we can't go back to our motel."

"I don't want to be away from you again," he moaned.

"Then we'll leave your car here and go in mine. We only need one now anyway," Sydney suggested.

Once they were in her car, they started to leave the lot, but then she stopped when she saw two police cars racing up to the hospital entrance. "Let's see if anyone else comes before we go," he suggested. They waited a couple of minutes, and then he said, "Maybe that's all. Let's go."

Jeremy's heart raced until they were clear of the area. "I think we made it," he said. And then he added, "I love you, Sydney."

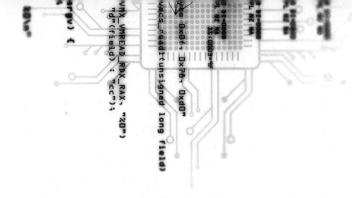

CHAPTER
TWENTY-EIGHT

LILIA WAS SO GLAD TO be heading back to Utah with her family intact that she didn't complain about the long wait they had before they could get on their flight. Timmy, however, seemed unusually nervous. Stetson, who was sitting next to her, also noticed the boy's agitation. He said, "Timmy, come sit here and let's talk."

He hadn't wandered far, but Lilia didn't want him to be anywhere but right here with them. Diana was standing nearby like a guard. She was ever alert, her eyes darting around the area. Stetson was not having a great day. He'd overdone it. He should have allowed more time for his injury to heal. But he, like the others, wanted to get back to Utah.

Timmy sat next to Stetson, holding his computer bag in his hand. Lilia leaned around Stetson and asked, "Something's bothering you, little brother. What is it?"

"It's nothing. I'm just nervous. I'm anxious to get home," he said evasively.

Lilia wasn't buying it. She said, "Timmy, please. What's wrong?"

For a moment he just sat there, his eyes down and his lips closed tightly. Finally he said, "What if Saul gets back home before we do?"

"Hey, kiddo," Stetson said with a cheerful smile on his face. "Do you forget that he's got every cop in England looking for him?"

"I know, but he got away from Utah with every cop there looking for him," he reasoned. "What if he has some of those guys he hires waiting for us when we get home?"

"We've talked about all of that," Stetson reminded him. "We will have some of Diana's friends and mine looking out for us. We'll be okay. We aren't taking any chances."

Just then, boarding for first-class passengers was announced. Lilia watched as they moved toward the gate. One guy carried only a small carry-on and a computer bag. Not that that was unusual, but he carried them both in the same hand. For some reason she couldn't grasp, that bothered her. A few minutes later, they were among those instructed to board.

As they passed through the first-class area, Lilia noticed the guy she'd observed earlier. He had a gray fedora pulled down close to the dark glasses he still wore. His head was bald, and he was clean shaven. He had not taken the large coat off even though it was not cold on the plane. She glanced at him as she passed. He seemed to take no notice of her. She went on, and they soon had their few pieces of small luggage stored in the overhead bins.

They were all seated on the right side of the plane, with Diana and Stetson on the aisle seats. They occupied six seats, three right in front of the other three. Timmy was at the window with Lilia between him and Stetson. Roland and Pamela were behind them with Diana watching people as they passed beside her.

Timmy was fidgeting with his phone. She wasn't sure why. They were not going to be calling anyone. They would soon be required to put them in airplane mode. Lilia's was in her purse, which she kept on her lap. She leaned over and whispered in Stetson's ear. "Timmy wasn't like this when we flew here. Something's bothering him."

Stetson reminded her, "He told us he's worried about Saul being there ahead of us."

She shook her head and whispered, "It's more than that. I can't figure it out."

"Well, he's safe here. So don't worry. When we get to Salt Lake, we'll see if we can get him to tell us. Just relax, Lilia. We have a lot to be grateful for. Your whole family is together, and we are on our way home," he said.

"I know, and I am grateful. I just wish that Saul hadn't gotten away," she said. "He could be anywhere by now."

***

Saul was gloating. He had the Dixons within his sights. He could barely suppress a chuckle. What were the odds of getting on the same plane with them for the flight home? He knew they had a plane change in New York, but so did he, and he was almost certain to still be on the same flight as them. He had a couple of calls to make on his latest phone. He'd already applied some heavy pressure to a couple of ex-cons he had some information on. Blackmail always worked well with the kind of men he used to do his dirty work. He hoped they would answer his call this time.

He pulled his phone out. The plane was still on the tarmac, but it wouldn't be for long. He punched in a number. He smiled when he got an answer. He said, "You know who this is. I'm on my way back to Utah. I'll need you at the airport when I land. The people I need disposed of are on the same flight as me. I'll text you the details."

Before the guy could respond, he ended the call. Then he made a second call to another man. He repeated what he had just said. Then he wrote a text message to both of them. He included the flight number of the plane from New York to Salt Lake that they would be on along with photos of the Dixons he'd carefully snapped as they'd boarded the plane. He explained where they were to be watching for them when the plane landed in Salt Lake City. He told them they were to trail the Dixons from the terminal and then take care of business when they got to the parking area.

He also texted them copies of the photos he had taken of the two officers who were with the Dixons as they'd boarded the plane. The young male officer was limping and using a cane. That was the officer he'd shot and wished he'd killed. The other one was the woman who had tried to arrest him at his home. It was her fault that he'd had to flee from the country. He had a burning hatred for both of the officers.

He gave his men instructions that they were to be eliminated as well. He told them if they needed extra help to get it. He reminded them of the consequences if they didn't do exactly what he instructed them to do. Failure was not an option if they valued their freedom, or for that matter, their lives. He sent the messages and then put his phone in his pocket and smiled to himself. He relaxed in the comfort of his first-class seat.

* * *

Timmy continued to be withdrawn as the big plane winged its way across the Atlantic. Lilia had a hard time sleeping. She was worried about her little brother. Stetson, on the other hand, slept most of the way, and she didn't mind since she knew how badly he needed the rest.

She wished they didn't have to change planes in New York, but it couldn't be helped. Diana and Stetson instructed them as they prepared to deplane that they were to stay between the two of them. It had taken some strong negotiating on the part of Detective Inspector Kinsley, but both officers had been allowed to carry weapons on the flight and would continue to do so after they boarded the next flight destined for Salt Lake City.

Lilia caught a brief glimpse of the bald-headed man in the fedora as he deplaned ahead of them. She wondered if he was also going on to Salt Lake City, although that idea seemed remote. As they started to walk up the concourse, Timmy suddenly ran ahead for some unknown reason. The man in the fedora had stopped and was facing them. Timmy stopped right beside him and shouted, "This is Saul!"

Saul's left arm shot out and caught Timmy violently on the side of his head with the cast. He flew to the side and landed in a heap as other travelers jumped out of the way. Saul followed up with a kick to the boy's head. One woman screamed as the man in the fedora shoved her violently out of his way, knocking her to the ground. He then fled at a run up the concourse. Diana shouted at Stetson, "Stay with Timmy. I'll try to catch Saul."

Lilia was stunned. She dropped beside her brother, as did her parents and Stetson. He was out cold. Stetson was checking his vital signs and said, "His breathing and heart rate are fine. We just need to give him time to wake up." They were joined by a stranger who announced himself as a medical doctor. Stetson looked at him suspiciously. Then he said, "He'll be fine, Doctor. He's just unconscious, but I don't think it will be for long."

"I am Dr. Black. I am a brain surgeon from Los Angeles. I think you should let me check him. He took a couple of very hard blows," the doctor said. "That man appeared to have something under his coat, something very hard."

"I'm sorry, but no stranger is getting close to him," Roland said as he stepped between Timmy and the doctor. "I'm sure your intentions are good, but we'll take care of him."

The doctor said, "Please, I should check him. He probably has a concussion. Let me check for that."

"Doctor," Stetson said as he stood up, "the man who hit him is a dangerous killer. I am a police detective. You can see that I have injures. That man shot me in England. We fear that he may have some confederates here somewhere."

"Let me show you my credentials," the doctor said. He reached inside his jacket. Stetson had his hand on his pistol but did not pull it out. "Here, look at this."

Roland took the man's credentials and looked them over, showed them to Stetson, and then handed them back. "Okay, you may check him," Roland said.

Dr. Black did just that. As he did, a couple of security officers joined them. Stetson explained briefly what was happening. "My partner is after the man who struck this boy. Please alert everyone to be watching for him. He is a dangerous killer."

Stetson gave the officers Saul's description, for he was convinced that it was Saul who had hit Timmy so violently. Timmy could not have been mistaken when he identified him. One of the security officers got on his radio. Stetson turned his attention back to Timmy and Dr. Black.

Lilia was fighting back tears. She couldn't believe this had happened. She kept looking up the concourse, hoping to see Diana leading Saul back, but she was nowhere in sight. Her stomach roiled with tension.

Dr. Black stood up and said, "This boy needs to be in a hospital. Let me help you make arrangements. In fact, I can get another flight to LA. I think I should stay with him. This could be serious. We need to make sure he doesn't have a brain bleed, but it's possible, as hard as he was hit. If he does, he'll need special care."

***

Diana had almost caught up with Saul once, but the concourse was crowded, and people kept getting in her way. Saul kept shoving people aside. One lady hit her head against a counter at a food booth. Diana shouted, "Someone take care of this woman. I'm a police officer, and this man is a killer."

She continued her pursuit. Saul looked back at her, and when he did, he ran into a man who hadn't seen him coming. Both of them went to the floor. Saul's carry-on bag and his computer case came free of his hand. The man Saul had run into was cursing at Saul. He started to his feet, but Saul hit him with his left arm, and the guy went down again as Saul surged to his feet.

Diana got there in time to get a hand on Saul's arm, but he shook her free, throwing her down hard on the floor. He took off running again, deserting his belongings, including the fedora, which had fallen off his bald head during the collision. A security officer showed up, and Diana pointed Saul out as she struggled to her feet. The officer asked if he was the killer they had been told to look for. She said, "Yes, he has to be stopped."

The man said that they would get him, and he took off at a sprint in pursuit. Diana turned her attention to the man on the floor. He was starting to get up again. Diana spoke to him briefly, explaining who she was and asked if he was okay. The man said he was and got to his feet. He started on his way again, grumbling to himself.

Diana picked up Saul's computer bag and carry-on luggage. She let the fedora lay where it had fallen. Her phone rang. She answered it. "Diana." It was Stetson. "We need to get Timmy to a hospital. There is a doctor here with us. I don't suppose you've caught Saul."

"I'm afraid not. But a security officer took off after him." She explained what had just happened. Then she said, "I'll head back your way."

"Okay, they are coming with a stretcher for the boy. He took a couple of awful blows. The doctor, a brain surgeon, is very concerned about him."

"I'll be right there," she said and started to jog back down the concourse.

* * *

Saul Greenbaum was not in very good physical shape, and he was rapidly running out of energy. He was breathing hard, his chest hurt, and his legs burned. He kept running into people, knocking them aside, but he didn't care. He was desperate to get away. He was aware of someone running behind him. Whoever it was shouted for him to stop. That only made him run faster.

A hand grabbed his shoulder from behind. He tried to swing the only weapon he had, his casted left arm, but he was unable to before he was dragged to the ground. He couldn't imagine where all the men in uniforms had come from, but he found himself surrounded. He kicked and flailed his arms. But it was to no avail, and he soon found himself unable to move his arms or legs.

Saul Greenbaum, deadly killer, hardened thief, hateful man, started to bawl as he was dragged away.

* * *

Two hours later, while waiting in the hospital for the still-unconscious Timmy to undergo tests, Stetson and Diana were busy on their phones. Stetson was talking to a security officer from the airport who told him that he had the suspect's phone. Stetson told him to keep it and someone would pick it up later. The officer told him that he would prefer to bring it to him at the hospital if he was going to be there for a while. That was agreed to. Stetson just wasn't sure how they would be able to open the phone with Timmy, the expert, out of commission.

Diana was on her phone with Sergeant Snow. She gave him an abbreviated version of what had occurred, assured him that Saul was in custody, and then said, "We will not be on the flight, Sergeant. I'll let you know what happens next. We are all terribly worried about Timmy Dixon. We are not leaving here until we know how he is."

"You and Stetson stay with the Dixons," he instructed her. "Even though Saul is in custody, there could be others who might present a danger to you."

"There is one other thing, Sergeant," she said. "I have Saul's computer, and Stetson just whispered to me that Saul's phone is being brought to us from the airport. Would it be possible to have someone prepare search warrants for both of them? If Timmy Dixon wakes up and is okay, he might be able to help us open them."

"We'll get on it," Sergeant Snow promised her.

An hour later, Stetson was holding Saul's phone. The security officer had wasted no time getting it to him. He tried to open it, but as he feared, even though it was a new and rather inexpensive phone, it was password protected. "If only Timmy would wake up," he said to Diana. "We could sure use his expertise."

Suddenly, the phone began to ring. Stetson looked at Diana, who said, "Answer it. Then we'll have the phone opened."

Stetson said, "Hello," as he put Saul's phone on speaker mode.

The voice on the other end sounded angry. "Boss, this is Jimmy, Snitch's brother. What's going on? We've been waiting for the Dixons and those two cops to get off the plane, but they haven't shown up. I have five guys waiting. We are watching all the exits. I'm not sure what to do."

"Keep waiting," Stetson said. "Their flight may have been delayed."

He glanced at Diana, who was already getting to her feet with her phone in her hand. "See if you can keep him talking," she whispered and stepped away as Stetson took the phone off speaker mode.

As soon as her call was answered, Diana said, "Sergeant Snow, this is Detective Franklin again. Saul has some men waiting at the airport for us to get off the plane. The idiot called Saul's phone, and Stetson is talking to him now on it." She quickly explained what they knew, including the name Jimmy Horentz.

"We'll see if we can catch them," Snow said.

After Diana had ended her call, Stetson again put Saul's phone on speaker. The crook on the phone with Stetson shouted, "You will owe me, Saul. You owe all of us. It's not our fault the people aren't here. We would have killed them by now had they been on time."

"The plane has been delayed," Stetson said. "Stay there. They will be getting off in the next few minutes."

Jimmy ended the call, but Stetson was able to keep the phone open.

"It sounds like Saul had a greeting party awaiting us at the airport in Salt Lake," Stetson grimly said to Diana.

"Let's hope Sergeant Snow and some others catch them while they're still there," Diana responded, equally as grimly.

They walked across the waiting room to where the Dixons were all waiting, their faces strained and their eyes red. Lilia got up and approached Stetson. She put her arms around him, and he hugged her tightly. "He'll be okay," he said.

"I wish we knew that," she responded, her voice choking.

"We've all got to have faith," he reminded her.

"We are trying, but it is so hard."

A few minutes later, Dr. Black, who had been allowed by the resident surgeons to go back with Timmy, came into the waiting room. "Mr. and Mrs. Dixon, Timmy will need to have surgery. And it needs to be now." His voice was filled with urgency. "You both need to come with me. They need a signature before they can take him down to surgery. I won't be able to be with him, but I have a great deal of confidence in the surgeons here. As soon as they take him, I'll come and wait with all of you."

After her parents had left with Dr. Black, Lilia said, "I am so scared. What if he dies? I can't stand it."

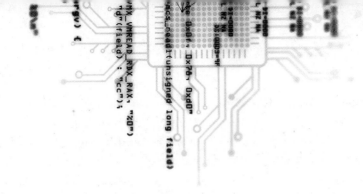

CHAPTER
TWENTY-NINE

THE HOURS DRAGGED. IT WAS like the clock had stopped. Lilia spent much of her time as she sat beside Stetson with her eyes closed, begging the Lord to spare Timmy's life. She could see that her parents were doing the same thing. She loved them so much. They had been through an unimaginable ordeal, and then to have it end with Timmy's life hanging in the balance was more than any parent should have to go through.

Diana had been on the phone from time to time. At one point, she had walked over to where she and Stetson were seated and said, "Stetson, Sergeant Snow says that all of the five men at the airport have been arrested. The leader of the group was the guy you talked to, Jimmy Horentz. He started talking almost immediately. He has told them a lot. Saul will never be free again. And he will almost certainly face the death penalty."

Diana joined them again later and said, "Mr. Dixon, I'm afraid I have really bad news. Harry Lundquist has passed away. On the other hand, Gabriel Schiller is doing very well and will probably be released from the hospital tomorrow."

Roland put his head in his hands. "I am just sick. To think that Saul and his greed has caused all this trouble and that even Harry lost his life because of that man's actions. I feel a heavy burden. I hope I can do what Harry wanted me to do. I'm not anywhere near prepared for so much responsibility."

Pamela put her hand on his and said, "You will do great, Roland. I have faith in you, and I know Harry did too."

A couple more hours passed, and Dr. Black came into the waiting room with the chief surgeon, a fellow Dr. Black introduced as Dr. Kellar. "He'll tell you about the surgery."

Dr. Kellar said, "Timmy's injury was very severe. His brain took a shock. There was some bleeding, but we were able to stop it. I have every reason to believe that he will recover, but I can't promise that he won't have some difficulties with things like memory, reasoning, and other skills. He will be in a coma for a couple of days. We want to keep him that way to give his brain time to sort itself out, so to speak. He will be in the hospital for a few weeks. But I am confident that he is going to live."

The sighs of relief were audible. It was Roland who asked, "So he will no longer be the genius that we've always known."

"Genius?" Dr. Kellar asked, lifting an eyebrow.

"Yes. He's only twelve, but he has always been extremely intelligent. He's had a photographic memory, and when it comes to things like computers, he's absolutely unbelievable," Roland said.

"Also, he is very physically fit," Lilia said. "Do you think he will forget things like his karate skills?"

Dr. Black and Dr. Kellar looked at each other. It was Dr. Kellar that said, "We can only hope he eventually recovers both his physical and mental skills. But I can't promise anything. Although I will say that I've never operated on anyone with a mind like you tell me he has. Who knows, maybe he'll surprise us all. I certainly hope he does."

"How soon will we be able to see him?" Pamela asked.

"Someone will come get you in an hour or so. But remember, he will be in a coma for a while. However, you should talk to him, express your love, and treat him as though he were awake. There's a lot we don't know about the human brain, but I know that many times people who have been in a coma remember things that were told to them, and sometimes very clearly." Dr. Kellar shrugged his shoulders. "Who knows, he may be one of those."

After the doctors had left, Diana said, "I need to make another phone call."

***

Sydney and the man she loved were sitting in a restaurant in Phoenix when her phone rang. She answered when she saw it was Diana, the one police officer she still trusted, and as far as she knew the only one who had her phone number. She said, "Hello, Detective. How are you?"

"I'm doing okay," Diana told her. "The big question is, how are you?"

"I'm fine," Sydney said, knowing that she was very much not fine. She still feared that she could be arrested if she returned to Salt Lake even though she had been assured she would not be.

"Listen, Sydney, have you been keeping up with things the past two days?" the detective asked her.

"No. I just wish my dad would be caught. He's ruined my life."

"He's ruined lots of lives. He's destroyed lots of lives. But that's over now. He's in custody, and he will not be getting out."

"Are you serious? Someone arrested him?"

"Yes. Sydney, are you somewhere we can talk for a little while?" the detective asked.

Sydney looked across the table at Jeremy. He was stressed almost to the point of falling apart. They'd talked a lot about going back to Salt Lake and turning themselves in. To the detective she said, "Yes, I guess so."

"Then let me tell you what's been going on." For the next few minutes, Sydney listened to Detective Franklin.

When the detective told her about Timmy Dixon and what her father had done to him, she felt like her heart would rupture. It was all so horrible. She said with tears in her eyes, "I'm so sorry about what my father has done."

"Listen, Sydney, you and your friend, whoever he is, should come back to Salt Lake from wherever you are. Your dad's boss is dead, and Mr. Dixon is now in charge of the law firm. Mr. Schiller is going to be fine. He has nothing but good to say about you and your friend. Sergeant Snow has talked with the District Attorney. He has promised both of you that he will not file charges on either of you if you will come back and testify against your father."

"I don't trust Sergeant Snow," Sydney said with a bite to her voice.

"Do you trust me?" Diana asked.

"Well, yes, I think so."

"Okay, so let's do this. I'll have a written promise from the DA that I will show you if you meet me somewhere. I'll see that you are both okay. You have my word. You saved my life, and I will be grateful to you for as long as I live. Please, do this," Detective Franklin urged.

"Are you back in Salt Lake?"

"No, but I will be by tomorrow. I'm still at the hospital with my partner, Detective Erman, and the Dixon family."

"Can I call you back?" Sydney asked.

"Of course. I'll be waiting."

After the call ended, Sydney told Jeremy what Detective Franklin had just told her. He sighed, rubbed his forehead, and then said, "Let's do it. I can't live like this anymore."

She called the detective right back. "It will take us a while to get back to Salt Lake. Can I call you when we get close? We both think we need to do this."

They agreed and the call ended. "Let's head back as soon as we finish eating," Jeremy said.

* * *

The next day, Lilia said to Stetson, who, along with Diana, was still waiting with the family in the hospital in New York, "Dad is worried about the firm. He's worried that he doesn't know where the money Timmy recovered is. He thinks maybe he can find someone who can figure it out for him. Although to him, that is not the most important thing; Timmy's recovery is what matters. But he feels like he needs to go back and do whatever he has to do to save the firm. He thinks he should return now and let Mom and me stay here with Timmy."

"I think he's right," Stetson agreed. "Diana is flying back to Salt Lake first thing in the morning. I will stay here as long as you'd like me to."

"You aren't well yet, Stetson," she said as she put her arms around him. "You should go and heal in your own apartment. I will miss you, but I think it's best that you go home."

So it was decided, and Stetson flew back to Salt Lake with Lilia's father and Diana on a red-eye flight that very night.

* * *

A week passed before young Timmy Dixon finally regained consciousness. Lilia and her mother were with him when he did. He opened his eyes and squinted, and the first thing he said was, "I need my glasses. I can't see."

His mother leaned down and kissed him while Lilia retrieved his glasses. Pamela put them on him, and the old familiar and much-loved look of big eyes behind thick lenses returned.

The second thing he said was, "I need my hearing aids."

They got them for him, and he put them in.

The third thing he asked was, "What happened to me?"

His mother told him. He stared at them through those thick glasses, and then he asked, "Is Mr. Greenbaum still free?"

"No, he's in jail," Lilia said.

The boy smiled. "Good. Where's Dad?"

"He's home," Pamela said. "He is in charge of the law firm now. He had to get back."

It seemed to Lilia that Timmy's amazing brain woke up when he did. He asked, "Did Harry die?"

"I'm afraid he did," Pamela said.

"What about Gabriel?"

"He's fine and he's home."

"Is everybody else safe now?"

"Yes."

"Good," he said. Then he closed his eyes and brought his lips close together. Lilia looked at his hands. They were both in a tight fist. After a couple of minutes, he said, "I need to tell Dad how to find the money."

"Can you still do that?" Lilia asked.

"Of course. Do you think I'm dumb or something?"

"No, little brother, I don't think that," she said as a surge of pure joy passed through her. He was back. And he was still Timmy, an amazing boy prodigy.

"Call Dad so I can talk to him," he said firmly.

As soon as Roland was on the phone and he'd had time to tell Timmy how grateful he was, Timmy said, "Dad, do you have your computer there?" It appeared to Lilia that his dad had responded that he did, for then Timmy said, "This will take a minute, but I need for you to follow my instructions exactly."

No, Lilia thought as Timmy rattled off instructions that rattled her mind, he did not lose his genius. It took ten minutes and then Timmy said, "Okay, Dad, as you can see, the money is back in the firm's account now. Love you, Dad. I want to come home now."

When he said that, to Lilia's amazement, tears began to stream down her little brother's face. But not for long. When he had recovered his composure, he asked, "Lilia, when are you and Stetson going to get married?"

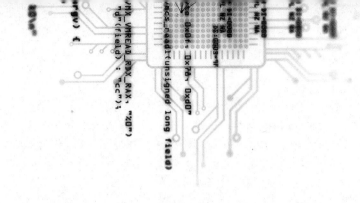

ABOUT
THE AUTHOR

CLAIR M. POULSON WAS BORN and raised in Duchesne, Utah. His father was a rancher and farmer, his mother a librarian. Clair has always been an avid reader, having found his love for books as a very young boy.

He has served for more than forty years in the criminal justice system. He spent twenty years in law enforcement, ending his police career with eight years as the Duchesne County Sheriff. For the past twenty-plus years, Clair has worked as a justice court judge for Duchesne County. He is also a veteran of the U.S. Army, where he was a military policeman. In law enforcement, he has been personally involved in the investigation of murders and other violent crimes. Clair has also served on various boards and councils during his professional career, including the Justice Court Board of Judges, the Utah Commission on Criminal and Juvenile Justice, the Utah Judicial Council, the Utah Peace Officer Standards and Training Council, an FBI advisory board, and others.

In addition to his criminal justice work, Clair has farmed and ranched all his life. He has raised many kinds of animals, but his greatest interests are horses and cattle. He's also involved in the grocery store business with his oldest son and other family members.

Clair has served in many capacities in The Church of Jesus Christ of Latter-day Saints, including full-time missionary (California Mission), bishop, counselor to two bishops, Young Men president, high councilor, stake mission president, Scoutmaster, high priest group leader, and Gospel Doctrine teacher. He currently serves as a ward missionary.

Clair is married to Ruth, and they have five children, all of whom are married: Alan (Vicena) Poulson, Kelly Ann (Wade) Hatch, Amanda (Ben) Semadeni, Wade (Brooke) Poulson, and Mary (Tyler) Hicken.

They also have twenty-six wonderful grandchildren and three great-grandchildren.

Clair and Ruth met while both were students at Snow College and were married in the Manti Utah Temple.

Clair has always loved telling his children, and later his grandchildren, made-up stories. His vast experience in life and his love of literature have contributed to both his telling stories to his children and his writing of adventure and suspense novels.

Clair has published over forty novels. He would love to hear from his fans, who can contact him by going to his website, clairmpoulson.com.